The Wounds of Time

S.L. Russell

ISBN 978-1-7397186-0-2

Cover design by Liz Carter

HIGHSTOWE BOOKS

The best stories are character-driven...but there must be good characters – realistic, vivid and interesting. Such is Janet Clarke. In 'The Wounds of Time' we share in her story – absorbing, moving and challenging all the way. **Paul Trembling, *The Hidden Libraries***

From the start we are faced with believable characters and an absorbing plot which twists and turns to its conclusion. A thoroughly enjoyable read. **Deborah Jenkins, *Braver***

A beautifully rendered exploration of the tangled relationship between self and soul. 'The Wounds of Time' is simply S.L. Russell's best yet. **C.F. Dunn, *Mortal Fire***

I enjoyed meeting again some of the characters from S.L. Russell's previous two novels, The Healing Knife and The Thorn of Truth. **S.C. Skillman, *Mystical Circles***

This contemporary novel immediately draws the reader in... A very good read with some thought-provoking moments. **Penelope Swithinbank, *Scent of Water***

From the first word to the last this book pulled me in and would not let me go. Gripping at its best. **Wendy H. Jones, *Killer's Curse***

Authentic, colourful characters, vivid settings and a plot that drew me in. Enjoyed it very much. **Liz Carter, *Catching Contentment***

Acknowledgements

To my beta readers, for your loyalty, good sense and eagle eyes, thank you.

To my writing buddies, for your nagging, encouragement and all-round wisdom, thank you.

To Jane Harris, for excellent suggestions and invaluable expertise, thank you.

Any failures are my own.

February 2017

Anna rang from court soon after 3 o'clock.

'Janet, I'm not coming back to chambers. The weather is appalling, and it's likely to get worse. Please, round everyone up and tell them to finish what they're doing and go home before the rush hour makes it impossible. Contact anyone who's out of the building, leave messages, whatever you need to do. I'm worried people will come to grief. The whole country's in a mess.'

I swivelled my chair round, the phone still clamped to my ear, and looked out of my tiny window. The two trees at the end of our back courtyard were whipping about wildly in the wind, and branches littered the paving stones. 'So that's what those crashes were,' I muttered. I turned my attention back to my Head of Chambers (we twisted her arm into taking on the title at a meeting before Christmas.) 'Did you take your car today?'

'No. I'll get a train back and walk from the station. Please, just get everyone out and lock up. I want you all safe. And that includes you, chum. No risk-taking. Let's hope it blows itself out overnight.'

'What about the interviewees? Want me to call them too?'

There was a pause. 'No,' she said. 'We'll see what they say on the evening news. If it looks bad we'll just have to call them at home. With any luck we'll be picking our way through the rubble in the morning and going on as usual.'

'OK, boss,' I said. 'Be careful on your way home. Hope there are trains running, no trees on the line or anything. How was your case, by the way?'

'As we expected,' she said. 'I'll probably phone you later. Get cracking, Janet – I can hear that gale howling from here.'

Storm Doris was the reason I was at home in time for the early evening news. Normally I would just be thinking of finishing up around that time on a quiet day, to say nothing of when we were busy. I was glad to have missed the rush hour, which is horrible in our city even when the weather is kind, because Anna was right: the wind was blowing the trees sideways, a cold rain hammered on my car's roof and the windscreen wipers were flailing manically and doing little good. Sitting forward in the car trying to see out, shoulders hunched, had given me a headache, so it was a relief to lounge on the sofa with a cup of tea and a painkiller, curtains drawn against the whistling of the wind, the pounding of the rain on the windows and occasional ominous crashes: someone's roof tiles flying along the street, or so I imagined.

The news was sombre: in places winds gusting in excess of 90 miles an hour. Snow in Scotland. Someone killed by falling debris in the Midlands. An aeroplane out of Edinburgh crashed in the Netherlands. Narrow misses when trees fell, crushing cars.

When I'd come in, blown up our front path by a following wind, coat flying everywhere, I'd heard noises from upstairs and was relieved to hear Drew was safely indoors. I frowned: where was Bob? Then I remembered I'd asked him to go to the supermarket for a few things, and sighed. Knowing Bob he'd go out if there was an alien invasion and the street was on fire. Being a paramedic had made him so used to emergencies he almost never panicked. Thinking back I realised I'd rarely seen Bob anything but calm, and I'm not one to flap either. I remembered he was on a night shift, and put a meal in the microwave for him. Ten minutes later he flew in, soaked through, hair wild, and muttering curses about the weather as he slammed the front door shut.

'The shopping wasn't that urgent,' I said as he came into the kitchen rubbing his hair with the hand towel from the downstairs loo.

'I've got to go out later anyway,' he said. 'I'll change into my uniform and come down and eat. I'm hoping the rain will ease.'

'You could take the car for once.'

He shook his head. 'You'll need the car in the morning. I'll take an umbrella if I have to.'

He disappeared upstairs and I set the table for one. He can eat and still be at the ambulance station well before his shift handover: it's just a fifteen minute brisk walk, which is why we can manage with one car. I would eat later at my leisure. I went into the living room and switched off the television. I wondered what humorist at the Met Office was responsible for the naming of storms. For something so dramatic and dangerous Doris seemed most inappropriate. I had a great-aunt Doris, my grandma's older sister, long gone now; she was five-foot-nothing, shaped like a barrel, and hard of hearing. Not a lot that was dramatic or dangerous about her.

I was just finishing my own meal when my son slouched downstairs.

'You want to eat?' I asked, indicating my empty plate.

'No, thanks,' he said. 'I'll get something later.' He went into the hall and returned wearing his coat. 'Bit rough out there.'

'It's really bad,' I told him. 'You need to be careful.'

'OK if I take the car?'

'Yes. But look after it. And bring it back.'

'I'm going to need it in the morning, Mum.'

'So am I.'

There followed five minutes of bargaining, a familiar ritual between my son and me. In the end we agreed he could have the car, but he would have to take me to work first.

'Early,' I warned him.

'Get me up, slave-driver,' he said, flashing me his lopsided grin.

'With great pleasure, idle boy.' I looked at him, shaking my head. 'You seeing Tiffany tonight?'

'Yep. We'll be at Jess's. See you, Mum.'

I called after him. 'Be careful with my car!'

The morning after the storm I was awake at half past five. I often woke early, even on those dark winter mornings when sensible mortals make a half-conscious trip to the toilet and then dive back under the duvet and surrender to oblivion. I got up, wrapped myself in a dressing gown of Bob's that was lying on the foot of the bed, and twitched back the curtains. The street looked much as it always did; if there'd been any damage, or rubbish bins rolling about, the neighbours had cleared it all up.

I turned away, and a small sigh escaped me. The room was cold. I was alone, of course; Bob's shift wouldn't be over for another hour and a half, and with all that was going on yesterday he would probably be late. I was, I supposed, used to it; he'd been a paramedic all our married life, and often enough we didn't cross paths for days, except in passing, but these days we weren't quite as good as we had been at making up for lost time. I assumed most people were the same after more than twenty years.

I showered and dressed, made coffee and toast, and did a few things on my laptop. At seven o'clock I woke Drew and told him he'd need to be ready in ten minutes. A groan was all I got in answer but if he wanted the car that was the deal. So, having driven myself while a dishevelled son huddled in the passenger seat with his eyes tightly shut, I was in chambers soon after seven thirty. The roads hadn't been too crammed at that hour, and I encountered no obstacles. The destroying wind had come and gone, and the authorities had been out clearing away any debris.

I switched on a few lights, turned up the heating and settled myself at my desk. The building was unnaturally quiet, but I found I liked it. Normally there was a buzz of activity, and my desk phone was rarely silent. This morning all was weirdly restful. I sat for a while, swinging gently this way and that in my office chair, hands idle in my lap, computer unopened, and thought about the interviews we were about to do that day. My former assistant, privately nicknamed Mouse for her twitchy, scurrying ways, had given notice in favour of a London firm. My own experience had been the same: to go up the ladder you moved chambers. I'd moved three or four times before fetching up at Hartington as Senior Clerk, but then I'd stayed. After almost twenty-five years it was my own fiefdom, so Anna told me.

We'd narrowed the field of applicants down to three, and they were due at ten. There was work I could be getting out of the way before that, but still, unusually for me, I sat, musing. I was thinking about Anna.

As Head of Chambers she was sort of my boss, but only sort of, because our fields of operation were different. She said often enough she couldn't do without me, because although we have other clerks I understand the way she works and the sort of cases she'd do best. I realised too that she was probably my only friend. Maybe that was because I had a high bar when it came to friendship, and most people call you friend when you're just a pleasant acquaintance. I had brothers and sisters and family members in droves, but for my own good reasons I kept away from them as much as I could. There were people I knew, of course: neighbours, women at my dance class, even some of Bob's colleagues, but they weren't friends – not by my reckoning. With a small chill I realised that over the past few months there'd been a growing distance between me and Anna; friendship needs some nurturing, and as so often happens life had been getting in the way. Quite apart from the normal demands of work, Anna was in the throes of applying for the post of Deputy District Judge, the first step in a reluctant plan to ensure some kind of pension in the future, and the only role she could fill and still retain her private practice as a barrister. The application form was an important part of the process, needing careful work on top of her normal load. I knew she was in the thick of it and had been trying to cut her some slack, but it wasn't always easy. I couldn't remember the last time we'd had the chance to sit down with a bottle of wine and talk. The thought struck me, out of nowhere it seemed, that although she was the only person I would call my friend, even she didn't know very much about me; but that wasn't surprising. Bob used to complain about my clam-like nature, but he doesn't bother any more.

I shifted in my chair, and decided it was time for more coffee. While it was brewing I wondered if there was something else, other than her career preoccupations, which was making Anna less approachable: friendly, of course, but somehow remote, in another sphere. Apart from vague mentions of dinner engagements nothing specific had been said, but my antennae are formidably attuned, so I am told, and I wondered if – at last – there was some man she was seeing. It wouldn't do her any harm to think about something other than work, though I am hardly one to preach on that subject.

Finally, a fragrant cup at my elbow, I opened my computer and logged on to the diary which rules all our lives. I hadn't been working long when I heard the front door open and close and the sound of footsteps along the passage. I knew it would be Anna, and a moment later she put her head round my door. I thought she looked tired.

'Morning, Janet. You're early.'

'I wondered if there'd be problems on the roads, but there weren't any. Not from my direction.'

She nodded. 'Are we ready for the interviews?'

'As ready as we can be. You read all their applications? Letters, CVs, references?'

She put her bag down and sighed. 'Yes. But honestly, on paper how do you know what they're really like? They are all so perfect, if you believe the hype. And who's going to choose a referee who says you're useless? Do you fancy any particular one? It's you that's going to have to deal with them.'

I nodded. 'Let's see how they perform later on. You ask the questions, and I'll watch. My nose will be twitching, my eyes will be beady.'

'As always.' She smiled.

'Who else will be sitting in?'

'Elizabeth, I thought,' Anna said. 'She's got her head screwed on. Anyway, they're all rookies, our candidates. We can't know yet how they'll fit, since they'll all be learning on the job. Maybe what we're looking for is teachability. Humility, even.'

I snorted. 'Not a common trait in these days of self-promotion.' I could hear the acid in my voice.

She smiled and said nothing, and in a moment was gone with a languid wave of her hand. I heard the door of her room open and close.

An hour or so later she reappeared in my room, in her stockinged feet and holding a cup of coffee. I looked up from my screen and raised a questioning eyebrow.

'Janet,' she said after a few sips, 'do you consider yourself to be happy?'

I wasn't expecting this. 'Why do you ask? Is it because you are? Or aren't? Or might be happier if…?' I left the thought hanging.

Her mouth quirked at the corners, and I saw amusement in her blue eyes. 'Maybe. But I asked first.'

I thought for a moment. 'Not sure why you want to know, but – well, I guess so. At least, I should be, I suppose. We could probably all think of ways we might be happier. Maybe I would be, if I could persuade Bob about moving house.'

'You still want to? Why?'

I shrugged. 'The house is OK. And we're not exactly cramped. Drew's hardly ever home. And it's convenient for Bob. But the area's on the edge of being rough. I'd like to be more central. Or on the other side of the river, if only we could afford it.'

I should never underestimate Anna's sharpness. Not only is she knowledgeable, well-educated and fearsomely intelligent, she is also uncomfortably perceptive. She gave me a considering look.

'Hm, OK. So would this be a movement towards, or a movement away?'

I sat up straight. 'What's that supposed to mean?'

I never got my answer, even if she had one, because at that moment, from deep inside my handbag, propped against my chair, my mobile rang.

Very few people even had my mobile number. Bob and Drew knew never to ring me at work unless there was a real emergency, and if the crisis was medical Bob was in a far better position to deal with it, to make the right decisions, than me – unless it's about him, of course. When I answered my phone and found it was my sister Pauline on the line I was astonished – I couldn't ever remember giving her my number – and then indignant. It was nine thirty in the morning – didn't she know I'd be at work?

'Jan, I'm really sorry to ring you so early.' She spoke fast, almost gabbling, as if she was out of breath.

'Whatever is it?' I knew I sounded sharp.

'You know I wouldn't bother you normally, but we just don't know what to do.'

I turned towards Anna, shaking my head, and she moved away down the corridor. 'Where are you?' I asked Pauline.

'We're outside the house, at Dad's.'

'We?'

'Yes, Christine and me. Dad won't answer the door. We had to shout through the letterbox, and the neighbours are looking.'

I heard the tears in her voice; she could be over-emotional, my sister. 'For goodness' sake, Pauline, never mind about the neighbours. What are you doing there in the first place?'

I heard her gulp. 'Ben rang me early this morning. He came home quite late last night, apparently – I don't know, maybe Dad was worried because of the storm – but they had a big row and Dad's locked Ben in his room! He can't come out, not even to use the bathroom, and he hasn't had any breakfast, and he's panicking because he can't get to work, and you know what Ben's like, he's really over the top about his job –'

'Slow down, Pauline, please. What do you suppose I can do about it? You do realise I'm at work, don't you?'

'I know, and I'm sorry. But Dad won't listen to us, you know him, he can be so unreasonable, and we all think he's been getting worse recently, and you're the only one who'll stand up to him.' I heard her beginning to cry.

I took a deep breath, closed my eyes and tried to swallow my anger. After a moment or two listening to her snuffling, I managed what I hoped was a reasonable answer. 'All right, I'll come. You'd better stay put, keep Ben on the phone. I don't want him doing anything stupid. Did you contact his work?'

'Yes,' Pauline said, her voice barely above a whisper. 'Christine went down there. The manager was very nice about it – said Ben should come in when he can. But you know Ben.'

'Yes,' I said. 'All right. But I might be a while. If you manage to sort it out by yourselves give me a ring.' I rang off without waiting for her reply.

Sighing, I pushed my chair back and went down the passage to Anna's room. The door was ajar, but I knocked. She looked up as I entered; her new glasses were on the end of her nose, and she was beginning, so I thought, to look like the judge she would one day be. 'Family trouble?' she said.

I nodded. 'If it was anyone but Ben, I'd tell them to get on with it.' I told her briefly what was going on. 'Look, I'm really sorry. I won't be able to do the interviews. I'll get someone else from the clerks' room, someone sensible, to stand in for me – Charlie's a good lad. I'll ask him now.' I looked at the carpet, feeling my temper rise, trying to put a lid on it.

'Janet, don't worry. If you have to, you have to. We'll manage, and I'll try to give the job to the best candidate. No guarantees, of course, but there wouldn't be even if you were here. Go on – sooner you sort it out the better.'

I took a deep breath. 'I'll be back as soon as I can.'

She nodded. 'I know. Off with you.'

What would have been a fifteen minute journey if I'd had my car took an hour by public transport, with a brisk ten-minute walk at the end of it. Luckily it rained while I was in the bus and had stopped by the time I got off. Even so my mood was darkening by the minute. My siblings, all of them, but especially my two sisters, were in awe and fear of Desmond Yates, our father. I didn't relish the idea of seeing him either; the years of bullying and confrontation, the sheer drudgery my teenage self had put up with, the sense of injustice I carried with me through the years, would stand between us till one of us died. I blamed him for everything, which in one corner of my mind I knew wasn't completely rational; there were no doubt other forces in play. As I'd said to Anna, if it was anyone but Ben, I'd have told my sisters to sort it out by themselves for once in their cowardly lives. But even though they were now in their forties, with their own families, neither was willing to stand up to Desmond. And Ben was vulnerable, Ben needed special consideration, we all knew that. I'd had the raising of Ben since he was less than two years old. I'd been with him through all the problems of his childhood, his health, his struggles with school, his ever-changing social workers. Plus I understood how important his job was to him. It wasn't much, perhaps, doing the donkey-work at a big DIY store, but it was what gave him status in his own eyes, made him an equal, a success in the world of the employed, worthy of respect. I understood that only too well. My work, knowing that I had got to where I was by my own efforts, knowing that there I had appreciation and esteem for my competence, formed a huge chunk of my own sense of self-worth. Sometimes I had to remind myself that Ben was not my child; he was a grown man, thirty six years old. But in some ways he was more my child than the one I had given birth to.

As I walked, picking my way through rubble and rubbish, the area grew less and less pleasant. Some people had made the effort to keep their front gardens tidy and their doors and windows painted, but not many. The further into the estate I went, the more overflowing dustbins I encountered, along with front yards barely visible behind untended straggly hedges. Then there were the dogs – either curled up pathetically or showing their teeth, depending on their temperament – chained up outside blistering front doors, and the inevitable cans and bottles rolling around in the gutters. I could hardly blame my sisters for hiding away in Pauline's car.

As I approached they climbed out. I suppose they could see I was in a black mood because the only greeting I got was a sketchy, nervous little wave. Pauline is the next oldest of us, five years my junior, and Christine a few years younger still. They couldn't be more different: Pauline takes after the Yates side, short, round, with thin, light brown hair; Christine, like me, is more of a Symonds, taller, wiry, dark.

'Hello, Janet,' Pauline said. 'Thanks for coming.' She frowned. 'Where's your car?'

'Drew has it,' I said. 'I had to come on the bus, which is why it took so long. Have you been in touch with Ben?'

Pauline nodded. 'We've been talking to him on his mobile. Chrissie told him she'd spoken to his manager at Wyatt's. He was pretty hysterical earlier, but he's calmed down a bit now. I told him you were on your way, so that helped.'

'Hm. Have you spoken to Dad again?'

Pauline bit her lip. 'No. We haven't tried. At least it's quiet now. The neighbours have all gone in.'

'For pity's sake, Pauline! Who cares about the neighbours? It's all a bit of soap opera to them, a nice bit of crappy daytime TV.' I glared at the pair of them. 'OK, let's get this over with.'

With some difficulty, because it was attached by a single hinge and grated on the rough ground, I shoved open the gate and strode down the cracked concrete path to the front door – the door which had always been that familiar, hated shade of green. To my knowledge it hadn't been repainted in twenty years. The place had the same rundown look I remembered, a look of neglect, shabby, unloved. I hadn't been here in several years; if I never came back it would be too soon. This was where we had all grown up, all seven of us, and until our mother died it was just chaos and noise and nowhere private to go and too many children and too much work; after that it was simply hell.

I pounded the door with the heel of my hand. Christine and Pauline had followed me reluctantly, but now they hung back, as if they expected the door to open and an army of roaring demons to pour out. There was no response. I thought of my calm office, the work I loved and did with efficiency; the interviewees waiting in the reception area, the faint aroma of coffee, the legal tomes on the shelves. And here I was, banging on the door of a house I never wanted to enter again, transported back into the world of an adolescent seething with rage. I hammered harder, until it hurt my hand. When nothing happened I bent down and yelled through the letter-box. 'Desmond Yates! Father! Open this door or I'll get one of the neighbours' lads to break it down – I'm sure they'd be happy to oblige. Then you'll have to pay to get it mended, because I certainly won't.'

After a moment there came the sound of heavy, shuffling footsteps on the other side of the door. I heard an old man clear his throat and spit noisily. 'Who is it?' he said, his voice grating. 'Pauline? Christine? Why are you still here?'

'It's Janet,' I shouted. 'Open the door before I break it down.'

'Oh, it's you, is it?' came the growling voice. 'What brings you here – slumming it, are we?'

'Let me in. I want to see Ben.'

'Tough. Get lost.'

'Do you want me to call the police? Tell them you're keeping Ben prisoner?'

I heard him laugh under his breath. It was not a pleasant sound. Then I heard a bolt slid back, and the door opened with a screech of swollen wood. A stale smell flowed out of the hallway.

My father stood there, leaning on a stick. He was unshaven, his hair long and greasy. He was wearing an old brown cardigan over grimy pyjamas, his great belly straining the buttons.

'Do come in,' he said in a falsely-sweet voice which made me want to be sick and with a smile that revealed teeth stained from years of smoking. 'How frightfully good of you to call.'

I stepped inside, my nose wrinkling. 'Grief,' I muttered. 'This place is a worse hovel than ever. Don't you ever clean?'

He shrugged. 'Can't. My arthritis. Ben does it sometimes, but these days mostly he's not here.'

'Can't say I blame him.' I looked around, my arms folded. 'So what's all this about locking him in?'

I saw his eyes narrow. 'He came in at half past one in the morning! Woke me up! I'm not having it, I told him. Teach him a lesson. He's a bad boy, sullen, disobedient, gobby.'

I lost it a bit then. 'You talk about him as if he was a kid,' I yelled. 'He's a grown man, thirty six, holds down a job. What's the matter with you? Are you losing your marbles?'

For a moment I saw something like fear flash across his face. 'Don't you dare talk to me like that!'

With an effort I made myself calm. 'Frankly, I don't want to talk to you at all. Just give me the key to Ben's room and you can go back to your beer and your TV and stew in your own foul juice.' I held out my hand.

For a moment he stared at me with those heavy-lidded, bloodshot eyes that I remembered all too well. Then he groped in his cardigan pocket, took out a small key and dropped it in my hand. 'Do what you like. What do I care? Nobody thinks about me anyway.' He turned and walked away, lurching from side to side. If it hadn't been for the stick I think he would have fallen. He disappeared into the living room and closed the door, and the blaring of the TV was muffled.

I turned to my sisters, standing back side by side, clutching their handbags. 'Come on, you two,' I said. 'Let's rescue Rapunzel from the tower.'

'What?' Pauline sounded dazed.

Without waiting for them I ran up the uncarpeted stairs and called through to Ben. 'Benj? It's Janet. I've got the key. Are you decent?'

A hoarse voice answered. 'Jan, open the door! I need the toilet!'

I unlocked the door. In a moment my brother pushed past me, dressed only in his underwear, and hurtled across the landing into the bathroom. From the foot of the stairs Pauline spoke in a low, shaky voice. 'Janet, do you need us anymore?'

I glared down the stairs at her. 'Don't even think of disappearing. What desperately important things are you missing anyway? A spot of dusting, maybe? Coffee with your pals? I'm the one who's missing work. The least you can do is give me a lift back to town when we're done here. Go and sit in your car if you can't stand the smell. I want to talk to Ben when he's finished.' I heard the toilet flush and a moment later the sound of the shower.

Christine spoke up for the first time, and I remembered she was the sibling with the most sense and kindness. 'Jan, remind Ben, please, if things are getting bad here, we have a spare room.'

'Yeah. Of course.' I watched them escape as fast as they could. A few minutes later the sound of running water was shut off and Ben emerged, dripping and wrapped in a towel. Through the steam I saw how neat and clean that shabby bathroom was, and remembered that Dad used the downstairs cloakroom: his damaged foot made the stairs too much of a challenge.

Ben clutched the towel. 'Got to get dressed,' he muttered. The bedroom door closed.

'Benj, I'm not going anywhere till we've had a talk.'

'All right – wait,' he called back.

I leaned on the wall, thinking about all I was missing back at chambers. I looked at my phone – it was now almost eleven. I sighed. They'd probably decided on the new clerk by now.

Ben's door opened. 'Hey, sis,' he said softly. I stepped into the room, and he allowed me to give him a brief hug. I sat on the edge of his neatly-made bed and looked around. The room desperately needed a coat of paint, but it was clean and orderly, and I could see he had tried to make it liveable: books and DVDs were tidily arranged on a set of rickety shelves that looked as if they'd been rescued from a skip, and there was a rug on the bare floorboards that might once have been vivid.

I turned my eyes on my brother, now fully dressed except for his shoes, still standing by the door, his hands in the pockets of his trousers, his fair hair damp from the shower. 'So what happened, Ben?'

He looked at the floor, avoiding my gaze. 'I was out. Waited for the rain to stop. It was really windy last night. There was a storm.'

'I know. What about when you got home?'

He shrugged. 'Dad was in one of his moods. He probably forgot to take his pills because I wasn't there. Look, Jan, it's OK. It's all OK now. I've got to get to work.'

I shook my head. 'Not yet, Ben. Not till we sort something out. Christine's spoken to your manager. I expect you can make up the hours you've missed. Your job's safe. But I've been hauled away from mine because of this. Christine's offered you a room at hers. You can get away from here, from Dad, all this aggravation.'

He shook his head violently. 'I don't want to go to Christine's.'

'Why not?'

'Because…because it would be worse than here. They don't really want me in their house. Honest, I'm OK. This was just – I dunno, Dad being stupid. Most of the time we don't interfere with each other. He stays downstairs. I keep the place clean. I do the cooking when I'm here. Anyway –' I saw him flush.

'Anyway what?'

'He's a sad stupid old man. He needs me.'

'What? What are you on about?'

'I make sure he takes his pills and stuff,' Ben mumbled.

I sighed and got up. 'Well, bro, you're a grown man,' I said. 'We can't make you do something you don't want. But just promise me something, OK? If things get so you can't cope, ring Christine, or Pauline, or me.'

'Yeah.'

'That's a solemn promise, right?'

He nodded. 'OK.'

'I've got to get back to work,' I said. I reached up – he's a head taller than me – and kissed his cheek. 'Look after yourself, Benj.' I turned back at the door. 'I think you'd better have this.' I dropped the key into his hand, and he looked at me and smiled.

None of us spoke much on our way back through the city. Pauline was a nervous driver, and the traffic was heavy. On at least one occasion she almost caused an accident by driving too slowly, but neither Christine nor I commented; we couldn't afford to add to the stress. Eventually we got close to chambers and I told Pauline to stop in an adjacent street where she could turn round easily without holding up the traffic. She parked and turned off the engine.

'Thanks for coming out today, Janet,' she said. 'I don't know how you do it, but somehow you can sort Dad out.'

I looked at her. 'Is he actually losing it? I mean, apart from being an awkward, cantankerous, unreasonable old bully, is there anything else I should know? Not that I really want to.'

Pauline looked down at her hands, twitching in her lap. 'We don't really know. But what would we do? He'd never see a doctor. He hates them.'

I sighed. 'Well, maybe after all we'll have to rely on Ben.' I turned in my seat to where Christine sat in the back. 'I gave Ben your message. But he won't move. Says he's OK where he is. At least now he has the key to his room. Anyway, I must get back to work. Thanks for the lift.' I opened the car door.

'Oh, Janet, I forgot to say,' Pauline said. 'You'll be getting a proper invitation soon.'

'Invitation?'

'Yes, you know, Neville's wedding. I told you the date ages ago.'

'June, isn't it?'

'June the tenth, yes. I'll be writing the invitations this weekend. What about Drew?'

'What about him?'

'Should I put him on the same invitation as you and Bob, or should I send a separate one for him and his girlfriend? I've forgotten her name.'

'Tiffany,' I said. 'But June's a long way off. Perhaps you'd better send an invitation to Drew plus one.'

Christine leaned forward from the back seat. 'Maybe you'll be the next one organising a wedding, Janet.'

I snorted. 'Please, do me a favour. They're barely out of school. Tiffany's only nineteen.'

There was a silence, and I suppose we were all thinking the same thing, but it was Christine who voiced it. 'You were nineteen when you got married, Janet. For the first time, I mean.'

'And look where that led,' I said. 'Please don't remind me.' I got out of the car and held the door for Christine as she took my place in the front passenger seat. She patted my arm, smiling uncertainly. It crossed my mind that our father was not the only family member my sisters were afraid of.

'Anyway,' she said quietly, arranging her coat as she settled into the seat, 'that's all a long time ago. And Bob's a very different kind of husband, isn't he?'

'Hm. Well, bye, you two. See you sometime.' I watched, shaking my head, as Pauline did a seven-point turn and drove slowly away.

I walked back to chambers, the gusting wind following me and blowing my coat around my knees. There was a spit of cold rain in the air, Doris' last spiteful reminder of a night that had wrecked buildings, torn down power lines and taken lives. I thought about my sisters, their daily existence so different from my own. For a start, neither of them worked. Pauline had married a man I didn't like, Colin Stevens, bluff, self-made, full of himself, loud and critical. If Pauline had ever had any great ambition – which I doubted – Colin would have squashed it flat. He was a member of what I hoped was a dying breed, the sort of man who regards his wife working in any but the most undemanding capacity as a personal insult. Oddly he was a doting father to Neville and Nicole, and on the rare occasions that I met them now that they were grown up I saw little of my gentle, self-effacing sister in them. I suspected that Pauline was a more or less willing doormat. Christine's husband Giles was a strangely faded sort of man, quietly spoken, easily overlooked, inclined to stutter when stressed. He and Christine seemed devoted to each other, though. They had no children, but lavished attention on a pair of yappy little terriers. Giles was something in a bank, and Christine did a bit of voluntary work in the hospital bookshop and spent her time at home doing a number of completely useless crafts. Her house was immaculate, of course. When I thought about these men, which I rarely did, it seemed Pauline had married a replica of our father, and Christine the opposite. Unsurprisingly, Colin and Giles disliked each other intensely. But what did I care? I saw them all as seldom as I could.

I pushed open the door of Hartington Chambers with a sigh of relief, and forgot about the family I would cheerfully have ignored for the rest of my days. It was almost lunch time, but I thought I had better tell Anna I was back and visit the clerks' room on the first floor to make sure all was well.

Anna's door was ajar as usual. I knew she had no clients coming today. I put my head round and she looked up from the papers on her desk and beckoned me in. 'Take the weight off, Janet. Are you all right? Did you manage to sort things out?'

I sat on the edge of a hard chair. 'Let's say we solved the immediate problem. I'm just sorry I had to leave you in the lurch. What did you think of the interviewees? Did Charlie contribute?'

Anna leaned back in her chair, flexing her shoulders. 'Charlie was a help, yes,' she said. 'He's no substitute for you, of course, but I can tell you're teaching him well. The only thing is, he's an impressionable young man. I hope his views on the candidates' qualities weren't coloured by their appearance.' She smiled wryly.

'Go on, put me out of my misery,' I said.

'Of course we discussed it afterwards, Charlie, Elizabeth and me. We are going to offer the post to Lauren Barclay. You said yourself she sounded good on paper, and she interviewed well. I just hope you like her, Janet, because you're the one that'll be working with her.'

'Pretty, is she?'

Anna smiled. 'Charlie seems to think so.'

'Luckily,' I said with some asperity, 'Charlie is far too busy with his BTEC course to be flirting at work. I'll have to keep an eye on this young woman, I suppose. But there are one or two others she can shadow, as long as I keep the overview. When is she starting?'

'That's one of the things that persuaded us about her,' Anna said. 'She's between jobs at the moment, so she doesn't have to work out notice. She can start on Monday.'

I raised my eyebrows. 'Between jobs? How does that work?'

'Well, she lives with her parents rent-free, so she told us. She's done a bit of temping. From what we gathered she's been looking for something she really wants to do.'

'Sounds a bit privileged to me,' I said.

Anna laughed. 'Janet, your prejudices are showing. What matters is how quickly she learns, how she gets on with the job and rubs along with us all. The rest doesn't concern us.'

'I hope you're right. Anyway, we'll see.' I stood up to go.

'Don't take against Lauren, will you, Janet?' Anna said, her voice soft but her face serious. 'Just because you weren't here giving her the once-over. The thing's done. You'll have to trust our judgment.'

Of course I trusted Anna's judgment, and Elizabeth Merchant's, but they are barristers, not clerks. Charlie, with four years' experience, whatever the BTEC course was teaching him, and me as a guide, should have been savvy enough. I still felt faintly uneasy, but I told myself I would meet our new Junior on Monday and see what could be done with her. I hoped she was made of tough stuff, because we often worked long hours under pressure and there was a lot to learn.

I trotted up the stairs quietly on the deep carpet, listening for the rowdy banter which often characterised the main clerks' room when I am not there. This morning things seemed normal enough when I slipped in.

Charlie looked up from his workstation, where he was on the phone, and gave me a wave. One or two others wished me good morning. They were mostly young, smart, fast-talking, and sometimes a bit cocky. There were more coming through with degrees, some even with law degrees, but experience still counted – or so I told myself. I had to do quite a bit of background work in my own time to keep up with all the changes in the law, but it was the sort of work I relished, not to mention the need to keep on top of my juniors.

Charlie finished his call and I beckoned him over. 'I hear you helped appoint the new girl,' I said, making an effort to keep my tone neutral. 'Easy on the eye, was she?'

Charlie pretended to look horrified. 'As if that would influence me! You are such a cynic, Janet. But since you mention it…' He grinned cheekily.

'You're welcome to pursue your interests, if that's your game,' I said severely, 'but strictly out of office hours, OK? She's got a lot to learn and needs no distractions. Anyway, for all you know, she may be spoken for. Right, we have work to do on your portfolio. We'll look at it in our lunch hour.'

'Slave-driver.'

'Maybe, but if you crash and burn it reflects on me. One o'clock sharp.'

Much as I loved my work, that day I was glad when it was over. I felt distracted, even a bit tired. I'd tried to dismiss my thoughts of Ben, but they circled annoyingly. What I needed, I told myself briskly, was some exercise. It was Friday, and my dance class was at six. Often if we were busy I turned up late or not at all, but today I got away in time and climbed onto a crowded bus just as the rain started up again. As we trundled through the busy streets I saw the rain turn to sleet and slap wetly on the windows. I huddled down in my seat; February was probably my least favourite month.

By contrast the sports hall where the dance class was held was hot, especially in the changing rooms. I kept my stuff in a locker, and was soon changed. The other women – they are all women, of course – drifted in in twos and threes, calling out greetings. I didn't know any of them well, but they were friendly enough and loved to chat.

After that it was an hour of loud music with a heavy beat, and no let-up, with our instructor – a beefy woman called Pamela – bellowing out instructions, and all of us, maybe thirty in all, jumping about obediently. I wouldn't have said it was enjoyable, but it kept me trim and released some of the stresses of the week. I usually felt like a wrung-out dishrag at the end of the hour, but a calm one.

I was finishing up under the shower when I suddenly started to feel quite ill. This could have been alarming, because I am rarely unwell, but I put it down to the demon menopause, and just leaned my forehead on the dripping tiles of the shower wall till the nausea subsided. I towelled myself down carefully, left the cubicle and retrieved my clothes. I thought it would probably be wise to sit while I dressed, so I found a space on one of the benches and pulled on a T shirt and some underwear. The other women were all milling about in various stages of undress, talking and laughing at their usual deafening volume.

I was trying to put on my trousers, which I would normally do standing up, when the faintness returned. For a horrible moment I thought I was going to throw up. There was a singing in my ears and a chill flowing through me, and the next thing I knew I was lying flat out on the quarry-tiled floor, looking up at a circle of faces and fighting for comprehension.

'What happened?' I sounded dazed and groggy.

Someone squatted down and put a folded towel under my head. 'You fainted, my love,' she said. 'How are you feeling now?'

'Awful,' I said. 'How embarrassing.'

Someone I knew vaguely loomed down from the circle. 'Not pregnant, are you, Janet?'

I closed my eyes, breathing deeply. 'Hilarious.'

The woman who had given me the towel pillow looked up. 'Not funny, Crystal. She might actually be ill.'

I sat up slowly. 'I don't think so,' I said. 'It's very hot in here. No need for alarm, ladies. I just need to get home.'

Someone else said, 'Perhaps we should call an ambulance.'

I hauled myself up onto the bench. My head was throbbing. 'Absolutely not! Anyway, my husband's a paramedic. I've got my own personal advice service at home.' I tried to smile. 'I'll be fine. Please don't worry.' One by one, muttering, they went back to dressing.

The first woman retrieved her towel. 'Are you sure you're all right?' she said. 'Have you got far to go? Should we call someone?'

I shook my head. 'It's just a short walk,' I said. 'The fresh air will do me good. But thank you.'

I had intended to take a bus, but the thought of close-packed bodies, stale air and diesel fumes deterred me. I even thought of ringing Drew to pick me up, but I had no idea where he would be or what he would be doing, and I didn't want to fuss and cause unnecessary alarm. The idea of a twenty-minute walk on a dark February evening with a fine, cold drizzle falling was not enticing, but I took it slowly and the chill air revived me.

When I got in the house was full of the smells of cooking. Bob was up and had made dinner. I hung up my coat and he came through to the hall, sleeves rolled up, drying his hands on a small towel. 'Hello, love,' he said. 'All right? You look flushed.'

'That's what a walk in the rain will do for you,' I said. I squeezed past him, patting his shoulder briefly.

'Where's the car, then?'

'Our son has it. I don't know why he wanted it – I don't ask these days. I made him drive me to work, but otherwise I've been on a number of buses.' I saw him raise his eyebrows as he followed me into the kitchen. 'First of all because I got called away from chambers at half past nine by Pauline, because Desmond had locked Ben in his bedroom and Ben was hysterical.'

Bob shook his head. 'Couldn't they sort it out?'

'Apparently not. Anyway, it all got resolved.' Feeling suddenly leaden, I planted myself on a chair at the table. Bob threw the towel over his shoulder and started to organise cutlery. 'I haven't seen my father for months. He looked dreadful. Old, grubby, tottery, neglected. Like the house.'

Bob leaned against the sink and folded his arms. 'And Ben?'

'Christine offered to have him. But he won't go. And part of the reason is some feeling of responsibility towards Dad, I think. Says he makes sure the old boy takes his meds.'

'And there's us, all these years, thinking it was Ben that needed looking after.'

'Yeah.'

Bob turned back to the cooker and gave something a stir. 'I just did some spaghetti – hope that's OK. Do you want a bottle with it?'

'No, I don't think I do, thanks. You have some if you like. I'll stick to water.' I was feeling very weary. Bob gave me a look but said nothing.

About half way through the meal the wooziness returned, and I laid down my fork.

'What's up?'

I took a deep breath, trying to steady myself. 'Not feeling too great, I'm afraid. Nothing to do with your cooking – this is fine. But I don't think I'll risk eating any more.' Hands flat on the table, I pushed myself up.

'Look at me.' Bob studied me with his piercing dark blue eyes, his professional face to the fore. 'You look like death.'

I smiled feebly. 'Is that a medical term? Hope you don't use it on your clients.'

'How are you feeling?'

'Dizzy. Lead legs. Very tired. Too hot. Don't go fussing, OK? It's just my age making itself felt. Just be thankful men don't get it, apart from psychologically.'

Bob stood up, came round the table, and took me by the elbow. I found myself leaning on him for a moment. 'Well, we have our problems later,' he said gruffly, 'when our prostates start acting up. You'd better go and lie down.'

'Yes, I will. No, don't come up, I can manage.'

He let go of my arm. 'I'll come and look at you later.'

At the door I turned back, and noticed his pallor for the first time. 'You don't look too chipper yourself.'

He shrugged. 'Tired, that's all. Getting too old for night shifts.'

'But you slept today, didn't you? And you've got this weekend off?'

'Ah.' He looked slightly embarrassed. 'I should have had. But I signed up for two days on. There are a lot of people off sick at the station. I've got Monday, Tuesday and Wednesday off instead.'

For no reason that I could fathom, this came as a blow. I decided I must be feverish, because this wasn't like me. I'm independent and adaptable – I've had to be. I'm never feeble and needy.

'You promised to help with the loft this weekend,' I said.

'I know, and I will do it. If you're feeling OK, you get started tomorrow as planned and I'll do a shift on Monday.'

I turned away. 'I suppose that'll have to do. Oh, and before you say anything, I know it's not because you've agreed to move. Just that it's a good idea to declutter once in a while.'

'Let's not worry about that now,' he said gently. 'Go on up. And if you feel really bad in the morning I won't go in. They'll just have to get on without me.'

Oddly, though, when Bob woke me at six o'clock the next morning I felt absolutely fine.

'Just checking to see if you're OK to be left before I go,' he said. 'I have to say you look better.'

'I'm in the pink,' I said dopily. 'Just not ready to get up. Go on, go to work. I'll see you this evening.'

He must have been concerned because, unusually, he bent over and planted a kiss on my forehead, which was the only part of me that was visible. 'Don't overdo it.'

I lazed around till eight thirty, then bounded up, put on my scruffiest clothes, made myself some cereal and toast and looked out of the window while I ate. I had thought of taking an early walk but the grey, lowering clouds and blustery wind deterred me. It was a day to be inside. Just before I got the loft ladder down Drew rang.

'Hey, Mum.' He sounded sleepy. 'Do you need the car?'

'Nope.'

'OK if I bring it back this evening, then?'

'I suppose. It's still in one piece, is it?'

'Of course.' He paused. 'Will you and Dad both be in tonight?'

'I think so. Unless he decides to whisk me away from the chores to some glitzy restaurant.'

'Be real, Mum. Good, because I need to talk to you. Now I'm going back to sleep.'

'Idle boy.'

I worked hard on the loft all morning, sorting through boxes of assorted papers, finding forgotten treasures, exclaiming over the folly of keeping rubbish, and getting filthy in the process. I made several piles: things to be thrown out or recycled, things of Bob's which he would have to decide about, things that could be put to use or needed filing. At lunchtime I came down, feeling a little stiff from squatting and kneeling in a confined space, and wallowed in the bath for half an hour. I warmed some soup and made a sandwich. The nausea of the day before had gone, and I was quietly pleased with my progress. If we never moved, a tidy loft was a good thing, and if we did, it was a job done. I wasn't certain of getting my own way, and I had to admit that Bob's reasons for staying were more weighty. Even with Drew at home, we weren't cramped, and he wouldn't be at home for ever – nor for much longer, I suspected. The nearness to the ambulance station was an advantage for Bob, and he always argued that with both of us having pressured jobs there was no need to add the stress of moving house. My own reasons were far vaguer, and not easily articulated; but I was not giving up, not yet. I regularly scoured the internet for houses on offer on the other side of the river, where gardens seemed greener. I knew what we could afford, and I knew how house prices were looking. I was prepared.

I washed up my few dishes and saw that the weather had changed: obviously it had rained while I was in the loft; now the clouds had rolled away, and a weak sun made the wet garden sparkle. I put on an old coat and trainers, ran a comb through my damp hair and went out. The pavements were awash, water gurgling briskly down the drains. I headed for the local park, ten minutes' walk away in the opposite direction to the ambulance station. A few people were about, mainly parents with young children, warmly wrapped against the February chill. Down by the lake a father and two small boys were kicking a ball, the children's voices high and sharp in the clear air. Two adolescent girls wandered the paths ahead of me, deep in quiet chat, one of them with a dog on a long lead. The girls seemed oblivious to the dog, which was snuffling around under the bushes, until it managed to wind the lead round their legs. I smiled as I passed, seeing them hysterically laughing as they tried to untangle themselves. I like dogs, but I had long ago sworn I would never have one. Still, at the same time I'd sworn I'd never have children – but then, Drew was mainly Bob's idea.

I went back to the loft refreshed, telling myself I would work till about four, then have a cup of tea and concoct something for dinner, with a sense of a useful day's job done. I was scrabbling about in a dark, dusty area under the eaves, pulling aside boxes of who-knew-what to be investigated, when I came upon something I instantly recognised but had forgotten for years. It was a small, battered white suitcase, the sort of thing a child might have, flimsy and squashed out of shape, its catches filmed over with rust. I hadn't seen it or thought of it in all the years we had lived in this house – more than twenty. But I knew exactly what was inside, and I felt a stab, a jolt, then a rush of memory which for a moment froze me where I knelt among the teetering boxes.

I pulled the case out into a small cleared area and squatted down beside it. I put a hand on each of the catches and hesitated. But somehow I felt compelled to open it; there was no question of returning it to its hiding place, just as there had never been, I realised, any question of simply throwing it away. I wondered why we so often keep things that we know can hurt us. With some difficulty I released the catches and lifted the lid, releasing a cloud of choking dust. Inside were a pile of notebooks, held together by rubber bands. On the cover of the top book was a date, a child's hand in faded ink, and my own name: Janet Mary Yates. Here were the diaries I had kept sporadically, from the age of about eleven, coming to a sudden stop two years later. I knew what was in them: the daily trivia of my life, the squabbles at home and at school, peevish complaints about chores and siblings, my thoughts about a book I was reading, small classroom achievements, friends and jokes. I set them aside. Underneath was a scatter of letters which had lost the band that held them together; now they littered the floor of the case in a random jumble. The nausea I had felt the day before returned, but this time it was not physical. My hand shook a little as I handled the fragile pages with no envelopes, and I wondered if I could face the task of putting them in date order. It would mean reading again the anguished, rage-filled words of a bewildered and bereft adolescent. Did I want to revisit those terrible weeks and months? No. I let the letters fall.

The only other thing in the case was a small book, bound in white leather, now stained round the edges, a Prayer Book, never used that I could remember. Something was sticking out of its end pages. I opened it up and pulled it out, realising that here was something I had completely forgotten: two black and white photographs, curling at the edges and stuck together. Carefully I peeled them apart. On the back of each one was a date: 7 December,1980. I turned them over, blinking away the momentary blurring of my eyes. Here were twelve children, boys and girls, the boys resplendent in their Sunday best, the girls in bridal white, some with veils and flounces, their faces variously solemn, grinning, smirking. I saw among them faces and even names I recognised, and in the front row, beaming, my sister Pauline, aged then almost eight, her little round face a picture of delight, her light brown hair fluffed out, holding her Prayer Book to her narrow chest as if it were a precious baby. But in the back row stood a skinny child who loomed taller than the others by a head or more, dark hair scraped back, and a scowl on her face black enough to darken the sunniest sky: myself, of course, aged twelve. I looked at my stance: arms held down straight and stiff, the unwanted book hidden behind the other children, the brows a straight line, the eyes narrow. How I had hated every moment of that day, a day I had stubbornly resisted for years, made to be where I knew I did not belong. It hardly mattered now.

I looked at the other image: this was harder to contemplate. There was my mother, so young – barely more than thirty – radiantly smiling, proud that her two oldest children were now received into the church and bound for heaven. Beside her, smiling also, but suitably reserved, his eyes hidden behind small round glasses, the black-clad figure of Father Gerard, tall, beginning to be fleshy, a man in his prime. My mother revered him, and all that he stood for, without question, second only to the Holy Father himself, the sainted Pope John Paul II. Angry Janet detested him, with a loathing that far outweighed his human failings. She had not, I remembered, quite dared to detest the Pope, because he, so she was told, was in direct communication with God, and He had the power to fling the sinner into outer darkness. Fostered by all she had been taught, some superstitious fear still lurked in her childish mind. For a brief moment I recalled with painful clarity the humiliations of that day. Then I remembered that Father Gerard would be an old man now, retired, if he was still alive, and whether he was alive or dead he had no power over me. I put aside the thought that maybe God still did, if indeed He existed. As to that, I told myself, the jury was out, a question for another day, if I could bring myself to consider it. I put the photographs back where I had found them, closed the case and propped it against the loft wall.

Bob got home about seven thirty, looking weary and drawn. He rarely said anything about his day anymore, and I wondered what he might have seen in the course of it: what near-misses, tragedies, frustrations, lost opportunities, time wasted, lives squandered, and sometimes lives saved. I didn't ask, because I thought he may not want to relive what could not be amended. It was a hard job, and he had done it gladly and faithfully all the time I had known him. From the occasions when we met colleagues of his in a social setting I gleaned how well he was thought of, and it didn't surprise me.

'Dinner in fifteen,' I said. 'You've got time for a speedy shower.'

He nodded. 'Good. Some hot water might do something for my aching muscles.'

We were just finishing our meal when we heard the front door open and close, and quiet voices in the hallway. I looked up, surprised. Somehow I had assumed Drew would be coming home alone, but when the hall door opened he ushered Tiffany in ahead of him, almost with a sense of ceremony, and I felt a shiver: it seemed this was no ordinary casual drop-by. We had met Tiffany on several occasions and thought she seemed a pleasant girl, if rather quiet, but there was humour in her eyes and speech and I suspected there were depths in her which were not often on view.

'Hello, son,' Bob said. 'Hello, Tiffany.' He waved the half-empty bottle of wine enquiringly. 'Can I tempt you?'

Drew slithered into an empty chair and pulled Tiffany towards him, his arm round her waist. 'I will, thanks, Dad, but Tiff's driving.'

Bob stretched over to the sideboard and found an empty glass. 'Sit down, Tiffany, won't you?' He poured wine into the glass and slid it over to Drew.

'Oh, no, thank you,' Tiffany said, and I saw a blush creep up her neck. 'I'm not stopping. Just thought I'd come and say hello, then I'm off home. I've got my car outside.' She glanced at Drew, her eyes wide.

Drew picked up his glass and took a deep swallow. 'Thing is, Mum and Dad, we wanted to tell you that Tiff and I are engaged. To be married, that is. One day.'

I found I had absolutely no idea what to say. I couldn't yell at Drew with Tiffany there, and no doubt he had brought her for just that reason. I was horrified, but I couldn't have said why; I liked Tiffany well enough, and I could hardly object on the grounds of their youth, having done exactly the same thing myself, as my sisters had reminded me.

Bob, who is a fond father seemingly oblivious to his son's faults, and who would have hated to embarrass Tiffany, rescued me. 'Well! You've knocked us sideways, son. What can I say – congratulations!'

Drew's grin was sheepish, and I saw he was avoiding my eyes. 'Yeah, well, thanks. We won't actually get married for a while, so don't worry, Mum.' Now his eyes slid towards me, and I remembered to shut my mouth. 'I've got my course to finish, for a start. But we've been making plans, haven't we, Tiff?' He gave her a squeeze.

'I should get home, Drew,' she said, her voice low.

'Right. I'll see you to the door. Then I'll come back and tell these old folks what we're going to do.'

Tiffany said goodbye, and I noted her sense of discomfort. For a moment I heard their voices speaking quietly in the hallway, then the front door opened and closed again, and a moment later I heard Tiffany's car start up.

Drew sauntered back, sat at the table and drained his glass. There was a definite gleam in his eye. There are occasions, even now when he is grown up – allegedly – when I could cheerfully box his ears, and this was one of them. But I said nothing.

'All right, Mum, you can bawl me out now.'

'No, I'm not going to,' I said. 'It's a done deal, isn't it? Don't get me wrong, I like Tiffany, she'll be good for you, but you're both too young and you don't have a job or anywhere to live or any money. I know you'll say I was only nineteen when I married Terry, but that was a disaster. Strangely enough, Drew, I don't want you walking into a disaster of your own.'

'I know, Mum,' Drew said, sobering. 'I get it. But we're not you and Terry, and nobody can say whether we're walking into a disaster or not, can they? Seems to me disasters can happen at any age. Anyway, let me tell you what we have in mind, then I hope you'll feel a bit less appalled and might even give us your blessing.' I nodded, and he went on. 'OK, you know our friend Jess? Her family live up at Thripp's Ford, remember? It's a great big old place, with sheds and shacks and outbuildings. They have a huge garage full of stuff, no room for cars, and there's a flat above which they had converted – kind of – for Jess's older brother Dan when he lived at home. He lives away now, Birmingham I think – he's doing a PhD or something, but he was in a band at school and they used to practise in this converted loft. It's a bit run down because that's where we meet with our friends mostly, but we can do it up and make it nice. Jess's mum and dad said we could have it for a really reasonable rent. It's got a shower and a toilet and a little kitchen, and heating, and you get up to it by an outside stair. We thought we'd start soon getting it all cleaned up and decorated. I even rang Uncle Ben to see if he could get us paint and stuff from Wyatt's on staff discount.'

'What? My brother Ben?' I said stupidly. I was beginning to feel quite dizzy.

'I don't have more than one uncle called Ben,' Drew said, shaking his head. 'Anyway, I'll be staying here most of the time while I finish college, just going up to the flat to work on it while we can, and Tiff's got a job as you know, but she's going to sign up for a course at my college at Easter so she can get some vocational qualifications. Once my exams are over I'll be looking for work too. We'll probably move in come the spring. And then we'll be saving every penny we earn.'

'Well,' Bob said, 'You seem to have it all worked out. Good on you, lad. I agree with your mum, Tiffany's a lovely young lady. I'm not sure you deserve her, but that's another thing.'

Drew pushed his chair back and stood up. He went over to where his father sat and patted his shoulder. 'Can't say I disagree with that,' he said, grinning. 'And I have yet to face my future father-in-law, who I am sure is certain I don't deserve his precious girl. Let's hope Tiff will soften him up for me. Anyway, I've got some college work to do, so I'll say goodnight. I'm knackered – must be all the excitement.' He looked over at me, and his expression was unreadable. 'Night, Mum,' he said softly. 'Don't be too mad at me.'

I shook my head. 'I'm not mad. I don't really know what I feel. Anyway, goodnight, Drew.'

When he had gone, Bob and I stared at one another in silence for a few moments. 'Did you have any idea?' Bob said.

'I thought something was in the air this morning, when he rang me to make sure we'd both be in,' I said. 'Before that? No, not really. We know he spends most of his time with Tiffany, but I assumed that was more a question of hay-rolling, not nest-building.'

Bob laughed. 'You would.'

I thought for a moment. 'I married Terry to get away from home,' I said. 'Do you think that's what Drew's doing?'

'No, why would he?' Bob said. 'He has a cushy billet here, and we're not tyrants. No, I think he's just making a bid for adulthood and freedom. It's only natural.'

'I suppose.' I said no more; but another thought had come to me when Drew mentioned his future in-laws. I had no objection to Tiffany, but didn't relish the idea of being related to the Leamans. I worked for and in the law, and it was embarrassment enough having two brothers who, I was pretty sure, often worked outside it, or at least on its dubious edges. Now, it seemed, I was going to be associated with a man who, less than a year ago, had been in prison, accused of murder. As it turned out he had been proved innocent of that charge, and the true perpetrator was now in jail, but Calvin Leaman still had a reputation – if he deserved it, I didn't know – as a supplier of illegal substances. And, whether he deserved that reputation or not, I didn't like him. In fact, he gave me the creeps.

Bob and I did the washing up almost in silence, each with our own thoughts. As he dried his hands, Bob said, 'There's some football on TV. You OK with that?'

I shrugged. 'Whatever.' But the Leamans were on my mind, and I followed him into the lounge. 'I don't have an issue with Tiffany,' I said. 'Too bad if I did, I guess. But I really don't relish the connection with her family, especially her father.'

Bob sighed. 'Yeah, I know. But what can we do?'

'Is Drew aware of everything that's gone on? He must be. Tiffany must have told him, and anyway, he lives here; he can't not know. He's never mentioned it, though.'

Bob threw himself down on the sofa with a groan. 'Look, if I get a chance I'll have a tactful word. See how the land lies.'

'Better you than me. He might just listen to you.'

Bob picked up the remote control and a moment later came the roar of an excited crowd. I left him to it.

Bob probably fell asleep on the sofa, or maybe he found something to investigate online. Not unusually I went to bed alone – gone were the days when such solitude would have been unthinkable – and lay thinking for a long hour before sleep claimed me. As for Drew and Tiffany, there was little to think about: they would do what they wanted with little recourse to us, and we would just have to get on with it. I would have another set of shoals to navigate, but I certainly had experience. I seemed unable to escape an association with shady doings, even though I had never fallen foul of the law myself – on the contrary; but it made for discomfort and shame, considering that I did my part on a daily basis to uphold that very law.

What really kept me awake was the thought of the battered little suitcase somewhere above my head. I knew what those letters contained, of course, even though I had not looked at them for many years. I could not now remember what had possessed me, a child of thirteen, to write them to a woman who could never read them, but they were some kind of an outlet for my shattered spirit at a time when I had refused all other avenues of help. Nothing much had changed, I realised. Those deep wounds had left scars which no one could see, and if they chafed still, well, no one would know.

Hours later I woke, heat rippling through my upper body and into my neck and face. I threw off the quilt and sat on the edge of the bed. By this time Bob was there beside me, making the odd grunting noises which are typical of him when he is in a deep sleep. My hair was damp with sweat, and my head throbbed. I hauled myself to my feet and shuffled to the bathroom, feeling a sudden urgency to pee. Pulling up my pyjamas, I noticed spots of blood. I cursed under my breath. As I washed my hands at the basin I looked up at the mirror and saw a draggled, heavy-eyed, bleary gorgon staring back, and in an irrational moment almost envied my mother: all those pregnancies, but she'd never had to put up with this.

Chilled now, I crept back to bed, shuddering as I pulled the covers up round my chin, and had a sudden urge to huddle up to

Bob's sleeping body and steal his warmth. I resisted. I told myself he needed his sleep for work tomorrow, but perhaps also I was afraid to lay myself open to acknowledging my own fragility. It would pass.

The next morning he was gone before I surfaced. All that remained was the smell of coffee and slightly burnt toast in the kitchen. Normally I would be relishing the prospect of a whole day to myself, but today I felt out of sorts. I wondered briefly if I should consult a doctor, but dismissed the idea as quickly as it had arrived: it was just the menopause and would have to be endured. Strong coffee, painkillers and a hot shower helped, and by mid-morning I was climbing the loft ladder again. As I continued with the sorting work, bringing down the boxes for throwing away and stacking the things we needed to keep more tidily, clearing space as I went, the hours flew by. I heated up pizza for lunch, prepared something for the evening and carried on into the afternoon. All the while that little white suitcase sat there under my eyes, so innocent, so deadly. Finally I came to a stop. It was enough. As I went to climb down the ladder I paused. It was as if someone else's will directed me as I grabbed hold of the suitcase and took it down with me.

I made a cup of tea and sat at the kitchen table, the case at my feet, the letters spread out in front of me, scraps of flimsy paper scrawled over in a child's uneven hand. I picked one up at random, unfolded it and smoothed it out on the table top.

'Mummy mummy mummy mummy…' twelve times, the pen scoring deep into the paper. 'Why did you do it? Why did you pick Davey up? Why didn't you look? Why did we have to go shopping anyway? If we'd stayed at home everything would have been OK. How could you leave me like this? Didn't you know what my life would be like?' Here the page was crinkled where my angry tears had fallen, as they were falling now. There was more, line after line of fury and grief, and no lack of self-dramatisation which would have been funny, in its bleak way, if it had not been so pathetic and raw.

'You called me your princess, but now I am just a slave, and it's all because of you. Selfish, to have so many children, careless, stupid. I'm condemmed, and it's all your fault.' All the underlinings, the moments of dodgy spelling, all the self-absorption, spoke of a bewilderment and misery whose intensity I had almost blotted out.

I wiped the feeble tears from my eyes with the back of my hand. What use was any of this now? I put the letters back in the case, closed the lid and snapped the catches shut. I would put it all back where I had found it, but next time we had a bonfire I would burn it all.

I lay in a warm bath, letting the heat soak into my muscles. I wanted to forget, but for the moment I had lost the knack. I wondered about my brothers and sisters – how did they cope? They were all so young, of course; perhaps time had erased their memories. The only one who might remember was Pauline, but even if I could have brought myself to ask her, it was Sunday, and she and Christine would be at Mass: another legacy of our mother which they had swallowed whole, which perhaps still consoled them, but from which I was shut out, and by my own will. I would stick by that rejection, that much I knew, refusing to be taken in, fooled, controlled; but it was, all the same, a cold philosophy.

On Monday morning I left Bob asleep and crept around, taking even more care than usual to ready myself for the day because today I was to meet our newly-appointed clerk, Lauren, and introduce her to her role in chambers. My plan was to offload her as soon as I could to one of the other more experienced clerks – though assuredly not Charlie. I dressed with particular care, selecting a brilliant purple top that clung, and a skirt soberly-striped in two shades of grey, ending below the knee, but leaving a space between the hem and a pair of soft suede ankle boots for shiny tights sprinkled with silver stars. The ensemble was completed by a boxy jacket patterned in black and purple, the whole pretty muted and conservative by my standards.

My outfits are a source of fascination, amusement and horror at work, though no one would dare comment – except, sometimes, Anna. Of course the way I dress is a statement: something along the lines of I'm not ordinary or I can carry it off. It takes some doing when you're rising forty-nine, but I have kept my figure by painful discipline. There are two small charity shops in the city which I like to investigate for unusual things, off the main shopping streets, where the staff know me and sometimes put aside items they think will suit. Once these garments have had a few airings I take them back, so that my wardrobe is always changing. Bob thinks of this as a harmless eccentricity, and I suppose it does seem odd that having had to endure hand-me-downs from my cousins throughout my childhood I'd be happy to wear other people's castoffs; but these I have chosen, and at least I know they will fit, unlike some of the things I was forced to wear as an embarrassed teenager: school shirts with too-long sleeves, tight jumpers, dresses with hems hastily taken up. That morning I inspected my reflection in the bedroom mirror with a critical eye, and decided, for the sake of a more sober image, I would refrain from gelling my hair into sharp spikes.

I set off for chambers early, wanting to be there before anyone else, and it was lucky that I did. I followed my usual route through the city, but before ten minutes had passed I was confronted with a closed road. Beyond the barriers men in hard hats milled around monster machinery, and it looked as if the storm had caused damage to the road surface, perhaps because of fallen trees. With a quiet groan I swung right and followed a series of yellow diversion signs, finding to my dismay that because of the layout of the city's one-way system I was being taken on a roundabout route which would add miles and minutes to my journey. My dismay deepened when I realised I would have to skirt the scruffy housing estate where I had grown up – though not, fortunately, in sight of the house where a few days before I had confronted my father.

Normally the traffic here would have been bearable, but today everyone was having to divert on their way to work within the city or to the ring road, and I crawled behind a line of cars before I could get back to my route. I felt my stomach clench as I drove all too slowly past familiar landmarks: the primary school where we had all gone long ago; the parade of shops where I might be sent for stamps or a pint of milk; and above the roofs of the houses and shops the tower of the Church of the Holy Cross, scene of many a torment. I uttered a quiet expletive, as if spitting something foul out of my mouth. At the end of the road, where a junction siphoned off some of the cars and where I was able at last to put my foot down and escape, stood a bus shelter, painted in dowdy cream and covered all over with graffiti, and I remembered with a small shock that it was here I had first met Terry Walters.

I knew of Terry, but he was a couple of years older, with all the cachet of seventeen, and we had never spoken. I had been given the job of walking our dog Paddy, who was the result of many random pairings and far from handsome, but with a sweet temper and a tolerance born out of years of children's careless affectionate maulings. That day it was raining hard, but I welcomed the chance to escape the house with its noise and dirt and crying children. Paddy and I had plodded round the local park, getting soaked. It was summer, so all I had on was an ill-fitting cotton dress in a colour that didn't suit me and someone else's sandals. I remembered how cold my feet were. When the rain strengthened we took refuge in the bus shelter, waiting for the dark cloud to pass, and it was then that an equally drenched figure hurtled into the shelter, cursing loudly. To my horror I realised it was Terry, heart-throb of many of my contemporaries, and here was I with my hair matted down and my uneven hems stuck wetly to my knees. I turned away, hoping he wouldn't recognise me, but after a moment of flicking his wet hair out of his eyes he exclaimed, 'Hey! It's little Janet Yates!'

I didn't much care for the 'little', since he was barely two inches taller than me, but the annoyance at being patronised was engulfed in a moment by the warm embarrassed pleasure of being noticed by the glamorous Terry Walters. He had a reputation for bad behaviour such that the school we both attended had been pleased to see the back of him. Word was he now worked in a local lumber yard and so had that dazzling rarity: money in his pocket. Years later he told me that I had a reputation too, for a sharp brain and a tongue to match, so to my surprise the awe wasn't all in one direction. That day he was apparently out to impress. From his pocket came a crumpled pack of cigarettes, and I was offered one – but here I was already wise, and declined. Choking and spluttering didn't do one's image any favours.

'So, what brings you out in the rain?' Terry asked, taking a deep drag of his smoke.

I indicated the dog, cowering under the bench seat. 'Dog walking duty,' I said. 'I swear, I'm never going to have pets or kids.'

Terry laughed at this. 'Why not?'

I thought. 'I like dogs, actually, and this one's a nice old thing. But they are quite smelly. And kids? Who would? For ever pissing themselves or falling over or chucking food on the floor.'

'So what's your plan, then?' Terry said, a spark of amusement in his eyes, eyes so blue that a fifteen-year-old, however cool she was trying to be, might have been forgiven for feeling wobbly.

'Me?' I said with all the nonchalance I could muster. 'A good job, and a nice flat all to myself.'

'No one to share it with?' Terry had said then, his tone making an innocent question sound suggestive.

This was too much, and I felt a hot blush turn my face fiery. Turning away from his grin I saw that the rain had stopped and the sun was creeping round the edge of the cloud, sparkling on the leaves that hung down over the bus shelter, making even that dreary road seem alive. 'I'd better go,' I mumbled. 'Come on, Paddy.'

'Hey, wait,' Terry called after me. I risked looking back at him. He was very blond, I remembered, now that his hair was drying, and undeniably attractive. 'Do you fancy a trip to the pictures some time?'

Me? Skinny, badly-dressed Janet Yates? Was I dreaming? But that was how it had begun, and years later, lying in a tangle of bedsheets one lazy Sunday morning, Terry admitted that he'd noticed how the rain had plastered my thin cotton dress to my girlish curves and sparked his predatory lust.

I didn't go to the cinema with Terry, not then. I knew enough to suspect that this was the beginning of many a traditional route to disaster – early motherhood, the one thing I had vowed to avoid. I declined his invitations unless they took place in the public eye, walking the dog or lounging on a crowded beach or in a café surrounded by friends, and this resolve served to fuel the fires of his frustration. I knew he had other girlfriends during those years, and I pretended not to mind. My friends thought I was mad, such was his allure, but it turned out I was right when one of my sillier contemporaries, after a fling with Terry, found she was pregnant and had to be whisked away for a timely termination. I was using those years to my advantage, anyway: finally, after years of patchy attendance at school because I had to be a little mother to my siblings, someone had noticed, and I was working for exams. But that's another story altogether. Turning eighteen, I left school with hard-won A levels and looked for a way to escape the family home, scene of so much drudgery, so many screaming matches between me and my father. By this time I was no longer a skinny kid, but a determined, if still naïve, young woman, and Terry made his move. Ever the hunter, he had a string of conquests to his name, but he wanted what he couldn't have. He had a flat, but – tempted though I certainly was – I refused all invitations, until one evening, sitting in silence by the river, he suddenly turned to me and said, 'All right, you teasy little bitch, you've got me cornered. How about if we get married?'

Knowing what I know now, I should have given him the final elbow; but the lure of finally losing one's virginity legitimately to the sexiest boy in the neighbourhood was overwhelming. Ironically I had no idea till much later what a great disappointment that would turn out to be. My second marriage was in all respects a vast improvement.

As I approached the city centre and the roads approaching chambers I hauled my mind back to the present. Things had conspired, it seemed, to bring the past close over the last few days. I didn't want it, and it wouldn't do. I had work waiting, and a new recruit to introduce to our ways.

Hartington Chambers, Brant: according to Anna, my personal realm. I smiled at the thought, but of course it wasn't true, except in the narrowest sense. This place was important for numerous reasons and many people. It served the people of Brant, and I served it. But where the clerks were concerned, there was a whisper of truth in her teasing words. That morning the place was quiet; the cleaners had been in very early, and the heating had been on for an hour or so. I hung up my coat, booted up my computer and looked at the electronic diary for the day. Seeing nothing that required immediate action, I idly tidied my desk, which required no tidying, and thought about what the day might bring. Foremost in my mind was the newly-appointed Lauren, and the things she needed to learn.

Sometimes people asked me what I did as a job. Most had no idea what went on in chambers, in the law generally, and certainly not what I did. 'Clerk' probably brought up images in their mind of a lowly dogsbody and penpusher – probably about right for when I first started – but with the rapid evolution of the past two decades it was sometimes a race to keep up, especially with the developments in technology. Increasingly we were expected to be masters of IT, marketing and property management as well as the traditional role of looking after the barristers. Hartington was a small provincial set so we were less high-powered than some of the big London chambers, many of which employed specialist staff to manage things like marketing, credit control and hospitality. Hartington, while equally under the vigilant eye of the Bar Standards Board, managed these things in-house, but while increasingly clerks had their own specialisms I kept an overview and considered it part of my job to understand every part of our role. Of course I would not expect a new recruit to have a handle on it all, but I would expect her to learn quickly; here was no milieu for plodders and dullards.

I heard the front door open and close, and a moment later Anna put her head round my open door.

'Morning, boss,' I said. 'You look tired. Must have been a hectic weekend.'

'The usual frantic social whirl,' she said. 'You know me, always on the party circuit.' She grinned – we both knew the reality. 'So, anything I should know?'

'I'll recheck and write you a list,' I said, 'and I'll deliver it to you with a cup of coffee.'

'That sounds wonderful.'

'But,' I reminded her, 'I'm going to be busy today getting our new clerk bedded in.' I gave her a severe look. 'I hope you've picked a good one.'

'So do I,' she said, pretending to shiver, 'or I'll never hear the end of it. I suggested she should get here by eight-fifteen today, so she'll probably be the next to arrive. Better get that coffee brewing.' I heard her chuckle as she went down the softly-carpeted corridor to her own room.

I went down to the cubby-hole where we make our own drinks and prepared coffee for Anna. When I crossed the reception area, mug in hand, there was a young woman perched on the edge of one of the chairs, clutching her handbag in her lap. She looked up at me with startled eyes.

'Morning,' I said. 'You must be Lauren. Sorry, I didn't hear you come in. I'll just deliver this to Ms Milburn and I'll be with you.'

I put Anna's coffee on her desk. She was on the phone, and nodded her thanks. Returning to my own room I found Lauren standing outside, arms tight by her side, almost to attention. She was slightly-built, fair hair in a neat knot, and soberly dressed in a dark skirt and jacket with a white blouse underneath. I thought I detected a look of surprise as she took in my own less sober outfit, and I suppressed a smile.

I held out my hand, and she shook it briefly. 'I'm Janet Clarke, Senior Clerk. Yes, I know, the name fits the function. Did you have a coat? I can show you where to stow it.'

She shook her head. 'No, I… my father drove me today.'

'Right. Can I get you coffee, tea?'

'No, thank you.'

'All right, so before the hordes start pouring in I'll give you a tour of the building and then we can have a chat about your duties.'

Hartington was a warren of a place, Victorian in origin and a pleasant building on the outside, rising three storeys on one side of a square. On three sides the buildings are similar, but the fourth is taken up by a big new supermarket. How they got planning permission for that nobody knew, but it was handy. I led Lauren along the corridor, away from Anna's room. I waved a hand in that direction. 'That just leads to our Head of Chambers' room,' I said, 'plus there's a small washroom.' I opened a door which led to steps going down. 'This goes to the basement. Just used for storage but you may need to go there at times. There's also domestic stuff, the cleaners' cupboard and so on.' She followed me further. 'These rooms on each side are for the barristers. They have their names on the doors, and you'll need to get to know who's where. That door ahead of us goes out to the courtyard, which you can use. The last door on the left is a small meeting room, and there's another, larger one opposite where we have management meetings. Right, let's go upstairs.' She followed me, and I showed her more barristers' rooms and the big open space where the majority of the clerks operated. 'There's another floor,' I said, indicating the stairs. 'About five more barristers' rooms up there. But I don't want to overwhelm you with information. You'll pick all that up as you go along. Let's go down now and I'll talk you through things and you can ask any questions you may have. Then I'll bring you back up here and introduce you to the other clerks. They should be in by then. You'll answer to me in the last resort but I'm going to assign you to one of the experienced clerks for shadowing. Apart from my own workload I'm mentoring Charlie at the moment – you met him at your interview – because he's doing the BTEC course, so I have plenty on my plate.' All this time Lauren had barely spoken, just nodding, nervously I thought, every so often. Was I so forbidding? I was doing my best to be pleasant, but perhaps my impatience was showing. I tried to remind myself what it had been like when I first started, and remembered only that I had to learn on my feet at a great pace and was often bawled out for the mistakes of others as well as my own. This young woman, it seemed to me, had it easy. I hoped she would soon develop the thick skin necessary for survival.

I sat her down in my little office. She again declined coffee, but I made one for myself. 'So, Lauren, tell me, what made you want to be a chambers clerk? Unfortunately, as you know, I was called away on Friday so I didn't get to ask you any questions.'

She leaned forward. 'I've always been around the law,' she said. 'My father's a solicitor. It was his idea, actually. I've been doing a number of temporary jobs since I left college, trying to decide what I really wanted to do.' She spoke softly, with little trace of the local accent. I, on the other hand, had never lost mine. It was not the sort of accent anyone would strive to achieve – guttural, full of glottal stops, in fact pretty ugly – but when you grew up on the Winstone estate it was hard to avoid. I think mine might have softened a bit over the years but I knew I still sounded a bit like a market trader shouting her wares. My sisters commented once on the contrast between how I sounded and the words I used, hardly surprising when you considered all the law reading I'd done, the courts I'd been in and the daily content of my work, not to mention my association with the barristers, especially Anna, who has, as well as a comprehensive command of the English language, the most amazing voice.

'Your dad's a solicitor?' I said. 'Here, in Brant?'

'Yes.' She named a large firm on the other side of the city. We'd had a few dealings with them over the years, but I wasn't familiar with all the solicitors, and had never heard of a Barclay.

'I see. So you had some idea what to expect. Well, it's the usual practice for a new clerk to learn on the job from others who are more experienced, and I see no reason to depart from that. Is there anything you'd like to ask me?'

'Yes,' she said, leaning forward. 'I'd like to know how you came to this work, because you've been doing it a long time, haven't you? And I think a lot has changed.'

I nodded, leaning back in my chair. 'It certainly has. For instance, when I first started, in 1989, in London, there were hardly any computers, and what there were were huge and slow. I didn't come across one for a long time. I was Senior Clerk here in 1993, and we still did everything on paper. It wasn't till 1997 that we put the diary on a computer, and there was no internet then, not for another couple of years.'

'A steep learning curve, then,' Lauren murmured.

'Yes, because once it got going the advances were very rapid. I understand you're pretty savvy in that department.'

'Most people of my age are,' she said modestly. 'You were telling me about your own career. If you don't mind. It's very interesting.'

I looked at her keenly. Was this genuine? Was she being subtly patronising? I decided not to be paranoid. 'I was about your age,' I said. 'Twenty-one. Went up to London to seek my fortune. Found a job as the 'boy' in a set in Gray's Inn. In those days females were rare, so I was a 'boy' even though I was a girl. Caused some huffing among the older barristers when a young woman in a short skirt carried their papers to court.' I watched her; she didn't smile. 'As I'm sure you're aware we moved up the ladder by changing from one chambers to another. I was a Third Junior in Middle Temple, Second Junior in Lincoln's Inn. Then I had a spell out of London: I got a job in Nottingham for a while, saw how things were done in the provinces. I came back to Brant in 1992 – I came from here originally – and found a job as a Junior at Hartington. That was in the days when Mr Weldon QC was Head. He was getting towards retirement then, and so was the Chief Clerk, Reg Fenner. Fenner was a funny old chap, could be brusque, but he was extremely knowledgeable and he taught me a lot. He retired first, and by then I'd tried to make myself indispensable. Mr Weldon asked me to take over, even though I was young for it. So you see I was here a few years before Ms Milburn, almost twenty five years now, and a huge amount has changed, as you say. The law itself is always changing, our roles along with it. Hartington has expanded its services, its clientele and its staff, and there are constantly new directives coming from above. We have to run to keep up.' I paused, sipping my coffee, watching her reaction; she sat very still, little moving except her eyes. I sighed. 'Sometimes I feel quite nostalgic for those days when I used to race from court to court, loaded down with law books and barristers' robes.' I looked at Lauren and smiled briefly. 'But we have to move with the times. That involves keeping up with the world of law in general, plus the expectations of our current clients and any new ones we might acquire, and then there's the need for getting all the data into new databases so we can expand our services online, and so on and on. Yes, you're right – much has changed.'

I heard the front door open, and looked up to see Elizabeth Merchant come in along with Claire, a clerk of some years' standing. They were both flushed from the cold air, laughing at some private joke. 'Ah, just the person I needed. Morning, ladies,' I called. 'Claire, can you spare a minute?'

I introduced Lauren to Claire, and left them to their own devices. 'I'm here if you need me,' I said. I hoped they wouldn't. More than that, I hoped to have as little to do with the training of Lauren Barclay as I could decently manage. At that moment I could not have said why, but there was something about her that set me on edge. This was no disqualification; as long as she did the work, I had no quarrel with her. It was not important enough to spend time on analysing my instinctive reaction, and I dismissed her from my conscious mind.

March

I got into work early, as I always did. It gave me a chance to settle my mind before things got busy. It was unseasonably warm that March, and I'd put on powder-blue linen crops and white sandals with a loose jacket in lemon and black. Bob looked up from his coffee and newspaper with raised eyebrows – appreciation or consternation? I wasn't sure – but didn't comment. Despite the summery outfit and the spring weather I was feeling a level of mental discomfort that matched the irritating physical ones: abdominal aches which I put down to the vagaries of menopause. I'd been sleeping badly, getting up in the early hours and pacing round the house, wishing for unattainable oblivion. It did my mood no good.

That morning I'd paused by the front door and looked back at Bob. 'I think I should give up watching the news,' I said.

He looked at me, cup in hand, and nodded. 'Yes. Most of it's pretty depressing.'

'Wars, bombs, maniacs. Nothing seems to get any better. Syria, Afghanistan, Somalia, Korea, Iraq.'

'Libya, Israel, Yemen,' he added.

'And things close to home. School shootings, bridge collapses, avalanches, even an axe attack! But do you know what really made me sick? When they found that mass grave in Ireland. Hundreds of orphans. You wonder if they'll ever find out what really happened. Poor helpless kids. No wonder I don't want anything to do with the church.'

'Ah, but,' Bob said enigmatically.

'But what?'

'The Pope donated 100,000 euros to the poor of Aleppo.'

'Did he? Well, that makes me feel a bit better, I suppose.'

Bob got up and took his cup to the sink. 'You know, a lot of good things do go on,' he said quietly. 'They just don't get reported much.'

'Why do you think that is?' I wondered. 'Do we really have such a thirst for bad news?' I heaved a deep sigh. 'Well, I have to get to work. Do my small part shoring up the crumbling ruin of the law in England.'

Bob turned to look at me and smiled. 'You need more sleep, love. It makes a big difference.'

'If only. Well, I'll see you.'

I was surprised when Claire came through the door when I'd been at my desk barely fifteen minutes.

'Couldn't you sleep either?' I asked her.

She came into my room and pushed the door to. 'I needed a word,' she said. 'Before anyone else gets here.'

'OK, go on.'

'It's our new girl, Lauren. You gave her to me to look after, and it's not been easy. I didn't want to say anything sooner – she's only been with us a month, lots to learn, and we all make mistakes. I know I have.'

'But?' Now I was all attention.

Claire sighed. 'Look, I don't want to be mean, but I'm not sure how bright she is, to be honest. Or maybe it's just that she's a bit slow. And you know better than I do – you have to be quick on the uptake in this line of work. There's no time for daydreaming or doing half a job.'

'Anything specific?'

'There've been a few minor things, nothing in themselves, but it adds up to ...well, an impression. And then I gave her something to do by herself. You remember the case Elizabeth was defending?'

'Birmingham? Went well, I heard.'

'It almost didn't. I asked Lauren to arrange the train and the accommodation for Elizabeth. Plenty of instructions – when the case was due to begin, recommendations for hotels. She noted it all down, seemed to take it all on board. The thing is, I can't be chasing her up every five minutes. I've got my own work to do. Luckily it got flagged up, because I found she'd just, well –' She paused, looking nonplussed. I waited. 'She just hadn't done it. I found out the night before Elizabeth was due in Birmingham, and she, Elizabeth that is, checked with me on her way out, you know, just "Everything OK for tomorrow, Claire? I haven't been told about any reservations." So I looked, and there was nothing. I was very embarrassed, I can tell you, Janet. Obviously it was OK, I put it all straight there and then, and Elizabeth went off to Birmingham the next morning. Lauren had gone home by then but when she came in the next day I tackled her about it and she was, how do I put this? Defensive. I didn't yell at her or anything, but all she could say was that she was sorry, though she didn't seem very sorry to me, and that everyone gets things wrong sometimes. I don't think she understands, Janet – what we do can actually make or break a case. If we don't get the details right someone's going to find themselves in the wrong court, or the right court on the wrong day, or with the wrong papers. Some poor person's case will be deferred, and it makes us look bad.'

I thought. Today hadn't started well, and it seemed to be continuing in the same vein. 'OK, Claire, just keep this quiet for now – it's true, we all get things wrong, and she's still pretty new. I'll have a word with Anna about it when she comes in. But thanks for telling me.'

Claire seemed reluctant to go.

'Something else?' I asked.

'Look, this is pretty cringe-making, and I'm not one for gossip, but I think there may be another distraction.' Claire's face was red.

'Don't tell me – Charlie.' She nodded. 'Which one's making the running?'

'Charlie. But she plays up to him.'

'No wonder she's losing the plot. All right, Claire, this is just silly. I'll have a stern word with Charlie. If he turns up with red ears you'll know why.'

She smiled, clearly relieved. 'I'm glad it's him, not me,' she said with a small giggle.

'So you should be.'

When Anna trudged in, looking loaded down with both files and weariness, she called to me. 'Will you come to my room as soon as you can, please?'

Breaking with tradition – one I'd instituted very early on – I made her a cup of coffee and put it on the desk in front of her.

'Janet, you are an angel.' She wrapped her hands round the mug and sipped. 'Perfect.'

'What can I do for you?' I asked.

'I've been up to the very small hours working on this wretched application. I wondered if you'd look at it for me, see if there's anything I've missed, or if there's anything that doesn't sound right. Not now, of course – maybe you could take it home with you this evening.' She took another gulp of her coffee. 'You know how long it's taken me. I'll be glad to see the back of it.'

'Of course, if you think I have anything to contribute.'

She looked at me keenly. 'I trust your judgment. You know that very well.'

I shrugged. 'Sure. I understand. It's important. This is what could get you an interview.'

She sighed. 'Lots of hoops to jump through. Great, I'll e mail it to you.' When I didn't leave, she said, 'Was there something you wanted to talk about?'

'Yes. I don't want to load you up with trivia, and of course it's for me to deal with, but you should know.' I told her, as briefly as I could, the gist of my conversation with Claire. She sat in her chair, swinging gently from side to side, listening, eyes closed. When I fell silent she drained her cup and set it down.

'OK, I see. But how long has she been working for us? A few weeks?' I nodded. 'It's not long, and there's a lot to learn. Happily the thing with Elizabeth's arrangements got sorted out. We should cut her some slack, shouldn't we? Once she's gained some experience she should shape up. Maybe you should keep an eye on her yourself, Janet.' This was not what I wanted to hear. 'Look, I must crack on. I've got court at eleven and things to prepare. I'll just pop to the loo first.'

She got up and went out in her stockinged feet, smiling at me as she passed, a distracted, distant sort of smile, I thought. I picked up her coffee mug, and as I did so her phone, which she had left on her desk, pinged to announce an incoming text. I wouldn't have gone out of my way to read it, of course, but it was there under my eyes. 'Looking forward to seeing you tonight. HoG xx.'

Who was 'HoG'? To be seeing her tonight, and sending her kisses? It was no business of mine, but there was a time, I thought, when she would have told me. Clearly it wasn't just the application for Deputy District Judge that was making her so preoccupied. A small cold fear eddied its way around the region of my heart. Was Anna, bit by bit, moving away? She had new friends now, I knew, in particular Rachel Wells, who had asked Anna to be a godparent to her baby daughter. If she got through the stages of her application, if she started to work as a Deputy District Judge, even though the commitment was not onerous, she would be less often in chambers, and inevitably in time she'd be looking to move up that particular ladder. Now, if there was some man in her life, there'd be yet another thing making her less and less dependent on our friendship. I didn't doubt her loyalty; but there was only so much time at any individual's disposal.

She put her head round my door on her way back from the washroom. 'Will you be able to look at the application tonight, do you think?'

I nodded. 'I should do. Bob's on nights again so I'll be on my own.' A thought struck me. 'But you know,' I said casually, 'there probably won't be time to discuss any issues at work. You've got a full day out of chambers tomorrow, and I'm always up to my neck in work. Are you busy tomorrow evening?'

She shook her head. 'Don't think so.'

'Come over to ours after work. Have something to eat, crack a bottle. Then we can work on your application, if it needs it.'

Her smile was tired, but warm. 'That sounds great, thanks. It's been ages since we had a chance for a chinwag. Around seven? Can I bring Gordon? He'll have been on his own all day.'

'Yes, that's fine.'

'Oh, and Janet. Don't worry too much about young Lauren. You're probably thinking we didn't do a very good job in your absence – Elizabeth, Charlie and me – but I promise you she came across very well at the interview. I'm sure she'll improve.' She laughed. 'Besides, what harm can one silly girl realistically do?'

When she'd gone I shook my head. I hoped what she'd said hadn't been prophetic; but if nothing else, that throwaway remark convinced me that Anna wasn't thinking straight.

My next job was to deal with Charlie, and after ten minutes I heard his voice as the front door opened, along with Claire's and Lauren's. All three were laughing. I called out to them. 'Morning!'

'Morning, Janet!' they chorused as they made for the corridor.

'Charlie, a moment, please.'

Charlie appeared, looking enquiring.

'Shut the door.'

I saw him frown. Perhaps he had noted my expression.

'I'll get straight to it,' I said. 'Word is there's some nonsense going on upstairs.'

'What nonsense? Says who?' A red flush crept up from his shirt collar.

'You and Miss Barclay. Frankly, you don't have time to waste. And she made a stupid mistake which could have caused us all some embarrassment. I am concerned that neither of you has their mind fully on work. And you have a portfolio to finish. For goodness' sake don't let it slide on account of some foolish flirtation.' He looked at the carpet, shifting from foot to foot, and mumbled something. 'What did you say?'

He looked at me. 'I just...Lauren's only been here a few weeks. We all make mistakes.'

I sighed. 'I'm aware of that. Look, what you do in your own time is up to you, but I don't want a lot of tomfoolery in working hours. What's the point of me taking time to steer you through this course if you're not giving it your full attention? I thought you had more sense. That's why I asked you to sit in on the interview when I couldn't be there. Now I'm wondering if maybe it wasn't her CV that persuaded you.'

He smirked at this, and I was reminded that he was little more than a boy himself, not much older than Drew. He noted my narrowed eyes and instantly sobered.

'OK, fair enough,' he muttered. 'I'll back off. But it's not all me, you know. The clerks' room's always full of banter.'

'Banter's one thing. Cock-ups are another. And if I have a go at you it's because I think you are capable of better things. As long as you are ruled by your brain, not some other item of your anatomy.'

For a moment he looked shocked; then he laughed. 'Hey!' he protested.

'Go on, scoot. Get some work done.'

That evening I prepared something ready for the following day so that I could just heat it up and waste none of the time I had with Anna. It would take a matter of minutes to knock up a salad and open a bottle. Bob went off to work with a perfunctory wave, and the house was silent. I spent an hour combing through Anna's application, and was surprised. There were some small errors in it, which was not at all typical of her; and it was far too modest when detailing her relevant experience and achievements, which didn't surprise me. There was enough to justify a meeting; but I hoped we could talk about other things as well.

She arrived early the following evening. I hadn't seen her all day in chambers; she'd gone home direct from court. She looked fresh and floral in a long cotton tunic over darker trousers, and wore a pastel-patterned scarf round her neck. She had a very small patch of scarring there from a scald she'd given herself last year, and she was unnecessarily conscious of it.

'I can't get over how warm it is,' she said as she dumped her bag. 'Most unlikely for March. Can I let this dog out in the garden, Janet?'

'Yes, of course.' I gave the pot a last stir and took off my apron. 'Pasta OK?'

'Lovely. It smells good!' She slid into a chair at the table, and I poured her a glass of wine. 'I have to be moderate,' she said. 'Water only after this one. I drove here.' She took a sip. 'I saw Bob. We bumped into one another at the gate – literally. Gordon managed to wind his lead round Bob's ankles.'

'Yes, he's at work at seven, and running late. So probably actually running.'

Anna looked at me, a small frown creasing her brows. 'I thought he looked a bit under the weather.'

'Really? He hasn't said.'

'You haven't noticed anything?'

I shook my head. 'What with work, and shifts, we're ships that pass in the night these days. By the time he gets in tomorrow morning I'll be out of the door. Then he sleeps most of the day. He did say he felt he was getting too old for shifts, but then he's been saying that for years.'

'He does very stressful work.'

'So do we, don't we?'

She shook her head. 'Of course we're busy, and what we do is important and can be frustrating, but we don't pick bodies out of mangled cars. It must tell on him.'

'Hm, I suppose. And he hardly ever talks about it anymore. But maybe he does, with his mates at the station. Right, shall we eat, then attack this application form of yours before I have too many more glasses of this lovely stuff?'

We worked on Anna's form and at the end of it I thought it was quite polished. The errors were gone, and more had been made of Anna's successes (she'd protested, but I'd insisted.) I closed the folder with the printed script in it. 'I don't see how they can possibly not call you for interview. I mean, if you received this application, wouldn't you be bowled over with admiration?'

'No,' Anna said with an unconvincing scowl. 'I'd assume it was utter hyperbole, if not an actual pack of lies.'

'Ha! I'll say nothing about Miss Barclay's application, in that case.' I saw her wince. 'OK, I promise to say no more about it – until she makes another blunder, if she does. I'll make some coffee, shall I? We can drink it somewhere more comfortable.'

When I came into the living room, tray in hand, Anna was stretched out on the sofa, shoes off, eyes closed. 'Do make yourself at home,' I said. I put the tray down on a low table and poured two cups of coffee. 'Shall I pass it to you, or can you manage to stretch out a limp hand, do you think?'

She sat up with a groan and took a cup from me. 'Thanks. Enough of your sarcasm – it's been a tiring week.' She took a sip and looked all round, as if taking in every detail of paint shades and soft furnishings. 'Why are you so set on moving house? This place is ideal. You've done it up most tastefully, if I may say so. The garden is manageable. It's a good size for three people and no pets. Which reminds me, Gordon's still out, and it's dark.'

'I'll get him,' I said. I went through to the kitchen and opened the door. 'Come in, old man,' I said to the grateful dog huddled on the other side of the door. 'Your mistress is getting forgetful in her dotage.'

'The cheek,' Anna muttered. 'You're at least five years older than me.'

'Four.'

'Whatever. Hello, Gordon – sorry I forgot you. Blame Janet's great cooking. Anyway, what was I saying? Why do you want to move? It's a nice house. Handy for Bob.'

I must have had more to drink than I thought, and I was certainly more at ease than I had been for some time, feeling that our friendship was back on its undemanding path. For whatever reason, I told far more than I would normally have done, breaking a habitual reserve. 'What you said the other day. About moving away from something, not towards.'

She raised an eyebrow. 'Away from what?'

'My family. What else?'

She eyed me thoughtfully. 'We've known each other for many years, but I don't really know very much about your background at all – apart from the fact that you've pulled yourself up by your bootstraps and so have a jaded view of everyone you consider privileged, me included. Which I suppose is fair enough. And I know you have a lot of siblings and a father but no mother. Do you really not get on with any of them?'

'My sisters are OK,' I said. 'My father's a nightmare. But I also have four brothers.'

'Four!' She looked startled. 'That beats even me.'

'Well, you know about Ben, the youngest. He's a good lad, tries to do his best, had trouble being born and then when he was little started having seizures, so he's not altogether, how do I put it? a hundred percent. And there's David, but he hardly counts – he escaped to Australia years ago and didn't come back. He's got a job and a wife and two kids we've never met. A life. I hope it's a nice one. He sends cards at Christmas, that's all. No, they're not the problem.' For a moment I closed my eyes, and when I opened them she was looking at me with that peculiar intense gaze she has, totally focused. I heaved a sigh. 'I have brothers who are twins. Matthew and James, Mattie and Jimmy. They are crooks.'

Her eyebrows disappeared into her hairline. 'Are you sure?'

'They've been trouble since they were about twelve, if not younger. Identical, so very alike, and they pulled stunts only they found amusing, covering for each other – you can imagine the kind of thing. It was because of them I came back to Brant, when I'd got away from them all, plus my first marriage, and swore I'd never come back. They were fourteen and got into trouble with the local police, a bit more than a boyish prank: property was missing and damaged, and there were numerous complaints. Because of my background in the law my father – very grudgingly – appealed to me and I – equally reluctantly – came home and helped to sort it out. Of course they swore they'd behave, and it did give them a fright, but what actually happened was they got cannier and more slippery. They've never been inside, though I'm sure they deserve it. I don't know where they get their money from, and I'm not sure I want to. Neither of them has a job as such – they just laugh and say they've made some good investments. Anyway, way back when they first got caught the job at Hartington was vacant and I took it – as a stopgap, so I thought. The rest you know. I would have gone back to London, but by then they'd offered me the Senior Clerk post and not long after that I met Bob. But maybe you can see why my horrible brothers make me want to run a mile. They're very shady, and that's being charitable. I work in the law. Embarrassing.'

'Ouch. I didn't even know you had twin brothers, Janet. You've never mentioned them.'

I shrugged. 'You can see why. The strange thing is, if you were to meet them you probably wouldn't suspect. They can be charming, in a laddish sort of way. They're good looking, full of fun, a bit flash. Neither is married, though they've had a string of girlfriends, a different one every time you see them. But you can't trust them. Not an inch.'

She frowned. 'Do you think they've ever been actually violent?'

'I don't think so. It's not their style. They're not gangsters exactly. Just unscrupulous, cheats, scammers. Whatever they can pull off and get away with, whatever makes money. I don't know the ins and outs of it. I try not to know.'

'And I thought my brothers were a headache,' Anna murmured. 'Well, not Alastair, obviously.'

'From what I gather your brothers are model citizens compared,' I said. 'But while I'm complaining about my relations you might as well hear the whole story. A few weeks ago Drew came home and told us he'd got engaged to Tiffany. If that comes off I'll be related by marriage to the Leamans. And there's not a thing I can do about it.'

Anna almost choked. She put her cup down on the table and flopped back on to sofa, howling with laughter. 'Oh, Janet,' she gulped when she'd regained a mite of control. 'I'm sorry – it's not funny really. But it also is.' She wiped her eyes with the back of her hand. 'I don't envy you. That's the thing – we never know who our kids are going to lumber us with.'

'It's not Tiffany I object to,' I said. 'She's a nice enough girl, and she'll probably be good for Drew. I guess there's more to her than meets the eye, even though she seems so quiet and mild. But only last year we were defending her father on a murder charge, and there's still that unresolved suspicion that trails him like a dirty cloud.'

'I know,' she said, sobering. 'You'll just have to meet as seldom as you can and maintain just necessary politeness.'

'Not so easy,' I said. 'One day Drew and Tiffany may have a child. Then we'll be joint grandparents.'

She shook her head. 'That's a long way off yet, Janet. Worry about it if and when it comes. Sufficient unto the day, and all that.'

'I suppose.' It occurred to me that the future may well hold more than one unwelcome change. If Anna did become a Deputy District Judge, the next step up would be to District Judge, and that was a salaried post, meaning she would not be able to function as a barrister. What would chambers be like without her? Who would replace her? And how would that affect me? I said nothing; but it was an uncomfortable train of thought.

'I should be getting home,' Anna said, heaving herself up from the sofa. 'Where did I leave my shoes?'

'I think they're scattered in the hallway.'

She didn't move for a moment, and I sensed there was something she wanted to say. She looked away from me, and I saw a pink flush creeping along her cheekbones. 'Since we're being confiding,' she said, 'perhaps I should tell you something.'

I folded my arms and pursed my lips. 'Let me guess: you're seeing some man or other.'

She turned towards me, and her startled expression was comical. 'How did you arrive at that conclusion?'

'You've been distracted lately, a bit not quite there.'

'That could have been the fault of this monster.' She patted the file which contained her application. 'It's taken up a lot of my time.'

'And you're always tired.'

'Ha! Well, don't read too much into that.'

'Go on, then. Who is he, this lucky chap?'

'Not sure about lucky. Jeremy. Jeremy Adebayo. He's a consultant Obstetrician and Gynaecologist at the hospital. I think he had oversight of Rachel during her pregnancy and delivery – not that he actually delivered Lucy himself. That might have made things awkward seeing as he knows Rachel and Michael socially.'

'Is that how you met him?'

'Yes, at a dinner party they gave before Christmas. Rachel swears she wasn't matchmaking, but I'm not sure I believe her. Anyway she's very smug about it all. Says she absolutely knew we'd get on.'

'Adebayo. That doesn't sound like it goes with Jeremy.'

Anna smiled. 'He's Nigerian. A widower. And he wasn't christened Jeremy. He adopted it for working here in the UK. His parents were very devout, and he's the only son. He was baptised Hand of God.'

'Good heavens. I can see why that might be a bit alarming for the average British patient, especially a woman at a vulnerable time of her life.'

'Terrifying.'

'Is he devout too?'

'Pretty much.'

'Well, you're a dark horse.'

Anna stuffed her feet into her shoes and pulled her coat down from the hook. 'I didn't want to say anything too soon, in case it turned out to be a damp squib.'

I pretended to look horrified. 'Are you telling me this might actually be serious? Not a fling? Not an indulgence of middle-aged lust?'

She looked pained, and I suppressed a grin. 'Oh, Janet. If only. I might have to marry him to enjoy any of that. He's quite stern on the subject.'

‘Good grief. I didn’t know anyone was, not anymore.’

She smiled. ‘But then you’re a dyed-in-the-wool heathen.’

‘Maybe not,’ I murmured. ‘I was raised Catholic. Extremely lapsed.’

‘Well, well.’ She shook her head. ‘That’s most interesting, and I shall insist on knowing more. A conversation for another day, I think.’

‘If ever. “Lapsed” is too kind a description for me, I’m afraid. More like “hopeless case.” It’s not something I think about if I can help it.’

‘We’ll see. I’m not a barrister for nothing, you know. I have powers of persuasion.’ She patted my arm. ‘Thanks for looking at my script, Janet. And for a lovely meal and your company. I’ll see you in the morning.’

‘I think you’re forgetting something. Didn’t you come with a dog?’

I fell asleep promptly that night, but woke again at four o’clock with a dragging pain low down in my abdomen, and when I tottered to the bathroom there was a gush of blood. I swore under my breath, cursing the day I was born female, and stayed where I was, perched on the toilet, till it had more or less stopped. I did what was necessary, took a couple of painkillers and went back to bed. Alcohol, analgesia and exhaustion served to knock me out as if I’d been hit with a sock full of wet sand, and it was only Bob coming in at half past seven that jolted me back to consciousness.

He put his head round the door as I sat on the edge of the bed, feeling less than fresh.

‘Are you ill?’ he said. ‘Why aren’t you dressed and going to work?’

‘Rough night,’ I mumbled. I got up and staggered to the door.

‘Wait.’ He took me by both elbows and gave me an assessing look, frowning and muttering as I stood there desperate only for a shower and a cup of hot tea. ‘You look awful.’

I squinted up at him. 'Thanks. To be honest, you don't look so good yourself. Kind of grey.'

'Tired. Night shift.'

'Is that all there is to it?'

'Maybe not. But you've just sneakily deflected my clinical observations.'

'I don't think "You look awful" is much of a clinical observation. And if you don't let me go I'll be late for work.'

'Is it just the usual thing? Or are you brewing up some infection?'

I wriggled out of his grasp. 'I'm never ill – you know that. Just my age. Did some bleeding in the night. I really need a shower. And you need to get some sleep.'

'All right. But I absolutely need to talk to you tonight.'

'Fine.'

The shower and the tea did their work, and by eight thirty I was on my way to chambers. The traffic was heavy and I knew I would be late, but it couldn't be helped. Bob's washed-out, baggy-eyed face came back to me and I wondered if I should be concerned. Bob was a natural stoic and never complained, but he was fifty-three and he'd been doing this job for twenty-eight years. Was it all getting too much for him?

If he hadn't been a paramedic we would probably never have met. I remembered with clarity the day I came to, lying on the pavement of a shopping street where I'd gone on a busy Saturday afternoon to buy some new shoes, a circle of goggling bystanders staring down at me, and a tall man in a green uniform squatting by my head. 'What happened?' I heard my voice slurring – not unlike the incident in the changing rooms a few weeks earlier, but for a very different reason.

A few moments later I found myself stretchered into the back of an ambulance, my head immobilised. A second ambulance was parked along the street, and I had time to see a crunched motorbike a few yards away and a car with its wing smashed in and one wheel on the kerb.

They took me into A and E but it turned out I was just bruised and scratched and mildly concussed, so I got sent home with painkillers and warnings and symptoms to look out for. I only found out what had happened sometime later – from Bob. I remembered hearing a loud bang and a scream, but that was all. Apparently a car had gone out of control, careering across the carriageway into a motorcyclist and knocking me off my feet so that my head came into jarring contact with a letterbox. After a few days the headache subsided, although the physical shock took longer. For several weeks, on and off, I was plagued with nightmares, and knowing the reason didn't stop me waking up at all hours trembling with fright. It happened not long after I'd been offered the Senior Clerk's post at Hartington; it was early July, a few days before my twenty-fifth birthday. A long time later Bob admitted it hadn't been easy maintaining his professional cool when my cotton skirt was rucked up revealing a lot of bare leg.

Weeks later I bumped into Bob again. I didn't recognise him for a moment because he was in ordinary clothes. I was in the restaurant of a department store, weaving my way through the tables with a loaded tray towards where a friend was sitting waiting. Now I couldn't even remember her name; she was someone who'd come into chambers on some work experience scheme, and she didn't stay long. As I pushed past I heard a vaguely familiar voice. 'Hello – how are you?'

I looked down and there was a man I knew I had seen before, but couldn't remember where.

He saw my puzzlement. 'Same old story,' he said with a smile warm enough to melt chocolate. 'We pick them up and put them back together and they forget us.'

'Oh!' I took a step back, and the tray wobbled. 'Of course I haven't forgotten.' I thought hard, and a name badge swam up to conscious memory. 'It's Bob, isn't it?'

'Well remembered,' he said. 'Are you all right now?'

'Yes, fine, thanks to you and your partner. What happened to the other guy – the boy that got knocked off his motorbike?'

He shrugged. 'We don't usually get to know what happens to people once we deliver them to the hospital, but I'm pretty sure he didn't die.' This was delivered so deadpan it startled me – but I realised that people dying was probably quite a common thing in his working day.

We exchanged a few pleasantries and I joined my friend.

'Who's that?' she demanded. 'He looks nice. A bit old, but nice.'

'Does he? I wouldn't know,' I said. This particular young woman was always asking me about my love life, and seemed to find its nonexistence personally affronting. I'd told her some time before, 'I'm divorced. I'm not interested in going down that particular route ever again,' but she was obviously not convinced. I told her, 'He's one of the paramedics who helped me the other week, when I was in that accident. That's all. So you needn't get all quivery with excitement.'

She'd had another friend to meet, and clearly I was of little interest, so once she'd downed her coffee she'd left, leaving me sipping mine and thinking of nothing in particular. A moment later Bob appeared at my elbow. 'May I?'

I was surprised, but said 'Of course,' quite casually, laughing inside at the thought of my friend missing what would have been, for her, a tasty morsel of gossip. And it was strange, thinking about it now, how an hour had slithered past unnoticed as we talked, mostly about our work. Like many people who didn't know much I was intrigued by the cases he had dealt with, and he was equally fascinated by what must have seemed to him a closed, arcane world of dusty tomes and bewigged dinosaurs in Victorian courtrooms.

We were both completely wrong, and the process of enlightening the other made us both chuckle.

Stuck for the moment in the inevitable traffic jam, I wondered what he wanted to talk about this evening. Could it be, finally, that he'd decided to look for some other role within the ambulance service? I'd floated this idea on a few occasions with no success; but I figured Bob was a grown up, he knew better than anyone what his job entailed and whether he felt equal to it, so it was his decision. The notion of moving house was a different matter altogether.

Momentarily the queue of cars snaked forward, but then there were traffic lights, and we all slowed and braked. I took the opportunity to text Anna and warn her I would be late. Once the lights changed, I managed to edge across the intersection, only to grind to a halt on the other side. The roads were, it seemed, in a constant state of being repaired, with all the snarl-ups that entailed. There was little use in getting steamed up about it, even with my tendency to impatience; the only result would be a rise in blood-pressure. Perhaps it was thinking about how I had first met Bob; perhaps it was the natural progression to accidents and ambulances, but I found my mind drifting back into the past in a most unwelcome direction.

From time to time – not often – I test my memories to see that they are safe, sanitised, unlikely to erupt disastrously onto the well-lit stage of my present preoccupations. That day, with nothing else to do, I allowed the connections to happen.

I had, long since, told Bob about the day we lost our mother, and after that it was almost never mentioned. I could see little point in rehashing something that couldn't be helped. Nothing would bring her back, and whatever damage had been done was a fact that couldn't be altered, only lived with. I was not a fan of navel-gazing emotional splurges; in my experience they just made you feel worse.

I loved my mother, just because she was my mother and because she was a lovable kind of person – in an exasperating sort of way –

but for as long as I could remember I had been angry with her too: for hooking up with Desmond Yates in the first place, then for getting pregnant with me and giving me an inadequate eighteen-year-old father. It was all fine for the first five years of my life: I was mother's pet, her precious baby girl, and no doubt I sunned myself in that glow of uniqueness. But she wanted more children, and eventually underwent some medical procedure to unblock whatever it was that was stopping that happening. (Given what I later became aware of, it certainly wasn't a case of denying my father his conjugal privileges.) When I was five Pauline was born, and any reduction in maternal attention was recompensed with the novelty of a cute baby sister. Unfortunately for me it didn't stop there. Sibling after sibling arrived: David, then Christine, then Mattie and Jimmy. The twins were a bad mistake. Apart from what they later turned out to be, their birth did her some damage, and she was advised to stop; but barely eighteen months later there was Ben, and Ben's birth was long and hard, depriving him of oxygen for vital minutes. By this time I was old enough to resent them all – the time they stole from me as I was forced to help look after them, the happily flustered distraction of my mother, the state of the house. The only good thing was the frequent absence of my father who was forced to work long hours at the docks to support his family. When I knew more I also, and with vengeful intensity, resented the church which I blamed for encouraging my mother's improvidence, the church to which she devoted herself all her life. I thought of the photograph I had found in the loft, my radiantly smiling mother standing beside her beloved Father Gerard, at my and Pauline's First Communion. Little more than a year after that photo was taken, she was dead.

January 4, 1982. It was a Monday, and the four oldest of us were due back at school the following day. My mother took it into her head that we all needed new equipment for school – a bag for one, a skirt for another, shoes, PE kit. The January sales were in full swing in the city, and we would all go – all eight of us – to take advantage of the bargains, despite the fact that it had snowed the day before and the pavements were slick. As we approached the department store I was at the back of our little procession, pushing a wriggling, whimpering fifteen-month-old Ben in a buggy that had been used by us all and had ominously wobbly wheels. Attached by reins to the handles on each side were the twins, then aged three, who had been bribed by a promise of sweets to behave. In front of me, constantly turning to see if I was still there and halting my already difficult progress, were Pauline and Christine, hand in hand and angelic, but nervous and cold. Christine had lost a glove and tears were running down her pinched little face. Unsurprisingly I was furious: why were we making this expedition on such a terrible day? Why had I been lumbered with the three little ones and a totally inadequate buggy? Why didn't my mother think things through? Not for the first time, I vowed to put myself up for adoption; I felt sure someone would want a daughter who was so handy round the house.

I didn't see it happen, but others did, because the pavements were crowded with shoppers. My mother was well ahead, in charge of David, who unusually was throwing a tantrum. I heard only a screech of brakes, a rumble of tyres, a series of bangs and crunches, a high-pitched wail. For a few seconds there followed an unearthly silence. Then there was shouting, screaming, people surging. For several minutes my brothers and sisters and I couldn't move, hemmed in by the crowd; then I heard a child cry, and recognised my brother David's voice. I think in that moment, at some subliminal level, I knew.

Time seemed first to slow, then to gallop; behind the noise was a great yawning chasm of silence. Eventually we heard approaching sirens and blue lights flashed. Reality seemed to crash back onto my unprotected consciousness, and I heard myself howl, 'Davey! Where are you?' People around me began to pay attention. A large woman in a brown coat loomed. 'Your brother, love? Go on, go and get him. I'll mind these little ones.' I gathered my terrified siblings round the buggy and fought my way through the crowd. I saw my brother immediately, held tightly in the encircling arm of an old man with a white moustache who was squatting beside him. David seemed unhurt, but he was struggling, weeping, his arms flailing. When he saw me he broke away from the old man and ran, throwing himself into my arms, his little body convulsed with sobs. I picked him up and soothed him, and over his shoulder I saw a sight that I have tried to blot out all these years, or at least to rob it of its power: my mother sprawled in the road, her arms outflung, her bag spilling its contents, her hat yards away. Her eyes were closed, her face whiter than the churned-up snow. A thin stream of blood was running down from somewhere beneath her, past her horribly bent leg, into the gutter. At that moment my first response was shame, that my mother was making such a spectacle of herself in a busy street, that her coat and dress were above her knees, her tights torn. Perhaps the thought that she might actually be dead was too huge and momentous to take on board; my stunned brain could not give it room.

After that, of course, adults took over. The big woman in the brown coat appeared with Ben and the twins. I put David down, and he clung to my legs. 'Where are the girls?' I said fiercely. 'Don't let them see.' I grabbed the handles of the buggy and turned it round. 'Boys, come with me. Davey, stop yelling – keep up.' The voice of familiar authority calmed them. I found my sobbing little sisters, and I took them all away to the plate-glass window of the store with its mannequins and glitter, and waited.

This was what I told Bob, many years later, when we were an item but not yet married. I thought he had the right to know why his girlfriend was such a hard nut. The years following my mother's death were chaotic, and I often wondered how any of us had survived as well as we had.

He'd asked me, 'Didn't anyone help you? Not your family, not your siblings, you yourself?'

I thought. 'My dad had to work. Sometimes the kids got farmed out to relatives – there were a couple of his sisters living locally – but they always came back. They'd take the girls, because they were reasonably well-behaved, but even they got sent back after a while, because my dad wasn't too regular giving my aunts any money for their keep. The twins rarely lasted more than days away: they looked like angels, but their behaviour was diabolical. Poor kids had lost their mum – they were all over the place. In the end it was better for them to be at home where they felt familiar. Such as it was – home, I mean.'

'Social Services?'

I shrugged. 'We saw them sometimes. My dad was dead against what he called interference. Maybe that was because his shortcomings would have been all too obvious. He was, is, an arrogant bully.'

'But what about you?' Bob was scowling, clearly appalled.

'I was a mouthy teenager. I told the social workers where to get off. For once my dad was dependent on me, and he held back on all his browbeating, yelling, his threats of taking the strap to us, especially me, even though it went dead against the grain. We were a train-wreck family. It was chaos. What could I do? Six little kids, no mum. I hated it, but I had to do it.'

Bob leant against the sofa back, his arms folded. 'I'd like to think it wouldn't happen nowadays. No wonder you're like you are.'

'What am I like?'

'Independent. Stand-offish. Not easy to get close to.'

I smirked. 'You seem to have managed it.'

He winced. 'I don't mean in that way.' For a moment he was silent. 'So you ended up as a household skivvy? A surrogate mother? At what? Thirteen?'

'Thirteen and a half. And I missed loads of school.' I saw his expression. 'Oh, they sent some woman round, and she tried to sort something out for us, but it never lasted long. See why I wanted to get away, soon as I could?'

'How did you manage? You were just a kid yourself.'

'Huh, even before Mum died I was pretty used to it. Looking after the kids, doing stuff around the house. But a couple of things happened anyway. When Ben was about three – nearly four? Can't remember exactly – he started having fits. Once doctors got involved it blew it all wide open. Then my dad had an accident at work – he was using some piece of machinery with a load on board and it hadn't been secured properly. His foot got badly damaged. There was no way he could go on working, and he'd been a docker all his life – he didn't know anything else, had no qualifications. He got some compensation from the company but that wasn't going to go very far. Luckily there was a sort of self-help scheme that some of the workers had set up and he'd been paying into it, just a few quid a week, for years. So what it meant was, once he was mobile again, he had to be at home and take responsibility. And that gave me as much pleasure as finally being able to get back to school. I had a canny head teacher. She realised what had been going on and made it easy for me, extra lessons after school, good advice. I had a hard time of it with the other kids, what with my dreadful clothes and bad language – I got into a few fights, actually. But I kept my head down, worked really hard and got my GCSEs.'

Bob smiled. 'I guess it didn't hurt that you had a sharp brain on you.'

'Yeah. So they said. Anyway, by the time I met Terry things had improved, but not that much. Dad would skive when he could and go to the pub or the betting- shop, and I'd be back child-minding. So I went out with Terry, worked for my A levels, and stayed away from home as much as I could – it was too noisy for studying, and if I didn't clean up nobody did. I suppose poor little Pauline had to take up the slack then, and she was always more biddable than me, and in fear of Dad.' I slid onto the sofa beside Bob, and gave him a narrow-eyed, sideways stare. He slipped an arm round my shoulders. 'Look, I've told you all this, the nasty little story. I don't want to keep going on about it. Let's forget it. And don't tell anyone, OK? It's done, I'm over it, I've made a life in spite of it. Plenty of people have worse. Lots of kids don't have a decent home. What good is it to go on talking, anyway? It doesn't alter anything.'

Now, as the cars began finally to roll and I accelerated away, I felt strangely upbeat despite my rough night. I'd remembered the day Mum died and I hadn't gone to pieces. Perhaps ignoring it really had worked, whatever the mournful head-wagging pundits said.

I had planned to go and see Anna as soon as I got into chambers, to tell her I was finally there. But when I entered and looked down the corridor I saw that the door to her room was closed. I shed my coat and scarf, went into my own little office and powered up the computer. I checked the diary, and was reminded that Anna had a client that morning. Then I became aware of a hubbub from upstairs. I slipped quietly to the foot of the staircase and listened. The clerks' room was normally noisy, with people shouting questions and making inane remarks, but this exceeded the norm, and if any one of them was on the phone – to a client, a solicitor, the police or another chambers – it was a poor advertisement for our operation if mayhem was erupting in the background. Luckily the position of Anna's room, especially with the door closed, meant that she and her client probably wouldn't be disturbed.

I crept up the stairs and stood in the open doorway for a minute or two before any of them noticed my presence. Claire had a phone clamped to her ear with one hand, and with the other was waving furiously at the others. I saw her press her phone to her chest and hiss, 'Shut up, you lot! I can't hear myself think!' Desks had been pushed aside and in the space that resulted Charlie and Lauren were dancing vigorously, with the others facing them in their swivel chairs, chanting encouragement and clapping. Then one looked towards the doorway and saw me. 'Whoops!' he shouted, and scooted back to his workstation. Moments later they all fell silent, some grinning guiltily, others looking worried, and began creeping back to their desks. Charlie's eyes were wide as he fell into his chair. Lauren alone, red faced and laughing, remained upright.

A bit of nonsense was normal, and I remembered the havoc of the clerks' rooms in several sets where I'd worked. As long as the work got done, I was inclined to be tolerant. But this exceeded all bounds.

'Good morning, everyone,' I said, my tone level, but decidedly chilly. 'I see you have taken advantage of my absence. Please get back to what you were supposed to be doing, and let's do it all in silence, unless you absolutely have to consult a colleague. Lauren, since you seem to have nothing to do, perhaps it's time you and I had a little chat. Come down to my office, please.'

Lauren opened her mouth, I assume to protest, but I ignored her and descended the stairs, and since all the others were now glued to their computer screens there was little she could do but follow. 'Close the door, please.' I sat behind my desk. The only other chair was behind me, by the window, and she didn't quite have the boldness to fetch it. I didn't invite her to sit, so she stood awkwardly, trying not to look at me, scowling.

I spoke pleasantly enough. 'I thought it was time we had a chat to see how you are getting on,' I said, 'and it seems today has provided a good opportunity.' I paused, but she looked at the floor and said nothing. I noticed a flush bloom across her cheek. Good. 'So, perhaps you are finding you don't have enough work to do? Is that it?'

'No, I –' I waited. 'But it wasn't just me! The others –'

I cut her off. 'There's no need to drag anyone else into this. I saw what was going on with my own eyes. Clerks' rooms often are a bit unruly, but as long as the work is done efficiently and they all know when to pipe down, that's fine with me. No, I am asking you how you are getting on, whether you like the work, because you are relatively new.'

'It's OK, I suppose. A bit more boring than I thought.'

'Do you feel you're getting a handle on all the things we have to do to make sure cases and queries that come in are dealt with properly? The necessity for carrying out instructions to the letter, for instance?'

Her flush deepened. 'You're talking about me forgetting to book Ms Merchant's hotel and that,' she muttered. 'Yeah, well, it got sorted out. Everyone makes mistakes, don't they?' She looked at me, a challenge in her expression. 'Even you must have, when you were new.'

'I'm sure I did,' I said icily. 'But I would have expected to be torn off a strip and threatened with dismissal if I didn't improve, not patted on the head and told, "There, there." You have to learn fast in this business.' Her eyes narrowed, and she said nothing. I tried again. 'You do realise, don't you – Claire must have spelled it out – that when a clerk, even a lowly one such as yourself, makes a cockup and it isn't noticed in time, what the end result might be?' I saw her frown at being described as 'lowly,' but she again said nothing, merely shrugged. 'Let's take your unfortunate lapse of memory as an example. If we had had to make arrangements for Ms Merchant at the last minute, she might have been late for her case, or perhaps never have got to court in time. That would have resulted in a waste of public money – preparing the court and its officers for something that had to be postponed. It would have damaged Ms Merchant's reputation, when it wasn't her fault, and also the reputation of this chambers. Too many gaffes and solicitors will think twice about hiring us. Not only that, but whoever had brought the action, the person who was relying on getting his or her case dealt with, would have had to wait even longer. That's very stressful.'

Lauren's face was flaming red. 'But that's not fair,' she said, her voice rising. 'That's putting too much on me when I haven't been here long. I can't be expected to know everything.'

'I quite agree,' I said, 'and I don't expect it. That would be unreasonable. I wanted to give you a worst-case scenario so that you were in no doubt as to the importance of the tasks you are set, however trivial or boring they may seem. But what I do expect is fast learning. If you don't understand something, ask. Write a list of what you are required to do, and check it, more than once. With so much to take on board I am surprised you have time for dancing in office hours.'

'But that was Cha –' she wailed.

I cut her off. 'I'm sure Charlie needed no encouragement,' I said. 'But Charlie does seem to understand, most of the time, the consequences of his actions. You can be sure I will be speaking to Charlie. But it's you I am talking to now. I hope it's all clear. If it is, we'll say nothing more about it. Feel free to go back upstairs and get on with your work.'

She flung out of the room, letting the door bang unnecessarily loudly behind her. I heard her running up the stairs. There was silence for about a minute; then I heard a howl of laughter. Someone must have closed the clerks' room door, because the sound was suddenly muted, but I could still hear it, and I felt rage and horror rise within me. What were they laughing at? Was it the laughter of relief that the storm had passed? Or was Lauren, as seemed all too possible, whispering something to them all, mocking me, perhaps even mimicking? Was I being paranoid, or was the little minx stirring up disaffection? I didn't expect to be grovelled to, but I did count on a level of respect. I let my indignation cool, and wondered how I should handle it.

About twenty minutes later there came a quiet tap on my door. At my invitation Claire sidled in. I looked up enquiringly, my expression bland.

'Janet,' she said in a rush, 'you must think I'm making a terrible job of looking after Lauren. But I'm telling you, it hasn't been easy. I didn't want to make a fuss, not while she's new, and I don't like dropping people in it, but really –' I waited. When she didn't continue, I said, 'I think you'd better tell me everything. Pull up a chair.'

She fetched the chair and sat down. 'I can't be long. I said I was going to the loo. And anyway, I'm waiting on a call from Mr Phelps.' She leaned forward. 'To be honest, Janet, Lauren's a nightmare. I mean, she's quite fun if you like that sort of thing, and some of the others do, especially Charlie, but there's a time and a place. Just because her dad's a solicitor she seems to think she knows better than everybody else, that she doesn't have to apply herself to learning how we do things. I've tried everything I can think of, but I'm coming to the conclusion that she's that awful combination – a bit thick, hates criticism, thinks she's God's gift.'

I thought. 'We keep a watching brief, I think, Claire,' I said at last. 'I have a bad feeling about this, but I don't want to be prejudiced. Perhaps she'll improve.' I saw Claire shake her head. 'I know, you've had to deal with it and I haven't. But now you need to keep me up to speed. I realise you don't like tattling, but we have to keep a close eye on her. We can't afford to have a snotty, dim, spoilt little miss with a sense of entitlement in our midst. We give her a chance to learn and improve and generally come on board, and if she can't or won't…' I let the thought hang.

Claire got up. 'I must go,' she said. 'I'm glad you know about it now, anyway.'

'Oh, by the way,' I said casually as she opened the door. 'What was all the laughing about when she came back up?'

I caught Claire's look of horror before she suppressed it. 'I don't think you want to know,' she said awkwardly.

'Just what I thought,' I said. 'All right, Claire. Off you go.'

The rest of that morning I sorted out a few routine tasks. I made phone calls, even exchanged a joke or two with people I knew well. Anna came in when she'd seen her client out, asked how I was. She seemed distracted, and I knew she had preparation to do for a case the following day. I was certainly not going to bother her with the doings of a potential loose cannon. If and when the need arose, I would deal with it. I considered myself to be reasonably forbearing, as Senior Clerks go, but I wasn't going to let the smooth operation I had built up over almost twenty-five years be threatened by a troublemaking pipsqueak like Lauren Barclay.

Twenty-five years is a long time to be in one job. Perhaps that was why I went home that day relatively unperturbed: I'd been in potentially difficult situations before, both before and after becoming Senior Clerk; and in any job where there are people, there are always awkward customers and clashes. I may even have been one of those awkward customers myself at times, even though I tried hard to keep my nose (and reputation) clean. Whatever the case, I went home that evening calm.

Bob was not only up, he had cooked and done some housework. 'Good day?' he asked.

'Yes, thanks, OK.'

'How's the new girl doing?'

'Ah, since you ask, a little issue may be brewing.'

He turned from the hob where he was stirring, and raised an enquiring eyebrow. 'Are you bothered?'

I smiled. 'I can handle it.'

'Should I warn her? Does she even know what might be coming her way?'

'The others will oblige, I dare say. Anyway, what do you know about it? I don't think you've ever been on the receiving end, have you? Not in living memory.'

'Probably not,' Bob said. He started putting cutlery on the table. 'I'm too canny. But I've heard you bawling Drew out a few times.'

'Hm, well, Drew's another matter altogether.'

Bob gave me a look. 'Drew's not a bad lad. He'll turn out fine, you'll see.'

'Ha, you're hopelessly biased. No, I know he's OK really. But it doesn't do to let him know I think so. Boys are so very prone to conceit.'

Bob laughed. 'Says you! OK, do whatever you need to, love, because this is ready.'

'Good – I'm starving.'

Bob pushed his chair back from the table. 'Leave the dishes,' he said. 'There's something I want to run past you.'

'I'll make some coffee.'

In the living room, mug in hand, I kicked off my shoes and stretched out on the sofa. 'Go on, then. Before I drop off.'

Bob took a deep breath. 'I've been thinking about work. My work. You've said before, when I've been doing nights on the trot and come home whacked – why don't I go for some other role? Well, before I've always said no, I can cope. But I'm beginning to wonder if that's true anymore.' He paused, and I waited. 'The thing is, the job's changed. When I first started, and for years afterwards, there was always something to go for – some new aspect, some new directive, a training course – and you know, I lapped that up. Obviously I was a lot younger and keener in those days. And it all seemed so worthwhile then – I felt that I was really doing some good, at least most of the time. I'm not saying it was all plain sailing – of course it wasn't. Things went wrong, stuff you can't do anything about, tragic unnecessary accidents, babies that die, teenagers that hang themselves because of lousy exam results – all those awful things that break your heart with the waste of it. But then there were the days when you actually got to save someone's life. It's why I wanted to be a paramedic in the first place. Maybe it's what motivates most of us in this job, at least in the beginning, because I don't suppose it's the pay or the hours.' He smiled crookedly. 'But you know, things are different these days. Our role has changed. When you get a 999 call it's less likely to be an old-fashioned emergency like a traffic accident. What I'm finding now is I'm doing a lot more with people with dementia, people with mental illnesses, self-harm, and a lot of drug-and drink-related calls. I'm not saying these things aren't important, but do I really want to spend my nights doing this sort of stuff? It's not really what I trained for, and it's not what I'm good at. And that's not even counting the prank calls and the timewasters and the abuse. Bottom line, a lot of what I do these days is plain depressing. It's getting to me.'

I sat up and put my cup on the low table next to the sofa. 'What's the alternative?'

Bob smiled, but I couldn't help seeing the sadness in his face. Twenty-eight years of giving a job your all, and then somehow have it die on you, must be hard, I suppose. 'There are other things, management roles, but they don't come along that often. I'm not keen on the idea of being a trainer – I'm not sure I'd be much of a teacher. I don't mind taking some rookie out and showing them how it's done, but a lecture hall? I don't think so. Anyway, what I'm saying is I'm going to put myself forward for something different. Away from the ambulances. Which would probably mean I'd be based at the hospital. And if that happened I wouldn't need to be near the station. So if you wanted to, we could move.'

I looked at him, taking in his expression of careful neutrality that didn't fool me for a moment. 'But you don't really want to move, do you? Even without the need to be within walking distance of work.'

He shrugged. 'I don't see the need, no. Especially with Drew gone, this house is plenty big enough for us. It's comfortable; we've got it more or less as we want it. If I was working more social hours I would have more time for the garden and so on. But I know you've got a yen for somewhere over the river, so you might as well see what's out there. Just be aware it could all take a while.'

I nodded slowly. 'OK. Sure, I'll look. But nothing's set in stone. See how you get on with finding a different role. Then we can talk about it some more.' I got up with a groan. 'I'm going to do the dishes. Then I think I'll have an early night. My lack of sleep is beginning to catch up on me.'

I left Bob watching TV and went upstairs with my laptop. There were several sites that I'd saved for hunting up suitable properties, and my search brought up some very desirable places that might be within our budget. I'd been visiting these sites for quite some time, and usually they gave me a sense of possibility, that life wasn't closing in and cutting off my choices. Somehow, though, that night I felt less invested in the idea of moving, and I wondered why. It certainly wasn't because I felt any slackening in my desire to distance myself from the family. Was it perhaps a faint, niggling notion that we wouldn't fit, on the other side of the river among the more well-heeled residents of Brant? Would I feel like a fraud? Or was it something to do with Bob, the settled sense of low spirits that I felt coming from him, the air of resignation? Should I be thinking more about him? Did I still have that hot ambition to be someone other than awkward, gobby Janet Yates from the Winstone estate? Could I ever really hope to escape?

April

April started warm that year, and maybe that was why I felt a strange sense of calm, as if I truly believed things were going to go well. On the other hand, perhaps my brain was addled by the volatile behaviour of my hormones, because my experience should have warned me that whatever the weather things rarely go well for long. Before many days had passed a sharp wind began to blow, knocking daffodils flat in the garden borders and whisking tender pink blossom from the trees, covering the grass verges with a cake-icing drift. Even I, who rarely noticed such things, thought it beautiful – until it started, after a few days, to turn brown.

With the wind came a downturn in my own well-being. I told myself I was never ill, that I simply didn't have the time, that it was all down to the monster menopause, with which subject I was heartily bored. But after consecutive nights of broken sleep, and spending far too many hours closeted in the bathroom, it became more and more difficult to look fresh and sunny – or to behave in a pleasant, professional manner.

That day Anna, instead of wafting past my door with a wave and a 'Good morning!' came in and sat down, dumping her bag at her feet and her files on my desk as if she meant to stay. I had that low-down ache in my abdomen, and all I could do was raise my eyebrows. She gave me the studying look I knew of old. 'Janet, you don't look well.'

I shook my head. 'It's just my age. You should know what it's like.' Anna had undergone a hysterectomy almost twenty years before, following the complicated arrival of her daughter, and had gone through an early menopause. I dare say she had to take all sorts of medication in the wake of that, and probably still needed to, but at least she had got it over with.

'You have to be careful,' she said seriously. 'It's all very well putting it all down to hormones, but for all you know it could be something else.'

'Thanks for the cheering thought,' I said.

'Janet, please, have some sense. Go and see your GP.'

'I did – don't you remember? Just after Christmas. He had a good look, asked me loads of questions. Even took some blood to check for hormone levels. He said there was no evidence of anything else.'

'Maybe it's time to check again. That was three months ago. What's Bob saying?'

'Nothing. He knows I'm fed up with his nagging.'

She narrowed her eyes. 'Well, now I'm nagging as well, and the only way to stop me is to do as I say. We can't have you sick. You're necessary to our operation. But that doesn't mean you push yourself to keep going. It means you go to your doctor, and if necessary you get a second opinion.'

'All right, all right. I'll feel like a hypochondriac fool, but I'll do it. Tomorrow.'

She beamed. 'Excellent. You see, I've been quizzing Jeremy, who obviously is an expert on female problems.'

I sat bolt upright, appalled. 'You've been talking about me to your – what? Your boyfriend?'

She chuckled. 'He's fifty-two: hardly a boy. And of course I haven't mentioned you. I just asked him some general questions. I even made out it was my own health I was enquiring about. But some of his answers were very interesting. Not to say alarming. Which is why I want you to go back to your GP – and don't get fobbed off. Even if you're actually feeling a bit feeble, give him the famous Janet Clarke treatment.'

'And what might that be?' I asked caustically.

'If you truly don't know,' Anna said with a broad grin, 'ask any one of your clerks upstairs. Speaking of whom, how are things going with our newest recruit?'

I shook my head. 'I haven't heard anything untoward. But that may be because I've got Claire to set her some tasks. If she hasn't got enough to do they'll keep her busy.'

'Tasks?'

'Yes. I've got her to research the latest on money-laundering legislation, and to familiarise herself with the Proceeds of Crime Act.'

Anna laughed aloud. 'Janet, you are a sadist.'

'No, there's no reason why she shouldn't have at least a passing knowledge. It's all good background. And if there's any trouble, I've told Claire that Lauren can sit in with me. There's not one of them would want to do that.'

'Seriously, though, Janet. Apart from damage limitation, do you think she'll shape up?'

I shook my head. 'I don't want to prejudge, but I'm not hopeful. She has attitude. I also had attitude at her age, but I also worked ridiculously hard. Maybe she and I got off on the wrong foot. Let's say we're watching, Claire and I.'

'And Charlie?'

I snorted. 'Charlie's a stupid boy, but a good clerk. I had a stern word with Charlie a couple of days ago. Anything that might be going on with him and Lauren is to be left on the outside steps. Within these walls it's to be all professional efficiency and sobriety.'

'That'll be a first,' Anna murmured.

I thought it was time to change the subject. 'What about you? Isn't it nearly time to step up to your own responsibilities? As a godmother?'

She smiled. 'Yes, Easter Day! Now I have to think of a present for the baby who has everything. And likely to acquire more. Rachel says not to bother, but I'd like to do something.' She sighed. 'It would be nice to think I might have a role in that child's life like Geoffrey's in mine. He's been a great help to me.' She pushed herself to her feet. 'I suppose I'd better get some work done.'

'You certainly seem pretty chipper these days,' I observed. 'Might that be down to a certain gent from Nigeria?'

'Do I? Oh, well, I suppose it might. You must meet him, Janet.'

'I'll look forward to it.'

She paused in the doorway, her bag over her shoulder and her files once more clutched to her chest. 'Make that appointment,' she said sternly. 'Do it now. And I want to know the outcome. Or I may have to discuss you with Jeremy after all.'

To my surprise I managed to get an appointment for early the following morning. I saw a different doctor – they always seemed to be changing, but that was probably because I hardly ever showed my face in the practice. This one was young, keen and attentive, tall, with brown hair that flopped over his forehead and heavy-rimmed glasses. I liked him – which was also unusual. He listened to my complaints, examined me and took notes. When I told him about my recent and more unsavoury symptoms, he decided there and then to take a swab for culture. 'I don't expect anything to worry about,' he said with a sweet, slow smile, 'but you are right to be cautious. Give the secretaries a ring in about ten days for the results.' I left feeling better than I had for a long time. When I got back to chambers I reported to Anna. 'I can't quite believe it,' I said. 'He didn't make me feel like a malingering time-waster. They must be teaching them the importance of the old-fashioned bedside manner these days.'

She nodded, knowingly, like one with inside information, and I thought it must be due to her having so many medical friends these days. 'I think you'll find the brusque old doctor-type is no longer in the majority.'

'Don't you believe it,' I said. 'Though I dare say Jeremy's bedside manner is exemplary.'

She grinned. 'That sounded almost salacious, you terrible woman.'

'As if. Anyway, I did as instructed, I was examined thoroughly by a charming young doctor, I am unlikely to be at death's door, and as it happens I feel fine.'

'Praise the Lord,' she said with feeling. Sometimes, not often, she said something that reminded me of her faith. It never failed to make me uncomfortable.

That feeling came back to me a couple of weeks later, and it was unwelcome, almost chilling. Even the weather had taken another downturn: there were two or three days when an unseasonal frost crisped the lawns and verges before the spring sun melted it. We all had Good Friday and Easter Monday off, and I thought I might actually do a bit of gardening. Bob kept the grass down but there was weeding to do, and I was feeling more energetic than I had for a while. We'd invited Drew and Tiffany for Easter Sunday lunch but they'd already agreed to go to the Leamans' so it was just Bob and me as usual. He'd been on duty the day before and I'd encouraged him to have a lie-in and catch up on some much-needed rest.

I was in the front garden, filling a collapsible container with weeds, when the bells began ringing. First I heard the familiar jangle from Holy Cross, our old church, which may not have been the nearest but was one of the noisiest – and, I thought sourly, the nastiest. Church bells always made me feel strange, almost uneasy. I straightened up, trowel in hand, and listened: from across the city the bells could be heard, some muffled by distance, others surprisingly clear. Perhaps it was just the direction the wind had taken, but I was sure I could hear the deep booming of the Abbey bells, from the very centre of Brant. That, I knew, was where Anna went, Sunday by Sunday; but today she wouldn't be there. She would be standing up at the font at Rachel and Michael Wells's church, All Souls, maybe even holding the infant Lucy, who, according to Anna, was quite a character even at the insignificant age of six months.

I was standing listening, probably looking a bit vacant, when Bob materialised at my side, making me jump.

'Morning,' he said, his smile quizzical. 'You OK?'

'Yes, I guess,' I said. I frowned and drew breath. 'I was listening to the church bells. Loads of them.'

'Of course. It's Easter Day.'

'Bob, do you ever think about – well, you know, spiritual things?'

'Sometimes,' he answered, and I detected a note of caution. 'Not often. Why, do you? I thought you were an atheist.'

I shook my head. 'No, not that. I am probably not brave enough to be an atheist.'

'What! I thought you were brave enough for anything. You're not getting old and soft in the head, are you?'

'I hope not. But atheism is a pretty cold creed, isn't it? And what do any of us actually know? As in, I know this trowel has a wooden handle? No, I'd say I was more of a sceptic. And I have been an enemy, a very bitter one, but I'm not sure what I am now. Do you know what you are?'

He shook his head. 'Probably a cowardly agnostic. Plenty of those about, I'd say. Bet-hedgers, fence-sitters. But I don't know much. If you want answers, Anna might be good for it.'

'I don't know if I want anything. It's just those bells –. Anyway, they've stopped.' I paused. 'Isn't it strange,' I said, almost talking to myself, 'how even when bells stop the air still seems full of them?'

Bob was looking at me strangely. 'I came out to ask you if you wanted me to peel some potatoes.'

Nothing in this world lasts, especially periods of apparent calm. In the middle of the night on Easter Monday, when I anticipated a busy week at work, I awoke suddenly, probably disturbed by wave after wave of heat that raced across my body from somewhere around my knees up to my face. I was so hot I felt I could have been an asset to the National Grid. I threw off the covers and lay sweating till the sensation abated.

I got up quietly; Bob was fast asleep. My pyjamas were more than damp. I crept to the bathroom and took a tepid shower, but while this cooled me down it did nothing for the headache that was now pounding my temples with sledgehammers. I dried off and crept downstairs in my bathrobe, took some painkillers – which had little effect – and curled up on the sofa with a magazine, but the print kept blurring and reading made the headache worse. Eventually I must have nodded off, because the next thing I knew Bob was standing over me, a steaming mug in his hand and a frown creasing his brows.

'Rough night?' he asked.

I groaned and sat up. 'For someone who's supposed to have nothing wrong with her, I feel pretty disgusting.' I took the mug from him and sipped. 'Thanks for the tea.'

'Should you be going to work? I have to ask for form's sake, even though I reckon I know the answer.'

I smiled feebly. 'It's not so bad. If I find I'm not coping, I'll come home. But this is not an illness, is it?'

He shook his head. 'Maybe not, but it has similar symptoms and they are just as debilitating. Promise me you'll use sense.'

'Yeah, OK.'

Probably due to the power of distraction, things did improve once I arrived at chambers, and nobody commented on my haggard appearance. I dealt with various items that needed updating and familiarised myself with upcoming cases – which barrister was due in which court on which date, chiefly. The online diary was as always our anchor; without it we would have been adrift. At lunchtime Elizabeth Merchant came through the front door carrying her briefcase; she'd come direct from court. I was on the phone to a firm of local solicitors with whom we had regular dealings and waved to her through the open doorway. Instead of heading down the corridor to her own room she lingered till I finished my call.

'Morning, Janet. Sorry to distract – hope this is a good moment.'

'Of course. How's the case going?'

'That's just it. It's going well – I have hopes of a satisfactory resolution. But it's as we expected – it's going to run into tomorrow. I hope it won't take longer than a couple of hours, because I have another case in the late afternoon which is out of town. I won't have time to come back to chambers and I don't want to take a load of stuff on the train. I'm going to need someone to bring my robes and papers back. Possibly books as well.'

I tapped my pen on the desk, thinking. 'That's not a problem. I think we'll send our new clerk, Lauren. It'll be good experience for her, and when you have a moment you can tell me what you think of her.'

She raised her eyebrows. 'Any particular reason? I helped to appoint her – I hope she's proving an asset.'

'Not sure yet,' I said, my tone deliberately bland. 'I don't want to prejudice you, but I'll be glad of your opinion.'

She nodded thoughtfully. 'OK. I'll leave it to you to set up, then. I'll need to leave for court about nine-fifteen.' She paused in the doorway. 'Don't know if you've heard – there's going to be a General Election in June.'

'Is there? I suppose it's not surprising with all the hoo-ha over Brexit.'

She shuddered. 'If I never hear that word again it'll be too soon.'

'I think you'd better brace yourself,' I said. 'Seems to me it's going to be around and on every politician's lips for a good while yet.'

I went up to the clerks' room and found it almost deserted. Most of the clerks went out for lunch, even those who brought their own, because if they didn't they would probably get no peace from the phones. Claire was still there, her phone at her ear, and rolled her eyes at me in greeting when I appeared in the doorway. After a moment the person she was waiting for obviously spoke. She replied, made some brisk arrangements, and rang off. 'Hi, Janet. Some people think I've got all day. How are you?'

'Fine, thanks. Glad I've caught you. Elizabeth needs someone to bring her papers back from court tomorrow. I thought Lauren could do it – it'd be good experience.'

'OK. I'll tell her.'

'She needs to be ready, downstairs, at nine-fifteen. You'll let her know, won't you, what she needs to do?'

'Sure.'

I hesitated. 'Any further problems?'

'Hm, not exactly. The jury's out, to use a legal term.'

I had no stomach to hear of petty issues, so I left it at that.

It so happened that I was coming along the corridor with a cup of coffee the following morning when Lauren arrived back from court. She was carrying two hefty files, a thick book, Elizabeth's court robes in their case and her wig in its box. Her expression gave away her state of mind: her fair brows were contracted, her eyes wide, her mouth a thin line. She halted in front of me. 'Where do I put these, then?' she demanded without greeting or preamble.

I raised my eyebrows at her rudeness, but chose to ignore it – for now. 'In her room,' I said. 'Put the files and the wig box on her desk, and hang the robe up behind the door.'

She flounced off down the corridor. A moment later I heard a door bang and she returned.

'Lauren,' I called from my office. 'How did the case go?'

She appeared in my doorway, her arms folded. 'How do I know?'

This was becoming intolerable, but I kept cool. 'Didn't Elizabeth invite you to sit in? It would be a normal privilege for someone new, to see the workings of the court.'

She shrugged. 'Yes, she did. But I said I wasn't bothered. I sat outside with one of the other clerks, the one from Palace.'

'I see.' But truthfully, I didn't. She baffled me. Why had she even applied for the job if the law was such a bore to her? What had she thought the work would entail? And what information, if any, had Anna, Elizabeth and Charlie given her at her interview? 'Right. Well, off you go. I dare say Claire will have something for you to do.'

She mumbled something then that I didn't catch, but the tone of it needed no explanation. I watched her go. I was worried and also annoyed: it shouldn't have come to this, that I had to deal with a recalcitrant toddler instead of a reliable and reasonably interested colleague. I shook my head as I went back to my computer screen. Reluctantly I decided that I would have to tell Anna what was going on.

I finished what I was doing and sat quietly for a moment, sipping my coffee. I thought of myself at around Lauren's age, working in a humdrum job in the office of a local factory, which was not at all what I'd had in mind when planning my escape from the family home. Unfortunately my marriage to Terry, hasty and ill-considered, was beginning to crack under the weight of his petty gambling and his flirtations, if that's all they were. Later I realised that Terry was a natural hunter; once he'd caught his prey he began to lose interest and seek fresh conquests. It was all to feed his ego which appeared insatiable, and I – the nagging wife at home, always in a bad mood – didn't help by questioning his decisions and berating him for wasting money on gambles that rarely paid off, leaving me to hold down a meaningless job just to pay the rent.

I'd contemplated another escape, but I saw that it wouldn't do. On my wages alone I couldn't afford to live independently. Terry was working, and I insisted we both put some of our earnings aside. His contribution was minimal, but it was the best I could do. Meanwhile I thought, and researched, and tried to come up with a plan: something that would take me far from Terry, from my father and my siblings, and from Brant. I was at a low ebb of near-despair when I received a letter calling me for jury service. I snatched at the opportunity, if only for a change from sweaty Mr Morton in the office, but it proved to be the turning-point I had been looking for.

Despite the activities of my twin brothers I had never been in court; they had, on a couple of occasions, but had always been accompanied by some kind of Social Worker, or even my father. The proceedings I attended were of a different order altogether than the petty misdeeds of my adolescent siblings. They concerned a woman who had come home early one morning to find her house burgled, and who had later been arrested for possession of firearms. A locked cabinet in her spare room had been wrenched open, it transpired, while she was at work – or so she claimed – and a number of guns stolen. This unfortunate woman, who seemed to me to be completely innocent (except for the poor decision she'd made in marrying her husband in the first place, but there I could sympathise), said she had no idea what was in the cabinet; that was her husband's business. She was a cleaner who worked at night; her family had all been asleep and the burglars hadn't woken them. The details of the case had been, for me, less interesting than the workings of the court. The barristers in their wigs and gowns, standing up to prosecute or defend, were an astonishment to me: their eloquent use of the English language (which I had never thought to encounter outside the pages of a book); their deference to the judge; the legal jargon; the contempt barely hidden beneath the theatrical civility, calling someone 'My Learned Friend' when it was clear the man in question was no friend and considered to be anything but learned, was all a revelation. Apart from all that, the very fact that these eloquent creatures were men was a marvel in itself. In my world men spoke in sentences if you were lucky, in grunts if you weren't, and could rarely be counted on to follow a logical argument, let alone set out something so compelling and in such rounded and flowing phrases. I was completely hooked, and in the course of the days it took to find this woman not guilty I had found the path of my future.

It didn't happen quickly. In every spare moment I read all I could find (which wasn't much – our local library was ill-stocked with legal books, which were little in demand.) I saved every pound I could squirrel away into what I privately dubbed my 'Running Away Fund.' I said nothing to anyone. In spare hours I haunted the public gallery of the Brant courts, and it served only to increase my hunger. Terry – usually out placing bets or cosying up to girls – had no idea, and the pleasure of knowing this made up in part for the deeply unsatisfactory nature of my day-to-day life. I made enquiries as to which of my old school friends might now live in London, and to my delighted surprise I found one, a girl I had quite liked even though she was a bit of an airhead. My plans were maturing, and so one Saturday I phoned her and cheerily suggested we might meet up because I was coming up to London to do some shopping. In the course of our meeting I found out she shared a modest flat with another woman, and if I was desperate, as a stopgap while I was looking for work and somewhere to live, she would let me have a camp bed in the corner of the living room if I contributed to the rent. Jubilant, my next step (at an expense I begrudged) was to consult a solicitor and trigger the ending of my marriage. Terry, when he got over his astonishment, put up little resistance. He was as fed up with me as I was with him.

London – what had I expected? I had been there a few times, but now I began to realise just how big, noisy, dirty and anonymous it was. But here was where it all happened; it was the beating heart of the world of law and where I was determined to find my niche. And I did – by some miracle which was a combination of sheer doggedness on my part and a slice or two of brilliant luck, I found the arcane haunts of the Inns of Court and the pubs frequented by the clerks who oiled the wheels of the whole complicated business. By now I knew where I might fit. I cultivated them, buying drinks, wearing my shortest skirts, making them laugh at my coarse humour, generally being one of the lads – because then there were no female clerks, and relatively few women barristers. These mythical creatures, on the rare occasions I came across them, filled me with envy and awe. How had they done it?

So it was that I wormed my way in, through the good offices of a clerk called Raymond on whom I had cast a few favours, and a forward-thinking senior barrister, Mr Arthur Waldegrave, QC, who thought it would be amusing to shock his fustier fellows by appointing a woman as a clerk in chambers. I worked long hours, I didn't mind what I did for work, I put myself out and generally became an eccentric feature of the set until, or so Mr Waldegrave claimed, they simply couldn't do without me. Ambitious, I moved up the ladder – but all that is history. I moved to a little flat of my own and finally shook myself free of Terry. I revelled in my work; I socialised with my fellow-clerks, and even had a light-hearted fling with one or two of them; but in every spare hour I read, and studied, and thought about how far I could climb. This was the world I still loved, even though it had changed; and this was the world which Lauren Barclay clearly held in contempt. It didn't improve my opinion of her one iota.

Anna was in court that day, involved in at least three cases, and she didn't expect to be finished early enough to warrant returning to chambers. I told myself I would speak to her the next morning as soon as she came in, when we were likely to be on our own. As it happened I'd had a reasonable night for once and got in to work even earlier than usual. Once I'd familiarised myself with the day's requirements I set myself to sorting out the post which had just been delivered and distributed whatever there was to the desks of the barristers.

As I expected Anna was next to arrive and she stopped by my office.

'Morning,' I said. 'How did yesterday go?'

'Better than I expected, mostly,' she said. 'It wasn't exactly thrilling, but it'll go some way to paying the bills.'

'If they cough up before Christmas,' I said.

'We can hope. Janet, I've been thinking.'

'Oh dear.'

She smiled. 'I know it's a long time ago, and that's the point. Do you remember, way back, a chambers meeting where it was agreed that you should draft a sort of manual? It was really an attempt to have something handy in case the Bar Standards bunch came asking awkward questions.'

'Yes, I do remember. It took me a week of evenings, in my own time. At the end of it I was almost brain-dead.'

She nodded sympathetically. 'I know. All those riveting rules about staff remuneration and how the rent gets paid, and arrangements for tenants' arrival and departure. Who's responsible for what. Things financial generally. Dispute resolution.'

I opened a drawer and pulled out a loose-leaf binder with a dull maroon cover. 'I have a copy here. It's a bit dusty. Oh, and it's dated: 2004.'

'Good grief – I didn't realise it was that old. I was talking to someone over a rather horrible cup of tea in court yesterday, and he mentioned they were overhauling their equivalent document, and it made me think we ought to do something similar. A lot has changed in thirteen years.'

'I suppose you want me to rewrite it.'

'Not rewrite – I can't see that'd be necessary. Just bring it up to date. You're best placed to do that, because you've kept up with all the developments. Nobody in these chambers has the comprehensive knowledge that you have, and that's not flattery – it's just a fact. I thought maybe you could have a look, see what needs doing and get a rough draft done so we can put it through the next chambers meeting.'

I sighed. 'I suppose I must.' Privately, I relished the task; it was just the sort of thing I was good at. And Anna was right: while people were masters of their specialisms, I was the one with the general overview. 'When is the next chambers meeting – did we schedule one?' The diary was on my screen. 'No, so perhaps we'd better do that. Leave it to me.'

'Thanks, Janet. I know I say it often, but you truly are a star. Now I'd better get on. I have some notes to write.'

When she had gone to her own room I remembered I hadn't said anything to her concerning the issues with Lauren. Perhaps I would take her a cup of coffee later; it might sweeten the pill. But before five minutes had passed she came flying down the corridor in stockinged feet, clutching a letter which she was waving like a flag, a broad grin on her face. 'Did you see this?' she wanted to know.

'I saw you had letters,' I said mildly. 'Why, have you won the lottery?'

'I don't do the lottery,' she said, shaking her head. 'I thought you might have seen what was on the envelope. It's from the JAC – they've called me for a Selection Day!'

'That's brilliant,' I said. 'See, I told you that was a cracking application. I'm not in the least bit surprised. Congratulations!'

'Thanks,' she said. 'They've given me a date next month. We'll have to work my cases round it.'

'I dare say I'll manage,' I said drily. 'So – a celebration this evening? With Jeremy, perhaps?'

'My goodness, yes – I must ring him now before he starts his clinics.' And she was gone again.

After that there was no way I could mention petty chambers problems; they would have to wait.

I should have known: far from fading into oblivion, 'petty' problems have an unwelcome tendency to grow and divide and thrive like an octopus on performance-enhancing drugs. A few days later Elizabeth Merchant arrived back at chambers in mid-afternoon and came straight into my office, closing the door behind her.

'Sorry to barge, Janet,' she said. 'I'm sure this isn't your doing, but I've just come away from a court that wasn't expecting me and a case that wasn't happening, and I felt like a fool.'

I frowned. 'What? What was the date and time on your papers?'

'Today. And I checked with the diary. But when I got there I was told the case has been deferred till next week. Apparently the solicitor informed us by phone.'

I pushed my chair back. 'I knew nothing about this, Elizabeth. I'm very sorry for your wasted time and embarrassment. Come with me.' I led her up the stairs, and with every step I felt my annoyance increase. Mistakes happened, clerks were human, but they still needed to be dealt with.

'I don't want to get anyone into trouble,' Elizabeth murmured as she followed me.

'Whoever's responsible is already in trouble,' I said. 'Perhaps what they need is a shame-making public roasting. Give me those papers for a moment, please.'

I paused in the open doorway of the clerks' room. Everybody was working quietly at their stations. 'All right, everyone,' I said. 'I need a word. If your phone rings, let it go to voicemail.' My tone must have alerted them, because every chair and pair of eyes turned towards me and nobody muttered. 'Ms Merchant has just returned from court. A court where she was not expected, despite the fact that her paperwork said she was and the date was right according to the diary, which, quite correctly, she checked beforehand. Apparently a call was taken from the solicitor involved, informing these chambers that the case had been deferred till next week. But the diary was not updated and Ms Merchant was not informed. Can we know who took that call?'

I looked around the room, and saw raised eyebrows and shrugs and shaking heads. Then Claire said, 'What case was it, Janet? And who was the solicitor?'

I looked at the papers. 'Banstead versus Legge. Hutchins and Phelps.'

I saw Claire make a perplexed face. Then I heard a chair scrape against the floor, and my eyes turned to where Lauren stood, her face flaming, her fists clenched at her sides. She said nothing, but gave a choking sound and rushed from the room, almost knocking Elizabeth Merchant off her feet as she hurtled down the stairs.

Claire groaned and shook her head. 'I've told her repeatedly,' she said. 'Sometimes things get changed. She didn't say anything to me about a call from a solicitor. Maybe I wasn't in the room. I'm sorry, Elizabeth.' She looked up at me. 'I've tried, Janet. But I'm really wishing you hadn't given me this job, because it's like babysitting, only worse.'

'Don't blame yourself, Claire,' Elizabeth Merchant said. 'Luckily the error was in the right direction – I was in court too early, not too late. It could have been worse.'

'If she doesn't sort herself out,' I said grimly, 'one of these days it will be worse. All right, Claire. I'm sorry to have to ask you this, but you're going to have to check every task she undertakes, however small, and report to me.'

Claire sighed and nodded. 'She won't like it.'

'Too bad,' I said. 'OK, everybody, carry on.'

At the bottom of the stairs Elizabeth hesitated before going along the corridor to her own room. 'Look, the kid's new. And I've done the prep. There's no real harm.'

'She's not so very new,' I said. 'She's had time to learn the basics. And Claire's conscientious: she won't have let anything slide.' I frowned, looking around. 'But where is she? Lauren? Can she have left the building?'

'Maybe she's in the washroom. Should I take a look?'

'No. Leave this to me.'

I took a deep, calming breath. It was time to bring my Head of Chambers up to speed. I walked up the short corridor to her room, found the door closed and tapped on it.

'Come in.'

When I opened the door, to my astonishment I saw Lauren sitting in a chair opposite Anna, who was behind her desk.

'Excuse me,' I said, and even I could hear the frost in my tone. 'I'll come back later.'

'No, don't go, Janet,' Anna said. I thought she sounded weary, as well she might. 'I need to speak to you. And I'm sending Lauren home. The day's nearly over anyway.' She turned to the younger woman. 'Collect your things and go now, Lauren. This will be dealt with.'

Lauren got up. 'Thank you, Ms Milburn,' she said, her tone oozing a humility which to my ears sounded utterly false. As she passed me, her back to Anna, she flashed me a smile that spoke of triumphant spite. I was so amazed and disgusted I just stood there open-mouthed.

Anna and I waited in silence until we heard the front door slam. 'I think I need some tea, Janet. Could you stretch a point?'

'Gladly,' I said.

A few minutes later I returned with two steaming mugs.

‘Do sit,’ Anna said. ‘Janet, Lauren says she is being bullied.’

‘By whom?’

‘Mostly by you.’

I almost choked on my tea. ‘Bullied? She calls what I said bullying? She made a mistake, and it’s not the first. I’ve barely spoken to her, and I’ve tried to be civil. But I have to make sure our clerks are doing as they should. It’s my job.’

Anna sighed. ‘Of course it is. I think she’s a bit, I don’t know, fragile. Sensitive.’

‘So what’s she doing in a job like this?’ I said, my voice rising in frustration. ‘Or any job, come to that, where there’s a level of responsibility? I can’t let her get away with repeated blunders. She’ll give us all a bad name. A name I’ve worked hard to uphold.’

‘I know,’ Anna said. ‘I wonder if Elizabeth and Charlie and I are partly to blame. Maybe we didn’t make it clear to her what was involved.’

‘I can’t comment on that,’ I said. ‘But the fact is she’s had time to find out. And if she can’t cope, let’s be rid of her. She’s a liability.’

‘No, no, wait, Janet. We have to cut her some slack. Give her a chance to improve. Please, for my sake, if nothing else. Her father’s a solicitor, and he could make things difficult. I can’t let something like this, which, let’s face it, is relatively trivial, compromise my application for the Deputyship.’ I opened my mouth to protest, and she held up her hand. ‘Obviously,’ she said quietly, ‘obviously if she proves to be the liability you suspect after we’ve given her a decent chance, then whether or not my career is on the line we take the appropriate steps, and we do everything according to the book. Right now it doesn’t seem to me she’s failed so spectacularly that I’m prepared to admit I made a terrible choice.’

I took a deep breath. ‘All right. I don’t want to see your application in any way compromised either. Not for the likes of Lauren Barclay. Because I don’t think she’d care. But I do. I’ll be watching her, though.' I shook my head. 'There's something really quite unpleasant about that young lady.'

'Just be careful, Janet,' Anna said. 'That's all I ask. Don't let any personal feelings of dislike colour your judgment. You're better than that.' I saw her flush, and she went on, 'Perhaps you think I am the one that's compromising. Letting things slide for the sake of my reputation, my career.'

'No. I don't think that of you. I know you too well. It's an awkward moment, I realise that, what with the Deputyship and all.'

'OK, let's leave it there for now. And hope for the best.'

I nodded and smiled as I collected her cup and left; but I was far from convinced.

A few days later I called both Lauren and Claire to my office for what I hoped would be a reasonably friendly chat. Claire didn't really need to be there, but I felt the need for a witness.

'I'd like you two to bring me up to speed,' I told them once they were seated. 'We should, I feel, have a debrief after what happened the other day with Ms Merchant's case. Lauren, can you tell me what happened?'

Lauren looked at the floor. 'I took the call from Mr Phelps,' she mumbled. 'Claire wasn't there. I don't know where she was. And then something else happened and I got distracted and forgot to say.'

'I see. Well, Ms Merchant is inclined to let it go since no terrible harm was done. But what if the case had been brought forward, and she failed to attend? I just want you to understand that what we do, even if it doesn't seem important, has an effect. Each one of us has a responsibility to maintain our reputation. The barristers rely on us.' She shrugged. 'Do you understand, Lauren?'

Now her head came up, and I saw her eyes were wide. 'Why do you treat me like an idiot? I don't know why you've got it in for me!' I saw Claire wince.

I paused for a moment, holding her gaze until she looked away. I was baffled by this young woman, but I kept my voice even. 'I haven't got it in for anyone, as you put it,' I said. 'But I expect efficient working and good manners. We haven't seen much of either from you lately. And for the record, I don't appreciate being called a bully.' I heard Claire mutter, 'What?' I waited, but Lauren was silent. 'I've spoken with Ms Milburn,' I went on. 'She wants to give you the benefit of the doubt. Please do your best to improve. Listen to what Claire tells you, and if necessary take notes. You can go now. Claire, a word.'

Lauren scuttled out, and we heard her run up the stairs.

I turned to Claire with a sigh. 'Bear me out, Claire. I am being as patient as I know how. What I actually want to do is wring her neck.'

Claire nodded gloomily. 'She was telling everyone how she went to Ms Milburn. As if it was some great victory. Honestly, Janet, she's not cut out for this job. She doesn't like taking any kind of instructions, and she's slow. I don't know what she's cut out for, but it isn't this.'

'What do the others think?'

'Well, at first they thought she was OK. Fun, a bit cheeky. But now they feel she's an embarrassment. We all like a laugh, but she doesn't seem to know when to stop. And sometimes I've heard her say things on the phone that would make your hair curl. If you say something to her she gets all defensive and says we're bullying her. Even Charlie is having doubts now, and he always used to tell me to back off.'

'I feel you've had a bad deal,' I said, 'having to keep an eye on her as well as doing your own work. If there are any issues from now on, just refer her to me.'

For a week or so things went quiet. Lauren kept out of my way, and Claire had nothing to report. But I had an uncomfortable sense that it wasn't over, and unfortunately I was right.

May

I'd had a run of nights when I was pacing the floor or closeted in the bathroom in the small hours. Four o'clock seemed to be a favourite for pain and bleeding and headaches that seemed impervious to any medication. I felt haggard, stretched taut, and now I was feeling nauseated much of the time as well, such that the thought of food was repellent. I made a huge effort to get to chambers on time every day, to look as smart as I could (in my own way), to deal with work, to maintain a professional demeanour; but perhaps in the circumstances I could have been forgiven for shortness of temper.

I arrived at chambers that Thursday morning knowing I had plenty of work to catch up on, as well as whatever might come in during the day. Tired as I was, I had no doubt that I would cope, but as it turned out far more than coping was demanded of me. I had barely settled at my desk with a second cup of strong coffee when a face appeared round my door. It belonged to Nigel O'Hare, our most senior barrister next to Anna, and the dull red flush on his normally greyish complexion warned me that he was suffering unusual emotion.

I spoke cautiously, since he seemed unable, for the moment, to say why he had come. I rarely see him, except when he arrives or leaves. 'Good morning, Nigel. How can I help you?'

He sidled round the door and closed it behind him. I saw he was, as ever, immaculately turned out: dark trousers with a knife-edged crease, crisply-pressed white shirt, black bow tie neatly knotted. I waited politely.

'Janet, this will not do.'

'What won't, Nigel?'

He put both hands on the edge of my desk and leaned forward. 'I rarely complain, as you know.'

'I hope,' I said mildly, 'there is rarely anything to complain about.'

'Quite so. I came in this morning to start work. There was a brief on my desk. Just left there, not handed to me. I had other things to tie up, so I didn't open it immediately. But when I did, and started to work on it, I was soon extremely puzzled. It was a family matter, something to do with children and custody, and all that sort of thing. I couldn't understand why anyone would have thought of me in such a connection. It's well known, not only here in chambers but by all the solicitors who normally instruct us, that my specialism is medical negligence. I haven't been involved in family cases for years. You know that.'

'Of course,' I murmured. 'Who instructed?'

'Blake's. I don't think I've ever had instructions from them.'

'How mysterious.'

He leaned further forward, breathing heavily. 'Well, it's not. I smelled a rat. I did what I should have done at the outset, but I often don't, because there usually isn't any need. I looked at the details on the front page. The brief wasn't even for me! It was for Michael Harwood. Someone had given me the wrong papers. What really worried me was the thought that Harwood might have been given a brief that should have been for me and did as I had done – opened it up. I'm sure he's a good sort of chap, though I don't really know him, but there are issues of confidentiality here, at the very least.'

'Yes, I see that,' I murmured. 'So may I ask what you have done, if anything?'

'I felt that time was of the essence. I went down to Harwood's room and fortunately found him in. My brief was on his desk but even more fortunately he hadn't opened it. Of course I apologised for my error, but I have to say he didn't seem unduly perturbed. Well, he's quite a young man, isn't he, and I think sometimes younger people don't take things so much to heart. I assured him I hadn't seen anything which would compromise his case, and we left it at that.'

'I apologise for the error, Nigel. But can we say, annoying as it was, that happily no harm has been done?'

He frowned. 'I suppose we can. But Janet, just think what might have happened? Supposing I hadn't checked? I might have rung Blake's and demanded to know why they had sent me, of all people, a family case. And then – well, there would have been consequences. Ones which we all would want to avoid.'

I knew, as Nigel did not, that Blake's were one firm of solicitors who would never instruct him for anything. Had he made that call, as he could easily and with some justice have done, it would have been extremely embarrassing. 'Look, Nigel,' I said, 'there has obviously been a mix-up. I will deal with it, you can be sure of that. I'm sorry for your inconvenience, and thankful that you acted so appropriately.'

He puffed a bit, but my words seemed to calm him, and after a few minutes of self-righteous muttering he went back to his own room.

I finished my coffee slowly, trying to damp down the rising tide of fury which, if I was not careful, threatened to swamp my normal good sense. A part of me hoped I was wrong, and that this was an error some other clerk had committed, not Lauren Barclay. I had come to hope she was learning a measure of basic competence. But whatever the case, I had to find out. Taking a deep breath, I left my office and stalked up the stairs.

There was a general buzz of talk in the clerks' room, but it was muted, and I saw as I arrived in the doorway that Charlie was on the phone. I waited, my arms folded; one or two glanced my way, one even attempted a friendly wave, but most, seeing my expression, glued their eyes to screen or paper file and kept their heads down. Charlie finished his call and turned to me. 'What's up, Janet? This is becoming a habit, you appearing among the lowlifes.'

I didn't answer, and he pulled a face.

'A situation arose this morning,' I said, speaking slowly and looking round at them as I did so, 'which shouldn't have occurred. Mr O'Hare, who as you know is a senior barrister of many years' standing in these chambers, came to tell me he had had papers delivered in error. He admits he should have checked whether it was indeed his name on the cover, but he didn't, and most of our barristers don't, because they trust us to do our part efficiently. And this particular task really doesn't need much skill, does it? It's a simple matter of reading. Of remembering to check. But it seems that someone here can't even manage this small matter.'

I saw that every pair of eyes was looking somewhere other than at me, and other than at Lauren. When my gaze arrived where Lauren sat I saw that she had swivelled round in her chair and was glaring up at me. Her hands were gripped tightly together in her lap. 'You think it's me, don't you?' she said breathlessly. 'You always think it's me. Because I don't know much, because I'm new, because – because you don't like me.'

'Was it you?' I asked, my voice sounding hard and grim even to my own ears.

I saw her swallow. Then her chin came up. 'Yes, it was me,' she said. 'So what are you going to do about it?'

I heard a general intake of breath, but I chose to ignore her latest rudeness. 'What I am going to do,' I said deliberately, 'is explain to you what could have been the consequences of this – what is it? Negligence? Or just sheer stupidity?' I saw her eyes widen at my choice of words. 'Mr O'Hare opened that packet of papers. He started to read their contents. He was extremely surprised by what he read, because this was not the sort of case he normally does, and because Blake's don't instruct him, for reasons which aren't relevant here. He was about to pick up the phone and ring Blake's when he decided to check if the brief was truly intended for him. And then he did the right thing – he took the papers to Mr Harwood, the correct barrister, and retrieved his own, which Mr Harwood, luckily, had not opened. I don't intend to spell out the potential fallout in every excruciating detail; most of you will be able to figure it out for yourselves. But it could have meant Blake's taking their instructions elsewhere.'

Lauren jumped up from her chair and seemed about to bolt. I stood foursquare in the doorway. 'Unless you plan to push me bodily out of the way,' I said, fixing her with a baleful stare, 'you can stay and listen. Because it seems to me that's something you haven't been doing much of, not since you came here. If Blake's had decided we were an unreliable setup, they might have thought twice about instructing us in the future. We can't afford to have that happen. Our reputation is our most important asset. Not only that, but it would have impacted other barristers who had done nothing to deserve it. There would also have been a loss of income, not only to individuals, but also to chambers in general, since part of the running costs of chambers is defrayed out of barristers' fees. I think you will have been told all this already. We have to run a tight ship, for everyone's sake. Yet recently there have been repeated failures, all pointing at you. Everyone has made allowances; Ms Milburn herself has been very understanding. But enough is enough.'

'What are you going to do, then?' Lauren said, her voice high and squeaky. 'Give me the sack?'

'No, that's not for me to do. Perhaps you might like to consider your position, though.'

'What's that supposed to mean?' she shrieked. 'You're victimising me! You've been against me from the minute I got here! Get out of my way – I'm not staying to be bullied.'

I stood aside and watched her gather up her things. 'That's just what you should do,' I said softly. 'Go home and think about everything you've said and done in the last few months.'

'I'm going,' she said. 'And I'll be thinking about everything you've said and done. To me, when all I was doing was my best.' Her voice caught, and she suddenly looked about five years old.

I wasn't about to soften in the face of her manipulation. 'If that was your best, I hate to think what your worst might be.' I stood back, and she ran past me and stumbled down the stairs. I heard the front door slam.

I heard a collective sigh from the rest of the clerks. It seemed they were as relieved to see her gone as I was. 'All right, everyone. You can carry on with your work now. I hope we've seen the last of Ms Barclay – unless, of course, it's her letter of resignation.'

Back at my desk, with a cup of strong coffee, I brooded on this latest development, and hardly knew what to think. The absence of Lauren Barclay from chambers had, or so it seemed to me, lifted a palpable cloud of heaviness. Even so, I couldn't allow myself to hope the situation was resolved – clearly there was more to come, and none of it pleasant. I examined my own reactions, trying to compensate for bias, wondering how far my own mental and physical state might have contributed to tension. Had I been too hard? Too lenient? Too laissez-faire? Had I left too much to Claire? It was unlike me to question my own actions so closely, and I resented the effect this young woman had had on us all. I disliked her, for certain – but had I let my personal feelings influence my dealings with her? I knew she represented something which could have led to a knee-jerk reaction; I knew there was in me an inverted snobbery, a suspicion of privilege, which might have led me to demand more of the likes of Lauren Barclay than was reasonable. I thought of my own experiences as a Junior, far more rough and ready than what I had meted out to her; but times had changed, and sometimes kid gloves were considered a requirement. In my own private and unregenerate heart, though I would never have admitted it, I considered she had got off lightly.

I didn't see Anna the following day: she was in court most of the day, and she'd told me that if she finished early she'd go home and start preparing for the Selection Day. She'd also told me that she was going to some special celebration with Jeremy and needed to shop for some new shoes. 'I need something with heels,' she said. 'Otherwise I feel such a midget next to him. But I don't want anything that's crippling to walk in.'

'You could be in for a long search,' I observed. 'I've got a pair you could borrow, but I think your feet are a lot smaller than mine.'

She smiled. 'By several sizes, I imagine. If I wore those I'd definitely fall over. But thanks for the thought.'

I hardly saw Bob that weekend: when he wasn't working he was asleep. I carried on sorting out the stuff in the loft, and I made two trips to the dump. Seeing stuff disappear into the container full of junk was most satisfying, and for the time being work problems faded into the background.

On Saturday I felt reasonably well, but on Sunday it all took a nosedive: pain, bleeding, headache and insomnia. I realised I hadn't rung the GP for the results of the swabs he'd taken, so on Monday morning I rang chambers to say I'd be a little late and waited for the surgery to open. I ran a deep hot bath and wallowed in steam till the water got too cool, and found that it had relaxed muscles I didn't know I was holding in tension – an attempt to deal with pain that was wholly unsuccessful.

When I finally got through to the surgery they kept me waiting for what seemed an age before my notes were retrieved. 'No, Mrs Clarke, there's nothing untoward on here that I can see,' I was told. 'And the doctor hasn't made any note that he wants to see you. He's on leave at the moment, so if you're concerned you could consult one of the other doctors, or wait till he comes back in a week's time.' I groaned inwardly, thanked her, and went to work. The only good effect of the delay was that the traffic had thinned out.

I hung up my jacket and booted up my computer, noting what I needed to know for the day. Then I went along the corridor to Anna's room to let her know I was back. Her door was ajar; I tapped on it and put my head round. She was on the phone, but waved at me to come in. I slid into the chair on the other side of her desk.

She ended her call.

'Good weekend?' I asked. 'How was the party – or whatever it was? Did you find any shoes?'

'It was fine, thanks.' She seemed distracted; I sensed something was amiss. Were things not going well with Jeremy? She picked up a sheet of paper from her desk. 'Janet, this was in the post. It's a letter from Lauren Barclay.'

'I hope with all my heart it's her resignation.'

'Well, yes, but I'm afraid it's also a formal complaint, against you.'

I found I had nothing to say, apart from something from my foul-mouthed adolescence.

Anna looked at me with a rueful half-smile. 'Given the language it's couched in, I doubt very much that this is Ms Barclay's own work. If her father is involved, that could go either way. He knows the potential cost – to us and to her. Here, read it, Janet. It's about you, after all. Maybe you can clear up a few points.' She slid the letter across the desk. As I read, I felt the bitter bile rise in my throat at the sheer disingenuousness of the tone: legal-speak meshed with injured innocence.

I looked up. 'OK. She complains that she wasn't given proper guidance, that she should have been under my wing, not 'palmed off', as she puts it, on someone more junior. You know what my workload is, and I'm also mentoring Charlie through his BTEC. I thought Claire was a good choice: another young woman, and sufficiently experienced.'

'I'll make a note,' Anna said. She pulled a pad towards her and scribbled something down. 'It's up to me to reply to this, at least in the first instance, since it was addressed to me.' She looked up. 'Go on, Janet.'

'I should tell you what happened last week. I couldn't tell you before because you weren't here on Friday, and I didn't see why I should cast a cloud over your weekend.' I recounted the scene with Nigel O'Hare and the subsequent drama in the clerks' room, leading to Lauren's flouncing out of the building. 'You know it's not the first blunder; I told you of previous instances, you asked me to be sympathetic, and I tried, believe me. But this could have been very embarrassing, and could have affected us all.' I saw that Anna was shaking her head – I hoped at Lauren's errors. 'I concede I may have used less than moderate language,' I went on. 'And if necessary I am prepared to eat humble pie for that. But otherwise I don't think I have done anything wrong. I have acted to uphold chambers' reputation. Oh, and also you should know that I haven't spoken to Lauren without at least one other person being present.' I passed the letter back to Anna. 'As for 'shouting and insulting,' that's simply not true.'

Anna glanced down at the letter. 'Did you actually call her stupid?'

I thought back. 'I didn't say, 'Ms Barclay, you are stupid.' But I might have implied it. It's possible to put that construction on it, I suppose.'

Anna was silent for a moment, and I let her think uninterrupted. 'Janet, you said that you'd be willing to apologise, for your tone, for causing unintended distress, at the least.' She held up a hand to stop my protest. 'What I don't want is to let this get out of proportion, and if an apology from you will defuse the situation, all the better. We can word it to save your pride.'

'It's not my pride – it's what's right,' I said grimly.

'I understand that. Sometimes we have to act judiciously. Damage limitation, and all that.'

'Well, of course I'll do it, if you say it will help. But will that satisfy her and her doting father?'

'That's what we don't know, but this is a way of trying to stop the thing escalating. If Mr Barclay knows what's best he'll persuade his daughter to be content with waiving the need to work out her notice, getting such salary from us as is owed, and a written apology from you. The legal world in Brant is not a big one; he won't want any taint on his own professional life. We have to hope it will go no further.'

A terrible thought came to me. 'And if it did,' I said slowly, 'would you want me to resign?'

The unfeigned look of horror on Anna's face gave me my answer. 'God forbid,' she said, 'that this business of ours should lose someone of your quality and experience for this –' she waved a hand at the letter – 'storm in a teacup. For which I am at least partially responsible, for hiring the little madam in the first place. It's all a ridiculous waste of time, but we have to handle it with great care.'

I stood up. 'Right. I'll leave you to compose your reply, then. Don't forget you're due in court this afternoon.'

'I won't.' She smiled warmly. 'Changing the subject entirely, how did you get on at the doctor's?'

'Oh, they say there's nothing wrong with me. Apart from my time of life, being born female, and sheer bad luck.'

She looked suddenly serious. 'I'm glad to hear that. But your symptoms do sound a bit extreme. If things get any worse, promise me you'll go back.'

'You're as bad as Bob.'

'Someone has to look out for you, since you're so rubbish at doing it for yourself.'

'Ha, thanks.' I got to the door and turned back. 'How was your weekend? Nice time? Things going well with the, er, new friend?'

I saw her blush and I smiled inwardly.

'I did have a nice time, thanks, and if you are referring to Jeremy, yes, I think so. Now I have some prep to do for this afternoon.'

'And I'd better go and see what's what upstairs. Should I say anything to the clerks about Ms Barclay's letter?'

'Not yet. Let's see what response we get to my reply.'

I had every intention of telling Bob about what the surgery had said. I might even have told him about the situation at work, although I was wary of loading it with a significance I didn't think it merited. If for nothing else, I would probably have told him as a way of reconnecting; we had both been so preoccupied – not just recently but for months, it seemed – that we hadn't really talked to one another for a while, except for the basic necessities of a joint household – such as 'We're running out of detergent' or 'What did the weather forecast say for the weekend?' I wasn't even sure if we had communicated on the subject of our son. I didn't recall either of us saying, 'Heard from Drew lately?' I knew things were drifting with Bob and me, and it did make me feel uneasy, but whenever I decided to do something about it some urgent matter got in the way; and I habitually assumed that things would always be OK, that everything was retrievable, because that was the way it had always been: the foundations were there, or so I believed.

When I got home that Monday evening to my surprise I found him sitting at the kitchen table, staring into space. He was on a day shift and shouldn't have been back till after seven.

'Hello – what happened? Aren't you well?' This was strange – like me Bob was rarely ill and unless he was at death's door or infectious he usually went to work anyway.

He looked up, and I was disconcerted to see his red, baggy eyes. 'I got sent home.' I looked at him, perplexed. 'I, um, I had a bit of a turn.'

'What? What sort of a turn? It's not your heart, is it? But you're strong as an ox.'

He shook his head slowly. 'Not that sort of turn. I, I don't know, Jan. I went to pieces.'

I stared stupidly. 'At work?'

He nodded. 'In the station. I was on a break, and a call came in. It was our turn to go out, and I couldn't.'

My voice came out faint. 'I don't understand.'

'No. Neither do I. After all these years, the things I've seen. I just couldn't do it. I don't know if it's just today, or if it's always going to be like this. And that's what I can't cope with. That it might suddenly all be over.' To my absolute astonishment and horror I saw a tear leak down his face, and he made no move to brush it away. 'Do you remember Dave Prentice? Years ago? That's what happened to him. They had to pension him off. And he was never the same.'

I crossed the kitchen and wrapped my arms round his shoulders. 'That's not going to happen to you,' I said, trying to convince myself as much as him. 'You're strong. Dave was always a bit, I don't know how to put it, but you're not like him. You're just exhausted. You've been working other people's shifts as well as your own. You need a few days' rest.'

'That's what they said when they sent me home. Don't come back till you feel better, that's what they said.' He looked up, haggard and grey. 'They said I should talk to someone.'

'Maybe they're right.' I pulled up a chair and sat next to him. 'You never have. And the things you've seen would be enough to turn anyone a bit loopy, let's be honest.' I paused, thinking. 'Bob, has something happened? Something specific that just tipped you over? Or is it general overload?'

He shook his head. 'I was getting fed up – you know that. With all the boring stuff – taking old folks to appointments – not that that's unimportant, but it wasn't what I trained for. I was almost wishing for an RTA, something I could really help with. But then we had a week of emergencies.' He laughed, a quiet, hollow sound. 'Be careful what you wish for, isn't that what people say?'

I frowned. 'You mean you went out on calls and couldn't handle them?'

'No. Not that. I did everything I could.' Again, to my dismay, I saw his eyes fill with tears. This wasn't the Bob I knew. He swallowed. 'We had a hanging. A sixteen-year-old boy. Strung himself up in his father's garage. Left a note – worried about his exams, convinced he was going to fail. His family are devastated. I did my best, but it was too late. Then there was a call from a neighbour – some old chap hadn't been seen for a while. The police came at the same time as us, and it was grim: he'd been dead a few days at least, and the weather's been warm, hasn't it? Flies everywhere, terrible stink. Poor old man. What a way to go. But that's not all. It's the call I hate the most, from a frantic young couple down on your old estate, not much more than kids in a squalid little flat, with a baby that wasn't breathing. We tried, Jan. You wouldn't believe how hard we tried. But it was no good. And I know the flat was grimy and the parents were just teenagers, but they were heartbroken. Four months old, that baby was.'

'This all happened over the last few weeks? You never said a word.'

'Just one week. The baby was yesterday. I didn't say anything because you haven't been well – I know you've been up in the small hours. And you don't say much either. All sorts could be going on, and I wouldn't know anything about it.'

I took his hand – his strong, capable hand – and squeezed it. 'You're right,' I said softly. 'We've let things go. Let the important things go by because of the urgent things. We have to do better, don't we? But you'll be OK. I'll make us some dinner, then for goodness' sake get some rest. Don't even think about work until you're back to yourself again.'

He looked at me, and I could see him take a deep breath, as if trying to steady himself. 'What about you? Are you OK?'

'Of course I am. I'm always OK.'

I had to be OK, because if I wasn't nothing would be. Ever since that taxi hit my mother, it had been this way. For the rest of that week I went to work, dealt with what needed to be dealt with: attended meetings, chased up payments, kept an eye on what the other clerks were doing; but without Lauren it was all as it usually was: busy, bustling, purposeful, but underneath the surface activity there was tranquillity.

Towards the end of the week Anna called me in to her room. 'See what you think of this,' she said, angling the screen of her computer towards me. 'It's just a draft – obviously I will reply on paper, since that's what they, I mean she, did.'

I read what Anna had written to Lauren Barclay, and it was a model of diplomacy. Her tone was conciliatory but she gave nothing away. 'Brilliant,' I said. 'If it had been me writing that letter, I'd have had all guns blazing.'

'The thing is,' Anna said thoughtfully, 'she didn't give any clue as to what her preferred outcome would be. If her dad was behind it, I would have thought he'd have included that. I did a bit of sleuthing as well, Janet. I rang David Phelps for a chat off the record, seeing as Hutchins and Phelps are the solicitors we get most of our work from, and also I know him reasonably well. I thought I'd see if he knew Mr Barclay.'

'And?'

'David has met Peter Barclay, he said, but he doesn't really know him. He knows the firm by reputation, and he says they are a respectable outfit. His impression is that a bit of tactful negotiation would probably get the result we want. Barclay won't want any public unpleasantness, David reckoned. So I'll get this reply sent off and see what happens.' She looked at me with a small smile. 'Better be prepared with that apologetic letter.' She must have seen the scorn in my expression, because then she said, 'Look, I realise you hate hypocrisy. You'd rather give Ms Barclay a piece of your mind. But that's what's got us into this situation to start with. So please, dear friend, climb down off your high horse for five minutes and appear to do penance for the sake of these chambers. And my sanity.'

'All right, you win,' I said. 'Oh, and I've done that revamping you asked me to do on the chambers manual. It's a bit like shutting the stable door after the horse has bolted, but I made a special effort with the Complaints Policy.' As I left the room (Anna would probably have said I stalked) I heard her chuckle.

When I got home every evening that week I found Bob had got some jobs done which had been waiting for attention for a long time. By Thursday he'd cleared the garage of junk. 'Once I can have the use of the car,' he said, 'I'll get it all down to the dump. Oh, and I've repainted the guest room as well.'

'Wow. You must fall apart more often.'

He looked away, clearly embarrassed. 'That was just a blip. Overload, or something. Too many shifts back to back. I'm fine now. I'll go back to work on Monday.'

But on Friday, when I got home after my dance class, I found the house empty and a note under my water glass on the kitchen table. 'Got called in. All sorts of mayhem going on – watch the news. I'll text you later. Your dinner's in the microwave.'

As it turned out I didn't have to watch the news. I was washing up when the phone rang. I dried my hands, thinking it might be Drew; but it was Anna. 'Have you seen the news?'

'No, I went to my dance class. What's up?'

'The whole country's been subjected to a cyber attack.'

'A what?'

'Something called ransomware, apparently. Lots of institutions affected, including great swathes of the NHS.'

'Ah, so that's why Bob went back to work,' I murmured. 'So what are you saying – people's computers are all infected? What about chambers – is there fallout there?'

'I don't think so. I think we might have got away with it because we upgraded our IT systems last year. But many hospitals and GP surgeries are in absolute turmoil.'

'What, patient records?'

'I'm not sure. From what I heard it's made a mess of appointments, communications generally. Ambulances are being rerouted to help with the worst-affected areas. But it's nationwide. It'll have an impact on Bob, I imagine.'

'What about our hospital and all your medical friends?'

'I rang Jeremy, but he doesn't seem to know the full extent yet. He's concerned about his daughter too – she's in Orthopaedics somewhere up Birmingham way. I expect they'll all be getting their IT people in as an emergency. I shouldn't think it'll be all over in a day, either. These things seem to drag on.'

She was right. It was several days before things got straightened out, and in the meantime there was a scramble to retrieve thousands of appointments, not always successfully. I saw little of Bob; he came home to eat, shower and sleep, but otherwise was driving an ambulance somewhere out of area to help with other beleaguered services. On Sunday evening he came home, tired and pale, but exuding a sense of purpose, almost of excitement, that I hadn't seen in a long time.

'Well?' I said. 'Are you winning?'

He shook his head. 'It's not over yet, not by a long chalk. But we've been stood down for now. I've got tomorrow off – I'll try and finish that bit of decorating. Then it'll be back to normal shifts.' He came into the living room where I was flicking through a very boring magazine and flopped onto the sofa beside me. 'It's been quite interesting, going to other trusts, seeing how they do things. And I met old Ron Williams – remember him?'

I shook my head. 'Vaguely. I think I met him once.'

'I trained with him. He's a good bit older than me – in fact he's coming up for retirement. But he's a good bloke; I learned a lot from Ron.'

'Didn't he move up north somewhere?'

Bob nodded. 'His son had a baby - well, his wife did, obviously – and Ron and his wife wanted to be nearer to the grandkids so they moved. I hadn't seen him for a few years. But he reminded me about that reunion I used to go to, up in London.'

'You reckon you might go this year, then?' I asked, idly turning pages, coming to rest on a large colourful photo of a Mexican dish, complete with recipe. 'You never seemed too keen before.'

He shrugged. 'I know. But somehow meeting Ron again reminded me about some of the people I've worked with, so yes, I might go.'

'When is it?'

'Quite soon – 3rd June. It's a Saturday. Just before the General Election.'

'And the week before Neville's wedding. Or had you forgotten?'

'I wish I could forget,' he said, scowling. 'Knowing Neville, not to mention his father, it'll be a noisy, tasteless bunfight.' He paused. 'You could come if you like. To the reunion, I mean, not the wedding.'

I shook my head. 'No, thanks. You'll have a much better time without me, talking over all your old horror stories.' I tossed the magazine on the floor and looked at him searchingly. 'You seem better. Are you?'

He got up abruptly. 'I told you: it was something and nothing. One of those daft things. I was exhausted. I'm not as young as I used to be – got to pace myself a bit more. I'm going to put the kettle on. You want anything?'

He came back a few minutes later and put a cup of coffee in front of me. 'I meant to say, I got a call from Drew on my way home.'

'You're honoured! We've hardly heard a squeak out of him for weeks, let alone seen him.'

Bob looked uncomfortable. 'No, he drops me the odd text, and I'm sure he means me to keep you in the loop, but I forget. They've been busy, him and Tiffany, getting that flat of theirs to rights.'

'Playing house.'

'I suppose, but we had fun once, I seem to remember, fixing this place up. Anyway, they've invited us over there tomorrow evening. They want to show it off, I guess.'

'Oh! Did you say yes?'

'I did – you aren't doing anything, are you?'

'I don't think so. Is Drew cooking?'

'So he said. And apparently there's someone he wants us to meet.'

I sat up, alarmed. 'Please don't tell me they've invited Tiffany's parents.'

'He didn't say. But you've already met her dad, or at least seen him, so it doesn't seem likely. Anyway, you might as well face it – we're going to have to meet them some time.'

I subsided back onto the cushions. 'Oh, boy. I can't wait.'

'Do you think we should take them something?' I asked Bob as I teased my hair into spikes. 'A bottle, maybe?'

'Drew's more of a beer drinker,' Bob said. 'And Tiffany hardly drinks at all, so he told me.'

'Let's leave ten minutes early. I'll pop into the garden centre and get some small flowering thing.'

In the car, clutching a pot of pansies, a thought dropped into my head. 'Bob, do you ever sit quietly somewhere and take stock – of your life, I mean?'

He gave me an incredulous look. 'What brought that on?'

'Anna. She asked me that very question today, out of the blue.'

Bob grunted as he slowed to take a sharp corner. 'Maybe that's what she's doing. With this bloke in her life now. He's still around, is he? Have you met him yet?'

'No, I haven't, but it must still be going strong because she's going up to Birmingham this weekend to meet his daughter. It's her birthday, apparently.'

'Anyway,' Bob said after a moment's reflection, 'isn't that what we were doing the other day? Taking stock?'

'Were we?'

He threw me another glance, shaking his head. 'When I was thinking about a different kind of job.'

'Oh, that. I suppose. But that was you, not me.'

'So do you? Sit and think about where you've come from, where you're going, and all that?'

I pulled a face. 'Not if I can help it. You know I don't like thinking about the past at all if I can avoid it. The present is all right as it is, except for the idea of moving, but that's on the back burner, you'll be relieved to hear.' I thought for a moment. 'There was a time when I got a lot of changes made at work – maybe you remember. But now things are OK as they are.' I wondered for a second if I should tell him about the situation with Lauren Barclay, but by then we were almost in Thripp's Ford, and the moment passed.

Somehow, though I didn't acknowledge it, or even really notice it at the time, that evening marked a bit of a turning point for me. It was a fine early summer evening, the light beginning to look tired and end-of-the-dayish, when we parked outside the garage whose upper floor was our son's flat. It was some distance from the main house, and between the buildings a long stretch of tussocky lawn sloped down to where the river ran, unseen now behind a belt of trees in full foliage. As I got out of the car, I looked at Bob. 'This is nice, don't you think?' He said nothing, but his look was eloquent. He knew I was talking about moving.

Drew appeared at the top of a flight of wooden steps which gave on to a small landing. Here were pots of flowers set on rough towers of house bricks. I smiled to myself, feeling a bit better about my modest pot of pansies.

I was never much of a hugger – it made me feel awkward, except, sometimes, with Ben. Bob had no such issues, enveloping his boy in a bear hug, and I followed suit a little less gracefully.

'Hey, Mum, Dad,' Drew said, giving his father an affectionate pat. 'Welcome to the bird's nest.'

We followed him inside, and were greeted by Tiffany who was swathed in an apron that went round her twice. 'Don't worry,' she said, a little anxiously, I thought. 'Drew's done the cooking. But I'm allowed to make salad. I'll get this done while he gives you the tour.'

'Which will take about three minutes!' Drew said, laughing.

The flat consisted of one large room with two doors leading off. A table was set up by a large window overlooking the garden. The kitchen area was partially screened off on the opposite side. On the far side of the room, against a wall, was a large, comfortable-looking sofa which I supposed converted into a bed. One of the doors led to a walk-in cupboard, the other to a tiny bathroom. It was all very light and fresh, painted white with soft blue curtains at the open window.

'You've done a good job, you two,' Bob said. 'It's great.'

'You'd better meet our new flatmate,' Drew said. He crossed the room and opened another door which I hadn't noticed before and which gave on to a small balcony. 'Come in, mate.'

A huge dog shambled into the room and strolled up to Bob and me. He came up to my waist, and I was so surprised I gave a small squeak.

'He's totally harmless,' Drew said. 'Huge and hairy, but no killer instinct. Meet Horace.'

A pair of intelligent brown eyes looked up at me, and I recalled for a fleeting moment how fond of our old mutt Paddy I had been as a child. Then I remembered that it was with him I had first met Terry, and how I had sworn I'd never have pets or children.

Horace had now left me and was inspecting Bob, who was making a fuss of him. 'He's huge! What is he?'

'Nobody knows,' Drew said. 'We got him from the rescue centre. I'd guess he must have some wolfhound in his ancestry, though. He's the right colour – grey.'

'What on earth made you get a dog?' I asked.

Tiffany, now minus her apron, fresh and summery in a mint green shirt and white jeans, joined us, a bowl of salad in her hands. 'He's supposed to be a guard dog,' she said. 'Please don't tell anyone, but I think he's a bit of a failure. Big, but soft as they come. I always wanted a dog, but we never had one when I was a child. And now Drew's got this evening job and he thought I should have some company when he's working late and I'm on my own.'

I turned to Drew. 'You've got a job?'

'Ah,' Bob said. 'That's one of the things I meant to tell you. Sorry.'

'It's nothing much,' Drew said. 'Just in a bar in town, three evenings a week and Saturdays. Helps with the bills, and we can put a bit away. Hopefully once my exams are over I can start looking for something more permanent. Hold on, I need to look after our dinner.'

The evening was full of surprises: not that my son could rustle up a good meal, because I had always been determined not to raise a useless undomesticated man. But Drew seemed different: no longer the amiable but rather thoughtless and idle youth growing up at home, but a settled, responsible grown-up. How had this transformation happened without my noticing? In such a short time? I could only assume it was Tiffany's influence. Here he was, studying (I hoped) by day, working in the evening, saving for an unknown future, with a flat, a fiancée and a dog, paying his bills, and apparently content with life. It gave me a lot to think about, not least that perhaps I had never paid my only child quite enough attention.

After the meal I volunteered to help wash the dishes, but Tiffany said, 'Let's do them later. It'll be dark in an hour. I suspect Drew wants to watch the football and maybe his dad will too.'

Sensing a moment of awkwardness, I said, 'Look love, don't stand on ceremony. We're just Bob and Janet.'

'Right.' She smiled shyly. 'I thought we might avoid the roaring crowds and take Horace for a walk. Unless you're into football, of course.'

I shuddered. 'No, thanks. Yes, let's give the old chap some exercise. How old is he, anyway?'

'They weren't sure. Three or four, maybe. Great, I'll get his lead.' She paused, looking down at my feet. 'Not sure about your shoes, though. They're very nice, but not exactly for dog walking.'

'Lend me a pair of Drew's. He's got small feet.'

We let the dog galumph down the stairs, and Tiffany attached his lead at the bottom. The shadows were beginning to gather round the foot of the trees as we ambled down the lane in the quiet of the evening.

I breathed in the air. 'It's nice here. Such a change from the city. You'd never think it was so close.'

'Drew said you wanted to move.'

'One day, maybe.'

We strolled on in silence, stopping for Horace to take in the scents and water the bushes. He seemed a peaceful sort of dog, content to amble. The quiet, the undemanding company, the snuffling dog, gave me a sense of peace as well. It was something I rarely felt.

'I suppose we'd better turn back,' Tiffany said at last. 'It's beginning to get dark. There's even a few stars coming out.'

I stopped to look. 'I can't remember the last time I looked at the night sky,' I murmured, almost to myself.

As we turned in at the gate, Tiffany said suddenly, 'Janet, there's something I've been wanting to ask you.'

'What's that?'

'Do you think we, I mean Drew and me, are a bit too young? To be thinking about getting married?'

I stopped to look at her, and for a moment the young woman looked like the child she had so recently been, her eyes wide, her face anxious. 'It's no business of mine, love. It's no business of anyone's, just yours.'

'Well, it is kind of your business,' she said. 'Drew's your only child, after all.'

'And you're your parents' only child,' I said. 'What do they think?'

She bit her lip. 'We haven't told them yet.' She glanced at me and saw my expression. 'They like Drew,' she stammered. 'They didn't much like the idea of us living here together, but… The trouble is, I know they'd want a huge wedding with lots of guests and glitz, no expense spared. I'd be whisked off to dress fittings and there'd be endless talk about table decorations and bridesmaids and all that stuff, and it's not what I want at all, but I don't think I'd be strong enough to resist.' She smiled a little sadly. 'My dad's really well off, he wants what he thinks is the best for me, and it's hard to say no.'

'It's your choice in the end, though.'

'You were married at my age, weren't you?' Tiffany said.

'Ha! Don't think of that as any kind of example! It was a big mistake. I only married Terry to get away from home. In those days it wasn't so easy to do it on your own, and I earned peanuts.'

'But was it a mistake because you were young?'

I paused, considering. 'Partly. But mainly because he liked gambling and girls. Other girls.'

'Did you know that at the time?'

'I should have.'

'Was that the only reason – getting away from home?'

'No. The other reason was sex.'

'Oh!'

I smiled at her startled expression. 'Things were different then, Tiffany. You're a lot freer now. And even that turned out to be a disappointment. But I suppose I learned from the experience: mainly that the only person you can really rely on is yourself.'

On the way home, Bob said, 'You're very quiet.'

'I'm thinking.'

'How did you get on with Tiffany?'

'I like her. She's a nice, sensible young woman – not giddy and self-obsessed. Older than her years. I was going to say she'd need to be, but Drew's different too. Don't you think?'

Bob smiled. 'That change has been going on for a while, I reckon.'

'And I just haven't noticed,' I muttered to myself. I looked over at him; he was staring straight ahead, concentrating on the road. 'Bob, do you think I am a really terrible mother?'

I must have startled him, because the car jerked suddenly. 'What brought that on?'

'I don't know. I've just been thinking, that's all. Seeing how he's living now. Anyway, we both know he's closer to you than me. I was never very maternal, not in the clucky-huggy-coddling sense.'

'Maybe you gave him different things,' Bob said quietly.

'Like what?'

'Principles. The importance of education. You taught him how to cook.'

'So did you.'

'And speak properly.'

'I don't even do that myself.'

'Of course you do. You sound like a textbook sometimes. It used to make me and Drew laugh. I admit the local accent's still there, at least the odd twang.' He turned into our road and slowed as he approached our drive. 'Anyway, what's all this thinking about? It's not like you to navel-gaze.'

'I know.' I shifted in my seat to look at him as he pulled on the handbrake and switched off the engine. 'I'm not sure I understand it myself, and it's not just about Drew. It's like there's something moving inside me, like an earthquake that starts deep underground. I saw a TV programme about that once – something about plates. Plates of rock, not dinner plates.'

'It sounds painful.'

I shivered. 'It probably will be. Anyway, I'm knackered, and we both have work tomorrow. I'm going to bed. Don't stay up half the night, will you? Wasting time on the internet.' I climbed out of the car.

'No, I think I'll have an early night as well.'

I gave him a look. 'I am honoured.'

He laughed as he closed and locked the car door. 'Chances are I'll be asleep before you get your makeup off.'

'We'll see.'

As I slathered makeup remover over my face and wiped it off with cotton wool, I thought about my conversation with Tiffany, and how things had changed since I was her age. What I'd said was true enough: as a green nineteen-year-old I was as keen as any of my giggly girlfriends to lose my virginity as soon as I could and find out what the whole business was really about. Now that I knew better, I could have chosen a likelier person than Terry to do my research with, and I needn't have committed myself to marriage, but of course there were other reasons for that momentous step. Terry was good-looking and charming, in a laddish sort of way, and he had a reputation for being someone who knew his way around. With hindsight I realised he didn't deserve it, but I didn't know that at the time; all I knew was a sense of disillusionment. Was this all there was to it? There was no way then that I could know. What I later came to realise was that Terry was a callow, vain, selfish boy who had no more idea of what women wanted than any other youth of his ilk, despite the hype. I suspected that many women of my age were still stuck with their version of Terry and probably believed that their feeling of disenchantment was somehow their own fault. My sister Pauline was almost certainly one of them; I wasn't sure about Christine. She and Giles seemed mutually devoted, but although I liked Giles well enough he was a bit lacklustre, somehow bloodless. So maybe their relationship was not exactly sizzling; and maybe she liked it that way.

I was on my own for a few years, and all my energies went into career-building. But then I got lucky, if you can call it luck that knocked me off my feet in the street and caused me to come round looking into the concerned blue eyes of a tall man in a green uniform. Because Bob was a very different proposition to Terry. But it wasn't the only factor. At twenty five I'd developed a pretty hard shell and quite a bit of life experience – in my job you did, even if only at second-hand. I really liked Bob from the start, but I was determined not to cave in to what I saw as sentiment. Certain criteria had to be met: he had to be faithful and sensible with money, hard-working and handy round the house, and when it came to sex he had to be, at the very least, willing to please me, not just himself. And Bob, bless him, ticked every box. He was five years older than me, and that helped. He wasn't perfect – who is? – but he was a good man and he had red blood in his veins, not sugar-water. These days we were usually too tired to bother, which was a shame; but that night I thought there might be a chance of mutual pleasure, and I grinned to myself as I threw my clothes into the washing basket and doused the lights.

Heavy rain woke me at five in the morning. It had been very warm for the first half of May, but now I heard thunder rumbling in the distance as it moved away. I lay for a moment, sleepy, sticky and content, until a familiar pain stabbed me in the belly and I moaned aloud. Bob turned over, but he was still asleep. I had no intention of waking him; we would both have to be up soon anyway, and if he'd known I was in pain he would probably have blamed himself. I clenched my teeth against the biting wave till it abated. The sweat was pouring off me, and I lay huddled, my arms wrapped around my stomach. At last I breathed more easily and drifted off into a doze riddled with nonsensical dreams until the alarm bleeped at six fifteen. Then I shook Bob awake and headed for the shower.

Driving to work through the puddles that morning my thoughts circled back to Drew, who for some reason had set me off thinking in unfamiliar directions. I would have described myself as tough and practical, and I think others would have agreed; what tendencies I may have had to self-analysis were buried very deep, if they existed at all. But something was definitely nagging at me, and I knew I had to settle it in my own mind.

I loved my son, of that I had no doubt, in my own way. And as much as I had no great desire for children I had loved Bob enough to give him this one child, and Bob had always been a devoted father. Pregnancy hadn't got in my way until the very end, and the rigours of labour resulted in a robust, loud, healthy baby with a fluff of dark hair and deep blue eyes. He'd never been a difficult boy, nothing beyond the normal, and I supposed I was quite strict with him, while Bob was a much more natural and easy parent, unafraid to show how much he loved his boy. They did a lot of man-things together when Drew was growing up, and they were close and affectionate still. I, on the other hand, was happy to be left behind and pursue my own interests, which were almost exclusively work-related. Even so, then and now, I would have given my organs to sustain Drew's life, and if that is a sign of love, then so be it. I was relieved he was grown up and had turned out to be a decent human being. I knew enough to ask for little else.

When I arrived at chambers I put my son out of my mind for the moment. No doubt he would pop up again before long, as one's children do. For now there was work to be done, and once I had inspected the diary and noted what tasks there were for today, I made a note of the firms who owed us money, intending to make a few polite phone calls later in the morning, and then started to search the internet for potential marketing opportunities. I spent a fruitful couple of hours, and then decided it was time for coffee. I padded along the corridor to where we kept the kettle, filled it and set it to boil. Then I climbed the stairs and put my head round the half-open door of the clerks' room. They were all at their workstations, on their computers or on their phones, and apart from a wave or two in my direction were getting on with their tasks. I was inwardly gratified by the scene of quiet industry and went back downstairs in time to hear the kettle click off.

As I was stirring my coffee Elizabeth Merchant came along the corridor from her own room. 'Morning, Janet. The smell of your coffee has enticed me out.' We exchanged a few polite remarks and I made to go back to my office. 'Wait,' Elizabeth said. 'I've been meaning to ask you: has anyone heard back from Lauren Barclay yet?'

I was taken aback. 'I didn't realise you knew.'

Elizabeth shook her head. 'I could hardly fail to notice her absence. I asked Anna, and she told me the bare bones, and of course I haven't said anything and I won't. But I was on the interview panel, so I feel responsible, as Anna herself does.'

'Anna hasn't said anything to me,' I said, 'and I'm sure she would have. She'll have sent the letter some time after receiving the complaint, but it's a bare week, so I don't expect anything yet.'

Elizabeth eyed me thoughtfully. 'You're very cool about it.'

I shrugged. 'You think I should be worried?'

'I don't know,' Elizabeth said. 'For what it's worth, I think it's all nonsense. But I've been in chambers where a stupid thing like this can cause major upheavals. Or at the very least a mountain of unnecessary work just to deal with it.'

I sighed. 'Don't I know it – having literally just updated the complaints policy!'

Elizabeth raised her eyebrows. 'Oh dear! Hung with your own rope, as my grandfather used to say.' She took her coffee mug and went back to her room, leaving me standing on one foot and wondering. Could it escalate? Of course it could, however trivial and undeserved. Was it likely? I had no idea.

I decided to check with Anna that nothing had come in with the morning post. I'd put letters addressed to her on her desk first thing that morning. I made a second cup of coffee and took both mugs along to her room. She never closed her door unless she was with a client and the door was ajar. I tapped lightly on it.

'Janet, if that's you, come in.' I pushed the door fully open with my foot and entered. 'Oh, coffee! Thank you – you're a life saver.'

'The kettle, cups and coffee are mere metres away,' I reminded her.

'I know, I know, but I got stuck into this brief and forgot.'

'Which one is it?'

'That custody case you decided would be good for me to do. It's more complex than I anticipated – lots of tangled issues.'

'That's why I sent it your way,' I said, possibly with a hint of smugness.

'Well, now, what can I do for you? I sense you have something on your mind.'

'It was something Elizabeth said. I wondered if you had heard anything from the Barclays.'

She frowned. 'No, nothing. They may be keeping us hanging on purpose – trying to undermine us. Such ploys are petty, but not uncommon, I'm afraid.' She looked up at me. 'Why – are you concerned? It's been barely a week.'

'Not at all,' I said coolly. 'But it would be nice to put it behind us, wouldn't it?'

'Yes, I suppose it would.' She paused for a moment, twisting her pen between finger and thumb. 'Janet, tell me, are you really as – what's the word? – impassive as you seem?'

'What do you mean? Am I really a seething mess of violent passions under this calm exterior?'

'Not quite that.'

'Well, if I was, why would I be admitting it?' I said with a grin. But I should have known never to underestimate Anna. She was able to see though things more than most people I know, which is one reason why she was so good at her job.

'You wouldn't, knowing you,' Anna said. She spoke quite unemphatically, but then she pulled the rug out from under me by saying, 'The thing is, I sometimes get the definite impression that you are hiding something.'

'Aren't we all?' I countered.

She took a sip of her coffee and sighed appreciatively. 'Maybe. Some more than most.'

'What do you think I am hiding? A secret admirer? A covert life of crime? Some unsavoury habit?'

She smiled. 'Probably not. Probably something rather less dramatic. But I know how much store you set by self-reliance, how you think any sign of weakness – as you would see it – is fatal. I worry about you, you know. You have every right to your attitudes, of course, but I have to tell you you've got it wrong.'

I stepped back in mock-horror. 'You're not trying to convert me, are you? I feel a sermon coming up.'

She shook her head; she wasn't smiling. 'Don't be ridiculous. Of course I'm not; I wouldn't presume. I just don't like seeing you locked in this cage of your own making.'

'Some would say it's you that's caged,' I said. My tone was still bantering, but I now had the feeling of joining battle.

'Would they? Why's that?'

'Always having to obey the rules, to be good, to do the right thing.'

'But Janet, that's exactly what you do! All the time – you can't deny it. It's just that you try to do it in your own power, without help – and I know it doesn't work.'

I drained my coffee. I was still standing in front of her desk. 'Speaking of work,' I said slowly, 'I'd better get back to mine and let you get on with yours. Have you finished your coffee? I'll take your cup away.'

There was a distinct small smile on her face as she handed me the cup. As I turned to the door I heard her mutter, almost inaudibly, 'The world and all that is in it belong to the Lord; the earth and all who live on it are his.'

I pretended not to hear.

If I was anxious about the Lauren Barclay affair, I couldn't show it to anyone. It was such a petty dispute, and my every instinct was to treat it with the dismissive scorn it deserved; but that morning I found myself looking around my little office and imagining what it would be like if I had to leave it – and this whole building, and what it meant in my life – and never return. The feeling almost of vertigo, of a great gaping hole opening up before my feet, was enough to remind me that imagining was usually a very bad idea. Crossly I rinsed out the mugs and stomped back to my desk.

That night, unusually, I was awakened by a dream, and it served to intensify my annoyance: until then I had been sleeping peacefully, uninterrupted by pain or waves of suffocating heat, and such nights were rare. Any details the dream might have contained were swift to fade, but I was left with an impression of something dark and formless haunting me, practically treading on the backs of my shoes, and yet it didn't seem especially malign, and in the dream I felt no fear. What it was I didn't know, but it was persistent, and I felt that it wanted me to turn round and speak to it, but I refused. My waking self, feeling weary and hard done by, berated my unconscious for being both obvious and insistent. Go away, I muttered. Go away and bother someone else. But of course I knew it couldn't, because whatever it was, it belonged to me alone; and in the morning I found it had manifested itself, irritatingly but not for the first time, in an itchy rash on the backs of my hands. I found some lotion in the medicine cabinet, and told myself sternly to leave it alone, but of course when I forgot I found myself scratching and that drew blood. Little by little, seemingly as a result of accumulating tiny pinpricks which were in themselves of no account, I felt my mood darken.

I saw little of Anna for the rest of that week. She was often in court, and it so happened also that she saw a number of potential and actual clients in chambers. When I did see her she made no mention of any communication from the Barclays, so I had to assume there had been no response to her letter. On Friday she breezed in carrying a suitcase, and it was obvious she had been to the hairdresser: her hair was now neatly cut just below the jaw.

'Morning,' I said. 'Nice hairdo.'

'I thought it was about time. I was getting split ends from sheer neglect.'

'Can't have that.' I raised an eyebrow at the suitcase. 'Going somewhere nice?'

She reddened: one of the drawbacks of fair skin which I, thankfully, don't suffer from. No one would know from my face if I was squirming.

'I thought I mentioned it,' she said. 'I'm going up to Birmingham with Jeremy for his daughter's birthday. We're staying over tonight.'

'Ah. High heels and posh frock?'

She smiled. 'More or less.'

'Sounds like it's getting serious if you're being introduced to his daughter. It'll be his mother next.'

'That would be more of a mission,' Anna said, her grin now broad. 'Since she lives in Ibadan.'

'That's where he grew up, is it?' I asked.

'Yes, and where he started his medical studies. So that's my weekend, or part of it – we'll be back tomorrow evening.'

'What about your dog?'

'Gordon's going on an adventure too,' Anna said. 'He's having a sleepover with his pal Dulcie.'

'Remind me.'

'Rachel and Michael Wells' collie. He utterly adores her.'

'So, are you looking forward to your trip?'

Anna frowned. 'I'm not entirely sure. I shall probably have to be on my best behaviour.'

I made a very sceptical sound. 'Seems to me if anyone's likely to feel intimidated it'll be her, not you. Seeing as her dad's girlfriend is almost a judge.'

She chuckled. 'I'll try not to be too scary.'

She started towards the door, and I called after her. 'Just remember to tone down the voice, that's all. The one you like to use on quivering ne'er-do-wells.'

Her reply floated back to me. 'It doesn't work anyway, more's the pity.'

I left chambers at my usual time, but unusually I wasn't the last to leave. As I started down the steps I noticed an unfamiliar sleek silver car parked in Anna's space. Leaning against it, looking at his watch, was a very tall, very broad black man, casually smart in an open-necked shirt and dark trousers, his skull-hugging frizz dusted with grey above the ears. His steel-rimmed glasses caught the early-evening light. He was, I had to admit, handsome in a middle-aged, established sort of way, and his very size lent him presence. I felt suddenly bold and cheeky, and walked up to him. 'Hello. I think you must be Jeremy.'

He looked up, and if he was momentarily startled he hid it well. He smiled, his eyes crinkling in well-worn lines, and offered his hand. 'And you must be Janet,' he said as I shook it. His voice was very deep and somehow full of laughter. 'It seems we have heard of each other. I am glad to meet you.'

'Likewise,' I said. 'Now I had better go before my beloved Head of Chambers finds me chatting up her bloke.'

'Too late,' he whispered, his eyes alight with merriment. 'Caught in the act.'

I looked behind me, and Anna was coming down the steps with her suitcase. Jeremy pushed himself off his car and went to meet her, and I beat a retreat. 'Have a lovely time!' I called back at them.

When I arrived home, sweaty and stretched from my dance class, my mobile rang from the depths of my handbag. To my surprise it was Drew.

'You and Dad around tomorrow, Mum?' he wanted to know. 'I've got something I'd like to run past you.'

'I'm not going anywhere,' I said. I checked the calendar. 'And your dad has the day off. Yes, come in time for coffee. You'll both come, will you? I'll buy some biscuits in your honour.'

Drew laughed. 'Wow, thanks. OK, see you about eleven. All right with you if we bring Horace?'

'Sure.'

They arrived the next day in Tiffany's car with the dog stretched out on the back seat. Tiffany parked at the kerb and Drew opened the car door for the dog, who made himself at home, strolling up the front path, sniffing the flowers and peeing on the lawn. He then came up to me and nuzzled my hand.

'Morning, Horace.' I looked up at Drew who was following. 'Has this beast had a walk this morning?'

'No. I thought Dad and I could take him down to the park after we've had our coffee.'

Horace stretched himself out on the carpet in front of the sofa so that everyone had to step over him, but he had claimed his spot and showed no inclination to move. 'He has a very, how do I put it, entitled air,' I commented.

'Don't beat about the bush, Mum,' Drew said, grinning broadly. 'Just say what you mean. He's big, he's spoilt, and he has no manners.'

'Ah, but,' Tiffany said, leaping to his defence, 'he had a hard time before we rescued him. And you spoil him just as much as me.'

I retreated to the kitchen. 'I'll make a pot of coffee. I think your dad's in the garden.'

Bob came in when he smelled the coffee, washed his hands, greeted Drew and Tiffany and made a fuss of the dog, who accepted his attentions with a lordly air. 'So what's this you want to talk to us about?' he asked.

Drew and Tiffany glanced at each other, and Drew said, 'Thing is, I've had an invitation to Nev's stag do, and I'm not sure what to do. I don't really want to go; it's a Friday night, so I wouldn't have to ask for time off work, but now that I'm working most weekday evenings I don't have much time to finish college assignments. It's not just that, though. If I know Nev and his mates, it'll be one of those nights where people go on a pub crawl, end up at a club, get totally wasted and do stupid things like taking the bridegroom's clothes off and tying him to a lamp post. That sort of heavy drinking has never been my thing. I did it once or twice when I was younger and that's enough for me. The hangover just isn't worth it.' He looked at Tiffany and smiled. 'I know it's traditional, what blokes do, but it seems a bit of an insult to your wife-to-be, turning up at your wedding looking like a wreck who's had no sleep and been vomiting half the night. But – I don't know, Neville's my cousin, it's a family thing, should I go to show my face? Or even to keep an eye on him? What do you think, Mum? Dad?'

I sipped my coffee and thought. 'Knowing my family, if you don't go, it'll be seen as another example of us thinking we're too good for family occasions. On the other hand, why should you spend your evening doing something you dislike?' I glanced at Bob. 'We didn't want a drunken rumpus either, did we?' I said to Drew, 'We invited your grandma and your aunt, your dad's family, but none of mine. We had a very quiet wedding and then a little celebration some time afterwards with my lot invited so they didn't feel too left out, and we managed to keep it pleasant rather than rowdy.'

'That's just it,' Drew said. 'Nev's wedding is going to be rowdy, isn't it? Starting with the stag night and all his mates from school and the football team he plays for, right through the wedding itself. With Uncle Colin involved how could it be anything else? There'll be a lot of money spent on it: you know the sort of thing, "nothing's too good for my boy" and all that garbage, and there'll be no limit to the drinking.'

'What's his fiancée like?' Bob said. 'I can't even remember her name.'

'Jodie. She's big,' Drew said succinctly. 'Tall, plenty of flesh, blonde. And loud.'

'So no restraint from her side, then,' I said.

'Not likely. What do you think I should do? I don't want to cause any bad feeling. We're not exactly the cosiest family on earth, are we?'

'And our branch of it's not the most popular, either.' I sighed. 'What do you reckon, Bob?'

Bob put his mug on the table. 'You're asking me? They're your family, love.'

'More's the pity.' I thought for a moment. 'What about you go to the stag do, show your face, have a few drinks but make them last, go along with it, but then say you're feeling ill and cut off home? Or even slip away to a prearranged spot where Tiffany can pick you up and send Neville a text later, making your excuses?' I turned to Tiffany. 'Have you been invited to the hen night as well?' I asked her.

'No, thank goodness. I hardly know Jodie at all, or any of her friends.'

'That might work,' Drew said. 'Not talking to Nev at the time – he wouldn't take no for an answer. He'd just get another round in and make sure I drank my share. But just disappearing quietly without them noticing – yeah, that's what I'll probably do. Thanks, Mum.' He got up suddenly from the sofa, causing the dog to open a sleepy eye. 'Anyone for a dog walk?'

'Yes, I'll come, son,' Bob said. 'I could do with some exercise.'

'Mum?'

I looked out of the window. 'No, thanks, Drew. It's raining.'

'Me neither,' Tiffany said. 'Unsuitable shoes.'

Drew laughed. 'Wimps. Right, come on then, Dad, before it really starts pouring.'

In a moment they sorted out waterproofs, roused the dog and were gone. A silence gathered in their wake. I looked at Tiffany and she smiled shyly. 'More coffee?' I said, hefting the pot. 'Might not be too hot now.'

'Lukewarm is OK with me.'

I poured coffee into her cup, trying to avoid disturbing the dregs. 'So, everything going all right with you two?' I asked casually.

She nodded, her pale young face serious. 'I did get a bit of opposition from my parents when I said I wanted to move in with

Drew. That's why we announced our engagement when we did. And I go to see them a fair bit. Once in a while I even stay over, just to keep my mum company. Dad's always busy with his business.' I kept quiet, sensing there was more she wanted to say. She looked up, biting her lip. 'You know,' she said in a rush, 'I get it, that you feel conflicted about your family. You do, don't you?'

I raised my eyebrows: I wasn't expecting this. 'That's one way of putting it.'

She was silent for a moment, then she said, 'I love my parents. Of course I do. They've always done their best for me, nothing too much trouble. But I worry as well: all that awful business last year, when that man wanted to hurt me and Jasper was so heroic.' She shuddered, obviously thinking of the time when her father's falling out with his long-term employee had almost had tragic results.

'Do you still have nightmares about that, Tiffany?' I asked softly.

She shook her head. 'Not now. But I still think about what people say about my dad. It's, well, it's really hard, thinking your dad might be a criminal. And I still don't know for sure. To me he has always just been a loving dad.'

'Would you want to know?'

'I think so. But I can't really ask him, can I? It would seem so disloyal, that I don't trust him.'

'There may be ways to phrase the question,' I said. 'You'd have to be very diplomatic. What about your mother? Would she have any insights?'

Tiffany shook her head. 'I don't think she'd be any help at all. If I started asking questions I think she'd go to pieces. I don't know why, but she seems, not scared exactly, but in awe of him. I've always felt I needed to protect her. It's not what I would call a happy marriage. Why do they even stay together? I wouldn't. And you didn't, the first time round, did you?'

'No. But every set-up's different, and none of us know the ins and outs of someone else's life.'

'I want to make a better job of it,' she said, suddenly intense. 'Drew and me. I want us always to talk to each other if there's a problem, like we do now.'

I smiled. 'That's good if you can keep it up. What usually happens is life gets busy, you don't make the effort, little annoyances build up, you let things slide. And then suddenly you're middle-aged and communicate in grunts every other Thursday.'

Tiffany laughed, and it changed her whole face. 'I can't believe it's like that with you and Bob!'

'You'd better believe it, love.'

'Seriously, though, the rest of your family's a bit of a burden to you, isn't it? You don't mind me asking, do you?'

'No, I don't mind. You probably know I try to keep a big distance between me and my father and brothers and sisters. I had enough of all that growing up – couldn't get away fast enough.' I almost mentioned my wish to dissociate myself from the shadier elements, but thought it would be tactless, considering what she'd been saying about her father – to whom I would one day be related by marriage. Yes, it seemed Tiffany and I had a few things in common.

She frowned. 'But it doesn't really work, does it? From what Drew's told me.'

I was startled by her question, not least at the thought of my son discussing me. 'What do you mean?'

'Well, just recently, didn't you have to sort your brother out when your dad locked him in his room and your sisters couldn't cope? Seems like you're always on call. And didn't you come back to Brant, all those years ago, before Drew was even born, because of your twin brothers being in trouble? When you really wanted to go back to London?' She hesitated, a small smile on her lips. 'I'm glad you did, though – otherwise you and Bob would never have met and Drew wouldn't exist!'

'I gather you are quite pleased he exists,' I said with some irony.

She blushed a charming pink. 'Oh dear. Is it that obvious? You probably think I am very naïve.'

I pushed myself off the chair and gathered the dirty cups. 'If you can't be idealistic now,' I said, 'when can you be?'

She smiled and got up to help me, and I found myself thinking that my son, whose judgments I had not always rated highly, had this time made a surprisingly fortunate choice – despite my misgivings about her father.

Tiffany's unexpected comments about my family had a strangely unsettling effect on me. I hadn't thought before of the notion that I was somehow 'on call,' as she described it, but to an outsider it must have seemed that way. For me the bottom line was to ignore them all as far as I could, and never to think about why. I wanted to keep the lid firmly on that can of coiling snakes; but was it even possible? What if the snakes were growing bigger and stronger with the passing years? Could the can hold? Wouldn't the lid burst open one day and release poisonous monsters into every dark corner of my life? I shook myself crossly: this line of thinking could lead only to muddle and madness. But would I be allowed to let it rest there, as I had always done, if Tiffany wanted to discuss her family issues, which were very much alive? Anna had said she thought I was hiding something. She little knew how much. The thought that my days of hiding might be numbered filled me with a horror I could not have explained.

All through the following week I was dogged by a vague sense of unease, as if something was askew but I didn't know what it was, so could not call it out, confront it and send it packing. Bob was in a strange mood, sombre and morose; I asked him what the matter was and he snapped, which was unlike his usual tolerant self. I assumed it was something at work worrying him, but he seemed to manage to put on an air of cheerfulness when we were with other people: if

Drew and Tiffany came round, or if we chatted to the neighbours. As soon as were alone the dark cloud descended, cold and suffocating. Was it me that had sent him into this despondency? Or was it simply that with me he saw no reason to pretend?

I didn't see Anna at all until midweek; she was either in court or working at home. But on Wednesday she breezed in with a passing greeting and ten minutes later arrived in my office, minus her shoes, and slapped a sheet of paper on my desk, grinning broadly.

I ignored it. 'Good morning. How was your weekend?'

'My weekend – ? Oh, you mean going to Birmingham with Jeremy. That seems ages ago! Yes, it was pleasant, thank you.'

'How did you get on with his daughter?'

'Fine. She's nice. And she didn't ask me if my intentions were honourable.'

'Very funny. And how was your case yesterday and Monday?'

'We won.'

'That's good. So what is it that's making you so cheerful this morning?'

'Something I hope that will cheer you up too.' She picked the sheet of paper up and thrust it at me.

'Why do I need cheering up?'

'Because you look down in the mouth. Your normally eye-catching outfits have become weirdly muted. When did the Janet Clarke we know and love descend to wearing beige?'

'It's taupe.'

'Whatever. Please, Janet, read this letter.'

I took it from her and scanned it while she stood there in front of my desk. I'd guessed it was from Lauren Barclay, and I didn't want anyone to know how my stomach had lurched when I thought, not of what it might contain – Anna's air of triumph seemed to imply that there would be no serious repercussions from our little falling-out – but of what I might have to do to seal the bargain and heal the breach. Anna was right when she said I hated hypocrisy. The letter purportedly was from Lauren herself, and the air of injured innocence definitely smelled of her, but the language was almost certainly her father's. She would, she said, accept our terms, but she went on to reiterate her self-righteous sense of grievance at how shabbily she had been treated while an employee at Hartington, and she expected a full apology.

'This stinks,' I said sourly when I got to the end.

Anna's grin faded. 'I know,' she said softly. 'But you'll do it, won't you?'

'I said I would, and I will,' I said. 'But for the record –'

'I hear you,' Anna said. 'And it does stink. I'm with you. But you know as well as I do how often we have to compromise in this business.'

I sighed. 'All right. Leave it with me. I'll have it on your desk by the end of the day.'

'Thank you.' She reached the doorway and turned back. 'Don't be too fulsome, will you? We don't want them smelling a rat.'

'Feel free to edit it,' I said.

She looked at me with a strange expression. 'Janet, I'm really sorry you have to do this. I'm on your side – I hope you remember that.'

'Yeah, OK.' I could hear my own grudging voice.

When Bob came home that evening I thought I might tell him about the letter, that after all my career was intact, that I was not about to be drummed out in abject dishonour, but when I began to tell him – we were washing the dinner dishes at the time – he looked at me in blank incomprehension and I remembered, to my discomfort, that this was the first time I had mentioned the situation. I had barely ever referred to Lauren Barclay at all.

'What on earth are you talking about?' he said. 'What's all this about your career going down the pan? Is it some kind of joke?'

'No. It was all about that new clerk that got appointed when I wasn't there – when Dad locked Ben in his room and I had to go over there and sort them out – you remember that, don't you?' He frowned and nodded, standing with hot water dripping from his hands. 'Well, it turned out she was totally useless – kept making mistakes even after she'd been there long enough to learn the basics – mistakes which could have cost us reputation and clients. We all tried to be understanding, even me, but in the end it was once too many and I bawled her out. And then she left and we got a letter of complaint.'

'About you specifically?' The frown had deepened.

'Yes. Anna wrote back straight away, offering terms, but it has taken till now to come to any resolution. I've had to write a letter of apology when I don't think I have done anything wrong, at least not as she claims. The trouble is, her father's a solicitor so he'd know how to be difficult if he chose to.' I looked at him, and I realised I was clutching the tea-towel in a fierce grip. 'I thought you'd like to know I wasn't about to be unemployed.'

He shook his head, and it was some moments before he replied. 'And it's taken you all this time to say anything? Like, months?'

I shrugged. 'Other things got in the way.'

'Weren't you worried?'

'I tried not to be. It was such a trivial bit of nonsense. I put it out of my mind.'

'Yes,' he said grimly. 'You're good at that.'

'What? What's that supposed to mean?' I was bewildered. Why was he so angry?

'You keep everything to yourself,' he muttered. 'Unless it's something unimportant, flippant, top-level stuff. You don't share anything, Janet.'

This was serious. He hardly ever called me by my full name. But I felt indignation rising. 'And you do?' I said. 'You've been in a state of misery all week and you refuse to tell me why.'

'That's different. I would have said something eventually. I wouldn't have kept it to myself for months.'

'Whatever.' I felt weak suddenly, definitely not up for a full-on fight. Silence was now my best defence. I dried the last few dishes and put them away, aware of him staring at me. 'I'm going to read my book.' I stalked out of the room, and he called after me. 'I thought we were supposed to be a team!'

I said nothing. I found myself thinking, Did you? Did you really? To my amazement and horror the ache deep in my chest was rising, welling, filling my eyes with tears. I had my back to him; he couldn't see, but my shame choked me. I'm strong, I told myself. I can cope. I never cry.

Days went by with no word spoken, and the resulting unease was a pinprick I found hard to ignore. At work I could put it out of my mind and concentrate on the things I was paid to do, but at home it met me at the front door: that palpable sense that something was wrong. In times past we had never let a disagreement last so long; any silence would be broken by one or other of us as good humour finally returned, and as often as not there would be feeble jokes and relieved laughter. Not this time: Bob went to work and came home, brooding and uncommunicative, and over the weekend he did a series of night shifts which meant that I was alone most of the time. I had plenty to do, so I told myself, but with constant rain deterring me from going out I found I was drifting, unable to settle. Then on Sunday evening, after a period of welcome calm, I had another bout of pain and bleeding, and I decided to ring the GP surgery in the morning. Enough was enough.

I made the call as soon as they opened, and got an appointment in the late afternoon, so that I would miss only an hour or so at work. I would have told Bob about it when he came in from his shift, but his abrupt change of mood derailed me. I was drinking a cup of strong coffee and attempting to cover the night's ravages with layers of makeup when he came in just before eight, letting the front door slam behind him, and called out to me as if we hadn't been locked in a sullen stand-off for days. 'Where are you? Aren't you late for work?'

I left the bathroom and stood at the top of the stairs. 'I'm just about to go,' I said guardedly. 'What's up?'

His expression was all delight. 'I had an amazing shift,' he said. 'The sort that makes it all worthwhile.'

I started down the stairs. 'So what happened?'

He grinned. 'Something you see in those dramas about life in an ambulance,' he said, 'which are usually so unrealistic: drama and heroics at three in the morning, blood and tragedy at five. Not the dreary hours watching someone trying to kill herself with drugs and drink, or some headcase hurling abuse and trying to bite you. It's only happened once before, years ago, and then I was completely terrified! We got a call from a frantic chap whose wife was in labour and he didn't think she'd make it to hospital. We didn't waste time getting to them but I took it with a pinch of salt: babies usually take their time to arrive. But it turned out he was right: there was no way we could even get her into the ambulance. She'd decided to have a warm bath to ease the pains, but found she couldn't get out. The water had all gone, and she was wet and shivering, and that baby was ready to be born. She was a big lass and her husband just couldn't get her out of the tub – she was slippery too from the water, making a right hullabaloo, and he panicked.

'We managed to wrap her in towels and lift her out of the bath, and we laid her on the floor and made her as comfortable as we could. Her husband was on the phone to the midwife when I delivered that baby – a big, strong girl with a good pair of lungs. It was quite emotional – we were all a bit weepy. By the time the midwife got there mum and baby were cleaned up and in bed and I was making us all a cup of tea.'

'Nice to have something positive happen for once,' I murmured as I squeezed past him. 'And well done you – I didn't know you had midwifery skills.'

'It's part of our training,' Bob said, 'but a long time ago.'

I collected my things. 'I'm off to work. Aren't you going to bed?'

'Not yet. I'm too awake from all the adrenaline. I think I'll mow the back lawn – the daisies are taking over.'

'OK, well, see you later, then. Make sure you get some rest.'

'Have a good day. I'll cook tonight if you like.'

'Yeah, great.'

As I got in the car my head was spinning. There was something slightly unhinged about Bob's abrupt change in mood, even allowing for what had happened on his shift. What was the word I had come across in a document recently that seemed to fit him so appropriately? Labile – that was it; and it was unlike Bob, who had always been steady and calm, withstanding both tragedy and triumph with stoical acceptance, qualities which made him so apt for the work he did so that it rarely overwhelmed him. Now I wondered, with a sickening chill, if he was heading for some kind of breakdown, and I had no idea how I could help him.

As I sat waiting in the surgery reception area that grey, muggy afternoon I admitted to myself that I felt lousy. Weeks of on-and-off menopausal symptoms and resulting lack of sleep were breaking down my normal resilience. In one way it was a good thing; usually when I made an appointment with the doctor, which was rare enough, by the time I got seen I felt better. Not today, though: anyone with eyes could see my drawn, colourless face, my mouth drawn tight with anticipated pain.

The receptionist approached me. 'Mrs Clarke, I hope it's OK – you won't be seeing your normal GP today – he's been called away. You'll be seeing someone new to the practice – Dr Kemsey.'

I shrugged. 'I don't mind who I see.'

Dr Kemsey turned out to be young, slim, tall and female, with an air of suppressed energy; I imagined her changing into running gear at the end of her working day and hot-footing it five miles home. I recited all my symptoms over the past few months, and told her if this was just menopause I was heartily sick of it.

She got me to lie down and pull up my shirt, and she gently palpated my abdomen. When I was seated again in the chair she scanned her computer screen, then she looked up and said, 'Looking at your notes this has been going on for some time. Does the flushing keep you awake on a regular basis?'

'Yes.'

'The thing is, it could all just be the hormonal changes taking place. But I'd like to check things out in a bit more depth, just to make sure there's nothing else going on. Even if there isn't, we should be able to help you with the more intrusive symptoms. I'm guessing you must be exhausted. Do you work?'

'I'm a barrister's clerk.'

She nodded. 'Quite full-on, then, at times.'

'It can be.' I managed a weary smile.

'I'm going to refer you for an ultrasound and a D and C. Ever had these before?'

'Ultrasound, yes, when I was pregnant with my son.'

'OK, it'll be a question of waiting for your appointment to arrive in the post. With any luck it shouldn't take too long.'

On my way home, I didn't know whether to be relieved or concerned. Something other than reassurance was going to happen at last; but might they actually find something unwelcome, even sinister? It was a sign of my unusual fragility that I couldn't quite thrust that cold thought from my mind.

'You're early,' Bob said when I came indoors.

'I went to the doctor – again. But I saw someone different, and she's referring me for some tests. Just to make sure it's not something other than menopause.'

'Good. It's about time,' he said. 'You've been running on empty.'

Considering his own state of mind, I was surprised he'd noticed.

Bob woke me from a troubled sleep. 'What time is it?' I said blearily.

'It's gone twelve,' he said. 'I wouldn't have woken you, but I'm going down to the station.'

'What – now?' I said. 'I thought you had tomorrow off. Why do you need to go in at this time of night?'

He was already in his coat. 'There's been a bomb,' he said urgently. 'I just caught it on the twenty-four hour news.'

'Here? In Brant?'

'No, Manchester.'

I sat up, trying to blink the fog from my brain. 'But they'll call out the Manchester ambulances, won't they?'

'Of course,' he said impatiently. 'But there are multiple casualties. They might need backup.'

'What happened?'

'A concert,' he said. 'In an arena, packed with people, all streaming out at the end, mostly kids. Parents waiting in the foyer to collect them. Some madman with a home-made bomb – blew himself up and took others with him.' He made for the door. 'It's rolling out on the news if you want to see. I may be ages, or I may be back in ten minutes. They'll probably call in ambulances from the north west, but you never know.'

I heard him run down the stairs, and the front door banged. Even in my fuddled state I felt that here was more evidence of Bob not thinking straight. If there was a disaster in Manchester, they'd hardly be needing crews from Brant. It was as if he had to prove to himself that his skills were still needed. Now fully and unwillingly awake, I felt conflicted: part of me grieved for him, because his work was as important to him as mine to me, that I knew, and for me the thought that one day I would have to retire and give my job to someone else was almost frightening. His apparent stoicism, his acceptance of the need for a different role, was a blind. Another part of me was irritated. Get a grip, Bob. Face reality. Nobody goes on for ever. We all have to get old. I wondered too which of us would have to be strong and prop the other one up. It seemed to me that right now we were both in a very uncertain place.

June

They'd promised us a heatwave, and before June was fairly upon us it struck. Chambers was unbearable: some years ago there had been an attempt to install air-conditioning but it had long since failed, and we were reduced to open windows and desk fans, which let in fumes and traffic noise or sent unweighted papers fluttering to the floor. Mentally and physically I was out of sorts; not so Anna, who breezed in one morning looking fresh and floral in a predominantly apricot-coloured cotton dress, new sandals on her feet and a wide smile on her face.

'Morning!' she hailed as she passed my door. Then she saw my expression and sobered. 'You look like February just returned. Are you still not feeling well?'

'It's the same old thing, only worse,' I said. 'But this time they're sending me for a scan. Anyway, what are you so chipper about?'

'I had a letter waiting for me when I got home yesterday,' she said. 'I've been invited to a Selection Day.'

'Well! I didn't doubt it, but congratulations.'

She looked at me narrow-eyed. 'You seem a little underwhelmed.'

'No, of course not. I'm very pleased for you, because it's what you want. Not so chuffed for chambers.'

'I'll still be here. You won't notice the difference.'

I shook my head. 'Maybe not now. But the next step – you won't be stopping at Deputy, will you? – is District Judge, and then you'll be gone.'

'Things move on, Janet,' she said softly. 'Like you, I've been here many years. Perhaps it's time.'

'Will we survive, do you suppose?' I hadn't intended to ask this question; somehow it asked itself.

'Of course. Hartington has several excellent barristers. I could drop dead tomorrow, but this place would go on.'

I squirmed a little. 'I didn't mean 'we' as in chambers. I meant 'we' as in you and me.'

Her eyebrows shot up. 'Why wouldn't we?'

I couldn't look at her; she was too full of light and positive energy, everything that I was not. I stared at the dust-free surface of my desk. 'As you say, things move on.'

'But some things go on, and I hope we will always be friends.' She paused, frowning. 'Janet, is something wrong?'

'Plenty.' I sighed. 'But I'm sure we both have work to do.'

'Nothing too desperate, not from my point of view. I shall put the kettle on, and you will come to my room and drink coffee.'

I opened my mouth to protest, and closed it again. Her expression told me she wouldn't accept refusal.

I planted myself in a chair in her room along the corridor, and a moment later she came in with two mugs. 'If anyone enquires, we are having a serious conference.' She took her seat behind her desk and leaned on it with both elbows. 'Tell me what's going on. I feel we haven't had a proper chat for ages, and that's probably my fault.'

'Hm. It's true your love life has been taking up a lot of your attention.'

She laughed. 'As these things do. But I'm sorry if I've been neglectful.'

'So, all going swimmingly, is it?'

'Pretty much, thanks. But I thought we were talking about you.'

'That subject is deadly dull. I am suffering from unusual physical pressures, and I'm not sleeping. Getting to work on time every day looking half-alive is more and more a challenge.'

She nodded. 'That must be gruelling. But at least something is getting done about it. Anything else?'

'Drew's left home. But that's no bad thing. He seems OK. In fact he is behaving like an adult. So we haven't failed utterly as parents.'

'Of course you haven't, you idiot!'

I hesitated, and drew breath. 'And then there's Bob. He's not himself. One minute he says he can't do this job anymore – in fact he was talking about applying for something less stressful, more administrative – then the next he comes home full of beans because he's delivered a baby. He doesn't seem to know which way is up. But a lot of the time he's silent and cranky. We were never ones for deep analytical chats, but lately we hardly speak.'

She was silent for a moment, then she said, 'And you need his support at the moment, I'd guess.'

'Do I?'

'Apart from not feeling at your best health-wise, there's all that business with Lauren Barclay. I know you made out you weren't bothered, but I didn't believe you, not completely. It's got to be a strain, living with a complaint against you, however unjustified.'

'Ah, that. No repercussions, I take it?'

'No. I hope we can say that tedious matter is closed. Tell me, Janet – what was it, really, that you disliked about her? It can't simply be that you weren't around at her interview.'

'Of course not! I hope my ego isn't quite that inflated. No, it was the combination of stupid and cocky. Maybe she was raised with that sense of entitlement, I don't know. And, if I'm honest, I couldn't help comparing her with me – all the privileges she seemed to have, all the barriers I had to surmount. I guess it doesn't paint me in a very good light.'

'I know you find dumb stupidity trying,' Anna said with a small smile. 'It's a good job Drew's no fool: you might have given him away.' She took a sip of her coffee. 'Seriously, though, Janet, there are many kinds of cognitive lack, just as there are many kinds of cleverness. I think of my nephew, Sam – he has a mental age of five or six. And, if it's not too indelicate to mention, you have a brother who has similar issues.'

'But Ben can't help how he is,' I protested. 'He had fits when he was a little lad which caused brain damage. He does really well, considering.'

'I don't doubt it,' Anna said. 'But have you thought that maybe we all have areas of stupidity? I know I do.'

'You? You are annoyingly clever.'

'No, not across the board,' she said, shaking her head. 'I can be very dense. And so, if I may say so, can you. As can every human being.'

'I suppose,' I said grudgingly, 'you are going to say we are all idiots compared with God Almighty.'

She laughed. 'Well, that's certainly true. Transient, easily-squashed little bugs. No more sense than a block of wood. It amazes me that He even bothers with us at all. It's beyond comprehension. But maybe stupidity isn't the right word, Janet. Not for you. You're very quick, knowledgeable, logical. Maybe what we're talking about are areas of blindness that as individuals we are hardly aware of.'

'Don't tell me.' I heard my own sour tone. 'You think I am blind spiritually.'

She shook her head. 'That's not what I meant. Perhaps more in denial. But since you mention it I do think (and maybe I'm wrong, so tell me to butt out if you like) that you are cutting yourself off from a source of help, guidance, support, call it what you like, that's freely on offer if you will take it, all out of completely misplaced pride. Or maybe,' she added thoughtfully, looking at me as if the answer was written on my forehead, 'it's not pride. Maybe it's fear.'

'Fear of what?'

'Oh, I'd guess the usual things,' she said with a smile that was all kindness and no mockery. 'Rejection, failure, abandonment, loss of dignity, loss of competence. Ring any bells?'

I gaped, unable to respond. Where had all this come from? I drained my coffee, my thoughts whirling, making no sense. 'Do you remember,' I said slowly as a memory began to form, 'that course you made me go on a few years ago? Some nonsense about team-building?'

'I made you? I don't think so.'

'Well, there was certainly heavy pressure. Anyway, one of the questions they asked us, right at the beginning, was what everyday object we would compare ourselves to. I wanted to tell them I saw myself as an antique wardrobe or a set of fire-irons, just to be difficult. But I reined myself in.'

'So what object did you settle on?'

'A stone. Chipped and shapeless and rough, but hard to break.'

'I see that. At least, I see you might see yourself that way.'

The ache that was there all the time – not the gut pain, but the ache deep in my chest that I had to squash down in order to stay calm and function – rose up, threatening to engulf me. 'I don't think it's true anymore, if it ever was.'

'So what would you say now?'

'I can't tell you. Because I don't want to collapse in a weeping heap. It never helps.'

'I think I might disagree with that,' she said. 'But –'

Her phone, that she had laid on her desk, started to trill. She picked it up, mouthing 'Sorry' at me, and I took the opportunity to gather up the dirty cups and escape. I was ridiculously comforted by her belief that our friendship would continue, even though I had my doubts. She had acquired new friends in the past few months; I had not. I was beginning to understand what my own area of stupidity might be, but I set that train of thought firmly aside. Not for the first time, her ability to see through things surprised and unnerved me. I didn't want to face any more probing, not that day; because if she had pressed me for an answer, I might have confessed that if I now compared myself to some common object, it would have been to a ball of string – one which had a long, loose, trailing end that, if casually tugged, would cause the whole thing to unravel. I hid in my office, behind a closed door and a computer screen. Unravelling was a terrifying prospect, and it seemed all too possible.

On Saturday evening I paused at the front door and called up to Bob, who emerged from the bathroom dressed only in a towel. 'I'm just off to Drew and Tiffany's,' I said. 'Have a good time with your old pals.'

'Yeah, thanks.'

I hesitated. 'And Bob – be careful.'

He leaned over the banister, frowning. 'What of?'

'London's a dangerous place. Full of lunatics.'

'Everywhere's full of lunatics.'

'Yes, but –' I bit my lip. 'There are more of them there.'

'There are more people generally,' he said. 'What's bugging you?'

I shrugged; I couldn't explain. 'I was thinking about that nutter who drove into people, back in March. Just ploughed into them while they were taking a stroll, minding their own business. And then didn't he stab a policeman to death?'

'Things happen all the time, love. We don't hear about half of them. And not only in London – what about the crazy who set off a bomb in Manchester recently? Nowhere's safe.'

'Now I feel reassured,' I groused.

He narrowed his eyes. 'It's not like you to worry. Are you getting a bit soft in your old age?'

'I'm younger than you, cheeky. I don't know about soft, but I have a bad feeling.'

'That's not like you either. Where did the cool logic vanish to?'

'Maybe it's my Irish genes. Just be careful, OK?'

He shook his head and disappeared into the bedroom.

Perhaps the turmoil in my hormones had indeed set off some unlooked-for premonition. I was late leaving Drew and Tiffany's, and I was getting into my car when my phone rang. It was Bob, and there was so much racket in the background I could barely make sense of what he was saying.

'What? Bob, I can't hear you.'

'Wait.' The phone went dead. A moment later it rang again. 'I've had to hide in the gents' toilet for a bit of peace,' he said. 'Look, there's been a – ' I heard him swallow. 'My God, Jan, I think you really must have the second sight. There's been an incident on London Bridge. And right here where I am, in Borough Market.'

'What? Are you OK?'

'I've got a small scratch – it's nothing. If you put the news on you might get something.'

'What happened?'

'Another bridge.' He sounded hollow, his voice flat. 'Lunatics with a vehicle. People dead and injured. And then they came running down here. You can imagine – it's a warm evening, people were sitting outside enjoying a drink, and three men suddenly appear, slashing and stabbing. Dear God, it was horrible. Carnage.'

'You saw them?'

'For a moment. Then we were all pushing and shoving to get inside the pub. My friends were dragging at me, but I wanted to see what was happening, I wanted to see if anyone needed help.'

'Oh, Bob.'

'People were throwing things at them, chairs, bottles. I saw a young woman go down – I was near the door.'

'And you went to help her.'

He was silent for a moment. 'It's what I do.'

Fury and pride fought a momentary battle. 'What then?'

'Look, I'm going to run out of battery any minute. I have to tell you I might not get back tonight. They've shut some of the tube stations and some of the mainline ones as well. I don't know if I'll be able to get back to Liverpool Street. But don't worry – I can go home with Len. Jan, I'm OK. I'll charge my phone at Len's.' There was a crackle and a crash, and the line died.

I said nothing to Drew and Tiffany; they'd already waved me goodbye and gone indoors, and there was no point in worrying them. I drove home more slowly than usual. The late news gave the bare bones, but there were frightening, if blurred, images, and I imagined Bob in the middle of the melee, and felt sick.

He called me the next morning. 'I'm at the station. Can you come and pick me up? There don't seem to be any taxis, and I'm too knackered to walk.'

When I pulled into the station carpark, after the usual battle with the traffic and the one-way system which was intended to help and did anything but, I saw him walking towards me. His clothes were crumpled, as if he had slept in them – and probably he had. There was a dirty plaster taped across his forehead. Seeing him so battered gave me a combination of feelings that were familiar enough: horror that he had put himself in harm's way, anger that when he did so he wasn't thinking about me or anyone else, fresh recognition of his bravery and a tinge of grudging admiration. Less familiar, and slightly alarming, was the desire to protect him from himself. I suppressed it: I knew he would have bristled and resisted.

He glanced at me and swiftly away again. 'Thanks for coming to get me,' he muttered.

I started the car up and joined the steady flow of cars on the road. 'You going to tell me what happened?'

'Did you see anything on the news?'

'Some. But it was difficult to make sense of. Anyway, I'm most interested in your part in it. Where did you meet up with your mates?'

'The usual place, just inside Borough Market. It's handy for the majority. We were drinking at a table outside – nice warm evening, people all around, chatting, laughing, summer dresses and shirtsleeves, all the doors and windows open, people going in and out with drinks, just a normal Saturday evening. Then there was some kind of rumpus, and I heard screams and shouts. I got up to see what was happening, and some men came haring up saying they were police, though they weren't in uniform, and that there was danger and we should all go into the pub. People were panicking, nobody knew what was going on, and there was a stampede. We were a bit left behind but we got indoors and I was looking out of the window. I saw a few people still outside and some of them were throwing things – bottles, chairs, even a skateboard – and I saw three men and they had knives and were shouting something I couldn't quite catch. That's when I saw her.'

I indicated to overtake a trundling bus. 'Who are you talking about?' I glanced at him and saw his shrug, his barely-contained misery. 'I don't know who she was,' he said. 'Just some young woman out with her friends, got separated I suppose. Two of the men were attacking her; she was on the ground, and there was blood on her jeans.'

'You went outside. Where there were killers with knives.'

'Yes.'

'Go on.'

'When I got to her there were two men trying to fight the attackers off. I knelt down in the road to see what I could do for the girl. I kept saying, 'I'm a paramedic, let me help.' The men with knives split up and ran off, but one of them caught me a passing swipe across the forehead. It's nothing much.' He paused. 'The knives were pink.'

'Pink?'

'Yes. Pink ceramic. It's weird, the stupid little things you notice.'

'What then?'

'The two guys were the same ones as before, off duty police officers. They came over to me and knelt down with me. They said it was no good, that she'd gone. There was blood all over. Some of it was mine – it was dripping down my face. They said I should go indoors, get my cut seen to. They helped me up. That's when I heard the ambulance sirens.' He looked at me, his face a mask of anguish. 'I couldn't save her, Jan. I tried to stop her bleeding, but she had so many wounds. She was conscious for a while, though. I spoke to her, tried to make her feel less alone. But she just bled to death.' He choked on his last words, and for the rest of the journey home he was silent, sitting with his eyes closed. He was grey with fatigue.

When we got indoors he said, 'I slept on Len's sofa. Except I didn't, barely at all. I need to crash out for a few hours. Maybe I'll feel a bit more with it then.'

'I'm going to clean up your cut first,' I said. 'That plaster looks unhygienic.'

Bob slumped onto a kitchen chair. 'A bit like Len's flat generally,' he muttered. 'He's really let things slide since Joyce died. I could probably use a shower too.' He yawned. 'Later.'

I peeled the plaster off, and revealed a long, shallow cut, ragged at the edges. 'I don't think it needs a stitch,' I said. 'But we need to keep an eye on it in case it turns nasty.' I washed the area with warm water and dried it before spraying it with antiseptic and covering it with a clean dressing. Bob was swaying in the chair from sheer fatigue. Suddenly he clutched me round my middle and buried his face in my shirt. 'I'm sorry if you were worried,' he mumbled.

I gently disengaged and took the bowl of bloody water to the sink. 'If? There's no if about it. Of course I was worried.' I turned to him, leaning on the sink, folding my arms and fixing him with a frown. 'It may surprise you to know that I would very much rather you were not dead.'

He laughed feebly and got up, holding on to the back of the chair. 'Well, that's something, I guess.' As he came towards me, making for the door to the hall, I was dismayed to see tears in his eyes. We didn't do weeping, Bob and I. Perhaps that was about to change. He stopped, the strangest look on his face, and ran his fingers gently down my cheek. 'Thanks.'

We got through the rest of that week somehow. Bob went back to work after a scheduled day off and by then his cut was healing. He told me to say he'd had an accident with a nail in the shed. 'Otherwise it'll be talked to death,' he said. On Thursday we trooped obediently out to vote, and then it was time to face the imminent reality of a family wedding.

On Friday evening I opened up my wardrobe and laid out my wedding outfit on the bed. It had taken me some time to assemble, and had involved the cooperation of the women who ran my two favourite charity shops. Since I was a loyal customer they were happy to oblige, and I'd given them a list of things to look out for. I knew I wouldn't get exactly what I wanted, but if anything there was a better chance of that than if I'd shopped in the city centre, where the dictates of today's fashion limited one's choices. I had a quite specific ensemble in mind, and the chief criteria were that it had to suit me and it had to be as different as possible from what I imagined most of the other women to be wearing: either a new outfit sourced from those very city centre shops or something kept for best from last year or the year before or many years before. This year's fashions ran to the floaty and floral, which didn't suit me anyway, but would be considered just the thing by most for a summer wedding.

I scanned my finds with a critical eye. The dress was of some metallic fabric, silver-grey, which when on shimmered with the wearer's movements. It was strikingly simple: clinging, knee-length with a scalloped hem, a high halter neck, and backless. This last feature was perhaps a bit daring for a mere aunt of the groom, but it looked, I thought, fabulous. The accessories I had collected over a number of weeks, and some of them I had been obliged to buy new online, including the high-heeled silver sandals and the pièce de résistance – not a hat, definitely not a fascinator, more a headpiece, in black. This sported a kind of deep skullcap, fitting close to the head from forehead to nape, topped with a huge voile bow and forward-leaning black feathers, with an all-round spotty veil. It would mean I couldn't have gelled purple spikes, and I would have to keep it on all the time because it would flatten my hair, but that was a small price to pay for something so over-the-top glamorous. A tiny black-and-silver bag, only a little used, completed the ensemble, plus a quirky pair of black fingerless lacy gloves, which I had found in the charity shop in a pile of things to be discarded, and carefully washed and returned to shape.

My evening had already been disturbed by a phone call from Pauline, which I'd been expecting. I suppose it was natural for the mother of the groom to be all fluttery and twittery on the eve of her only son's wedding, and she'd probably worn Christine out with endless worries.

After describing her outfit in detail, and asking my opinion more than once on whether I really thought eau-de-nil was a good colour for her complexion, she wanted to know what my family would be wearing.

'Bob will put on his best suit, a clean shirt and a tie of his own choosing,' I said. 'That won't take long, as he only has three, and one is black, for funerals. He hasn't said, but he may even have splashed out on a new one for the occasion. I hope Drew will look respectable, but I don't know if he even owns a suit. Tiffany will look charming, I'm sure, but she hasn't told me her plans. As for me, you'll just have to wait and see. I can tell you it's not eau-de-nil, so we won't be competing.'

The mention of Drew sent Pauline off on a new tack. 'I do hope those boys aren't doing anything too stupid,' she said. 'You do hear of such goings-on – some of them quite dangerous! Is Drew with them? Perhaps he can keep Neville out of trouble. Some of his friends are a bit wild, and Neville has always been rather easily led.'

'Drew did say he would go,' I said. 'I don't know how successful he'd be at keeping anyone out of trouble, though. Look, Pauline, don't worry. Try to get a good night's sleep. I'm sure it will be a wonderful day, and the weather looks set fair, so you should have some good photos.'

After she'd rung off, I thought about my nephew and niece. Neither of them resembled their parents: Pauline was rounded, with a fluff of light-coloured hair, and Colin was florid and stocky. Both Neville and Nicole could have been my children; they were slender, on the tall side, with dark hair and sharp features. I wondered if Colin had ever thought they weren't actually his. I wouldn't have put it past him to accuse my sister of cheating on him. To me she seemed the last person to have an affair, but people are ever mysterious, and frankly if Colin had been my husband I'd have had a string of them. But then, I wouldn't have married Colin in the first place. And if I were being realistic and charitable, Pauline, even if tempted, would have resisted – not just out of fear of Colin, but because of her genuinely-held beliefs. Anyway, tall, skinny and dark were in our genes, from our mother's side.

In reality I barely knew my nephew and niece, and if I'd had to choose Neville would have won out every time. He was a silly, excitable young man with a high-pitched laugh a bit like a horse's whinny; he didn't have a lot of gumption and would go along with whatever was suggested even if it was foolish, so I understood Pauline's concern. But he was harmless and pleasant enough, and I imagined he was in thrall to his big, blonde, determined bride-to-be, in every way that mattered. Nicole was another matter. At nineteen – was she? Or was she twenty? I'd lost track – she worked in one of the city centre stores on the beauty counter, and she was certainly decorative, with her sinuous figure, perfectly-cut hair and predatory nails. Her face seemed to me to be set in a permanent slight sneer, and if not in her looks then certainly in some of her nature she reminded me of her father, who in general I thought a horrible man. She condescended to her brother, treated her mother with contempt, and clung hypocritically to her father – because, I guessed, he held the family purse-strings and was open-handed to his precious princess. Ugh. My thoughts slid sideways to another young woman I was getting to know. Tiffany was her own father's little jewel, but she was genuinely a good-hearted young woman, whose shyness hid both sense and determination, and I was thankful for Drew's excellent choice. If I was ever disgruntled with my own family, I had only to compare it with Pauline's to feel a sense of relief.

I awoke on Saturday to a fine, settled day. The wedding was at midday and we had time to prepare at leisure. I knew from the invitation that a double-decker bus had been laid on for guests to be transported from the church to the hotel where the reception was waiting, so that those who wanted to could drink without restraint. Some of the bride's guests were coming from Spain, so Pauline told me, and they would be staying at the hotel afterwards. Bob and I had decided we would take our own car, to be free to leave when we'd had enough, and we were certainly not staying for the evening party, which I had no doubt would be deafening.

I was just emerging from the shower, wreathed in steam, my bathrobe clutched around me, when Bob appeared at the top of the stairs. 'Just had a call from Drew. He said to tell you the cunning plan worked.'

'Ah, good. So presumably he won't be green around the gills as I imagine Neville and his mates might be.'

'He got Tiffany to collect him at a prearranged spot when he rang her. And they're going to take their own car today too. They don't want to leave Horace too long. I suppose Drew might well be working tonight anyway, so he can't afford to be late – or hungover.'

'Shouldn't you be getting ready?'

'Yeah, I'll shower now. Don't worry – I won't get in your way. I know how long it takes to get your face just right.'

'It's OK for you – no one minds if a bloke looks craggy and weatherbeaten.'

'Just as well, then.'

With my face done more or less to my satisfaction – there was no way to hide completely the evidence that in a few weeks' time I would be forty-nine – I put on my wedding clothes. It took quite a few minutes of adjustment and critical mirror checks to get the headpiece angle exactly as it should be. Bob, of course, was long since ready and called to me from the hallway. 'We'd better be off. You know what Saturday traffic's like, and we'll need to find a parking space.'

I picked up the tiny bag, which contained almost nothing, tightened a sandal strap and paused on the landing above him. 'Well?'

Bob's eyes widened visibly. 'Wow. Wait a minute, let me stand back and admire this vision coming down the stairs. Careful – those heels look like a disaster waiting to happen.' He watched me as I took the stairs with, I hoped, sufficient elegance. He shook his head slowly. 'That dress is enough to make a priest forget his vows, let alone a lowly paramedic.'

'That was the idea. Not the priest bit – I have no designs on Father Gerard, or his replacement.' I held up a warning hand. 'And the paramedic can rein himself in as well. I didn't spend half the morning achieving this level of perfection to have you mess it up.'

Getting into the car was a challenge, but I managed it. Bob concentrated on negotiating the back roads and I thought idly about clothes and why I tried, even on ordinary days, to make a statement. It didn't take much psychological perception to see that I was putting as much distance as I could between the skinny kid with the hand-me-downs and the terrible haircut and the super-groomed, mature (if idiosyncratic) career woman of the present; what might have been less obvious was that, rather than my clothes showcasing the Janet Clarke of today, they served as something to hide behind. I allowed myself to wonder, just for a moment, what or who I was hiding from, that day of Neville's wedding; because, as I acknowledged only to myself, it was a day when I would feel besieged and battered by unwelcome memories. The church itself would be the first hurdle; I hadn't entered it since the day of my mother's funeral on the bleakest of January days thirty-five years before, and I knew that the feelings of an unregenerate teenager were likely to resurface. Would Father Gerard be there as a guest? I was aware he had retired, and the service would be conducted by his successor, but it seemed probable he would have been invited, having had such connections with our family for so many years, and being held in such reverence and esteem by my sisters. Equally to be dreaded was meeting with my father on an extended social occasion. I wondered if Pauline also had misgivings. I thought I could count on myself to behave with dignity and restraint, but with Desmond you never knew. I wondered if now Desmond was in the early stages of dementia – his behaviour and speech certainly seemed to suggest it – and I shuddered at the implications.

Bob slipped into a parking spot outside a convenience store with an exclamation of triumph. 'Close enough for you not to have to teeter too far in those charming, but extremely hazardous, sandals.'

I extricated myself from the car, tugging down my skirt. 'I plan to lean on you,' I said. 'They weren't actually intended to walk in – just to show off a well-turned ankle and a shapely calf.'

Bob looked down with a small but wicked grin and offered me his arm. 'As they do.'

The Church of the Holy Cross stood between the dual carriageway and the very edges of the Winstone estate, behind a railing which enclosed a small garden and steps at the front and a cemetery at the back. It was an unprepossessing building of grey blocks, with a stubby tower. That day the doors were open and people were streaming in. As it happened we met Drew and Tiffany at the foot of the shallow steps. Drew was unusually tidy in light cotton trousers and a blue shirt, his dark hair combed down, his stubble barely visible, and Tiffany looked pretty and wholesome in a summery free-flowing dress in various shades of coral and tangerine. Drew's eyebrows shot up when he saw me. 'That's some outfit, Mum. You look amazing.'

'Thanks. So, how did it go last night?'

He smiled. 'Brilliant. I had a few – a very few – drinks and slipped away early. Texted Nev later saying I had the – um, a stomach upset. Tiff was waiting by the roundabout.' He patted her backside fondly and she frowned at him. 'My getaway driver. We roared off into the sunset.'

'It was dark, actually,' Tiffany said with some asperity. 'Shouldn't we go in?'

Inside we were greeted by two portly men in shiny suits who handed us orders of service. Little had changed inside the church: the nave was plain, with rows of dark polished pews, but nearer to the altar light streamed through two stained windows, one on each side. The altar area was a jumble of religious artefacts added at different times: candles along the steps; statues of saints in niches, clutching items with which they were associated – one a book, another a lily; a blue-robed Virgin on a pedestal, her eyes raised heavenwards; a gloomy painting of a bleeding heart. Behind the altar I noted the shallow dome of an apse for whose decoration Father Gerard had, I remembered, raised funds many years ago, depicting the unlikely azure of heaven sprinkled with cherubic angels, complete with flowing robes and golden wings. My spirit, even now, revolted at such pious nonsense. Religious bling, I thought sourly.

Places were reserved with name cards, and as family members we were seated a few rows from the front on the south side of the nave. I looked around as people came in, and found to my satisfaction that the women of a certain age were, as I had thought, all in floating florals, dresses and long light jackets, with huge hats in shades of oyster, magenta and teal. The guests on the other side of the aisle, the bride's family, were notable for their iridescence, flashing jewellery and loud chatter.

Pauline, Colin and Nicole were already seated in the front pew. I saw my sister's jaw drop as I walked in and took my place. A few moments later I heard a grunting and a puffing and Ben was there in the aisle, pushing our father in a heavy-looking wheelchair. Both of them were wearing suits; I recognised Desmond's as the one he got out of the wardrobe for such occasions, shiny from lack of dry-cleaning. Ben, as ever, looked well scrubbed and neatly pressed, if not comfortable. He parked the wheelchair next to Pauline, and I saw Colin scowl. Desmond acknowledged no one. He didn't seem to know where he was, and I wondered about the wheelchair.

A moment later Christine and Giles slid into our pew from the other end and whispered greetings. I could not easily turn round, and wouldn't have if I could, but then I heard a stage-whisper from behind, and with a sinking of my already hammering heart realised that my twin brothers had arrived. 'Hey, sis. Long time no see.'

Hands stretched forward to shake Bob's and Drew's, and clumsy kisses were planted on my cheeks.

I managed to turn my head without undue whole-body movement. 'Hello, Mattie, Jimmy.' No longer the impish boys I remembered, no longer the louche adolescents always in trouble, here were two prosperous-looking men in grey suits, and obviously trying not to look like identical twins. Matthew had a full head of dark hair, and James' head was shaved. But their features were the same, if fleshier, and their hard blue eyes were still full of mischief.

In the pew with them, settling themselves on broad bottoms, a waft of strong perfume accompanying every movement, were two women I'd never seen before. The twins had always attracted women and on each occasion appeared with a different pair.

'This is Prissy,' Matthew said. 'And that's, um, Theresa.'

We exchanged greetings as best we could. 'Fabulous outfit,' one of the women simpered. 'So different.' I muttered thanks and turned back to face the front with a sigh of relief. The dress was tight.

No one expected David, so it seemed the entire Yates clan was assembled. It was a rare occasion, and not one I relished in the least. I hoped the twins would behave, but with them you never knew.

I glanced around the church for my other nemesis, but saw no sign of Father Gerard. Instead there was a flurry of activity from behind, and Neville appeared, accompanied by his best man, one of his school friends I vaguely recognised. Both were smartly turned out in morning dress, but both, especially Neville, were almost yellow in their pallor, with darkly-circled eyes. Neville staggered a little as he approached the front, and steadied himself on the end of our pew. By this time the church was almost full, and at last the chatter diminished and a hush fell as the priest, a young man I'd never seen before, emerged from the vestry resplendent in his robes. With a small but heart-wrenching shock, I saw that behind him, simply clad in a black suit with a huge silver cross round his neck, came Father Gerard, leaning on a stick. He was thinner, stooped, and his hair was white. He settled himself in the north choir stall; then he looked up and – deliberately, I thought – caught my eye. He smiled faintly. The years rolled away, and despite my steely outer demeanour, I cringed.

The organ struck up, a bright trumpet tune, announcing the arrival of the bride, and with a collective sigh the congregation rose to its feet in a ragged surge. I remembered Pauline saying confidingly on the phone a week or two ago, 'It's Jodie's mother who's chosen the music – Jodie hasn't a clue and neither has Neville. But they didn't go for the usual Bridal March, Jodie being a rather big girl. I can just imagine what people would be thinking if they'd had that! They stuck to tradition for the way out, though.' I'd smiled to myself, imagining the wedding guests, half of whom were probably well in their cups already, breaking into 'Here comes the bride, all fat and wide, Here comes the groom, thin as a broom.' It was all too appropriate.

Jodie appeared on her father's arm, in a cream satin confection that if anything accentuated her ample curves. The dress was full-skirted and low-necked, revealing plump arms and a massive bosom. I heard Drew choke on a laugh, cut short by Tiffany's elbow in his ribs. Four bridesmaids followed, looking severally smug, hot and uncomfortable in apricot satin and matching shoes. The bride was duly handed over with some ceremony and the service began.

Seated where we were, close to the bridal couple, we saw every nuance of the proceedings. For me, despite the priest's attempts at solemnity, it had an air of the circus, especially the bride's heavily made-up face and false eyelashes, which she batted coquettishly and far too often. I stared straight ahead. Even the floating cherubs behind the altar were preferable to the spectacle beside us, and when it was over and the vows duly pronounced, the newly-married pair, without the usual invitation from the priest, indulged in a kiss so prolonged that chuckles and even catcalls erupted from the congregation. I saw Bob compress his lips in an effort not to laugh, but the whole show was beginning to take on the vaudeville flavour which I had gloomily anticipated. On another day I too might have found it funny, but I was beginning to feel unwell, and was holding on as best I could. This was no moment for the aunt of the groom to be falling over in church.

While registers were being signed and the usual photographs taken, I shut my eyes and concentrated on quelling the waves of pain and nausea that were sweeping through me. Everywhere people had broken into chatter, with no attempt at subdued voices. At last a loud series of notes from the organ heralded the appearance of the wedding party. To my ears the traditional wedding march always sounded triumphant – as if they were saying 'Hooray! We did it!' – and triumph was certainly the dominant expression on the faces of the bride and her parents, with the Stevens contingent only marginally more decorous, apart from Nicole, who was scowling.

When we finally managed to get outside, the fresh air revived me. The congregation were milling about, greeting acquaintances, lighting up cigarettes, jostling and laughing as the photographer attempted to marshal them.

'That,' I muttered to Bob, 'was not a wedding; it was a comic opera.'

He glanced at me, shaking his head, smiling. 'Snob.'

'Maybe. I always used to like the Wedding March – it's such an optimistic piece – but I think today might have ruined it for ever.'

'Be thankful they didn't choose the theme tune from Match of the Day,' Bob murmured. 'Jodie's father is a big football fan, I believe.'

After what seemed an eternity the tedious palaver of being shepherded here and there for the photographs, the endless combinations of parents and relatives, friends and acquaintances, was deemed complete and the party broke up for the moment. As we made a discreet departure back to where our car was parked we saw most of the congregation piling onto the red bus which had pulled up by the church gate, blocking the traffic. We saw windows wound down, annoyed shouts, blaring horns, but also encouraging waves and raucous jokes.

I slumped into our hot car with a sigh of relief. 'Now for round two.'

'Are you all right?' Bob asked. 'You're very pale.'

'There was no air in there. All those packed bodies, I suppose. Better now that we're out.'

By the time we'd found a space in a city centre multi-storey, and I'd teetered to the hotel on my crazy heels, we were among the last to arrive at the reception. There was a long line of people being greeted by the bride and groom at the door to the suite of rooms which they'd hired, and we duly joined the end of it. Neville and his new wife were giggling as they greeted their guests, and I was reminded just how young they were. Did they have any idea what a momentous thing they had just done? Probably not; I had the benefit of hindsight. We shook their hands and murmured congratulations when it came to our turn, and were supplied with flutes of champagne by a liveried waiter as we joined the throng. I saw Drew and Tiffany and we made our way towards them.

'You took your time,' Drew said.

'Parking,' I said. 'The usual problems.' I nodded back in the direction of the bridal couple. 'Neville looks more pink than green now, I see.'

Drew grinned. 'A visit to the hotel's restroom to get rid of the last of last night's excesses must have done the trick.'

'Ugh. You're putting me off my champagne.'

I cast my eyes over the throng and noted where my family members were. In a corner I saw Desmond in his wheelchair, and Ben bending over him. As he straightened up and saw me, he began to signal urgently. I remembered with a small shock a code we had used when he was small; he, obviously, had not forgotten it, and now he was telling me with discreet hand signals that he needed my immediate presence.

I gave my glass to Bob. 'Back in a minute.'

I threaded my way through the crowd. 'What's up, Ben?'

He looked all round as if worried that someone was eavesdropping. 'I need to talk to you, Jan. It's dead urgent.'

It was unusual for Ben to ask for anything, any help, any advice, and I felt a ripple of alarm. 'It'll have to be later,' I said quietly. 'After the meal and the speeches. I think everybody's arrived now – they'll be calling us through soon.' I waved in the direction of an inner room where long tables, sumptuously decorated, could be seen through open double doors. 'Can it wait?'

Ben nodded. 'I suppose,' he said reluctantly. 'But don't go, OK?'

'I won't.' I patted his arm.

The party seemed interminable: getting so many guests seated in their prearranged places when few of them seemed in any hurry, then serving their starters and dealing with complaints from people with particular dietary requirements, was all rendered even more leisurely by the rate at which the table wine was consumed and fresh bottles ordered. The servers were efficient and patient, but a starving person would have slipped under the table dead before getting anything of substance.

The food was fine, but I picked at it, and drank in tiny sips; my nausea had subsided but I was taking no risks. Finally, between courses, the tables were cleared, glasses charged – again – and we sat back to endure the speeches. Jodie's father, tall, bald and red-faced, expounded her many virtues, telling us she had given her parents never a moment of trouble or anxiety, at which point his wife shrieked, 'What? I told you he was losing his marbles!' to much hilarity. Neville's speech was mercifully very brief. Public speaking was definitely not his forte, but to my surprise he held off on the risqué jokes and sounded admirably sincere. His best man, who was a member of the same football team, was a different matter. His speech was larded with innuendo which became more and more cringe-worthy, though most of the company seemed to be enjoying it, especially football-related jokes about Neville being useless in every position. The young man had clearly been trawling the internet for inspiration. He concluded his speech by instructing the bride and groom to look deep into each other's eyes. 'Statstistical –', he said, slurring over the awkward word, 'er, statistically, you are now looking at the person most likely to murder you.' As the company erupted in laughter, Bob pinched my thigh through my dress, and I gave him a killing look.

In the interval before the next course, I looked for Ben. He was seated further down the table among all the younger men, with Desmond in his wheelchair beside him. I signalled to him to be ready to follow me. 'I'm just going to the ladies',' I told Bob. 'If they serve the desserts you can have mine. I'm not in the mood for cream-laden sugarbombs.' I got up, smoothed down my skirt and squeezed my way between tables where people made the going difficult, leaning back in their chairs to shout at a distant cousin, passing bottles down the table, or waving their arms expansively. I didn't look back, but when I got to the door and turned into the corridor I saw Ben standing, bending down and speaking to the young man seated on his right. I kept on going; I knew he would follow me. Halfway up the carpeted corridor I saw Father Gerard coming towards me, walking stiffly and leaning on his stick. I nodded curtly and slipped into the restroom. But if I'd thought I would now have a space to gather my strength, I was mistaken. The ladies' was thronged with women, touching up their makeup or their elaborate hairdos in front of the long mirror, hugging each other, squealing with laughter at each other's jokes. The only quiet place was the toilet, and I let myself in and shut the door. After a few minutes of noise I heard them leave, their voices fading as the door banged shut.

I let myself out, and inspected my image in the mirror. Everything was in place; I was still immaculate even if my face was pale and my eyes shadowed. I straightened my skirt and my shoulders and left the room to face my brother, just as three more women came charging in.

No one was waiting for me, and I frowned, puzzled. I looked up and down the corridor, tapping my foot. Then to my consternation a door almost opposite, which had been slightly ajar, opened wide, and Father Gerard stood there, beckoning me. I hesitated, then as his gesture became more insistent I approached him. 'What's going on?' I whispered. 'Where's Ben?'

'Please,' he said, his voice soft and urgent. 'Come in. Shut the door.'

I followed him into the room. It seemed especially dark, and I saw that the heavy curtains were drawn. There was a table in the middle covered with a thick crimson cloth, and six chairs ranged around it. In one of them my brother Ben was sitting, his head in his hands, and he was crying.

'What the heck–?' I muttered. I slid into a chair beside him. 'Whatever is it, Ben? Bro, speak to me.'

He lifted his head. His fair hair was falling over his forehead, his face was wet with tears, his nose red and dripping. I turned to look at Father Gerard who had come up silently behind me, and he handed me a large white handkerchief, perfectly laundered. I passed it to Ben.

Ben mopped his face and blew his nose, stiff snuffling. 'Got to tell you something, Jan.'

'Do you want me to go?' Father Gerard asked quietly. 'Perhaps this is a private family matter.'

Ben shook his head. 'You've known us all for a long time, Father,' he said. His voice was husky. 'Maybe you can help.'

The priest looked at me, his white eyebrows raised. I shrugged; I wasn't keen, but it was Ben's call. Father Gerard pulled out a chair on the other side of Ben and sat down, wincing at some undeclared pain.

'Tell us, Ben,' I urged.

Ben grabbed my hand. 'Jan, I don't want to go to prison.'

'Prison? What? What are you talking about?'

A bout of fresh sobbing broke from Ben's throat and eyes, and he couldn't speak. I put my arms around his shaking shoulders. 'Calm down, Benj,' I said softly. 'We'll help you if we can, but we have to know what's going on. Why are you talking about prison? What have you done?'

With an effort, gulping down his tears, Ben said, 'I didn't want to do it. I knew it was wrong. I mean, stealing is wrong, isn't it? But stealing from someone who's been good to you, that's worse. Mr Wyatt's been like a father to me ever since I went to work there. He's a really kind man.' He began to cry again, and I squeezed his hand with my free one.

'You've been stealing from work? But why, Ben? This is so not like you.'

He nodded miserably. 'I know, and I really didn't want to do it, but they said I had to help them, because there were some bad men after them, and they had to give them, the bad men I mean, lots of money, and they didn't have enough, and they were afraid something worse would happen –'

'Hold on, Ben,' I said. 'Who are we talking about here? Who wanted you to help them?' A horrible thought had entered my head, and a moment later my fears were realised.

Ben sniffed. 'Mattie and Jimmy. They said they were scared, and – what was it, they had a money flow problem, was that it? I offered to give them some of mine, and they took it – they said they'd pay it back – but they needed more, and they wanted me to steal some of the really expensive power tools from Wyatt's. They said they could pass them on to someone they knew who could sell them, and then they'd be out of trouble. And it wasn't hard to do. I put a few in my backpack every few days when I took my bike to work. I know what the valuable ones are, and nobody would think it was me, because they trust me.' Tears started in his eyes again, and he blinked them away. 'Mr Wyatt knows some stuff gets stolen all the time. He says we have to write it off. He'd never ever think it was me.' Ben looked up at me, his face a picture of bewilderment. 'Jan, I knew it was wrong,' he whispered. 'But they're my brothers, and I didn't want the bad men to get them. Only I've been thinking about it, like what would Mr Wyatt think, and would he call the police and get me sent to prison, and then who would look after Dad?'

'Oh, Ben.' I looked over at Father Gerard, who was shaking his head. 'Listen, bro. Where are those tools now? Did you hand them over to Mattie and Jimmy?'

Ben shook his head. 'No. They said they'd talk to me today about taking them, because they want to get them to this other bloke, and then they're going abroad, they said. Dunno where. But I've been keeping out of their way. The tools are all locked up in the shed at home.'

'Where's the key?'

Ben patted his pocket. 'I've got it.'

I looked at Father Gerard and back at Ben. 'It's something you've still got the stuff you stole, Ben. Maybe we can sort something out. You know we will have to tell Mr Wyatt, don't you?'

Ben nodded, and a tear leaked down his cheek.

I pushed myself up out of the chair. My gut was churning, my heart hammering. 'But right now,' I said slowly, 'I'm going to find those crooked little brothers of mine and call them out. They're going to wish they'd never been born. They've done some horrible things in the past, but to drop your own brother in it stinks to high heaven. It's them who should be in prison, Ben, and frankly I'd cheer to see the little bastards locked up.'

Ben looked up at me, his mouth and eyes wide.

'Wait, Janet. Please, wait. Think.' Father Gerard spoke quietly but with urgency. 'This shouldn't be done in public, causing a scandal, at your nephew's wedding. It would taint the whole family. People who have no love for any of you would be revelling in it, enjoying the spectacle. I can't believe that's what you want.' I hesitated. My blood was up, and what I most wanted was to bang their treacherous heads together. But Father Gerard was right. 'It's very likely,' he went on, 'that they'll have noticed you and Ben are both absent. My guess is they'll have gone.'

'Hang on,' I said. I scrabbled in my bag, fished out my phone and dialled Drew's number. I was pretty sure Bob didn't have his phone on him.

Drew answered, sounding puzzled. 'Mum? Where are you? We were getting worried – Dad thought maybe you weren't well.'

'I'm OK,' I said grimly. 'Drew, look around, can you? Are your uncles still there? The twins, I mean.'

There was a pause, and I heard murmured voices. 'Mum, Tiff says she saw them leave about ten minutes ago. With their plus ones. They didn't say goodbye to anyone, and they seemed a in a bit of a hurry.'

'Thanks, son.' I ended the call. 'You're right,' I said to Father Gerard. 'I don't know how you knew, but you did.'

'What do we do now, Jan?' Ben said in a small voice that reminded me of the little boy he had been.

'We go and see Mr Wyatt now,' I said. 'The sooner the better, before those brothers of ours cook something else up.' Reluctantly I turned to the priest. 'Do you agree, Father?'

'Yes. I have my car, and it's quite close. I'm parked in a disabled bay in the hotel's own car park. I can drive both of you to Wyatt's, discreetly.'

'I have to see Dad's OK first,' Ben said. 'Do you think Bob will take him home, Jan?'

'I'm sure he will,' I said. 'Let's go.'

We went back to the reception, with me leading the way, powered by my fury. Ben stumbled behind me, still clutching Father Gerard's handkerchief, and the priest hobbled some way behind.

When we entered the room, a few heads turned, but most of the guests were eating and drinking. Jodie and Neville, I saw, were circulating, as were some of the other young ones, including Drew and Tiffany, stopping to chat with this or that family member or friend, and the noise was deafening. As I approached Bob looked up, and he was frowning. 'Where have you been?' he said. 'What's going on? What's with all the cloak and dagger?'

'Keep your voice down,' I said. 'We've got a crisis, and there's no time to explain. I'll tell you later. But I need you to take Dad home when you go yourself.'

'Wow, thanks,' Bob said sarcastically. 'That'll be a lovely job.'

'Why?'

He nodded to a corner of the room. Desmond, in his wheelchair, was surrounded by women, including my sisters. Ben, who'd been looking for him all round the room, was now on his way to the little cluster of cluckers, his face a picture of dismay. 'He got hold of some beer,' Bob said. 'Apparently Ben asked one of the lads to keep an eye on him and not give him any alcohol, because it clashes with his medication. But the lad got distracted and Desmond saw his chance. So now he's puked up all over his suit and his wheelchair, and a few of the women are trying to clean him up, and he isn't very cooperative. The car will stink.'

'I'm sorry, but it can't be helped,' I said.

'Aren't you going to tell me what's going on?' Bob demanded.

'Not now. Now we have to go.'

'Who's we?' Bob was beginning to raise his voice, and people were staring.

'Ssh! Me, Ben and Father Gerard.'

'Father Gerard? What's he got to do with anything? I thought you couldn't stand him!'

'Please, Bob. Trust me. I will explain later.'

I beckoned to Ben, who by this time had reached our father. He hesitated, but he came, and we pushed our way through to where the priest waited by the door.

In silence we followed Father Gerard out of the hotel and along the crowded pavement. It was slow going: the priest with his stick and me with my heels, but the car park was at the back of the hotel and soon reached. Ben piled into the back of the venerable car, which was all polished chrome and well-worn leather, and I took the front passenger seat.

As the priest started up and edged out into the road I leaned back. 'Ben, what's Wyatt's number? And what's the name of your manager?'

'It's Mr Streeter.' He reeled off the number, and I dialled. It rang for some time before it was answered, and then a smooth male voice came on the line. 'Good afternoon, Wyatt's, Rod Streeter speaking. How can I help you?'

'Mr Streeter, my name is Janet Clarke, and I am the sister of one of your employees, Benjamin Yates.'

'Ah yes, Ben,' he said, his tone warm. 'Not at work today. At a family wedding, I believe.'

'That's right. But at the moment, Mr Streeter, we are on our way to Wyatt's and we need urgently to speak to Mr Wyatt himself. Is he in?'

I used my crispest and most businesslike tone and Rod Streeter was momentarily nonplussed. 'Oh! Ah, well, let me see.' There was a pause while, I assumed, he checked his computer. 'Right, well, Mr Wyatt is in the building, as it happens, but he's in a meeting. Can I help?'

'Thank you, but this is a sensitive and confidential matter and it's imperative we speak to Mr Wyatt himself. When is his meeting likely to end?'

'It could be soon, but then he is due elsewhere.'

'Please, would you be so kind as to detain him till we get there? It's extremely important.'

'Well,' he said dubiously, 'I'll try, but it would help to know what it's all about.'

'I'm sorry – no reflection on you, but it is him we must speak to.'

'I'll see what I can do.'

'Thank you.'

Father Gerard drove carefully through the Saturday traffic, speeding up only when the city centre was behind us. Five minutes later he pulled into Wyatt's yard and parked. 'Should I come in with you?' he asked. 'If you'd rather I didn't, I'm happy to wait in the car.'

'You might as well, Father. In for a penny.'

He smiled faintly.

A thought struck me. 'Father Gerard, do you actually know Mr Wyatt?'

'Oh yes,' he said as he locked the car. 'Roly Wyatt was one of my altar boys when I first came to the parish. I don't often see him in church nowadays, though.'

'Roly?'

The priest nodded. 'Yes, poor chap. His father died before he was born, and his widowed mother, who was a charming but rather fanciful lady, named him Roland Percival. You can imagine how well that went down with the other lads.'

'I never heard that,' said Ben. 'I've heard Mr Streeter call him RP, but I didn't know what it stood for.'

'Better not let on,' I said.

We went into the store, and immediately the typical smells of timber and paint were all round. It was busy, with queues at the tills. A man looked up from behind a desk in a glassed-in cubicle and waved to us. 'Mr Streeter,' Ben whispered. Rod Streeter got up and came out, smiling. 'Mr Wyatt's happy to see you in his office,' he said. 'You know the way, Ben.'

If he was surprised by Ben's look of mingled misery and terror, he didn't comment. Ben led us up a flight of open stairs to a door at the back of the store. The door was slightly ajar, and I tapped on it.

A hearty voice answered. 'Come in!'

As far as my heels allowed, I sailed in. Mr Wyatt was standing behind his desk, a tall, well-built sixty-something, with a fluff of white hair and a pleasant ruddy face. He was casual in summer trousers and a blue checked shirt.

'Come in, come in,' he said, smiling. 'Mrs Clarke – good to meet you.' He extended his hand, and I shook it. 'And Father Gerard! This is a surprise. Hello, Ben. I thought you would be at your wedding party.'

No one answered, and his expression changed. 'What's this? You all look very solemn. Has something happened?'

I opened my mouth to speak, but at that moment a choking sound came from Ben, who was lurking behind me, and he suddenly began to sob.

'Oh, dear! What's the matter?' Mr Wyatt was clearly alarmed. 'Shall I ask someone to make us some tea?'

I gripped Ben's elbow. 'Hush, Ben. This isn't helping.' To Mr Wyatt I said, 'You're very kind, but we know you have an appointment, and when you hear what we have come about you may not be so well-disposed. Perhaps I'd better explain, since Ben is clearly in no fit state.'

'All right, but at least pull up a chair.' He now sounded worried.

Seated on the edge of my chair, I leaned forward. 'Mr Wyatt, not to beat about the bush, Ben has just told me he's been stealing from you.'

A moan came from Ben, who was sitting with his head in his hands.

Mr Wyatt's eyebrows disappeared into his hairline. 'What?'

'It's not entirely what it seems,' I said. 'I wonder if you've heard of my twin brothers, Matthew and James.'

'Anyone who's been around Brant for several years has heard of them, I'm afraid.' He shook his head.

'I thought so. Well, my brothers are not above a spot of villainy, as you are aware. They spun Ben some story about being pursued by threatening creditors and persuaded him to steal valuable items from here to pass on and sell. As far as I can work out, today they were going to take the goods. But Ben found he couldn't go through with it, and he told me. I hope we may have stolen a march on them.'

Ben suddenly jumped up, brushed aside Father Gerard's restraining hand and lurched towards the desk. 'Mr Wyatt,' he said, his voice rough from all the crying, 'please, I'm really sorry I did it, I didn't want to, after all the years I've worked here, since I was eighteen, and you've always been really good to me, I feel so bad, I can't tell you, but please, I know I deserve it, but please don't send me to prison.' He was tearless now, but his eyes were wide and wild with horror.

'Sit down, Ben,' Wyatt said, slowly subsiding into his own seat. His face was serious, but he spoke gently. 'We don't need to think about prison. As you say, you've worked for me for a long time and you've never given me anything but loyal, cheerful service. But I can't lie – you've shocked me, Ben. I must have time to think about this.'

'Forgive my rudeness,' I said, 'but thinking will have to wait. Ben says your property is all intact, locked in his garden shed. If we act quickly, we can retrieve it. You can decide what to do with Ben when your goods are back where they belong.'

'I see,' Wyatt said, his face a picture of astonishment. 'One moment.' He picked up his desk phone and punched in a single number. 'Rod? Can you cancel my appointment and reschedule it for the earliest they can manage? And get one of the boys to bring a van round to the yard.' He stood up. 'We must deal with this now, I think.' We followed him out of the office, down the stairs, across the store and into the yard. 'Ben, you come in the van with me. Father Gerard can follow with Mrs Clarke.'

A moment later I was back in Father Gerard's car, trying to follow a plain white van with the Wyatt's blue logo on the side as it took the mile or so to my childhood home at speed. By the time we parked outside Mr Wyatt and Ben were standing in the doorway of the garden shed. Wyatt had his hands on his hips and was shaking his head in disbelief. 'How long did it take you to shift all this, Ben?' he asked. 'I have to say you've picked the best stuff – but then, you knew what you were doing.'

'I put it in my backpack,' Ben said in a small voice. 'A couple of times a week. It took me about two months.'

Wyatt turned to me. 'This is unbelievable. There's about seven grand's worth in here. All boxed up and neatly stacked.'

'Didn't you miss it?' I asked.

'There's always goods going missing,' Wyatt said with a rueful smile. 'Shoplifters are very canny. Yes, we noticed there was more stuff disappearing, but we wrote it off – we have always had to deal with theft. There's not much we can do about it, and the police don't want to know when it's small scale.'

'Isn't there some sort of security system on goods as expensive as these?'

'Yes, but it's a bit outdated, and Ben would know how to get round it – any employee would. We're looking to update our system, make stuff harder to steal – that's what my appointment was about.' He turned to Ben. 'I think you and I'd better get it all in the van.' He still spoke kindly, but his look of disappointment must have cut Ben in two.

It took them no more than twenty minutes, and then the van was full and the shed empty, apart from a few flowerpots and an elderly mower. Wyatt locked the van and turned to us as we huddled on the pavement. Despite the warm afternoon I was beginning to feel chilled, and my feet were in pinched agony.

Wyatt laid a hand on Ben's shoulder and made Ben look him in the face. 'We've got the goods back,' he said quietly, 'thanks to you telling your sister in time. I understand you've been taken for a ride, but you still knew you were doing wrong. You should have come and told me what was going on, shouldn't you?' Ben nodded dumbly. 'I'm going to have to think about what to do,' Wyatt went on. 'I will go home and talk to Mrs Wyatt about this. She knows you, doesn't she, Ben? And she's a wise woman. Give me till Monday, and I'll be in touch.' He turned to me and the priest and shook our hands. 'Thank you both for your quick action.' He got into the van, turned round, and sped away.

For a moment we were all silent. Then Ben said, 'What do you think he will do, Jan? Maybe he won't tell the police and send me to jail, but I suppose he will sack me now, won't he?'

If I'd had a gun in my hand and my twin brothers standing against a wall, at that moment I could cheerfully have shot the pair of them.

We were still standing on the pavement, unsure what to do next, when I saw my own car come slowly down the street from the opposite direction. As it came to a halt I saw Bob in the driving seat with Pauline next to him, and in the back Desmond, lolling against Christine, who was trying unsuccessfully to push him upright. A second car glided to a halt behind mine, and Giles got out.

'Where have you been?' Bob hissed as he joined us. He was clearly not amused. 'Thanks for leaving me with this mess.'

'Sorry, but it couldn't be helped,' I said, reining in my temper. 'Shall we get my father inside?'

Bob hauled the wheelchair out of the boot and set it up. Between him and Giles Desmond was manhandled into it and passed to Ben, who pushed it indoors. Pauline and Christine, their wedding finery crumpled, their hats in their hands, came to where I still stood with Father Gerard. Pauline was in a state of agitation, as well she might be. She greeted the priest and then she moaned, 'Why, oh why, did Ben have to disappear? You can't trust strangers with Dad. And now we have to go and get him cleaned up, and it's my son's wedding day, and Colin will be furious!'

'You could argue,' I said coldly, 'that our father is the concern of all of us, not just Ben – who has had a very pressing matter to attend to. Yes, it's a shame how it's all turned out, Pauline – but I assume the wedding party is breaking up now, isn't it? Won't they all be getting ready for the evening festivities? Wouldn't you be going home now anyway, to change? Surely Colin and Jodie's parents can deal with the stragglers.'

Pauline said nothing, but looked crushed, and for a moment I regretted my tone. I felt a hand on my elbow, and as Pauline and Christine scurried up the path after the men Father Gerard said quietly, 'I don't think you need me any more, not today. I'll go and leave you to your family business. You'll be able to get home, of course.'

'Yes. Thank you for all your help and support, Father. I appreciate it.'

He seemed reluctant to leave, as if searching for the right words to say. 'Look, Janet,' he said at last, 'I had been hoping, today, to have an opportunity to speak to you, but things rather got in the way.'

'Really?' I was surprised. 'What about?'

'There are things I've been wanting to tell you for a long time,' he said. 'The moment never arrived. Will you come and see me? I'm retired now, of course. I live in a home for superannuated priests.' He smiled a little sadly. 'Could you come tomorrow – after morning service, say eleven o'clock? Unless you're too busy, of course. There are things – well, about your mother, and other things, that I feel you should know.' He caught my look. 'No, no, nothing dramatic, nothing to worry you. But even so. Will you come?'

What could I say? 'Oh, well, yes, I suppose.'

He handed me a card. 'This is where I live now. It's very pleasant, very peaceful. If it stays fine, we might sit in the garden.'

A few moments later the old car purred into life, and I was left standing on the pavement, wondering. My painful feet brought me back to the day's reality, and I bent down and eased my sandals off with a groan of relief.

Sandals in hand, I walked gingerly up the path to the scaly green door, trying to avoid loose stones. The door was ajar, and as I pushed it fully open the stale smell wafted over me at the same time as a loud bellow came from upstairs. 'Get these women out of here!'

Pauline and Christine came down the stairs, jostling each other in their haste. Pauline was carrying an old pink plastic laundry basket. She pulled a face. 'This smells dreadful,' she said. 'Ben said to just throw it away. Dad won't like it – he's only got one suit.'

'I don't believe he really can't afford another one,' Christine said. 'Anyway, how often does he need one?'

'Chuck it,' I said. 'If he ever needs another I'll find him one in one of the shops I go to. It's not worth cleaning.' I looked up the stairs. 'What's with all the racket?'

'Ben and Bob have put Dad in the shower,' Christine said. 'I don't know how they got him up the stairs – he was fighting them all the way. But he isn't very strong these days, is he, Pauline? He saw us getting his clothes and he got really mad. He thought we were going to help wash him!'

'As if we'd want to!' Pauline shuddered. 'Ben and Bob are welcome to it. Right – to the dustbin with this lot.' She disappeared in the direction of the back door.

'Where's Giles?' I asked Christine.

'He's out the back, hosing down the wheelchair.' She sighed. 'What a mess, Janet. On Neville's wedding day as well. I feel sorry for Pauline – she wanted it to be so nice. And she's still got Colin to deal with.'

'If Colin cuts up rough we'll unite against him,' I said grimly. 'It's time someone did.'

'That's just what Giles said.'

'Did he?' I was surprised. 'Good for him.'

'There's no love lost between Giles and Colin – you know that,' Christine said.

'Anyway,' I said, 'most of the guests will either have left or they'll be taking a break before the evening do, I would have thought. If Colin and Jodie's family handle it tactfully there shouldn't be anything for people to gossip about.'

'Colin? Tactful?'

I had to laugh. 'Good point. I don't know about you, Chris, but I could happily sink a cup of tea. I wonder if there's any milk. And it would be a treat to put our feet up for five minutes.'

Thanks to Ben the kitchen was spotless, there was milk in the fridge and everything was to hand. Christine made a pot of tea and poured us both a cup. We'd barely sat down and taken a sip when there was more furious shouting from upstairs, then silence as a door banged shut.

'He's getting worse, you know,' Christine said timidly.

'I didn't know how bad,' I said. 'I haven't seen him for a few months – not since that business with Ben getting locked out of his room.' I looked at her, frowning. 'Has it got to the point where we have to do something? It's a heavy load just for Ben. He has work, after all.' Privately I wondered, Has he got a job any more?

Christine looked at the floor. 'Pauline and I help when we can, but it's not much.'

'Why haven't either of you told me?'

I didn't get to hear her answer, because at that moment we heard heavy footsteps on the stairs and Ben and Bob appeared, jackets and ties discarded, shirtsleeves rolled up.

Christine jumped up. 'I'll get you boys a cuppa. There's plenty in the pot.'

'There's some biscuits somewhere,' Ben said, and followed her into the kitchen.

Bob flopped down onto the sofa beside me. 'I'm sorry, love.'

I narrowed my eyes. 'What for?'

'Being shirty with you. Ben just filled me in with what's been going on. Him and Wyatt's. You could have told me.'

'There wasn't time.'

He shook his head. 'You don't tell me much where there is time,' he said quietly.

To my dismay I felt weary enough to weep. I leaned back against the sofa, closing my eyes. 'You know what, Bob,' I said, 'you must have noticed how I do my damnedest not to get mixed up in the doings of my family. I look around and I see just why I feel ashamed of them. It's like a cheap little soap opera.'

'Boy, you're bitter, Jan. It's not a good way to be. And anyway, they're not all bad. The twins, yes, I grant you. And your dad is definitely losing it, but he wasn't the sweetest old gentleman even when all his wits were in place. Worse, if anything. But Pauline and Christine are decent souls, and so's Giles. And even you think Ben's OK.'

I sighed. 'I wouldn't have chosen to get involved, but I had to. You understand that. And you're right – they're not all bad, and even I don't think so. I'm tired, to be honest. I carried this family all my teenage years, and I was glad to get free. But it seems I'm not.'

Bob shook his head. 'Of course you're not. You never will be. Even when no one needs you, they're where you came from; they're part of you. Sure, you could do what David did: scarper half way across the world and send a card at Christmas. But that's not really you either, is it?'

I smiled feebly. 'It's all right for you. Your dad wasn't an ignorant bully. You had a perfectly nice mother, and your sister's OK too.'

'I know. But they're what we've got, just like Drew's choice means we'll be connected to the Leamans. You might as well grit your teeth and accept it.'

'Seems like I'll have to. Someone's got to do something about Desmond, and it's not fair to dump it on Ben.'

Ben came into the room, carefully carrying a tray with four mugs of tea and a plate of biscuits. Christine, Pauline and Giles came in after him. Somehow everyone managed to find somewhere to sit in the cramped little living room, and we all sat round with our tea, looking at each other in silence.

'I got the wheelchair cleaned up all right,' Giles said. 'We'll have to let it dry.'

'Thanks, mate,' Ben said. 'It's a borrowed one.'

I took a deep breath. 'Look, everyone, I didn't know things were this bad with Dad. What have you done with him, by the way?'

'I gave him his pills, put some clean pyjamas on him and put him to bed,' Ben said. 'It's a bit early, but he's had enough.'

'Right. Like I said, I didn't know, and you didn't tell me, but I didn't bother to find out, and that's my fault. But it seems to me we have to do something. We can't expect Ben to play nursemaid for the rest of Dad's life – why should he?'

My sisters looked at each other and Ben mumbled something.

'What?'

Ben flushed. 'Maybe I won't have a job. So I'll have loads of time to look after Dad.' He looked at me. 'I told them, Jan. About what I did, and what Mr Wyatt said.'

'Even so, it's still not fair. We have to hope you will have a job, Ben. This one, or another one. And we have to decide what to do about Desmond.'

Giles said, 'We need to talk to Social Services. He should have carers coming in. He can't look after himself.'

'He won't like it,' Ben said gloomily.

'He'll have to put up with it,' I said. 'Meanwhile we can all help.'

'You have work, Janet,' Pauline said, her hands gripped tightly round her mug. 'Important work. You're busy.'

'Well, you know what, I never thought I'd say this, but work isn't everything.'

I heard Bob snort with laughter, and then to my surprise everyone was chuckling.

Bob looked at his watch and drained his tea. 'Sorry, I have to go. Speaking of work, I'm on a night shift tonight. Not great timing, I know.' He turned to me. 'You coming home with me? No need if you want to stay – I dare say Giles would give you a lift, because you certainly can't walk far in those sandals.'

I hauled myself up. 'I'll come with you. This party's over, I reckon.'

My sisters came with us to the door. 'Janet, don't worry about sorting out things with Social Services,' Christine said. 'We'll see to it, won't we, Pauline?' Pauline nodded, a little reluctantly, I thought. 'You've got enough to do. But we'll keep you posted.'

'Thanks,' I said. My view of my sisters, Christine in particular, had not been altogether fair, it seemed.

Bob made us something to eat while I stripped off my finery, put everything away, removed my makeup and showered. I put on a pair of old jeans and a loose top and brushed my damp hair flat. I avoided the mirror – I knew I looked weary and old. I remembered something my niece Nicole had once said, and nasty as it was, it applied: 'Ooh, Auntie Janet, you've done so well to keep your figure,' she'd cooed, falsehood oozing from every syllable. 'They do say, don't they, you have to sacrifice something as you get older – figure or face. Not sure what I'd choose.' How had someone so inoffensive as Pauline raised such a mean child? I guess I knew the answer to that; but then, Tiffany was doted on by her parents and I guessed had wanted for nothing material, and yet she was, in her own way, kind and wise. Bob looked up and smiled at my transformation, but said nothing. At half past six I was flopped on the sofa, half-listening to the evening news, when he appeared in uniform, waved from the doorway and went to work.

I must have been in an unusually weakened state, because I felt disinclined to do anything. Part of me wished Bob was there, dispensing reassurance, confident and strong. But another part, the realist, knew that was a hopeless wish. Bob was no longer any of those things. He was as fragile as anyone; and besides, it seemed he no longer cared about me as he had once done, and that was my own doing. I had pushed him away too often. Even now, with a building headache and a threat of tears, I berated myself for being feeble. That kind of self-indulgence was simply a waste of time and achieved nothing. Before the shadows covered the garden I gave up on the day and went to bed.

I had a mercifully unbroken night and felt a shade more optimistic in the morning. At half past seven I was dressing when I heard voices and a car door slamming, and glanced out of the bedroom window. Bob was on the pavement outside our gate, leaning in at the window of an unfamiliar silver-grey car. As he straightened up and waved the car pulled away, and I caught a glimpse of a female profile with long, wavy hair.

'Someone gave you a lift?' I asked idly. 'You walk normally.'

He yawned. 'Yeah. Serena, my new crewmate. I told you about her, didn't I? We had a really busy night, one call after another, and I was knackered, so she offered to drive me. I'm going to get my head down. I'll see you later.'

At eleven o'clock I drew into the gravelled car park at St Agatha's, a large, redbrick Victorian house whose austere outlines were softened by a pink climbing rose which frothed and bowered over the front door. The day's heat was already building, the sky an uncompromising blue, the sun hard and bright. I pushed open the front door and found myself in a tiled hall, with light pouring in through a high skylight. There was a desk to one side and a brass bell. I hesitated for a moment, then rang it. It echoed musically in the open space.

A few moments later a large woman in a voluminous floral dress appeared from an inner door, wiping her hands on a towel. ‘Good morning, my dear,’ she said. Her voice was low, her accent lilting. ‘What can I do for you?’

‘I’ve come to see Father Gerard Sinclair. He’s expecting me.’

‘Of course he is. You must be Mrs Clarke. Do excuse me,’ she said, smiling, indicating the towel. ‘We’re a bit short-staffed at the moment. Father Gerard is in the garden. Why don’t you go down and find him? I’ll organise some coffee.’

‘Thank you,’ I murmured, and followed her down a short passage to where glazed double doors led out onto a smoothly-mown space with substantial shrubs and colourful borders. An elderly man in a wide-brimmed hat was moving slowly down one side, deadheading roses as he went, dropping the petalled heads into a basket.

‘There he is,’ the woman said, pointing. ‘By that little table, in the shade of the cherry tree. Reading, of course. Always reading.’

I thanked her again and walked across the soft turf to where Father Gerard sat, his glasses on the end of his nose, deep in his book. He glanced up, blinking, as I approached.

‘No, please, don’t get up,’ I said. I slid into the chair opposite.

‘You found me, then,’ he said, smiling. His face was a map of lines. ‘Did Mrs Underdown show you the way?’

‘A pleasant lady in a floral dress? Yes. She offered to bring us coffee.’

‘Excellent.’ He laid his book down. ‘I hope you didn’t have any trouble finding this place.’

‘Not at all.’

A silence fell; I had no idea what to say and had no energy for small talk, even if it had seemed appropriate.

Father Gerard hesitated, absent-mindedly tracing the cover of his book with his finger. 'I dare say you're wondering why I asked you to come.'

'You said you wanted to tell me things about my mother.'

'Yes.' He paused for a moment. 'Yes, yes I did, but that wasn't all...You know, Janet, I've thought of you over the years, more so since I retired, and I've asked myself whether there's more I could have done, if I could have been of more help...' he sighed deeply, and I felt a surge of puzzlement and discomfort. What was I doing there, truly? Why did he ask me to come? Why did I agree? What common ground did we ever have, then and now? And what on earth could we hope to achieve, raking up a dead past?

Father Gerard looked up, and seemed to be collecting himself. 'Dear Mary. It was a terrible thing, to be taken so young. In her thirties, wasn't she?'

'Thirty-three.'

'And leaving such a family.' He looked up at me, the sun flashing suddenly on the steel rim of his glasses. 'You probably don't remember, don't realise, quite the – how shall I put it? – level of contact I had with your family, certainly before she died, and after, though that was more difficult.'

'I remember she was devoted to you, and to the church,' I said, my voice hard. 'I remember her determination to have me take my first communion, even though I protested. And those dreadful Saturday morning lessons she made me go to, in the church hall, with Pauline.'

To my surprise he chuckled quietly. 'Yes, I remember your expression on those mornings. The nuns had a hard time of it with you – and that was when you deigned to stay.' He caught my look. 'Oh, yes, I knew about the days you dropped Pauline off and vanished. Where did you go?'

I shrugged. 'To the park sometimes, to see if any of my school friends were there. Sometimes I didn't go anywhere – just mooched around, looking in shop windows.'

He looked up then, and I saw a young fair-haired girl coming towards us across the lawn, carrying a tray. She put it down on the table.

'There you are. Father. Shall I pour, or can you manage?'

'I'm sure we can do very well, thank you, Maddie.' He stood up shakily, leaning for a moment on the table. 'How do you like your coffee, Janet? Is it all right to call you Janet still?'

'Yes, of course.' We attended to the ritual of coffee in silence. I declined a biscuit.

'So, tell me,' he said, sinking again into his chair. 'From your point of view, when you were eleven, twelve, perhaps earlier, what was it that you so detested about the church? Or maybe me?'

Despite myself, I had to smile. 'You and your church were the source of all my troubles. That's what I believed.'

'Do you still think so?'

I thought, and he watched me, sipping his coffee. 'I don't think it's quite so black and white, no, not now. My views have broadened a bit, I hope. I saw my mother in thrall, blindly obedient. I believed that church teaching influenced her to have so many children. Too many, so she had to have help. Help my father could not or would not afford. Which is why it fell to me. It might have been bearable if she'd stopped at David, but the twins did her damage, from what I gleaned from the whispers of the ladies in church. She should never have gone on to have Ben.'

'I agree,' Father Gerard said calmly. 'I tried to dissuade her.'

'You did?' This was a revelation.

'Yes. On medical grounds. But you see, Janet,' he said, leaning forward, 'Mary loved children. Especially babies. Looking after very young children was where she felt most needed. And you're right:

she did rely on you, her home-grown helper. Did you resent your brothers and sisters?'

'Yes, at times. Most times, though, I pitied them. Especially after she died, of course. They were so lost. So young to be left with no mother and a useless father. I was angry with her, though, for what seemed such careless procreation.'

Father Gerard was silent for a moment. He put his empty cup carefully onto its saucer. 'She was enormously proud of you, you know,' he said. 'Especially with your progress at school. Neither she nor your father, nor your aunts and uncles, had ever had much schooling, and you were clearly very bright. You were reading to baby Pauline when you were six.'

'I loved school,' I said. 'And I remember her exclaiming when I brought some childish piece of work home. She sometimes tried to show my father what I'd done, but he wasn't interested. In fact, he was deeply suspicious of any educational attainment. I think it made him feel inadequate.' I shook my head, the old disgust rising up. 'What sort of father resents a five-year-old's success? What does it say about him?'

Father Gerard said nothing for a moment. 'He was a difficult man, I grant you,' he said. 'And unfortunately that hasn't improved with age. He may have resented you, innocent as you were, because you trapped him into a marriage he didn't want, not then, when he was so young himself. He'd wanted to go to sea.'

'Well, he did have something to do with my existence,' I said acidly. 'And none of it was my fault.'

'Quite. But to do him some justice, Janet, he could have abandoned her, and he didn't. He worked hard to support the family; that was his role, as he saw it. He was a traditional sort of man – he saw children as women's province, as many did.'

'Huh! Well, that's certainly true. Before she died he never lifted a finger. Nor after, if he could avoid it. He was quite happy to have me as an unpaid skivvy, and he thought I'd had quite enough education by then.'

'I know,' the old priest said quietly. 'I tried to persuade him, on more than one occasion, to get some live-in help, so that you could be freed. After your mother's death, I visited your house many times, but in the end he refused to let me in.'

I frowned. This too was new to me. 'You did? Why?'

'Mary had been a valued member of the church. I felt some responsibility to you all. But especially I was concerned about you.'

'About me?' I heard my voice rise to a squeak.

'Yes. You were being used. And you were missing such a lot of school. In the end, after many attempts to get something done, attempts which were foiled mainly by your father's attitude, I went to see your head teacher.'

I looked at him, my eyes wide. 'I didn't know that.'

He shook his head. 'She hadn't been aware of what was going on, not the whole story. She knew you were missing a lot of school, and there were times, usually after some official had come by to check, when your father sent the little ones away so that you, and Pauline, Christine and David, could go to school, but mostly he refused to have any contact with anyone who, as it seemed to him, wanted to undermine his prerogative.'

'That I remember,' I said grimly. 'But they always came back, didn't they, the little ones, because he didn't pay for their keep regularly. And the twins were a nightmare. But I also pleaded with him not to do it. Especially for Ben. He was too young, and he missed his mother. So I guess I brought it on myself, but I hated the idea of those poor little blighters in the so-called care of strangers.'

'I know,' Father Gerard said. 'I know a lot of all this story, because many years later your sisters told me. How you were a little mother to them, keeping them clean, feeding them, reading them stories, shielding them from your father.'

I smiled sourly. 'Did they tell you how I got money out of him, threatening to withdraw my services which were so convenient for him? No, I suppose they didn't know that. The whole situation turned me into a hardnosed little tyrant who could argue him into a corner and stood up to him, many times. That was after he had his accident, when he knew if I didn't look after the kids he'd have to do it himself. So every time he felt inclined to take his belt to me for being such a gobby brat he'd have to check himself – he needed me, and he hated me for it.'

'I'm not sure it was hate exactly,' Father Gerard demurred. 'I think in his way he quite admired your spirit. But it was that accident that started to blow things open. He had to have a nurse, those first few months, to see to his foot. And she saw what was going on in your house. She was one of my parishioners too.'

I bit my lip. 'I truly didn't know you knew so much.'

He smiled. 'And you didn't help either, Janet. When I came to see how you were, you refused to see me. You even resorted to bolting out of the back door to avoid me. And I was coming out of the goodness of my heart.' Now his smile was full of amusement, and despite myself I was smiling too.

'I would never have seen you as a saint,' I said.

'And you would have been quite right, then and now.'

I finished my coffee. 'I've learned something today, Father.' He raised an eyebrow. 'Apparently my mother wasn't dragooned into having so many children because of the policies of the Catholic church, abetted by her priest. And that very priest tried to help the motherless Yates children.'

'That part shouldn't surprise you. It's what most priests would have done.'

'Clearly I was prejudiced. But you were telling me you went to see my head teacher. I guess that's when things changed for me.'

He shifted in his chair. 'I'm getting a bit stiff, sitting here so long. Do you mind if we take a turn around the garden? I'm afraid I'm very slow.'

He rose creakily to his feet and picked up his stick, which had been resting against his chair. We strolled down the sloping garden, and he nodded and murmured greetings to fellow-residents who were sitting, or dozing, in the sunshine.

'Your head teacher, once she knew, set things in motion with great determination. By then the twins were in school and that left just Ben. Your father claimed he couldn't cope with Ben because of his own damaged foot, and not long afterwards Ben started having fits, poor lad. So doctors got involved and once Ben's condition was stabilised a nursery place was found for him, and a childminder.'

'I remember. Pauline was in the top class then, so at the end of school it was her job to scoop up the young ones and take them home. I stayed at school catching up until the caretaker threw me out. Then I'd pick up Ben from the childminder and race home to get everyone's tea.'

We paused for a moment by a sumptuously-flowering rosebush, where Father Gerard inhaled the scent, closing his eyes. 'Beautiful,' he breathed. 'It's been such a year for roses. Did you know I was a keen gardener myself before I moved here?'

'No, I didn't. I am beginning to realise how little I do know.'

'Ah, but then you were a child with a child's limited perspective.'

I glanced at him. 'And now?'

He smiled a little sadly. 'Now, I suspect, among the many things you have achieved, the many successes despite your unpromising start, you are wondering if there is something missing.'

'Ha! I know there is. But you can stop there if that's a conversion attempt, Father! I'll find my own way, and it won't be back to your church or any other.'

'That was not my intention, I promise,' he said mildly. 'I am aware you have chosen a path in direct opposition to your mother's.'

'What, divorced, and only one child?'

He sighed. 'Shall we turn back? This is where the garden ends. You can just see the river from here.'

We walked in silence for a few moments, then he said, 'I have to admit my heart quailed when I heard of your marriage to Terry Walters.'

'You weren't wrong. As I guess you realised, it was my escape plan.'

'Out of the frying pan…?'

I grinned. 'Something like that.'

We arrived back at the table, and I said, 'I should go and leave you in peace.'

He laid his hand on my arm. 'Please believe that conversion was not in my plan. That's a mysterious process unique to each individual. But I would ask you not to close yourself off from spiritual things. That would be a great loss. And of course, if you were ever to have questions, I would be happy to try and answer them, but there's no need for you ever to come back here if you choose not to.'

I sighed and looked down at the perfectly-tended grass. 'No, Father, I should thank you. For taking the time and the trouble. Then and now. For keeping the Yates children in your sights.'

'And in my prayers.'

'How effective is that?' I asked sceptically.

He smiled, and there was a hint of mischief in his faded blue eyes. 'Oh, well, as to that, it might be something to do with your willingness to come and see me today.'

'You have to be kidding!'

'I assure you I am not. Your sisters also pray for you, they tell me.'

'Good heavens.'

A bell jangled from inside the house, and Father Gerard looked up. 'Ah! It's lunch time. Sunday is usually a good one.'

'Then that's my cue to leave,' I said. 'Enjoy your lunch, Father. You never know, I may come back one day. I guess you believe in miracles, don't you?'

'Every day,' he said seriously. 'And you'd be welcome.' We started to walk slowly up towards the house, accompanied by other residents who'd been in the garden. At the door Father Gerard stopped suddenly. 'Oh! I almost forgot! I must be going senile. Last night, when I got home after the wedding, I rang Peggy Wyatt.'

Light dawned. 'Roly Wyatt's wife? Don't tell me – she's a member of your congregation too.'

'Well, she was. And still is a member of my successor's. Father Daniel, who presided at your nephew's wedding. But yes, I've known the Wyatts a good long while. I told her about Ben. I can't guarantee anything, because obviously Roly makes the business decisions, but she'll have something to say.'

'And she knows Ben too, I dare say.'

'Oh, yes. She's very fond of Ben. We will see.'

At the door to the dining room, now noisy with the clatter of plates and cutlery and voices, I turned to him. 'It's going to take me some time to digest all these surprises, I think.' I paused. 'And maybe I owe you an apology.'

'For what?'

'For thinking so ill of you all these years.'

'Well, well, not to worry. If forgiveness were needed, I forgave you years ago. Maybe now you can see your way to forgive me. God speed, Janet.'

Bob was still asleep when I got home, and I debated whether I should tell him where I'd been. Perhaps I would, especially since he'd not long ago accused me of keeping things to myself far too much. On the other hand, I didn't want to be grilled. I had too much to think about, and I needed time to process it. As it happened I didn't have the opportunity. Bob woke up with a headache and a sullen temper, ate lunch almost in silence and disappeared into the garden shed, where he said he had some tools to mend. I went for a walk, to get some fresh air and time to think, and while I was out it came on to rain so I arrived home soaked. I wallowed in a hot bath for a while, and by the time I'd made tea and a sandwich it was time for Bob to go to work. As I heard the front door slam and silence roll back towards me it occurred to me that sometimes it seemed I didn't have a husband at all. If I'd had the energy I might have applied myself to working out how this had happened; as it was I shrugged and sighed and got ready for a week at work.

Monday didn't start well. Anna came in looking preoccupied; she passed my door with an absent-minded greeting, then backtracked. 'Janet, you have remembered I won't be here on Wednesday, haven't you?'

'Wednesday?' I looked at the diary which was up on my screen. 'No note of anything on Wednesday. Oh, except you have an appointment with a Mr and Mrs Evans at three.'

'It's the Selection Day. I told you.'

'You told me it was happening, but not when, as far as I recall. I'd have put it in the diary.'

I saw her frown. 'I'm sure I told you the 14th. Maybe you forgot.'

It was more likely she'd forgotten to tell me, but I didn't make an issue of it. 'Well, maybe I did. I'll reschedule Mr and Mrs Evans.'

'Thanks.' She seemed flustered, and I said nothing more, but she'd made me doubt myself, and that was uncomfortable. Had I forgotten to log it? Nothing is impossible, but it would have been a shocking rarity. Was I beginning to lose my grip at work? In a tiny corner of my mind I conceded that things had not sat quite right ever since the debacle with Lauren Barclay; although I expected no further problems in that quarter, it hinted to me that my control was slipping. I had spoken immoderately, and a complaint had landed on us; not only that, but her very presence in chambers had resulted, even if only momentarily, in a slackening of the respect due to the

Senior Clerk. I recalled with a shudder the laughter in the clerks' room at my expense. I had no doubt that they sometimes joked about me, but they had never before done so in my hearing.

When I got home that evening, Bob called to me from the kitchen. 'There's a letter for you. I left it on the hall table.'

I picked the letter up, noting the blue NHS logo on the outside, and went through to the kitchen. I dumped my coat and bag on the table and tore open the envelope. 'Ha! Great timing!'

Bob turned from where he was stirring something on the hob. 'What?'

'This is my appointment for the scan and the D and C. Both on the same day – July 7th!'

He looked blank for a moment. 'But that's your birthday. Are you going to reschedule?'

'Not likely,' I said. 'Unless you're planning some fabulous surprise? No, I thought not. Anyway, if I put it off, who knows when I might get another appointment?'

He turned back to his cooking. 'I guess we can celebrate your birthday another day.'

'It says in the letter I'll need someone to bring me home. They're going to give me a general anaesthetic. And I have to be off work at least two or three days. What shift are you on that day?'

'I don't know yet,' he said. 'But if necessary I'll make sure I'm around.'

'Thanks.' I looked up at the clock. 'Why are you cooking this early?'

'I'm doing another night.'

'What? That can't be right!'

He put a steaming pot on the table. 'I'm covering for someone.'

'Again?'

'Yeah.' His voice was unnaturally flat.

Halfway through that silent meal I took a deep breath and said what was in my mouth, ready to be spat out. 'Bob. Look at me, not your plate.'

He glanced up and immediately away. 'What?'

'Are we unravelling? Just lately I've been feeling that I am – that everything's coming unstuck. But what about us – you and me? Is that what's happening?'

He still didn't look at me; he just stared at the table, breathing heavily. Finally he said, 'It's just life, isn't it. It happens.' He put his fork down. 'Sorry, but I'm going to work.'

Five minutes later, he was gone, leaving me bewildered. Was he heading for some kind of breakdown? Was he, crazy thought, having an affair? I thought immediately of the woman in the silver car who'd given him a lift. He was behaving like someone I didn't know. There was a time when we'd always discuss things rationally, even if neither of us were great soul-barers. I got up from the table, opened a bottle of wine and poured myself a large glass. It was not much help, and I had no intention of drinking myself under the table, but the world was rocking around me, and I didn't know what to do.

Later that evening, as I was doing the last of the washing up, the phone rang. It was Pauline. 'Great news, Janet!' she trilled. 'I just had a call from Ben. Apparently Mr Wyatt called him in to his office earlier today, gave him a stern talking-to, and said he could come back to work, no questions asked.'

'Wow. I didn't expect that,' I said. 'What other businessman do you know who'd let off a thieving employee, even given the circumstances?'

There was a pause. 'I don't think Mr Wyatt is your usual kind of businessman, though, is he?' Pauline said with some hesitation. 'I mean, I know you have to think about making a profit and all that, otherwise you couldn't pay your bills or your staff, but…I don't know, he doesn't seem the grabby sort, does he? I wouldn't say I knew him well, but I do know his wife, and –'

A light dawned. 'Don't tell me, Pauline. You've been saying prayers for Ben. You and a few others, including Mrs Wyatt.'

'Well, of course!' she said, as if it was the most obvious thing. 'Why wouldn't I? I pray for all my family, Janet, even you.'

'Me?'

I heard her laugh quietly. 'You really had no idea, had you? You're a funny one, Janet. So clever, but so, I don't know, out of touch somehow.'

Was I? Maybe I was. 'Well,' I said, 'I'm delighted Ben still has a job.'

'He hasn't quite got away scot-free, though,' Pauline said. 'Mr Wyatt felt some sort of penance was in order, I suppose. He's got Ben completely reorganising the warehouse, which will be a big job. It'll take weeks, and he's to do it in his own time and unpaid. The daft thing is, Ben will love it. He's no fool, is he? Mr Wyatt, I mean.'

'I guess not. If you think about it, he's being kind to Ben. That job will make Ben feel very responsible and worthy. He'll be even more tied to Wyatt's.' I thought for a moment. 'I wonder if Mrs W had anything to do with that suggestion, Pauline. She sounds like a lady with her head screwed on.'

'There may be more to it than that,' Pauline said. 'Ben's been at Wyatt's since he was eighteen. Mr Wyatt took him on and trained him. I think there's a bit of fatherly feeling going on there too, don't you?'

'Maybe you're right.' As I rang off, I thought, It's a pity our actual father isn't a bit more like Roly Wyatt. But then, I guess there aren't too many like him around.

On Wednesday morning I got to chambers early as always. I'd just made a cup of coffee and booted up my computer when my mobile rang. I was surprised, and even more so when Anna spoke.

'Where are you?' I asked. 'What are you calling for? Did you forget something?' I knew she was on the way to the Selection Day in London, and she'd said she would start early to make sure she could find where she needed to go.

'I've just got off a bus, and I'm walking down to the venue,' she said. Her voice sounded strange. 'Haven't you seen the news this morning? There's been a disaster, Janet – a terrible fire, right here in London. A residential tower block. Lots of people may have been killed. They were all asleep in their beds. Can you think how that must have been? People were talking about it on the train. I feel shaken by it all. It makes our concerns seem petty.'

I'd missed the news that morning; I don't always bother to put the radio or TV on. But I was concerned: she sounded unusually shocked. 'That's dreadful,' I acknowledged. 'I'll check it out in a minute. But are you all right?'

She sighed. 'I don't know. It's really got to me, I admit.'

'Anna.'

'What?'

'When you say our concerns seem petty compared to this sort of tragedy, I agree. They do. But if you mean our work seems petty, no, it isn't.' I spoke firmly; today was an important day for her, and she needed to be on form, not dazed. 'Stand still a minute and listen. If there's some sort of official enquiry into this catastrophe, who do you think is the likeliest person to head it up?'

'Er, probably a retired judge.'

'Exactly. In my view what we do every day, even though sometimes it does seem petty to us, is part of what holds our country together. Who was it who said, "Janet, the law may be an ass, but it's all we've got to pull the cart?" Remember that?'

She laughed quietly. 'Of course. I said it myself.'

'You have to give it your best today,' I said. 'Don't let this throw you off course. It's terrible, but you can't help. What you can do is be a good judge. The country needs every one.'

I heard her take a deep breath. 'You're right. Thanks, pal.'

Later, surfacing from work, seeing it was almost lunch time, I thought, I can run this place, no problem. I can straighten out my Head of Chambers; I can help my brother. The person I can't seem to help is myself.

For a moment that evening I hesitated to call Anna, but decided to anyway. If she was busy or with Jeremy, she didn't have to answer, but I wanted to know how the Selection Day had gone.

To my surprise she picked up the phone straight away. 'Actually,' she said in answer to my question, 'I think it went pretty well. There were a few people I knew there, like me being scrutinised, and that helped. When it came to the role plays I pretended I was in court, and with all the years of experience of different judges it wasn't difficult to put myself in their shoes. Not so sure about the interview; there were some tricky questions. But we'll see.'

'Are you on your own? I thought you might be with Jeremy.'

'I spoke to him this afternoon as he was about to get on a flight to Stockholm – he's at a conference for a few days.'

'All going well?' I asked delicately.

'Um, yes, fine.' There was a pause. 'On that subject, I am feeling the lack of your worldly wisdom.'

'Not sure I have any.'

'Well, you do. Any chance of a meet and chat?'

I thought. After his run of nights, Bob had told me tersely that he was now due a few days off. At the moment he was working in the garden while the light lasted. He seemed civil enough, but I sensed he wanted to keep out of my way, and while he was in this mood I was only too happy to avoid him. I'd tried to ask him what was going on and had met with a blank wall. If he had anything to say to me no doubt he would – eventually; meanwhile I had other things to think about. 'Shall I come to yours tomorrow evening?' I suggested to Anna.

'That sounds good.'

'Oh, by the way, just so you know,' I added, 'I've got a date for that tedious little medical procedure I have to have. July 7th. It's a Friday, so with any luck I'll be back at work on Monday.'

'July 7th is your birthday.'

'So it is. But I have no special reason to celebrate being forty-nine.'

'Survival?' she asked, and I could almost see her expression. 'As to getting back to work, you are not even to consider it unless you are feeling completely OK. It may be a "tedious little procedure," but you'll still need to recover.'

'Whatever. I'll come down about eight tomorrow, shall I?'

'Great.'

I'd barely hung up when the phone rang.

'Mum? You in?'

'Hello, Drew. When am I not in? I don't have hobbies, I don't play golf, I don't belong to a knitting circle.'

I heard him chuckle. 'Maybe you should take something up, Mum. Get a break from work and thinking only about work.'

'I think about plenty of things,' I shot back. 'Not that you'd know.'

'I would if you ever told me,' he said mildly. 'I want to talk to you and Dad – I could be there in minutes.'

'Again?'

'Yeah. It's getting to be a habit.'

'Your father's outside somewhere,' I told him. 'You can collect him on your way in.'

Ten minutes later I heard Tiffany's car slow down in the road outside, and then, to my surprise, it roared away again. I put the kettle on for coffee, and as it boiled I heard Drew's and Bob's voices at the back door. Bob sounded perfectly normal when he was speaking to Drew, I realised. It was only with me that he was so taciturn.

'You on your own?' I asked Drew.

'Yeah – Tiff's gone to her mum and dad's.'

I thought he seemed uneasy. 'Everything OK?'

'Sure.'

I poured coffee for us all and we sat at the kitchen table.

'What's all this, then, son?' Bob said.

Drew took a breath. 'Tiff and I have decided to get married.'

I frowned. 'That's not news.'

'In two weeks.'

'What? Why? She's not pregnant, is she?'

Drew grinned. 'If she is, she hasn't informed me. No, Mum, she isn't. Actually we gave notice a few weeks ago. We'd already decided to bring it forward, but we hadn't got round to deciding on a date. Nev's wedding clinched it. That, and the stag do I mostly avoided. We both hated it. We thought we'd try and do it our way.'

Bob grunted. 'It was a bit of a circus, I grant you.'

'Neither of us want anything like that,' Drew said. 'And I don't think either of you would ever put any pressure on us. But Tiff's parents are another matter. She's their only child, her dad's really well off, not to mention he's a powerful character and likes to get his own way, and she's convinced they'll want something big and flashy. That's where she is now.' He bit his lip, and I saw where his mind was. He fished in his pocket and brought out a small sheet of paper.

'We made you both invites,' he said. 'She'll be delivering hers about now. I don't envy her.'

'I get the impression,' I said, 'that under that shy exterior Tiffany is a determined young lady. Well able to stand up to her dad if her mind's made up.'

'Yes, she is,' Drew said quietly. 'But she'd much rather it wasn't some kind of confrontation. She doesn't want to hurt their feelings.'

'Whereas we,' I said acidly, 'don't have feelings to hurt.'

Drew shook his head, smiling. 'Give over, Mum. Of course you do. Just, I hope anyway, not about something like this.'

I looked down at the modest flyer he'd laid on the table between us. Wednesday, 5th July, two o'clock at Brant Register Office. 'Good job it's not later,' I said. 'I go to hospital on 7th.'

Drew frowned. 'What for? Are you sick?'

'Just a minor investigation,' I said. 'Nothing to worry about.' I wanted to change the subject, so I said airily, 'Looks like I'll be visiting my favourite charity shops, then.'

Drew tilted his head. 'Not recycling that glamorous outfit you wore at Nev's, then?'

'No, because this time I won't be dressing to kill. Or to have my feet mangled.'

Drew laughed. 'Mum, you are priceless.' To my surprise he picked up my hand, which I'd rested on the table, and dropped a kiss on my palm. 'So, you will both come, won't you? It'll be OK to get time off work?'

'Of course we'll be there,' Bob said. 'As if we'd miss it. Big or small, your son's wedding is a massive deal.'

Drew heaved a sigh. 'Thanks. I just hope Tiff's getting on OK.' He looked up at us, and for a moment I saw the defiant face of a little boy. 'Because it's going ahead, whether or not they choose to come.'

'Let's hope they can swallow their disappointment and be gracious,' I said. 'They had their turn – now it's yours.'

'It'll be a small party, then,' Bob said. 'Are we going anywhere afterwards to celebrate?'

'Yes!' Drew said, grinning. 'In keeping with the quietness of the event, we thought we'd have cake and bubbly at our little loft. I don't suppose you'd like to provide it, would you, Dad? Neither Tiff nor I have any spare cash right now.'

Bob laughed, and I realised with a small shock how long it had been since I'd heard that sound. 'You've got a cheek,' he growled. 'But of course we will.'

'So,' I said, 'it'll just be you two, and us, and the Leamans if they accept.'

Now Drew beamed. 'Plus two more! Millie is coming up specially to be Tiff's witness and supporter, and Jasper's coming as my kind-of best man.'

I felt a wash of relief. Millie was Anna's daughter, Jasper Rachel's stepson, and with those two young people part of the scene it would be far less awkward. 'Has their term finished, then?' I asked.

'Yes,' Drew said. 'Millie would have come home this weekend anyway. And Jasper took his last exams a few days ago. He'll go back for the results, I guess.'

'What's he going to do?'

'No idea,' Drew said. 'He was talking about travelling.'

'Were they ever an item, him and Millie?'

Drew shook his head. 'No. Good mates, of course, but last I heard they were both with someone else. They're really pleased for us, though. Said they saw it coming from the start.'

His phone rang, and he pulled it out of his shirt pocket and answered, turning slightly away. 'Hiya. You OK? Right. See you in a minute, then.'

'Tiffany? How did it go?'

He shrugged. 'She didn't say much. I think she'll leave them to think about it.' He paused, obviously thinking. 'I said to her there might be some leeway. Not for the wedding itself, but maybe later, if her dad wants to do something. We're open to a bit of compromise. It would be better to be on reasonable terms for the future, and I know Tiff would rather they were on board.'

'How do you get on with them?' I asked.

'Hm, yeah, OK. He's a bit of a force to be reckoned with, but as you say, Tiff's no pushover, and neither am I. Between us we'll try and make it work.'

I loved his optimism, even while I feared for him. I wondered where on earth ours had gone.

I decided on a whim to walk to Anna's the following evening; it was fine and warm, with a soft breeze that barely moved the heavy summer foliage of the trees on my route. Walking, I reasoned, was good for my health, despite the city's pollution; it saved having to sit in traffic; and if I took Anna a bottle we could legitimately share it.

I kicked off my shoes in her hallway and went through to the lounge. She had made some effort to tidy: the books and papers which were normally in heaps on every surface had been neatly stacked on the floor.

She saw me looking and smiled. 'Yes, I know, I should get more organised. I'm not as efficient as you.'

'As long as there's a place to sit and a spot to put my wine glass, I'm not complaining,' I said.

She came through from the kitchen with the uncorked bottle, two glasses and a bowl of nibbles on a tray. 'I hear news from your camp,' she said. 'Regarding another wedding in the offing.'

'Oh, so Millie told you?' I said, accepting a brimming glass. 'Drew only told us yesterday.'

Anna settled herself on the sofa opposite me. 'Word has it they left announcing it till now to give the Leamans less time to expostulate.'

I took a sip. 'Do you think they're being selfish? Drew and Tiffany, I mean.'

'No, I don't,' Anna said robustly. 'What they do is up to them. There's far too much nonsense talked and money spent when it comes to weddings. I read somewhere that statistically the likely success of a marriage is in inverse proportion to the amount of cash spent on the day. I don't know how true that is.'

'Drew and Tiffany are operating on a shoestring,' I said. 'But of course the Leamans are rolling in it.'

I saw the glint in Anna's eye. 'What do you reckon – Tiffany doesn't want to benefit from her father's ill-gotten gains?'

This made me snort with laughter. 'Poor girl. It's probably a subject she'd rather not dwell on. Anyway, what was it you wanted to talk about?'

She looked away, and I saw her blush. 'Oh, you know, nothing really. We just haven't had the chance to chat for a while.'

'Now you're prevaricating. You said you wanted to take advantage of my worldly wisdom. Go on, spill.'

'You're such a bully. Completely devoid of tact and sensitivity.'

'Overrated qualities. OK, let me guess: you have some issue with the lovely Jeremy.'

Anna sighed. 'Matrimony is clearly a prevailing theme. He wants us to get married.'

'Hm. I suppose that's preferable to him wanting to dump you. Just.'

Anna laughed aloud. 'Janet, you are a cynical woman. And a tonic. But why the jaded view? It should be me, shouldn't it, that's wary of commitment?'

'I got divorced once, you know,' I said.

'So you did. But it didn't stop you taking the risk again.'

'Perhaps I should have thought twice,' I said. 'But I was young and over-confident. Bob was a very different proposition to Terry, so I believed. And if I'm honest I was probably not thinking straight.'

'Overcome with sheer adoration?' Her eyes gleamed with amusement.

'Huh. Overpowering lust, more like. Which I suspect might be half your problem.'

'How did you guess?' She shook her head. 'We haven't known each other long. I have experience of a marriage gone wrong, with all the horrible rejected feelings that go with it. I wouldn't willingly suffer that again.'

'And Jeremy, as part of his beliefs, and because of the way he was brought up, is opposed to the idea of a mere affair.'

'Well, it's more than that anyway,' Anna said quietly. 'I guess I am scared, and it seems a bit too soon, but it's not easy for either of us.'

'How much do you like him?' I asked bluntly.

'A lot. He is altogether admirable and lovable.'

'Not too many like that around,' I said. I took a large gulp of my wine, and it went down smoothly. 'You don't need me to tell you what to do. Not really.'

'No, I guess not.' She looked at me keenly. 'That's me sorted out. Now what about you?'

'Me? There's nothing wrong with me. Apart from having to have my most tender parts investigated. But at least I won't know anything about it.'

She frowned. 'You're not still thinking about all that nonsense with Lauren Barclay, are you?'

'I hope I don't need to. It's over, isn't it? I admit, for a split second it threatened to make my pedestal wobble a bit. But I am back in control.' I grinned and proffered my glass for refilling.

She settled back against the cushions and folded her arms. I knew this body language of old. 'Janet, do me the honour of honesty. There is something going on.'

I thought. She was not going to be fobbed off with trivialities, but there were some things I knew I couldn't discuss with her – not yet, and maybe not ever. 'I have had a few family issues, yes,' I said. 'It's not an attractive story, but you can hear it if you like.' Briefly I recounted what had happened at Neville's wedding, Ben's revelation of our brothers' plot, the interview with Mr Wyatt and its surprising outcome.

Anna was appalled. 'Poor Ben! I'm so glad it didn't turn out badly for him. Mr Wyatt sounds like a truly Christian gentleman.'

'There's more,' I said as I drained my glass. 'I went to see Father Gerard.'

'Who?'

'I must have told you, but maybe it was a long time ago. He's retired now, but he was the priest at our church when I was a child. I hated church, and him, and the grim Saturday morning lessons we had to attend, delivered by a brace of nuns, in preparation for First Communion, which I tried to avoid. I thought it was the fault of the church, and by extension him, that led to my mother having so many unnecessary children. Children I was responsible for in large part, especially after she died. But it turns out I was wrong.'

Anna's eyes were wide. 'What made you go to see him?'

'He asked me to. Wanted to set the record straight, I suppose. And I have to admit he isn't the monster that young Janet painted him.' I sat thinking for a moment. 'It makes me wonder if I haven't got a lot of other things wrong as well. For instance, I've always thought of my sisters as slavish obedient little sheep, in thrall to the church, but it seems their faith is real. Pauline even told me she prays for me!'

'That doesn't surprise me at all. Why does it surprise you?'

'I don't know. I'm just dyed-in-the-wool prejudiced, maybe.'

'Oh, Janet. I pray for you too sometimes, you know. I certainly will when you go in for your op. But not only then.'

'Good heavens. As Pauline said, I am out of touch. Certainly with the wacky world of prayer. Are you quite sure it works?'

Anna shook her head, smiling. 'Positive, but not in any way I could possibly explain. It has to be experienced. I'm sorry if that sounds like a cop-out to you, but not everything is subject to human reason.'

'Hm. Food for thought indeed.'

We talked of other things: work; the horrific tower-block fire that had so shaken her yesterday; the prospect of weddings to come; the children – hers and mine – and her own potential career changes. Not once did I hint at what was really on my mind, and she, apparently, had no notion that something else might be. To the outside world Bob and I were as solid as a settled old impermeable boulder, weathered, maybe, but unshakeable. Only I, it seemed, had any notion that we were far from immune to normal human trouble.

I was almost exactly halfway home when it happened – too far to turn back to Anna's. It was just after ten o'clock, and dark, with the streetlights on, and depending on my route there were people about or almost-deserted pavements. I was walking briskly, bag swinging, thinking about what Anna and I had been talking about, wondering what her life would be like married to Jeremy and working as a judge, when I became suddenly aware of a dragging sensation in the pit of my abdomen which became stronger as I walked, so that I stopped, my breath coming in heaving gulps, and perched on a garden wall for a moment. It was the unmistakable sensation of my troublesome organs misbehaving, a sensation which almost any woman from teens to old age would recognise – and maybe dread, because it could so easily result in bleeding, sooner or later. The dragging, binding feeling soon escalated to pain, and I felt a fine sweat break out on my face.

I fumbled in my bag and found my phone. For a moment I considered calling a cab, but soon dismissed the idea: no driver would want a bleeding woman in his taxi. I rang my home number, and it went to voicemail. I was puzzled, because I'd left Bob watching sport on TV. I rang his mobile, and the same thing happened. As the pain came in waves I cursed through gritted teeth. Where are you when I need you?

The pain was bad enough, but almost worse was the horror of public bleeding which I felt sure was something else any woman would share. I was wearing pale blue linen crops and had no defences. I couldn't go back, and I couldn't go on – at least, not here. I briefly thought of a different route which would take me through a park where privacy would be more probable, but it would make my journey longer, and anyway it was a known haunt of drug-dealers and others who might find me fair game for mugging. Still perched on the wall, rocking slightly back and forward in an attempt to control the pain, nauseated and scared, I rang Bob's mobile again. It rang and rang, and I was mentally composing a desperate message when to my huge relief he answered. 'Hold on, I'll pull over – I'm in the car.' Moments later he was back. 'What's up? Where are you?'

'Please, come and get me. I need a lift home.' I gave him a brief description of my predicament and where I thought I was. 'And Bob, bring a towel.'

'I'm not far from there,' he said. Hearing his voice, calm and reassuring, brought a rush of relief. 'Hold on. I'm on my way.' One thing I could be sure of with Bob: he always responded well to a medical emergency. Whether it was because he was a kind husband, or whether I was more interesting when sick, was a moot point, but at that moment I was in no state to debate it. He drew in to the kerb in less than ten minutes and was out of the car, its engine still running, and helping me into the back seat and strapping me in, with barely a word spoken.

Another ten minutes found us back at home and parked. Again he leapt out and helped me indoors. 'I need a shower,' I said.

'OK, but don't lock the door,' he said. His face was serious. 'I don't want to have to break it down if you pass out. If you feel faint, get your head as low as you can and shout. I'll be hovering somewhere close.'

Standing under the warm water as it cascaded down my back and legs, I wondered why he had been out in the car that evening. Where had he been? Obviously he could go where he pleased, but he hadn't said anything about a meeting. I towelled myself down, defended myself against further bleeding, and put on pyjamas. My nice pale blue crops were soaking in a basin of cold water, and I wondered about the state of the car.

I emerged from the bathroom to find Bob waiting on the landing. 'Come on, let's get you into bed. How are you feeling?' He put an arm round my shoulders and supported me into the bedroom.

'Better. Good to be clean and safe,' I slurred. 'Need to sleep.'

'Don't even think about going to work in the morning,' Bob said sternly. 'I'll ring someone.'

'Where were you, anyway?' I asked him sleepily. 'What were you doing driving around?'

There was a pause, very brief but sufficient, half-asleep as I was, to alert me. 'Oh, I just went to see a friend,' Bob said. 'From the station.' What friend, Bob? There's something you're not saying.

But then he was straightening me out as I lay down, and pulling the covers up over my legs, and I thought, D'you know what, right now I don't care if you've got a harem of willing women scattered about all over the city. Or a troupe of naked dancing-girls hidden away in the shed. I closed my eyes, and then there was nothing.

Happily after this minor crisis everything went quiet. I was not fooled, however: I saw my problem as a muscular wild beast awaiting its chance to pounce, and I knew it was merely taking a nap. I took a day off work with poor grace, but inwardly I acknowledged that the drama of the night before had left me uncharacteristically shaky.

Over the next few days things were quiet domestically as well. I kept my more interesting thoughts largely to myself, and Bob was solicitous, in a distant kind of way. This situation seemed false – it leaned less to the muscular beast than to a curled-up snake, if I was being metaphorical – but I had no energy to confront it. The weekend passed without upheaval. But then on the following Tuesday people in chambers were abuzz with something that had happened the night before, that had been reported on the early news, something that had nothing to do with me at all, and yet served to give another unlooked-for shove to the rocking pedestal of my insulated life.

At a quarter past midnight worshippers were congregated on the pavement about a hundred yards from the Finsbury Park Mosque, following midnight prayers, trying to help an elderly man who had collapsed at a bus stop. A van mounted the pavement and ploughed into them, the driver shouting, 'I want to kill all Muslims!' and 'This is for London Bridge!' The elderly man died at the scene, and ten people were injured. This was, of course, appalling: yet more innocent people harmed for ideological reasons by another lunatic with hate in his heart. But what really struck me was the interview with the Imam of the mosque which was on the TV news later that day. He, so it was reported, along with some others, had stopped a vengeful mob from lynching the perpetrator, urging them not to beat him but to wait for the police so that due legalities could be pursued. He was calm, dignified, and wholeheartedly on the side of peace, and he stood up unflinchingly in support of the true tenets of his faith. He spoke of good community relations between people of different beliefs, and his attitude of acceptance and tolerance, his repudiation of revenge and hatred, made a deep impression on me. Alarmingly, though, I also made the connection between this much younger man and Father Gerard. They may have been of different religions, but their demeanour was the same: peace-promoting, hate-denying and compassionate. I felt again that shift of perception within me that I had noted some months ago, and I asked myself, Has this been an especially bum year? Or is something happening inside my head, so that these events, which once I would have noted dispassionately if at all, are having such an unforeseen effect?

Drew and Tiffany's wedding was a very different affair to Neville and Jodie's, less than a month before. I felt sufficiently stress-free to go into work for the morning and take only the afternoon off: there was no church to worry me with its oppressive memories, and no family to face behind a barrier of carefully-selected clothes. It was a warm day, if overcast and humid, and I chose a simple summer dress, two shades of pale purple in broad diagonal stripes, and low-heeled sandals which were kind to my feet. As we drove to the Register Office I thought about who knew whom in our very small gathering.

The young people all knew each other well: the most recent acquaintance was that of Millie and Jasper, who had attended different primary schools, but they had made up for it since. Because of my friendship with Anna, Millie and Drew were old friends, and had (sometimes reluctantly) turned up at each other's birthday parties when they were children. Drew and Jasper had attended the same primary school, though in different years, so I had probably seen Jasper on the occasions when I collected Drew from school. Now I felt as if I knew him from what both Anna and Drew had told me. As for the Leamans, I had only seen Calvin briefly, and had not been introduced, nor to his wife Sonia.

At half past one most of us were there – all but the bride and her supporter, who kept us waiting in the traditional manner. Drew, looking smart and handsome in a suit and tie and with all facial hair removed, introduced us and Jasper to the Leamans, and we were all very polite and awkward.

I studied the Leamans covertly. Calvin seemed taller and stringier than I remembered from my fleeting glance in chambers. His thinning hair was scraped neatly back over his scalp; his pale blue eyes, while full of sharp intelligence, were red-rimmed and watery, and his skin had a dull, colourless look about it. To my eyes, despite his affluent air – the expensive suit, crisp white shirt and hard-to-ignore watch – he didn't look well, but I had no way to tell if this was normal for him. Perhaps he spent too much time in front of a screen late at night. I glanced at Bob, and thought how much better he looked: well-built with just a hint of stomach straining his best blue shirt, and still with plenty of hair, brown and wavy, a sprinkling of grey above his ears. He caught me looking and raised his eyebrows. I turned my attention back to the Leamans, trying to banish the uncomfortable thought that my husband of twenty-four years might well be attractive to another woman.

Sonia Leaman was small and thin, with jutting collar-bones and sharp elbows. Her blonde hair was immaculately styled, her makeup was perfect, and she had a tan which I felt sure hadn't come from sunning herself on a beach. Her straight pink dress was simple enough but it was accompanied by an eye-watering amount of jewellery: bracelets, swinging ear-rings, even an anklet which drew the eye to a tiny mermaid tattoo. Apart from polite murmurings she said hardly a word, and seemed nervous: she glanced at her husband and immediately away again many times, and she opened and closed the gilt clasp of her minute white handbag without ever looking for anything inside.

Conversation, such as it was, threatened to dwindle into embarrassing silence despite the efforts of Drew and Jasper to jolly us all along. At last, with ten minutes to spare, Millie arrived through the double doors with great panache, and went round the room dispensing hugs to Bob and me and the young men and warm handshakes with the Leamans. I was struck anew by Millie's resemblance to her mother: taller, breezier perhaps, but with the same fair hair and something also in her expression that I couldn't quite identify.

'Where's the bride?' Jasper said with a look of comical alarm. 'Did she change her mind? Can't say I blame her. Sorry, Drew, it looks like you'll have to marry Millie instead.'

Millie pulled a face. 'Do me a favour, Jasper! I've never recovered from that peculiar episode when he thought smoking a pipe was cool. Tiffany is a woman of saintly tolerance. She's just coming. Had to visit the ladies' for the ninth time. Must be nervous, and who wouldn't be!'

Tiffany made her appearance to our relieved laughter, and she looked lovely: her dress was flowing and shin-length, white cotton sprigged with green and yellow flowers, echoed by the flowers in her dark-blonde hair. 'Thanks for giving my secrets away, Millie! Hello everyone, sorry we kept you waiting. We had a job to park, and if I'm nervous it's because of Millie's driving.' She circled the room, decorously hugging and kissing everyone, and landing finally at

Drew's side. I had never seen my son with such a wide, unaffected smile. He pulled Tiffany into his arms and kissed her. 'Hey, mind my flowers,' she said, smiling back at him. I surprised myself by a keen pang of loss. Had we, Bob and I, ever been so besotted? Maybe, once.

The wedding itself was charming, the ceremony serious when it needed to be, otherwise pleasantly informal, and soon over. Back in the waiting room, where another wedding party was already assembled, we all hastily congratulated the bridal pair and agreed to meet up again at their lofty flat, where, Millie whispered gleefully to me, food and drink awaited. 'That's if Horace hasn't learned how to open the fridge.'

On the way through the city Bob broke the silence. 'Drew told me the other day he's been having important chats with his father-in-law.'

'Oh. When was that?'

'He rang me. You were at work. Seems Calvin Leaman wanted to buy them a house, and Drew declined. Politely and gratefully, of course.'

'Good.'

I saw Bob glance at me. 'He doesn't want to depend on Leaman's largesse. But they came to a compromise. Otherwise they'll never own their own place. It's completely out of their reach.'

'What compromise was that?'

'That Drew and Tiffany would accept the deposit on a modest property as a belated wedding present, but not until they were both in good jobs and in a position to afford mortgage repayments. So I guess they'll be in their current place for a while yet.'

'Sounds like a plan. Calvin wants to help them out, and that's nice of him, and they don't want to seem ungrateful, but even with the piffling rent they pay now it'll take time to save.' I frowned and turned to him. 'Can we help them out a bit as well?'

'Not to the tune of house deposits,' Bob said. 'But yes, probably. Let's talk about it later. I have a few ideas.'

The afternoon's festivities, fuelled by fizzy wine, various savoury nibbles and cake, swung by in energetic disorder. The young people were excited, as much to see each other as by the occasion, and so we were spared the awkwardness inherent in the tentative joining of the Leamans and the Clarkes. I wondered if Calvin Leaman might collar me and ask after Anna, but happily he didn't. After an hour or so, in which they tried to look as if they were enjoying themselves, the Leamans left. 'I've got an important business meeting later,' Calvin Leaman said. 'As we had such short notice for today I just couldn't reschedule.' He and Sonia did the rounds, shaking hands, congratulating afresh. Tiffany and Drew escorted them down the steps to their car. As I looked out of the window I saw Tiffany hug her parents goodbye, and then I heard the muted roar of a powerful engine as their sleek silver car turned into the road and disappeared.

Not long afterwards I was beginning to feel worn. It seemed not too long ago that I would have stayed the course; it was my son's wedding day, after all, and I was unlikely to see another. I was forced to admit, if only to myself, that the physical challenges of the past few months were beginning to have an unwelcome effect.

'That's a shame, Mum,' Drew said when I told him I needed to go home. 'Uncle Ben said he might drop by after work, with his girlfriend.'

'Ben has a girlfriend?' I think I actually gaped for a moment.

'Oh yes – didn't you know?' Drew was all innocence, but his eyes gleamed with mischief. 'Remember when you had to go and rescue him – when Grandpa locked him in his room – in February, wasn't it? The night of that awful storm. That's why Ben was late home. He was waiting out the storm, with Hattie. She has a little flat above a convenience store somewhere.'

'I think you'd better fill me in, since obviously I'm the last to know. How long have they known each other?'

'Oh, I don't know, a while,' Drew said. He turned to Tiffany, who was collecting dirty plates. 'How long's Ben known Hattie, Tiff?'

'About eighteen months, I think.' She looked at me and smiled. 'She's nice. Small and slightly chubby. Fair wispy hair. Looks about fifteen, but is actually in her early thirties. Works in one of the branch libraries. Obviously thinks Ben is the bee's knees, but has him absolutely taped.'

Drew smirked. 'He doesn't seem to mind.'

'Well, he wouldn't, would he?' Tiffany said briskly. 'Most men are easily pleased, don't you think?'

'How do you know?' Drew said in mock-horror. 'How many have you been familiar with?'

Tiffany shook her head. 'Do give over. I have eyes, you know.'

I thought, The more I know Tiffany, the more I applaud my fool of a son's choice. Perhaps he's not such a fool after all.

'Sorry to abandon the party,' I said. 'But you'll have more fun without the creaky old codgers.'

'Speak for yourself,' Bob muttered.

'I was,' I said. 'But maybe not for much longer. In a couple of days with any luck I'll be getting my problems ironed out. Then there'll be no holding me.'

For my son's sake I put all the confidence I could muster into this utterance, but even if he believed it I was far less convinced.

July

When it came to it my day in hospital brought little drama. A long wand-like object probed my troublesome parts in search of information and images. I could see the screen but the blurred black and white lines and smudges meant little to me. Then they knocked me out and I was unaware of the rest of the day's proceedings.

They kept me in till late afternoon and fed me biscuits and weak tea. I was woozy and disorientated from the anaesthetic but they assured me I would be fine if I rested. Eventually they let me get dressed and go home. Bob was lounging in the waiting area reading a newspaper; he rarely reads the papers so I assumed he'd found one lying around and was passing the time. I saw him before he noticed me, and I was struck by how healthy he looked; but that might have been because I was feeling worn and old and washed out.

He threw the newspaper down, took my bag from my unresisting hand and put a firm arm round my shoulders. 'All right?'

'I suppose I am. Anyway, I guess they've done what they wanted to, so we can go home.'

They'd told me I would probably experience some bleeding and cramping as a result of their investigations, but that was no more than I had been suffering over the past months, so I took it stoically. All I wanted to do was sleep, but I wasn't so gormless that I failed to notice a huge bunch of flowers in a vase on the kitchen table, and a small card resting against it. Their perfume filled the room and made my head swim. 'Happy birthday,' Bob said with an awkward smile. I'd actually forgotten.

I spent a large part of that weekend oblivious to everything, surfacing just to eat and drink and totter to the bathroom. What Bob was doing all that time I had no idea. In my moments of consciousness he reported that people were asking after me: my sisters, Drew, Anna; and I registered vague gratitude. But on Sunday evening I definitely felt more human. I showered, dressed and came downstairs; Bob was washing up.

'I'm going to work tomorrow.'

He dried his hands on the kitchen towel. 'Are you sure you're fit enough?'

'I've spent too much time away this week, what with the wedding and hospital.'

He shook his head sceptically. 'Will the place go to ruin if you're absent a day and a half?'

I folded my arms. 'I can't take the risk.'

He sighed. 'Well, I guess you're a grown up; you can make your own decisions.' He waved a hand toward the corkboard on the kitchen wall. 'I've written my shifts up.'

'OK.' And that was the sum of our conversation that evening. We'd never been especially chatty or forthcoming; but even for us this way of being was beginning to seem extreme.

On Monday I barely admitted even to myself how fragile I felt, but anyone with an ounce of self-knowledge would have seen the significance of that morning's careful wardrobe choice: a cherry-coloured top with spangles, my black and silver ankle boots, and a shin-length black swirling skirt with silver worked into the hem so that it glittered as I walked. I had teased my hair into spikes, and I saw that I needed to visit the hairdresser soon: the colour of the tips was beginning to fade.

Work was as it always was. With the start of a new week there were calls to make, the diary to check and update, solicitors to contact, queries to field, and if there was any time in between articles to read online. I made sure my juniors were all happy and properly occupied, and distributed the day's mail myself to the barristers' rooms. The rhythm of work, familiar but ever-changing, did much to soothe the anxiety which lurked below the surface of my habitual sang-froid.

Anna came in lugging a heavy bag which she unceremoniously dumped on the floor of my office with a groan. 'How are you, Janet?' she wanted to know. 'Are you sure you should actually be here? Shouldn't you be taking it easy?'

'I definitely should be here,' I said firmly. 'I took it easy over the weekend. Thanks for phoning, by the way.'

'How long before you hear about results?' she asked. 'Did they say?'

'I can ring the GP surgery in two weeks, if I haven't heard anything by then.'

'Well, as you have so recently been under the knife, however much you like to downplay it, I shall make your coffee myself this morning.'

I sketched a mocking bow. 'Too kind.'

'Now I suppose I should get on with some work. I've got court all day tomorrow, and I didn't get anything done over the weekend, so today's my only day for prep.' She picked up her bag and strode down the corridor to her own room.

Five minutes later I heard a shriek from her direction and she was back. 'Janet! I have had a letter. In a very posh envelope, on beautiful thick paper. No expense spared. Our masters on high have plenty of cash, apparently.'

'Well? Don't keep me in suspense.' But of course I knew what her letter was about: her beaming smile was evidence.

'Seems I am going to be a judge, Janet. A very minor, humble one.'

'Minor for now,' I said. 'I'm not surprised. They're lucky to have you. Congratulations!'

'Thanks. I must text Jeremy before he starts his rounds.' She disappeared again, and I heard her quiet humming.

I was glad for her, of course. It was, I thought, about time she had some cause for jubilation. But for myself, my heart sank a little. Too many things were changing, and few of them boded well.

Bob was on a short series of night shifts that week, and I barely saw him. By the time I was ready for work on Tuesday he was still not home, and I assumed he had encountered an emergency that made him late. That morning I awoke at five thirty from a troubled night and took extra care to dress and put on makeup, in an attempt to hide what the mirror was telling me. I went for an outfit that was all pink, though not necessarily in the same shade. It matched the fading tips in my hair and I reminded myself again to make an appointment with my hairdresser. I went to work and drifted through the day, feeling oddly disconnected from reality. I must have done whatever I needed to do because nobody commented, but I caught a puzzled stare from Claire at one point when she came down to tell me something. Anna didn't appear in chambers; I guessed she would cover her cases and go straight home. I didn't expect her the following day either; she had no appointments and had said she'd work in the comfort of her own living room.

At the end of the day for some reason I found it difficult to galvanise myself into leaving. I saw barristers and clerks go out of the door one at a time or in groups, saying goodbye to me as I sat in my office pretending to look intently at my computer screen. They were used to seeing me there, the last to leave, and thought nothing of it. Eventually, with a deep sigh, I stretched my back, switched off my computer and collected my things. At least I made sure the front door was secure.

By the time I got home Bob was in uniform and about to leave. He frowned slightly when he saw me, but simply said, 'I left you a meal in the microwave.'

I washed and changed, ate and drank, read a magazine, watched the news, all the while feeling very odd, almost as if my brain had shut down, leaving only top-level mechanical functions intact – and yet I didn't care, which was odder still. Before I went to bed I thought to pick up the phone in the hall to check if we had any messages, and what I heard cracked through my dazed state like a pickaxe through ice. An unfamiliar female voice spoke: 'Good afternoon, this is the Brooke Road surgery for Mrs Janet Clarke. Mrs Clarke, please would you ring this number as soon as you can when you receive this message.' She reeled off a number which wasn't the usual one for the surgery, and after a couple of fumbling attempts I managed to note it down.

That night I lay awake for an hour or more, weary but sleepless, while a hollow feeling akin to nausea spread in my stomach and chest and up into my throat. Was my heart actually beating harder? I had never been one for useless speculation, but this was different. Why did I need to call the surgery – and on what seemed to be a special number? It could only mean one thing: that something worrying had been found from the investigation on Friday, the GP had been informed and was calling me in as a matter of urgency. I tried hard to banish thoughts of life-threatening illness, surgery, even early death. At some level a very quiet voice was telling me that I knew nothing yet, there may be no cause for panic, and I wasn't helping myself by letting these dark thoughts overwhelm me. Eventually I must have simply fallen asleep – an unlooked-for mercy, since there was no other escape.

I awoke later than usual the following morning, feeling almost drugged, and dragged myself out of bed. Breakfast consisted of painkillers and black coffee: my stomach refused to contemplate anything else. I knew the surgery didn't open till eight o'clock, and I decided to call from the car before I started for work. Again I dressed carefully, this time in an outfit predominantly green: not a favourite colour normally but one which seemed to reflect my mood. Instead of the dazed state of yesterday, I felt a silent howl from deep within, and suppressed it with faltering determination.

At five to eight, chin up and teetering on too-high heels, I walked down the pavement to the car. I'd noticed the evening before that our neighbour's son had once again left his car in the space outside our gate, which he was entitled to do, but it had meant I was obliged to find a space further down the road. I slid into the driver's seat. The car was already warming up, the sun glinting through the windscreen.

A few minutes after eight I keyed in the number I had been given and spoke to another female voice. She was friendly but brisk. 'Can you come in and see the doctor at eleven-thirty?'

I said I could, and ended the call. I contemplated making an appointment with the hairdresser, who I knew started her day early, but then I checked myself. What was the use of getting my hair done when in all likelihood I was desperately ill? I heard the little distant voice in my head snort and tell me not to be so dramatic, but it wasn't loud enough, not against a rising tide of dread.

I thought I would go to work, just taking time out to go to the surgery – it would be a distraction, at least – but then something else happened. I'd seen the neighbour's lad slam his front door and hurry out, pulling on his jacket, no doubt late for work, then jumping into his car and roaring away, leaving our space empty. As I thought about my day at work, I paused, my hand on the key in the ignition. From the opposite direction a silver car, one that I recognised, rolled slowly up our road and slid neatly into the space the neighbour's boy had vacated. I was on the other side facing the silver car, and I saw who it was: the driver was a young woman, her dark hair in a ponytail, wearing a green paramedic's uniform, and in the passenger seat, similarly clothed, Bob. I watched them, holding my breath, as they talked animatedly, often smiling, she with expansive hand gestures, and then they hugged one another, it seemed for several long moments. I felt as if my eyes were stretched, and there seemed to be something lodged in my throat. I saw Bob leave the car, closing the door but leaning in at the open window. I saw the young woman – Serena, hadn't he called her? – stretch out a hand and pat his wrist. Then she pulled out of the space and drove past me, waving back at Bob who was still standing on the pavement. A moment later he disappeared indoors.

What could I make of it? He was an hour late back, and if I thought about it he often had been later than expected over the past weeks. The little voice was arguing that it was probably innocent. Crewmates were usually supportive friends. But I wasn't listening. I rang into chambers and told them I had an appointment and hoped to be back in the afternoon. Then I started up the car and drove, not really planning any particular direction. I knew I had to get as far away as I could from my house, my street, that scene.

I managed somehow neither to have nor to cause an accident. Perhaps, with the traffic swelling into noisy, surly normality, that was a miracle in itself. Somewhere on the outskirts of the city I found myself on the road that led to Thripp's Ford, but even if I'd thought Drew and Tiffany might be home I didn't want to see them, not today. I turned the car round, and after half a mile I came across a farm track and turned down it. It looked overgrown and little-used, but I parked the car up against a fence so that I was well out of the way of any tractor. I had no strength to withstand an irate farmer.

I sat there, eyes closed, just breathing, while behind me the traffic rumbled almost incessantly along the main road. Otherwise there was silence, punctuated occasionally, when the cars and lorries abated for a moment, by the song of invisible birds. Bit by bit my mind cleared of its fog, and at last the small voice, the voice of reasonable Janet – hard to scare, hard to throw off course – began to gain in strength until it was almost as clamorous and insistent as the terror that boiled in my guts. On the one side there was the looming unknown: whatever it was that was lodged in my body, malevolent and menacing, and whatever had to be done to combat it; on the other was sanity, the possibility of healing and hope, the wells of medical expertise I could rely on. Then on the black side there was Bob, seeking comfort, assurance, perhaps even excitement, with another woman – younger, fresher and undoubtedly more appreciative. Did twenty-four years count for something? I couldn't really claim much in the way of shared endeavours or joint efforts, apart from raising Drew; but we were part of one another, it was a given, we belonged, joined in some unspoken mysterious way, unshakeable – or so, until recently, I had thought.

I took a deep breath, sighed it out, then another, and opened my eyes. In the field to my left a large brown cow was chomping the long grass growing under the fence. I switched on the engine, and the cow looked up, startled. The dashboard display told me it was ten fifteen; I had been sitting and pondering a long time. But there was still some time to go before my appointment, and now I surprised myself by what seemed at that moment, and to my disordered thinking, an utterly random impulse. I looked in my handbag, and at the bottom of an inner compartment I found the card that Father Gerard had given me on the day of Neville's wedding. I took out my phone and dialled the number for St Agatha's.

A moment later I heard the pleasant voice of the woman I had met on my earlier visit and remembered Father Gerard calling her Mrs Underdown. I asked if I might come and speak to him.

'Is that Mrs Clarke?' she asked. 'I thought I recognised your voice. Of course, my dear, do come. He'll be pleased to see you.'

I wondered about that, but now was no time for debate. Still with no clear idea why I wanted to see our old priest, except that he had been welcoming and kind when I'd spoken to him last, I turned the car round in the track with some difficulty, and in a moment or two rejoined the stream of traffic heading back into the city.

Twenty minutes later, having been held up by inevitable roadworks, I parked outside the house with the bowering rose. As I climbed out of the car I felt the heat rising from the pavement and pounding down from the cloudless sky. In the lobby it was cool. A middle-aged woman was on the phone at a desk just inside. She waved and smiled at me and indicated I should sign a visitor's book. As I did so I mouthed 'Father Gerard?' at her and she mouthed back: 'In the garden.'

I followed the same route as before and found him under the same tree. I wondered if he had been alerted to my coming; whatever the case, he didn't seem surprised. He looked up from his book, shading his eyes against the sun, smiling. 'Janet. How good to see you again.' He gestured to the vacant chair opposite and I slid into it gratefully. 'I don't get many visitors these days – none of us do – but your sister Christine has promised to call.' He looked at me searchingly. 'How are you?'

'I am OK, thank you, Father,' I said. Then, 'No, I'm not, that's nonsense. I'm not OK at all. But how are you?'

'Well enough, thank you,' he said quietly. 'Is that why you are here? Because you're not OK?'

I swallowed. Suddenly it was hard to speak. What was I doing here? How could he help? He was a celibate priest; I was a woman with female problems and potentially a marriage in tatters. 'I don't know. I suppose so. But now I'm not sure why I came.'

'Why don't you say what's on your mind? There's no need to go into detail. And I have plenty of time.'

I bit my lip and thought. 'Later this morning I have a doctor's appointment. I think it will be bad news. I guess I am afraid of dying. I know that sounds dramatic.'

He shook his head. 'What greater drama is there in most of our lives?' he said softly. 'And who isn't afraid of dying, if they are honest?'

'Even you?'

'Of course. The part of me that is merely human, the animal if you like – except that animals don't contemplate their end, not as far as we know – the physical part, the part that's so wedded to this familiar world – yes, that part of me is afraid, even though my spirit looks ahead with joy and anticipation of far better things. I might add that even Jesus was afraid, even he was overcome with horror and sorrow, for a dark moment, knowing that he was facing death.'

'I see,' I said dubiously.

'Do you?' He smiled. 'Is your fear of bad news, of dying, all that is bothering you?'

'Isn't that enough?' I shot back. 'No, you're right. There is something else. But the dying thing is enough for now.' I managed a painful smile.

'I gather that other thing might be a private matter – is it? Well, there's not a lot I can do for you, not much counsel I can give, but I do have a powerful weapon at my disposal, and if you are willing I will wield it.'

'Prayer, I suppose.'

He nodded. 'Living here, with these dear brothers, all of us sliding into a decline day by day, it's all I can offer. But it's far from nothing.'

'I see that. Please, yes, do pray for me. I can't do it for myself.'

He nodded. 'One day you might. Now, have you time for coffee? I can ask one of the helpers.'

Ten minutes later a tray with steaming cups and a plate of biscuits appeared, brought by a smiling blonde young woman. As I sipped and nibbled, I began to feel better – at least my stomach did.

I put down my cup and looked around the garden. 'It's lovely here. Very peaceful.'

His old eyes glinted. 'Just right for the anteroom of death, isn't it? But you're right – it's a great blessing, and all the staff are so kind.'

'I'm glad you have a good place to rest,' I said. 'I'd better go: the traffic is its usual self.' I stood up. 'Thank you, Father, for your kindness. I'm counting on your backup.'

'You have it, Janet,' he said. 'Before you're even out of sight, I'll be praying.'

I didn't doubt him. But, far from sensing the rustle of angel wings just out of sight, as I sat in the surgery waiting room I felt like a woman going to the scaffold. At last I was called, and the young GP I had seen before, Dr Kemsey, greeted me.

'Mrs Clarke, nice to see you,' she said. 'How are you?'

'Wondering why I am here. Thinking it can't mean anything good.'

'Please, do sit down.' She turned to her computer screen. 'Normally with tests such as you had on Friday it would take up to two weeks to get results. But if there are areas of concern they tend to arrive much more quickly.' She turned to face me. 'Look, I don't want to alarm you, but your scan showed something that shouldn't be there, and your D and C resulted in some cancerous cells.' She named the thing; it was a mouthful. So there it was, that doom-laden word. 'You're going to need another, different scan to find out if the mass is contained or if there has been any spread to other organs. Mrs Clarke, are you all right?'

My lips had gone numb. 'It's not the nicest news.'

'No, I understand that. It's a shame you don't have anyone with you. But it's not necessarily all doom. Hang in there, OK? Basically, because your previous tests didn't show anything up, and because these severe symptoms have been present just for a few months, there's a very good chance that the tumour is relatively small and restricted to the endometrial wall. Whatever the case, you are going to need a hysterectomy. If, as I hope, there is no spread then that will be curative. You'll need monitoring for some time, and there'll be medication you'll need to take, but that will be it – home free.'

'And if it has spread?' I heard my voice, and it didn't sound like me.

'You'll still need the hysterectomy. But other treatments as well. Look, let's not get ahead of ourselves. One step at a time.' She smiled sympathetically.

I had to ask. 'I've been feeling rubbish, on and off, for a while. Could this have been detected earlier?'

'It's hard to say. Honestly, this isn't the first time cancer has been masked by normal menopausal symptoms. It happens, I'm afraid. But the main thing now is to get you booked in for that operation. You'll get a letter very soon.'

She turned back to her computer, and I sat there feeling as if I had been in a fight: dizzy, knocked senseless. After a moment I gritted my teeth, gathered my wits and stood up. 'I'll wait for that letter, then.'

She looked up, a small frown between her brows. 'Is there someone you can talk this over with?'

'Not at the moment.'

'What are you going to do now? You've had a shock.'

'I'm going to work.'

I sat in the car outside chambers. The dizziness had receded but my stomach felt as if it was stuck to my spine. I remembered I had had nothing all day but two cups of coffee and a ginger biscuit, but I couldn't face visiting the supermarket and the very idea of food was repellent.

I was about to haul myself out of the car when the front door of chambers opened and Anna emerged, dressed in gym gear and trainers, carrying a small stack of files. She trotted down the steps and at the bottom she must have spotted my car; I saw her frown, and she came over. I wound the window down.

'You're not supposed to be here,' I said dully.

'I needed these,' she said, indicating the files. 'You know I sometimes like to work from paper copies. It gives my eyes a change.' Her frown deepened. 'Janet, you look terrible. Are you unwell?'

I smiled bleakly. 'You could say that. I've just come from the GP. She told me I have cancer.'

Anna said nothing for several seconds. I saw her gape and swallow hard. When she spoke her voice was barely above a whisper. 'Janet, this is awful. Look, you can't possibly go to work. What you have to do is come home with me, now.'

'I should check on my juniors.'

'No need,' she said firmly. 'Everything seemed quiet and productive in there.' She nodded her head towards the building. She came round the front of the car and let herself into the passenger seat. 'Do as I say for once, dear friend. Drive me home.' I was in no condition to argue.

We parked outside her house and she hustled me indoors. 'Sit,' she commanded. 'Have you had anything to eat?'

'A ginger biscuit. I might throw up if I eat.'

'We'll take that risk. I'm going to make you something very simple, comforting and full of glucose. Take those crazy shoes off and put your feet up.'

'I'm stopping you working.'

'For goodness' sake, Janet! Let's have a sense of proportion here.'

I lolled on her sofa with my stockinged feet on a footstool. A few minutes later she came back with a plate and a mug. 'Toast and honey,' she said. 'And a herbal tea. Nothing to irritate. Plenty of energy. Trust me, you'll feel better.'

Annoyingly, she was right. I finished the last mouthful and washed it down with the peculiar concoction which she assured me would do me good. I lay back with my eyes closed and felt a tear leak down my cheek.

'Feel up to talking?' she asked gently. I nodded. 'OK, so who knows about this?'

'You. Me. The medics.'

'Bob?'

'Sleeping off a night shift.'

'What did the doctor say?'

I told her briefly what was going to happen, and she nodded. She had been through it herself almost twenty years before.

Something that had been wound tight inside me was beginning to unravel. I couldn't hold on to it much longer, and a big habitual part of me wanted to bolt and hide and bawl alone. But I knew she wasn't going to let that happen. I looked up at her from my slouch on her sofa, seeing her concerned blue eyes, her hair half pinned up and half falling down from her time at the gym, and I thought about all the things I would miss if I didn't make it, and it hit me like a falling wall. I held my head in my hands and howled. She planted herself on the sofa next to me and wrapped her arms around my shoulders, saying nothing. Eventually the fit passed, and she handed me a box of tissues, and I mopped my face.

'Don't you dare apologise,' she said sternly. 'Like it or not, I'm going to make you another of those teas. Rachel swears by them.'

Moments later she was back, and put the mug on the table in front of me.

'Anna,' I said huskily. 'Call me an idiot, but I don't want to die, and I don't want to lose Bob.'

'There's every reason why you won't die,' she said firmly, 'though I understand your shock and fear. It's totally normal for you to fall apart a bit, getting news like that. My dear old thing, even you are only human. But what's all this about losing Bob?'

I told her how he had been, and what I had seen, and telling her even I thought it sounded flimsy and foolish, but she didn't laugh or tell me not to be stupid, and I remembered that she had been through the trauma of a faithless husband and an unwanted divorce. She was quiet for a moment, with an expression I knew of old that told of concentrated thought. 'Janet, from what you've told me, and what I know of you and Bob, there's probably nothing in it. But there's no way round this, pal – you have to talk to him. Sounds like you've got out of the habit.'

'What if he wants to leave me?' I said miserably. 'Me being ill will mess up his plans.'

'For heaven's sake! Playing 'what if' is not going to help. You've resisted it all these years – please don't start now. Anyway, if the unlikely scenario you postulate comes to be, what he'll almost certainly do is see you're OK after your operation and *then* run off into the sunset with his little trollop.'

An hour before, I wouldn't have thought it possible, but we have always had the ability to make each other laugh.

'It's not funny!' I spluttered.

'I know it isn't. But you are being just a tiny bit ridiculous.'

I sipped the weird concoction and made a face. 'You sure this isn't poison?'

'Positive.'

'I might give you another surprise.'

'OK. Hit me with it.'

'I went to see Father Gerard – you remember, the priest from my childhood.'

'Good heavens!'

'Yeah, I know. I'm not even sure why. He's hardly going to have a handle on women's ailments.'

'He's probably had a lifetime of experience with family issues and marriage troubles, though,' Anna said. 'Even if it's not first-hand.'

'Yeah, well, I didn't give him chapter and verse. I spared him that. But he said he'd pray for me.'

'And?'

'And I haven't changed my mind. It's always seemed to me that people like me, dyed-in-the-wool sceptics who don't give God the time of day, and then fall on their knees when disaster strikes, are weak, hypocritical and dishonest.'

Anna shook her head. 'No, no,' she said quietly. 'You've got that wrong. That's pride speaking. Because that's exactly what we are, all of us, to a greater or lesser degree – weak, hypocritical, dishonest. In my experience God isn't proud at all. He'll take you just as you are – in a mess, still trying to go it alone, doubting his existence, all of it. He values you infinitely, even if right now you don't value yourself.' I goggled at her, speechless, and she smiled. 'I'll add my prayers to Father Gerard's,' she said. 'Now, if you feel up to it, you know what you have to do. Wash your face first, because you look as if you've done several rounds with a heavyweight boxer. Then go home. Talk to Bob.'

'OK. But I can't wear these shoes anymore. My feet are not happy.'

'Let me see if I have an old pair of Millie's trainers. My shoes will be way too small.'

She found me a pair of battered shoes, and I paused by her front door. 'I did a bit of research,' I said. 'I wanted to know the correct form of address for that mythical creature, the Deputy District Judge.' I smiled inwardly at her pained expression. 'Unfortunately it's nothing very honorific.'

'Good,' she muttered.

'You'll just be 'Madam' in court. However,' I added wickedly, 'there's an alternative. You could be addressed as 'Your Worship.' If you chose.'

'Do give over,' she said, wincing. 'It's all getting embarrassing. And anyway, it won't happen for a while yet. You know how it is.'

'I do indeed.' I turned to her in the doorway. 'Thanks. Not just for today. For all the years before.'

'Now you're talking as if you're thinking of leaving it all behind. Anyway, you'd do the same for me. You have done – remember last year, when I had that accident?' She touched her neck lightly. 'Go on, go home. It's where you should be right now. Consider taking a day or two off work, just to process and digest the whole situation. Whatever you think, chambers won't fall to rack and ruin in your absence.' She gave me a hug. 'Let me know how it all pans out. It's far better than the soaps.'

'You don't watch soaps.'

'I don't need to with you around. Oh! Um, by the way, I meant to say, but you sort of pulled the rug out on me today. I said yes to Jeremy. After much heart-searching.'

'Good for you! That's great news. Well, I think it is.'

'Don't get too enthusiastic, will you.'

'No, seriously, I'm very happy for you. So – does this mean a trip to Ibadan?'

'That's the other thing! When Jeremy rang his mother to tell her I had finally given in – not that he put it quite like that to her – she immediately announced that she would come here! They have relatives and friends in the UK she hasn't seen for ages, not least her granddaughter, so she's planning a trip quite soon.'

'That's quite an undertaking for an elderly lady. How old is she?'

'Eighty-something. But she'll come with two of her daughters.'

'Do they all have fabulous names like Hand of God?'

'They do. But for the purposes of a sedate visit to England they'll just be Dorothy, Alice and Marion.'

I had to laugh. 'Rather you than me. Meeting your prospective mother-in-law. That's some rite of passage.'

'Don't I know it.'

It was strange, arriving home on a weekday at two o'clock in the afternoon. I couldn't remember the last time I'd seen my street at such a time, with hardly anyone about. I wondered if Bob was still asleep, but when I put my key wearily in the lock and kicked off Millie's trainers in the hall I heard the sound of running water and Bob's tuneless singing. It gave me pause; he didn't often sing. I thought perhaps I wouldn't hear that sound much longer, and it was like a knife turning in my insides.

I padded through to the kitchen and filled the kettle, then stopped, turning the tap off, frowning, and shaking my head. This was all automatic – did I even want a cup of tea? All I really wanted was a shower, and that would have to wait till Bob was done. My head was throbbing, and I slumped onto a kitchen chair and pressed my hands to my temples. I must have dozed for a few seconds, because the next thing I knew Bob was there, dressed in nothing but a towel, his hair wet and plastered to his head and neck.

'I thought I heard you,' he said. 'What are you doing home at this time of day? Are you ill?'

'I'll be OK,' I said. 'Now you're out of the bathroom I'll shower.'

'Can it wait for a moment?' Bob said. He seemed impatient, buzzing with unusual energy. 'Let me get dressed – I won't be long. There's something I need to talk to you about.'

I shrugged. I felt too beaten, too exhausted, for anything but weak acquiescence.

Ten minutes later he was back, in cotton trousers and a blue shirt, its sleeves rolled to the elbows. His feet were bare, and he was rubbing his wet hair with a towel. 'Shall I make some tea?' He didn't wait for an answer, but filled the kettle and set it to boil, humming under his breath. I was still at the kitchen table, motionless. It seemed he had seen nothing of my sorry state. Clearly whatever was on his mind was making him blind.

He brought two cups to the table and slid into a chair opposite me. Now at last he noticed me, and he visibly flinched. 'You look awful,' he said. 'Grey. What is it? There's gastric flu going round.'

'It's not that,' I mumbled. 'You said you had something to say.'

'Yes.' He hesitated, sipping his tea. Then he looked up. 'I feel a bit bad,' he said. 'I haven't been entirely upfront with you. I had my reasons, but maybe it wasn't the right decision. Thing is, I knew you were going through a bad patch health-wise, and I didn't want to add any more pressure.' I said nothing, and he took a deep breath. 'Remember a few weeks ago, or maybe longer, I had a bit of a blip? That's what I called it anyway, which was stupid, because it was more than that, only I was trying to tough it out.'

'Yeah, I remember.'

'Well…' he paused. 'It didn't go away, that sense of not being able to cope any more. People at work began to notice I wasn't doing well. They're just used to me being some kind of rock, but I'm not, it's all a front. Then my old crewmate Radu – you remember him? – decided to transfer and that's how I got partnered with Serena. She was the one who saw it, maybe because she was new to the station and saw things with fresh eyes.'

'Saw what?'

'That I was, how did she put it? Brewing up for a meltdown. One day she cornered me and said I had to stop pretending everything was OK. I had to get some help. And she was right. So I signed up for some online counselling. Had about six sessions, in one of the rooms at the station, every week or so. Today was the last one. I fitted them in round work, so today I had a session after our night shift. Serena, bless her, hung around instead of going home, to see how it went. She's been backing me all the way.' He saw me looking at him open-mouthed. 'What?'

'You didn't think it was something you should have told me?'

He shrugged, clearly embarrassed. 'Like I said, I didn't want to load you up with more worry. And I suppose, if I am honest, I didn't want to seem weak.'

From the flaccid, pathetic creature of a few minutes ago, now anger boiled up in me and it was all I could do not to shriek. 'But it wasn't all about you, was it?' I snapped. 'What you've done is make me worry far more. For I don't know how long you've been distant, dismissive, moody, absent – and not just physically, always at work. I know I'm not the best at communicating. I know you take it for granted that I'll always cope, because I always say I can. But this morning,' my voice rose, 'this is what I saw: you, arriving home from work in a woman's car, not for the first time, more than an hour late, and then chatting and laughing and hugging – which is more than we do these days – and now you've positively got a spring in your step, and this has probably been one of the worst days of my life, and even now you barely notice.'

I came to an abrupt halt, breathless, tears standing in my eyes, and he looked at me with a frown of bafflement, and then light seemed to break in and he said slowly, 'What are you trying to say?'

'Just tell me you're not having an affair with Serena. And please tell the truth.'

He gaped. 'What? That's mad – she's twenty eight! I could be her father.'

'And that doesn't happen?'

'Of course it does. But not to me. And I don't want it to.' He stretched out and took my hand, and I couldn't pull it free. 'Look. Serena is a lovely young woman, kind, caring, observant. She is a loyal colleague, and that is all. She lives with her boyfriend, who runs a gym in town, and they live in a ground floor flat with a miniature dachshund. There's no way she'd be interested in an old man like me! This morning was my last session. She's seen, everyone's seen, how I have got myself together – with help. She gave me a lift, and that hug was perfectly innocent – she was just pleased for me. How can you even think it? How could you ever think I would cheat?'

'Because of the way you were.'

'Oh, Jan. I'm sorry. I did what I thought was the right thing, but seems I got it very wrong. I'm sorry I made things worse.' He frowned. 'But where were you when I got home this morning?'

'In the car, about to go to work, or so I thought. Except I didn't. The lad from over the road parked outside our house so I had to park further up when I got home last night. By the time you arrived he'd gone. So I saw you.'

'I had no idea. I felt so much better; I'd made a decision. And I never even thought of you. That was wrong – I should have. But you've been very silent too lately. I'm pretty sure there are a few things you haven't told me.'

I heaved a deep sigh. Why was everything so difficult? 'Yeah. I can't contradict that. I had reasons too, but maybe not very good ones. And there were times when I would have told you, but something happened to get in the way, and I let it go.'

'So why weren't you at work? And why are you at home in the middle of the afternoon?'

'I thought you might have wondered about that before now,' I said.

'Sorry. Too full of my own things. Stupid. Tell me now.'

'Last night,' I said slowly, gathering my thoughts, 'when I got home you'd already gone to work. Before I went to bed I thought to check the answerphone. There was a message from the surgery, asking me to call them as soon as I could. That's what I was doing in the car when I saw you – making an appointment. To be honest, I imagined the worst. And I am not a great one for imagining, as you well know.'

'Oh, no,' he whispered. 'And what happened?'

'I got an appointment for eleven thirty. I couldn't face work. Rang in, said I'd be back after lunch. I spent some time in a farm track with a brown cow for company. Thinking.' He was silent, staring at me, his face drained of colour. 'Then I had a whim and I went to see Father Gerard.'

'What?' His eyebrows shot up.

'That wasn't the first time. I visited him, at his invitation, the day after Neville's wedding. I was going to tell you, but the opportunity passed. He told me things about my mother, and my childhood, and his part in our lives: things I never knew. It gave me a lot to think about. I'll tell you about all that one day; right now I don't have the energy. Anyway, I went to the see the GP. It was the same one who'd referred me for the scan and the D and C. Seems I have something called endometrial adenocarcinoma.'

Bob groaned, and he gripped my other hand, so tightly it hurt. 'I know what that is,' he said, his voice low. 'I'm sorry, love. I wasn't there when you needed backup. I've got a lot of things wrong. Terrible timing.'

'Well, I can't hold you responsible for that,' I said. 'You didn't know what was going on.'

'So what did you do then?'

'I went to work.'

'You and work! I don't believe it – why did you do that?'

'What else was there to do? Anyway, I didn't even make it into the building. Anna intercepted me and took me home and fed me toast and honey. Spoke sense to me and told me to go home and talk to you.'

'And when you got here I wasn't listening, was I?' He looked so cut up I almost considered forgiving him. 'Look, just tell me what's going to happen now.'

I told him about having to have more scans and an operation and waiting for a letter. 'Dr Kemsey said it wouldn't take long.'

'I hope not.' He was silent for a moment, just looking at me, his brow creased. 'Jan, my dearest girl. Please believe me when I say I had no idea you were ill, or worried, or thinking I was playing around with a girl half my age. I would have been horrified. I've never strayed, because I've never wanted to. It's as simple as that. You're the only one I want to be with, but I see I haven't really made that very clear.'

'No. But then, I haven't exactly been forthcoming.'

'I think we need to change our ways.'

'Yeah.' I paused. 'Look, I don't feel great. I had a rough night. I'm going to get a shower and put on some PJs and sleep for a century.'

'Don't you want anything to eat?'

'Maybe tomorrow.' I got up from the chair, pulling my hands free from his; my legs felt like wet paper, and I held on to the table. He shoved his chair back and came round to my side.

'Do you need help up the stairs?'

'No. Just give me a minute.'

He put his arms round me then, and held me close. I sagged against him, taking in his smell of washed skin, lemon shampoo and clean cotton, and felt the tears drip down my nose.

'I'm going to look after you, whether you like it or not,' he murmured. 'Until your surgery and while you recover. I've got a few days off, so we'll start now. And I won't take no for an answer.'

'Right now,' I told him, my voice muffled, my face half-buried in his shirt, 'that word has disappeared from my vocabulary.'

'Not before time.'

Halfway up the stairs I paused and turned back. 'What decision? You said you'd made a decision.'

'Yes. A job has come up, at the hospital. I'm going to apply for it. If I get it I'll still be working for the ambulance service, but more in a support role.' He smiled, but there was sadness and regret in his face. 'So you see, if I was based at the hospital, it might make sense to move.'

'Ah, that. A discussion for another day.'

The next few days were strange: I felt as if I were in some alternative universe where nothing whatsoever was demanded of me. I had no need to work, or read, or decide, or even to think. I knew it couldn't last, but it was good while it did. I was afloat on a warm sea.

Bob did everything: in my waking moments I heard him mowing the lawn, cleaning the house, cooking, fending off telephone calls, and often humming as he did so. He brought me drinks and meals and generally did penance for the fright he had given me. Better still, he spent time lolling on the bed beside me, or later, when I got up, on the sofa, and we told each other many things. I realised we had almost never done this. In the early days, before and after our marriage, we were always busy, focused, pursuing our working lives, bound up in our ambitions, and later looking after our son. Now his work at least looked set to change, our son was grown up, and I was making an effort not to think about chambers without me. I came to realise that, whether I was fully aware of it at the time or not, I had made a fine choice when I responded to Bob's proposal all those years ago, with my usual tendency to profound understatement, 'OK, if you like.' (I am not so sure if the same was true of him.) Privately I grieved, a little, for the time we had wasted letting it all slide.

He told me about the uncertainty that had led to his counselling sessions, his sense that his very foundations were shaking, and also about the things he had learned about himself, his upbringing, his thoughtless assumptions. I told him about my talks with Anna and Father Gerard, how my attitudes to my family were changing. 'I think I got stuck at thirteen and a half,' I said. 'There was always that anger and bitterness boiling somewhere in the depths.' I reflected for a moment. 'But maybe it's not just what Father Gerard told me; that was more a sweeping away of obstacles. I've seen my siblings in a different light recently, and I see them more as fallible people trying to do their best, just as I am. Obviously I don't include the twins in that. I just hope they aren't beyond redemption.'

'Steady, girl,' Bob said with a broad smile. 'Sounds like you're almost edging towards compassion.'

'Perish the thought,' I said, glowering. 'I don't go for all that 'everybody's wonderful' rubbish. Mattie and Jimmy aren't lovely. And neither is my father. Compassion, as you call it, has its limits. We shouldn't stray too far from reality.'

'You're a hard woman,' he said fondly.

'The other thing,' I said, hesitating, wondering if I could carry this off, 'I've also been thinking about God. Maybe it's inevitable when you are taking stock of your life and that life is suddenly threatened. I guess I also blamed him for letting my mother step out in front of a hurtling taxi, but I see now my view on that was a bit simplistic.' He looked at me and said nothing, but his eyes were wide. 'OK, I see you're wondering if I'm feverish. Maybe I am. I know I've got a lot of work to make up, a long road to take, but let's say I'm thinking about it. It's about time. You can't stay thirteen and a half for ever.'

We were lying on the bed having this conversation, me in my pyjamas, Bob fully clothed. He rolled over and kissed me.

'Let me know if you come to any conclusions,' he said, brushing the hair from my forehead with his fingers. 'I would be happy to be informed. But now there's a stack of dirty saucepans in the sink.' He heaved himself up and put his feet on the floor.

I wriggled down in the bed, closing my eyes. 'Good on both counts. I'm in need of sleep.' I sensed he was looking at me from the doorway and opened one eye. 'I'm glad we've got that little matter sorted out.'

'What little matter?'

'You deserting me for a younger, more nubile and less crotchety woman. Now I can give all my energies to the weightier matter of not dying.'

He laughed softly. 'Nice to know where I come in the pecking order of your priorities,' he said. 'And will you please, I beg you, stop talking about dying.'

Over the next few days, before I went back to work, we continued to talk. Bob ruminated aloud on what he had learned from his counselling sessions, and I listened, and learned things I had never bothered to ask: inconsequential things in themselves, memories of his long-dead father, the ambitions of his childhood, patchwork pieces that made up the man he had become. He'd said we should change our ways, and that weekend I told him about the little white suitcase in the loft and he climbed up and fetched it down. 'I didn't even know you had this,' he said, shaking his head.

'I'd forgotten it myself until I started clearing up there, months ago,' I said. 'I can't even remember how or why I ever brought it with me. To be honest, I decided I'd put it on the next bonfire or add it to the next load for the dump. I'm glad I didn't now. It's a painful little memory, but it's my past, and I suppose I should try to assimilate it, not deny it.'

He opened it up and spread out its contents. The photos of our First Communion day made him smile because of my black-browed mutinous face, such a contrast to little Pauline's beatific smile. 'Looks like angry Janet started before your mum died,' he said.

I sighed. We were downstairs on the sofa, with the contents of the suitcase spread out on a low table in front of us. 'I was very conflicted, though I couldn't have articulated it clearly then,' I said slowly, gathering my thoughts. 'I loved my mother with a simple child's love, and I'd enjoyed the sunshine of her undivided attention for five years. I was her pet, her little treasure, until she started producing children every couple of years. But she made me angry as well, and my anger made me guilty. Even then I hated feeling guilty. I still do. Too many kids, not enough money or organisation or sense, too much landing on me as time went on. And then there was her devotion to the church – no wonder I rejected everything they told me, those dear old pious nuns. And yet –' I paused, because something had become clear to me that I hadn't wanted to think about and had buried. I turned to him, biting my lip. 'I realise how much of what they tried to teach me did sink in, became a part of my mental background, just as they meant it to. You can take rotten parts out of your body – cancers, bits that don't work – but you can't take out those embedded ideas; you can't rationalise them away.'

He took my hand, rubbing the backs of my fingers with his thumb. 'Another case for assimilation, maybe.' He took the little white prayer book out of the case. 'I don't think this has ever been opened.'

'It hasn't.'

He found the bundle of letters then, and opened one of them up. 'What's this? You wrote these? Who to?'

Tears had already started to brim in my eyes, and pain stabbed my chest. 'My mother.'

He looked at me, bewildered. 'When did you write them?'

'After she died.'

'After –?'

'I know it seems crazy, but I had no way of expressing what I felt, the anger and grief and helplessness.' My voice broke, and I tried to swallow the tide of misery that swept over me.

Bob put his arm round my shoulders and drew me to him. 'You poor little wretch,' he said. 'Didn't anybody try to help you?' There were tears in his eyes too.

'I told you, didn't I,' I said when I had control of my voice, 'there were people who came and tried to do things for the family, but it was piecemeal, and Desmond didn't help.' I pulled a tissue from my pocket and blew my nose. 'Anyway, now you know what a strange kid I was, writing letters to her dead mother.'

'You did what you had to.'

'Yeah, I guess.' I picked up the letters, the prayer book, the photos. 'Let's put these away. I'm glad you know about them, but I don't want to dwell on them any more. I grew up and survived, somehow.' I gave him a watery smile. 'I have a better idea. Why don't we work on your job application? It'll be the second one I've helped with recently.'

'What was the first?'

'I'm sure I told you : Anna came over, oh, ages ago, back in the spring, one evening when you were on nights. You collided on the front path and nearly tripped over Gordon's lead.'

He nodded. 'Yeah, so I did.'

'I helped her polish her application for the Deputy District Judge post,' I said. 'And we must have done a good job, because it got her to a Selection Day and now she's heard from them and it's all systems go.'

'So,' Bob said thoughtfully, still with his arm round me, 'it's all change for her.'

'That's not the end of it,' I told him. 'I forgot to tell you – she's getting married. It's taken her a long time to make up her mind; I guess the first time around has left her with a few scars.' I told him what I knew about Jeremy, including his given name. 'I'm ever so slightly worried,' I said, 'that he might be the consultant in charge when I go to hospital.'

'I doubt that,' Bob said. 'Women's health may be his specialism, but with cancer the Oncology people will take over – unless he's a Gynaecological Oncologist. Anyway, even if he is, he's far too important for something so routine. Routine for him, I mean, not routine for you. Especially with a name like Hand of God.'

I laughed. 'I know. Poor man. It's a lot to live up to.'

'You mentioning Anna, though,' Bob said, straightening up and flexing his shoulders, 'made me think: if you wanted to talk about God and stuff, she'd be the person to talk to. I know she's very persuasive, but she'd respect your point of view. She wouldn't try to sell you a line.'

'You're right,' I said, surprised that he'd considered the matter at all. 'Much as my opinion of Father Gerard has changed – he's a good man, I think, in his own way, honest, quietly trying to support and lead his flock – but I don't share all his beliefs, his world view. I suppose it is all in there, in my mind I mean, but I've come a very long way since then. I can't go back.'

'None of us can go back,' Bob said. He heaved himself up from the sofa with a quiet groan. 'But we have to accept that we carry a lot of stuff with us. It's part of who we are. We might as well –'

'Assimilate?' I said. 'Was that your word or mine?'

He looked down at me, smiling. 'I don't know. Anyway, all this talking has made me thirsty. I'm going to find a cold beer. And it's very nearly lunch time.'

On Monday we both went back to work. I wasn't feeling at my best, but the status quo would have to do. As I parked I thought about that conversation I had had with Anna, when she talked about our various areas of stupidity, and I realised what mine must be – probably one of many, but at that moment this one seemed the most glaring and the hardest to understand: how could I not have seen just how crucial Bob was in the complex equation of my life? I was embarrassed at my own blindness, and relieved that somehow, despite the shifts and turns of the last few months, it seemed I had got my man back.

In chambers I made my presence known to the juniors and checked they were all managing well, which they were. I summoned Charlie with a crooked finger and a raised eyebrow, but he stayed in his seat, simply swivelling round to face me with a broad grin. 'If you're going to ask me about my portfolio, Janet, don't bother. I submitted it. And I wasn't late.'

'Well done, Charlie! You've achieved the almost impossible and surprised me. Now all I need to hear is your success when they've marked it.'

Charlie gave me a thumbs-up and went back to his screen. I gestured to Claire. 'Got time for a brief chat?'

She followed me downstairs and I led her to the smaller of the conference rooms and closed the door behind us.

'This looks serious, Janet,' she said. 'Did I do something terrible?'

'Not that I'm aware of,' I said. 'Sit for a minute. I want to bring you up to date with what's on the horizon. Not sure when – I'm waiting for a letter – but very soon, I hope, I'll be having a stay in hospital.'

'Oh!'

I waved a dismissive hand. 'Nothing to get too steamed up about, but I will probably be out of action for a while. You're the most senior clerk now, and probably the most sensible, so I'm hoping you'll step up and be me while I'm not here.'

'Nobody in this world could be you, Janet,' she said with a wry smile. 'Are you sure I'm not in the doghouse for failing to curb Lauren Barclay?'

I shook my head. 'I doubt anyone could have succeeded with her,' I said. 'Luckily we're coming to a quiet part of the year, but then you'll also be dealing with staff on holiday so whoever's still here will have to cover for them. I might well be off till the autumn.' I explained briefly what was going to happen, and she listened solemnly.

'That's bad luck, Janet,' she said. 'I'm really sorry you've been poorly.'

'Well, let's hope they can sort me out,' I said airily. 'There's one thing outstanding and I think today we'd better get some of the prep done in case I am called in sooner than I expect – I mean Mr O'Hare's big case that's coming up, the one concerning the hospital trust. We'll need to make a detailed schedule of all the conferences with clients and solicitors, so that nothing gets forgotten.'

She nodded. 'I'll make a start on the paperwork today.'

'Good. You know how Mr O'Hare likes everything sewn up well in advance.'

'Is that it, Janet?' She got to her feet. 'I'm expecting a call from Mr Phelps.' She paused in the doorway. 'I hope your surgery goes OK,' she said. 'However will we get on without you?'

'Perfectly well, I imagine. Anyway, the experience will be good for you, being in charge for a while. It won't be long before you'll be ready to move on, maybe even look for a Senior's post. Not that I'm trying to get rid of you – on the contrary.'

'Oh, I don't know,' she said, pausing in the doorway. 'Tim and I are thinking of having a baby quite soon.'

'That's no obstacle, is it?' I said.

She smiled. 'I know you combined work and motherhood,' she said. 'But we may have more than one, if it all goes according to plan, so I'd take a few years out. Work is great, but it isn't everything, and I'm thirty-four so I need to get my skates on.'

'Fair enough. I hope you'll still be here when I get back. Because I think in September we'll need to start looking for a new clerk. And this time I'll keep a close watch on the applicants, and maybe you can help me sift the wheat from the chaff.'

She laughed. 'That's one way of putting it. Of course I'll help. As for being here, if I got pregnant today, which is unlikely, I'd still be around at Christmas.'

She waved and left, and the cold thought came to me: 'Will I still be around at Christmas?' Then I told myself not to be morbid and turned on my computer with a defiant flourish.

I was lucky. The following Monday I had a phone call from the hospital. There had been a cancellation; could I come in for a CT scan on Wednesday? I could, and did, and was back at work by the afternoon. I had been told to expect a letter, and to my surprise one arrived less than a week later, offering me an appointment with a Consultant Oncologist, Mr Jennings, on Tuesday, 8 August. Although I realised this was the NHS operating at top speed, especially considering that it was now the holiday season, the time between these developments seemed interminable. I wanted to know the results of the scan, and I wanted my surgery as soon as was humanly possible. I spent the time as fruitfully as I could, getting things in shape at work and at home, though there was little to do domestically: Bob was more than capable of looking after himself.

I kept my appointment with Mr Jennings on a dull afternoon, sticky with humidity. He was a short, round, balding man with rosy cheeks, and gave the impression of immense cheerfulness, which seemed odd for someone dealing with such a miserable illness. I took comfort, though, from his bustling welcome and his breathless patter.

'Now, Mrs Clarke,' he said, beaming benevolently across his desk, 'unusually I have a smidgen of good news for you. Yes, sometimes that happens, but not often enough, I'm afraid. Your CT scan showed a moderate-sized mass but it's restricted to the endometrial wall – no visible spread.' He paused; was he expecting me to leap up, shout Hurrah! and waltz round the room? I waited for the next instalment. He cleared his throat. 'That means we can confidently proceed to laparoscopic surgery – keyhole, in layman's terms.' I nodded curtly; did he think I wouldn't have looked it all up online? 'That's the least invasive method and reduces any tendency to cervical prolapse.' Still beaming, he said, 'Do stop me, won't you, if there's something you don't understand? It's a pity you came alone.' I closed my eyes briefly, then smiled at him encouragingly. No doubt he was used to idiots. No, I corrected myself sternly. He is used to very frightened people who don't take everything in. 'We'll take the uterus and the cervix,' he went on, slightly more subdued now, 'but there seems no indication at present to remove the ovaries and Fallopian tubes. It is possible, of course, that ovaries left with no blood supply can fail after some years, but we'll face that if we have to. The less we have to do, the better. That's my view. Nothing unnecessarily radical.' The beam was back. 'Everything clear so far?'

'Yes, thank you,' I murmured obediently. I was in this man's hands; I decided to be malleable and demure.

'Excellent,' he said. 'Now, on the day before your operation you'll come in and everything will be explained. After the operation you'll be quite tired, and you may have some pain, but we can help with that, also if you experience any nausea, as some do, from the anaesthetic. You'll have to wear elastic stockings, and there'll be a drip in your arm, and your bladder will be emptied with a catheter, at least for a while. But if all is well we'll get you up the next day. Much better to be on the move. Are you generally fit?' I mentioned walking and my dance class. 'Good. The fitter you are, the quicker you'll recover. You'll probably only be in hospital three or four days, and we'll get a physiotherapist in to suggest some exercises for when you're recovering at home. Now, do you have any questions?'

I had looked all this up on the internet, but I thought I'd better ask what his policy was. 'When can I go back to work?'

He chuckled. 'Good heavens, you're keen. It all depends on what your work entails. Do you have to do any heavy lifting?'

'A kettle,' I said, straight-faced. 'Perhaps the odd file.'

'I see. Well, if you are recovering without any setbacks, somewhere between four and eight weeks. About the same time-frame for driving, provided you are comfortable wearing a seat belt and confident that you can execute an emergency stop. Your insurance company may need a doctor's letter.'

'OK.' Was this consultation over? I started to get up, but he wasn't finished.

'After the surgery you may experience some disturbance to normal functions,' he said solemnly. 'That's quite usual. But not to worry, if you don't remember everything I've told you, the staff will remind you before you go home, and give you some leaflets.'

'Thank you.'

Now he stood up, and so did I. He extended a chubby hand, and I shook it. 'I hope we'll be able to get this done without undue delay,' he said. 'Then you can get back to normal. You'll get a letter.' He paused, as if a thought had struck him. 'Yes, you said you like to walk, good, that's excellent exercise, but once your wounds have healed you might consider swimming.'

I nodded, smiled, said goodbye and left. By the time I got to the carpark, I was laughing so hard my eyes streamed – partly at the charming Mr Jennings, partly with relief. Perhaps, after all, I could stop thinking about death.

August

Coming round from anaesthetic was strange. Afterwards Bob said I'd surfaced, or seemed to surface, several times before I truly felt conscious again, and during those brief times, though my eyes were open they were unfocused, and what I said was slurred and senseless. I had some vague recollection of curtains billowing in the breeze, but it had a dreamlike quality and may have actually been a dream. When the fuzziness receded and I managed to stay awake for more than a few minutes, I found myself alone, lying flat out on a white-sheeted bed with a drip in my arm. Moments later I heard laughter in the corridor outside; I recognised Bob, but not the woman he was speaking to. The door opened and he slipped cautiously into the room.

'Hey.' He bent over me. 'You're awake. Or are you?'

'What? Yes, of course I'm awake. More or less.'

'How do you feel?'

'A bit sore. A bit gormless. How did it go, the surgery?'

'Textbook.'

I sighed and closed my eyes. 'What's the time?'

'Around four.'

I opened my eyes again, frowning. 'Have you been here all day? Haven't you got anything better to do?'

'Yes. And no. Except I did go home and make something to eat, once I knew it was all over and you were OK.' He pulled up a chair and sat beside the bed. 'You look a bit washed out.'

'So would you if you'd just had various vital bits removed.'

He took my limp hand in both of his; he felt warm. 'People have been ringing, asking after you.'

'What people?'

'Pauline, Christine, Drew, Ben, Anna.'

'Didn't know I was so popular.'

'Silly.'

'Not Desmond, then?' I asked with heavy irony. 'Concerned as ever for my welfare?'

'Ah! No. To be fair, he might have wanted to, but he couldn't. I wasn't going to tell you this yet, but he's here, Jan – in the hospital. While you were under the knife he was being bluelighted into A and E. Ben found him collapsed – he'd had a stroke.'

'Oh! How is he?'

'Not great.'

I heaved a sigh. 'So now my siblings are having to divide visiting time between me and our father. What ward is he in?'

'Fleming. Your sisters are giving him priority. They say they'll come and see you at home because you'll be out soon. He won't be, even if he survives.'

'Bad as that?'

'Yeah, so they say.'

The thought of my father's death, which had been so fiercely wished for when I was a furious adolescent, now stirred no strong feelings in me. I hardly knew what I felt, but I put the news deliberately aside. When Bob had gone, when I was alone, I would think about it.

'Bob, who was that you were laughing with just now, in the corridor?'

'Oh, a nurse. She was telling me about a chat she had with you yesterday.'

'Young, blonde, a bit overweight?'

'Yes. Said her name was Lottie. Apparently you made her laugh. "Your wife's a bit of a character" is what she said.'

I smiled, remembering. 'She'd been deputised to remind me of all the things I had to do, all the things I shouldn't do, once I got home. Exercises, elastic stockings, wound care, and all that. She also said, with a giggle and a blush, no sex for six weeks. And I said it would give you time to get in training.'

'No wonder she was laughing, then,' Bob said. 'She probably thinks we're too old.'

'I may have persuaded her otherwise,' I said innocently, 'because I also told her about something I found out in the course of my researches into this particular procedure. Studies have been done which suggest that for some women the loss of their reproductive organs leads to a substantial increase in the strength of their libido. So you probably do need to build yourself up, just so you can cope with my unreasonable demands.'

Bob laughed aloud. 'The way you look at the moment I reckon I'm safe. But I'll take your word for it.' His eyes glinted. 'Fifty press-ups before breakfast – that should do it.'

'Show-off.'

They got me out of bed the next day, and I walked up and down the ward leaning on a walking frame. My legs felt weak and uncontrolled, but as the day went on and I tried again I began to feel more normal. Bob was working, so I knew he wouldn't be in to see me till after his shift, but Anna came after work. 'You look pretty good, considering,' she said.

'Considering I've had surgery, or considering I haven't got any makeup on?' I said.

She chuckled. 'It's true, I've rarely seen you barefaced. Or in such plain, boring clothes.'

'Yeah. Hospital sheets. White was never my colour.'

She sighed. 'Well, we're managing in chambers. But we miss you.'

'Really?'

'Yes, it's dull. Get well soon, please.'

Drew came briefly. 'Hey, Mum.' He leaned down to where I was sitting out in a chair and kissed my cheek. He smelled of fresh air, and his chin was bristly. 'Looking good.'

'Am I?'

'Yep. Better than Grandpa, anyway. I just popped in to see him. I don't know if he was aware of me, though.'

When he'd gone, I pondered. Was the old monster at death's door? Should I go and see him? Considering what a deadbeat father he had been, should I bother? Would he care? Would he even know who I was? When the nurse came with my painkillers I asked her. 'My father's in the hospital,' I said. 'In Fleming Ward. He's had a stroke. Is there any chance I could go and visit?'

The nurse – not the blonde this time, but a thin, dark, serious-looking woman – frowned and said, 'I'm very sorry to hear that, Mrs Clarke. I'll have to ask.' Half an hour later she came back with a cup of tea. 'Once you've drunk that,' she said, 'I've organised someone to take you up to Fleming in a wheelchair.'

'Thanks, but can't I walk?'

She shook her head. 'We can't risk you falling,' she said. 'Not yet. You're doing really well – keep it up and there's every chance you can go home on Saturday. But we must be careful.'

A little wiry porter in blue overalls turned up with wheelchair and the dark-haired nurse helped me into it. I was wheeled with some ceremony along several corridors and up two floors in a lift, then through a set of double doors into my father's ward.

He was lying flat in bed, much as I had been, his mottled old hands lying above the sheet, and he appeared to be asleep. His stringy grey hair straggled across the pillow, and his mouth had dropped open. Pauline and Christine were there, one on each side of him; Christine was doing a crossword, and Pauline was staring rather vacantly out of the window. When they saw me approaching in my chariot of state, they both leapt to their feet, and Christine dropped her puzzle book.

'Oh, Janet!' Pauline said breathlessly. 'What a surprise! Are you all right? We wanted to come and see you too, but then this happened with Dad, and we knew you'd soon be home –'

I waved an impatient hand. 'It's all right, honestly. I don't feel neglected.'

Christine took my hand and spoke softly. 'How are you, Janet?'

'Better than him, by the look of him,' I said, nodding towards the bed. 'What are the medics saying?'

She shook her head. 'They're not really sure yet. It's quite bad, I think. His lifestyle hasn't helped, of course. He never exercised, did he, because of his arthritis and his bad foot, and his diet's been terrible.'

I heard Pauline sniffle, and I looked up and saw her red eyes. 'Move this wheelchair a bit nearer, can you,' I said to Christine. She manoeuvred me closer to the side of the bed. The porter was waiting by the nurses' station. I leaned over and took one of my father's hands. It was more an experiment than a gesture of affection. His hand felt heavy, dry, lifeless. I looked at my sisters' anxious faces. 'Tell me something, girls,' I said softly. 'After I left home, after I married Terry, what was he like? Did he ever take his belt to you?'

I heard Pauline stifle a sob. Christine shook her head. 'He threatened it a few times, but he never did,' she said. 'He seemed to, I don't know, soften a bit after you went. Anyway, he knew he had to rely on us to see to the younger ones. He gave David a few knocks, though, but Dave kept out of his way, and as soon as he could he was away, as far away as he could get! I think it was you that made Dad mad, Janet. Pauline and me, we never answered him back.'

'That figures,' I muttered. 'Pauline, why are you all weepy? I can't believe you thought so much of him.' Pauline said nothing, dabbing her eyes and hiccupping. Then something strange happened. Desmond's eyes were still shut, but I felt him squeeze my hand hard. It hadn't seemed he had any strength left in him. My fingers felt crushed, and I pulled my hand away. 'Ow!'

'I think he's trying to say something,' Pauline whispered. 'Look, he's trying to open his eyes.' It was true: his eyes were open a slit, and what we could see was bloodshot. He was mumbling something, but it was nothing we could understand. I saw a tear leak down one seamed cheek.

'He's been completely out all day,' Christine said. 'Now you're here and he's trying to speak! What can that mean?'

'Perhaps he's trying to ask you to forgive him, Janet,' Pauline said timidly. 'For all the times he was so horrible to you.'

'Ha! More like he's wishing he'd caught me more often and beaten me black and blue for being lippy,' I said.

Desmond, exhausted from his effort, sank back. His hands went limp, his eyes closed, and he snored.

'Is he going to make it?' I asked abruptly.

Christine shook her head. 'We don't know. Even if he does, he's going to need twenty-four hour care. A nursing home. And now he's in no state to refuse. Giles has been looking into it. But Janet, are you all right? We had no idea you'd been feeling unwell all this time.'

'I'm OK. They've taken the dodgy bit away, and if I go on behaving they'll probably let me out before the weekend.'

She patted my hand. 'Good. We'll come and see you then, won't we, Pauline? Maybe do a bit round the house, give Bob a break.'

For once, I found I didn't want to thrust them away. It was kind of them to bother, though I hardly knew why. 'Yeah,' I said. 'Thanks. That'd be great.'

It was a strange summer that year. To be resting, feet up, while others bustled round me, was a great rarity. My sisters, true to their word, dropped by frequently, making tea, bringing me reports of family matters, or bringing carloads of shopping and cleaning the house when Bob was working or sleeping off a shift. Desmond survived his stroke, but it had the effect of accelerating his dementia, and he was left unable to speak coherently, so that it was impossible to tell if he was making any sense. Once he was discharged from hospital, with a sackful of medication, a nursing-home was found for him and he was duly installed. I told myself that once things returned to normal, as far as they could, I would visit him there. Pauline reported sorrowfully that Neville and Jodie were often arguing. I kept quiet about Drew and Tiffany: they seemed to be doing well. Drew passed his exams with a comfortable margin, and was actively seeking employment in his field, while Tiffany signed up for a course at the college from which he had just graduated.

Left alone, I applied myself conscientiously to the exercises suggested by the hospital physiotherapist, and soon enough began to feel stronger. I'd been warned that as well as the physical discomforts following a hysterectomy I could also fall prey to depression, but the very reverse happened: along with better health I felt liberated.

Bob and I worked together on his application for the hospital job, and he went for an interview looking unusually smart in his suit and tie but full of self-doubt: it was a very long time since he'd put himself through this particular trial. He must have conquered his nerves because two days later he was offered the job. Now he was working out his notice before starting in September. His feelings were mixed; he knew he would miss the work he had done for so long and to which he had given so much skill, dedication and heart. But he remained firm that this was best for us, and now, not before time, 'us' was a priority. We had a number of long talks over those weeks of my recovery, chewing over our past mistakes, often getting distracted and laughing immoderately, but always returning to the ways we could find never to repeat the misunderstandings and miseries of the past few months. Bob called it 'shoring up defences,' and if that was a cliché it was an apt one.

I had a surprise one evening. Bob was on a day shift and I was watching the six o'clock news; it was the day Big Ben fell silent in preparation for a three-year conservation programme. The doorbell rang, and I got up stiffly: I'd been on a longish walk that day and was feeling the effects. Standing on the doorstep was Ben, smiling rather painfully and blushing, and with him a small, rounded, youngish woman with fluffy blonde hair and a determined expression.

'Well! This is a surprise!' I said.

'I, um, just thought we'd come and see how you are,' Ben mumbled. 'And I thought, well, Hattie thought...she wanted to meet you.'

'Come in,' I said. 'I'm very pleased to meet Hattie too.' Once we were seated, and they'd declined tea, I said, 'You're a dark horse, bro. I didn't even hear about Hattie until Drew told me.'

Hattie giggled. 'Isn't that just like Ben,' she said. 'Never tells you anything.' My poor brother looked uncomfortable. He'd never quite got used to being teased; but I got the impression that with Hattie he would soon have to. I liked her, but even if I hadn't it wouldn't have mattered. If my baby brother was OK, I was too. Seeing them together, holding hands on my sofa, bickering in an undertone, made me want to laugh, but it was from pleasure, not from any desire to mock. They didn't stay long, but they promised to come again. Before they left Ben told me the old family home was now empty. My father had only rented it all those years, and now there would be another tenant. Ben had moved in with Hattie temporarily.

'We're looking for somewhere else,' Hattie told me. 'My flat's a bit small for two, even though Ben's really tidy.' As I watched them walk away down the street I thought about the house with the cracked green door, and consigned it gladly to the bin of bad memories.

Anna was a frequent visitor. She seemed a bit wistful, I thought, remembering the previous summer when she'd spent time with her new friends the Wellses at their farmhouse in France. They'd invited her again, but she'd decided to stay at home to spend time with Jeremy. Work was slacking off for her, but for him it was just as busy, and they had little enough time together as it was. 'I'm hoping to persuade him to take a few days off at the end of the month,' Anna said. 'He'll need to build up his strength for that visit from his mother and sisters – as will I! Millie's not going to France either this year: she's got herself a holiday job in the city, in one of the bars, and then there's a certain Hugo…'

'So is Jasper taking his current love-interest?' I enquired idly. We were lounging outside on the lawn, covered in sunscreen and sporting sunglasses and inelegant hats. Anna shook her head. 'She had other plans, Rachel said. So they'll be a very small party this year – just Rachel, Michael, Jasper and the two children.' She sighed. 'With all the uncertainty around Brexit, they may even decide to sell up. Sad for them. Michael bought that place when Jasper was four.'

'Many changes afoot,' I murmured. 'Not least for you. When do you take up your new duties?'

'Oh, probably not even this year!' Anna said. She wriggled bare toes in the grass. 'You've got me around for a while yet, just as it always was.'

'Not quite. There's a wedding coming up before then, so I hear.'

'Yes, yes.' She closed her eyes. 'Some time.'

'Not getting cold feet, are you?'

'No, not at all. I just feel exhausted thinking about all the arrangements. We should do what Drew and Tiffany did, I reckon. Maybe I'll suggest it to Jeremy.' She chuckled to herself. 'Anyway,' she said abruptly, 'what about you and Bob? Are you OK? Did you sort yourselves out?'

'I think so. At least we're actually speaking now. Quite a lot, actually. But as you're here, there are a few things I'd like to run past you.'

'OK, but do you mind if we go indoors? This sun's hot, and I'm beginning to feel over-toasted. A nice long drink in the cool would be just the thing, especially if you're going to grill me.'

'Who said I was?'

'You have that look on your face. I know it of old. There's no escape.'

We went indoors and provided ourselves with cool drinks and nibbles, and Anna subsided onto the sofa with a sigh. 'What was it you wanted to talk about?'

I hesitated. 'It's hard to explain. I don't know…look, this year has been rough. But now it's not, and I can't take any credit for the change, because most of the time I've been working against it.'

'Go on,' she said softly.

'Like, I kept trying to cope with things in the way I always have, the way I learned when I was a kid: take it on the chin, if you fall down get right up, cope with whatever comes, never ask for help, because it gives people power over you.' A horrible thought struck me. 'Maybe that's something I picked up from my father, the obstinate old monster. Or even, perish the thought, inherited.'

Anna said nothing, but she was grinning.

'Anyway, things got worse. I wanted to move house, just to try to dissociate myself from my family. I was really quite unwell, but I got up and put on my most in-your-face clothes and a bucketful of makeup and came to work, regardless. Maybe that's why I lost it – just for a moment – with Lauren Barclay. And then Bob – he told me he was worried, that he felt he couldn't cope with the job anymore, and I saw him go up and down and it's so unlike him, but I thought, he'll be OK, he'll sort it out. So I wasn't much help to him at all, but then I got really ill and he's been an absolute brick.' I paused and glanced at Anna. She just sipped her drink and watched me, and I knew from her expression that she was taking in everything I said and processing it with uncanny speed. I took a deep breath. 'And then there was all that trouble with Ben, and going to see Father Gerard, and seeing my sisters in a different light. Bob's got this new job at the hospital, so we could actually move, and now I find it's nowhere near as attractive a prospect as I thought. Here's fine. And things have come out better than I expected and much better than I deserve, and there's part of me that wants to apologise for being pig headed.'

Anna put her empty glass on the coffee table and sat back among the cushions. 'Not to mention, perhaps,' she said quietly, 'to say thank you as well.'

I opened my mouth to protest, but I realised that she was right. I was thankful. But I was also guarded. 'Look,' I said, 'you know I have never actually been an atheist. Just a narrow-eyed sceptic, very suspicious.'

Anna's eyes crinkled and she laughed, shaking her head. 'My dear old thing, what are you suspicious of? What do you think is going to happen? That Pauline and Christine and Father Gerard and the Wyatts will roll up one Sunday morning, manhandle you into a car and haul you off to Mass, singing loud hymns? Or that I will ring you up at six o'clock every morning and demand to know if you are saved? You're still thinking like that twelve-year-old bane of nuns.' I was silent, and mortified. 'Janet, this is one area where I think you need to apply your celebrated rational brain. Look at the thing as it is. You can say anything you like, sorry or thank you or whatever, in the silence of your own mind. Nobody is likely to challenge you in any way – certainly not the people I mentioned – though I don't doubt they may all be praying. Why don't you try it and see? Seems to me there's a crack in your carapace, and I for one would love to see it get wider and wider so that the new liberated Janet can come out dancing.'

'Now you're being daft,' I said grumpily.

'Not really,' she said. 'Think about how just talking to your husband has improved your life, and no doubt his. Why wouldn't it conceivably be the same with God?'

I couldn't think of any answer to that. I gaped a bit, then said sourly, 'You are definitely in the right profession.'

She laughed aloud. 'So my dear godfather reckoned when I was ten, and he hasn't changed his mind,' she said.

'I hope Jeremy knows what he's in for.'

'Who knows, eh? It'll be a great voyage of discovery for him.'

'Should I warn him?'

'No! You'd be spoiling the fun.'

After four or five weeks I went back, as planned, to the GP. Dr Kemsey was on holiday, I was told. The tall young doctor with the floppy brown hair examined me and asked me questions.

'You've been in the wars, Mrs Clarke,' he said as I put my clothes back on behind a screen. 'But you seem to have made a remarkable recovery.'

'I feel very well, thanks.' I sat back in the chair next to his desk. 'What I'd like to do is go back to work. I'm a barrister's clerk, not a labourer on a building site. No heavy lifting.'

'Long hours?'

'Sometimes,' I conceded. 'But I'll try and learn to delegate.'

He accepted this without comment, which showed how little he knew me. But somehow I reckoned that between them my various supporters would be doing their best to frustrate my workaholic tendencies. The GP and I agreed on a date, somewhere around the third week in September. I couldn't wait.

Before that, though, it was Bob's birthday, and Drew and Tiffany came round for dinner, and we sank a couple of bottles between us, which was a fair amount since Tiffany was driving and drank only water. She looked around the littered table with a bemused expression as Bob and Drew and I got more and more flushed and loud and uproarious and no doubt wondered what sort of family she had married into. They insisted on helping with the washing up and left before ten; they seemed to be in a hurry to get home.

'What do you think?' I said to Bob as we stood at the front door and waved them off. 'Still in the first flush of wedded lust?'

He looked at me and raised an eyebrow. 'Maybe,' he said. 'But I reckon they've gone home early to give us some space.'

'Why would they do that?' I could hear myself slurring a bit. I leaned on him and he pushed me gently indoors and shut the door.

'Because, drunken numskull, they are not deaf, blind or stupid. You told them you'd seen the GP and all was well?'

'Yes,' I said, and giggled. 'And by my calculation the dreaded six weeks are well and truly up.'

Bob folded his arms and put on a severe expression. 'Which, I'm afraid, you also very indiscreetly hinted at. Not to mention it's my birthday.'

My eyes widened. 'So it is!'

'I will even forgo the news,' he said. 'Otherwise you will be snoring in sozzled slumber before I've even got my socks off. For goodness' sake try not to fall up the stairs.'

I wasn't half as drunk as he thought I was, and for a moment I felt completely sober. 'Bob.'

'What now?'

I put my arms round his waist and leaned against him. 'Thank you.'

'What for?'

'For not giving up on me. I know it hasn't been easy.'

He held me close and kissed the top of my head. 'It's never been easy,' he said gruffly. 'I'm just a natural born martyr. Now will you please get up those stairs while you can still stand.'

I grinned. 'With pleasure.'

My return to chambers after unprecedented weeks of absence required careful planning. I made a long-overdue visit to my hairdresser, and startled her by my instructions.

'Cut off the pink tips,' I said. 'They look faded anyway. I don't want any extra colour at the moment – just my own. I'm not too grey yet, and maybe those – shall we call them silver? – hairs at the sides lend distinction. What do you think?' Wide-eyed, she simply nodded. 'I've found a photo in one of your magazines,' I told her. 'Perhaps you could cut it something like this.' So it was I left her salon that morning with a short layered face-framing cut, just my own dark locks with no embellishments.

I'd phoned the manager of my favoured charity shop the week before and laid out what I had in mind, so she was prepared. She knew me of old, and regarded my eccentric tastes as a challenge, but this time was different. Today a revamped Janet would take up her work with renewed purpose, and her clothes needed to reflect that. I was aware that my wardrobe selection was a matter of interest and amusement among my colleagues. I didn't want to disappoint them, but sometimes wackiness itself can be predictable; plus there is always the law of diminishing returns.

'I've found a few things for you to choose from,' the woman at the shop told me. 'But I'll be interested to see what you like, because there's one thing I think will be ideal.' The shop was quiet, and she came out of the back room with items draped across her arm and laid them out on the glass-topped counter.

It took me less than a minute. 'This.'

She gave me a look of triumph. 'That's what I thought.'

It was a top with two layers: plain underneath, patterned and floaty on top, fairly loose and cool, with elbow-length sleeves, in two shades of a fiery orange-red and a faint pattern which was reminiscent of flames. I looked up at the woman with a smile. 'All guns blazing,' I said. 'Just the message I hope to convey.'

'It's a size bigger than you usually need,' she said. 'But you've put on a bit of weight, haven't you, and I have to say it suits you. So this will be perfect, I think, and if it's a bit loose it won't be too hot. Obviously you'll need to try it on. But before you do that, have you thought what to wear with it? Normally you'd be asking me for a clashing shade – maybe a different red, or something to hurt the eyes. But from what you said on the phone I guess you're after something different.'

'I've decided,' I said, 'on this occasion, to go for tasteful, but not boring.'

'I have a nice dark grey skirt,' she said, looking me up and down with a critical eye. 'Slim-fitting. Just below the knee. Ideal for your figure.'

'That sounds absolutely right,' I said. 'And this time I'm going to ditch the crazy heels. Not flat, of course. There are people I need to look in the eye. But a bit kinder to the feet.'

At Anna's suggestion I went back to work on a Friday, a deliberate choice to ease myself in when things were beginning to wind down and before the hectic activity of a new week. I'd checked what was going on during the previous week, so it was a matter of making sure everyone was doing what they should and all the barristers were happy. People were pleased to see me, greeted me warmly and asked after my health, but there was no great sense of occasion. Perhaps I hadn't been as much missed as Anna had claimed, and I felt faintly foolish to have made such careful preparations. There was quite a lot of discreet bustling, and when I went upstairs to check on the clerks some of them were missing. 'I expect they're about somewhere,' Claire told me innocently.

Anna had a client that morning and remained closeted with her, her door firmly closed, until coffee time. She accompanied the woman to the door and shook her hand as she left.

She put her head round my door. 'You busy?'

'Nothing that can't wait.'

'Come down to my room,' she said. 'I'll make coffee.'

'I'm honoured.'

Unusually she closed her door again once we were settled, and I half expected her to discuss some weighty and private matter, but she barely mentioned work at all, apart from a passing reference to a case she was preparing. She seemed most interested in my health, although I had kept her updated all along.

The strangely subdued atmosphere in chambers persisted all morning, but I only noticed it when I raised my eyes from my computer screen and realised that the phone hadn't rung once and not one of the barristers had emerged from their rooms in pursuit of some favour. But a little after half past twelve Anna appeared in my doorway again. 'Come with me,' she said.

'Where to? I was just going to think about lunch.'

'Forget that. Just do as you're asked for once.'

I got up and stretched. 'You're being very mysterious.'

She smiled and said nothing, ushering me down the corridor to where the door to the back courtyard stood ajar. She opened the door to the larger of the meeting rooms, scene of many a wearisome chambers meeting, and stood aside to let me enter.

To my astonishment and dismay the room was full of people: all the clerks, all the barristers who weren't in court, even a couple of people representing the solicitors who most frequently instructed us. They were all standing round quietly with glasses in their hands, but as we entered the whole room erupted in cheers and catcalls and whoops of laughter – probably at the expression on my face. Anna propelled me into the room and pressed me down into a vacant chair. Someone put a glass of something fizzy into my unresisting hand. Anna gestured for silence and the hubbub diminished and then stopped altogether, apart from the odd giggle.

Anna cleared her throat and looked down at me. I was giving her my most baleful look but she didn't seem at all fazed. 'Friends, colleagues – thank you for your amazing occasional ability to do something discreetly,' she said, to a ripple of laughter. 'I think we can be sure from Janet's expression that for once we have completely astonished her. It's not often we can get one ahead, and I predict it's not going to last.' There were rumbles of amused assent. 'Janet, we couldn't let today pass without acknowledging how much you have been missed at Hartington these last weeks and how delighted we are you are back with us and so well.' I heard a hearty 'Hear, hear!' from someone whose voice told me he had already downed more than one glass of the fizzy stuff. 'But it's not just because you have been away that we decided we must celebrate today. I don't know the exact date, and nor does anybody here, because you, my dear friend, antedate us all. But somewhere around now you started working at these chambers twenty five years ago. That's a quarter of a century of dedicated service and ruthless efficiency, and we would all, I am sure, like to say congratulations and thank you – because the success of our operation here is largely a result of the hard work you have paid into it, year in, year out. You have used every method in your considerable armoury to keep us focused and systems running smoothly. Occasionally you might have used persuasion, but oftener, as many of us can attest, it was more like terror.' Another upsurge of laughter greeted this and Anna paused. 'But to be quite serious for a moment, we couldn't have got where we are without you, we're relieved and delighted you're back, and we look forward to a resumption of normal service, knowing that with you in charge there will be no slippage or half-measures.

'Ladies and gentlemen, let's raise our glasses to Janet – necessary and beloved tyrant.' My name echoed round the room, and there was a great deal of slurping, guffawing and noise. I took a swig of my own drink to calm my reeling thoughts. People were now talking in clumps, and had moved away from the tight circle they had occupied, to reveal tables laden with food and bottles of all descriptions. But refreshment, I decided, would have to wait. I had no doubt who had orchestrated this party and I was determined to answer her. I stood and tapped on my glass. People quieted down and looked at me inquiringly.

'Ladies, gentlemen,' I said. 'Barristers, solicitors, fellow clerks. I'm amazed you haven't remembered to invite the cleaners.' There was a chuckle from the gathering. 'Anna is right: for once you've pulled the rug out from under my feet and it's a miracle I'm not flat on my backside. I can promise you I will be exacting a spectacular revenge when she least expects it.' Someone hooted and was hushed. 'I don't often do public speaking, thank goodness, and I can't do it anything like as well as she does. She's got the years of experience and the inimitable diction and turn of phrase, whereas I'm pretty much pure Winstone Estate. So it's a good job she's the barrister, soon to be a Judge, and I'm the clerk. I won't say 'just the clerk', because we all know it's a demanding role that not everyone can cope with. So yes, I'm back. No more sloppy, no more slapdash, no more stretched-out lunch breaks or slipping away home early.' Someone called out, 'You listening, Charlie?' and there was more laughter.

I continued, 'You are all very kind and I appreciate your gathering here to mark the occasion of my twenty-five years – which, as it happens, isn't for another few weeks. If you'd let me organise things, rather than our revered Head of Chambers, I'd have got that detail right.' I said this with a straight face, but everyone laughed, and I was amused to note the flushed faces of people who were either unused to alcohol at work in the middle of the day or, in some cases, all too familiar with it. 'So thank you all, let's keep on doing what we do, and if anyone is daring enough to mention the word 'retirement' in my hearing there'll be hell to pay – plus a month of filing in the basement.'

Later that day, well fortified by food, wine and company, not all of which I would have chosen, I slipped into the little washroom at the end of our short corridor, to find Anna there, washing her hands. There wasn't much room, and she stood aside, hands dripping, to let me pass.

'You,' I said severely, 'are an absolute stinker.'

'So I am,' she said amiably, stretching for the paper towels. 'But we couldn't let it pass, we really couldn't. Quite apart from anything else, it was pure delight to see you so gobsmacked.' She gave me a considering look. 'I note a change in your appearance too,' she said. 'Positively toned-down. I assume that's deliberate?'

'Of course,' I said. 'The new, liberated Janet, as you'd put it, has no need of dazzling disguises. In fact I've turfed out some of my more interesting outfits.' Her eyebrows shot up. 'Not all, of course,' I added. 'After all you never know… You ran quite a risk there, you realise,' I said abruptly. 'The trouble with reclaiming one's humanity is a tendency to public weeping at moments of heightened emotion or shock. And if that had happened I would never have forgiven you.'

'Oh, I know,' she said airily. 'But I had faith in your aplomb. Never mind the velvet glove – you're the iron fist in the chain-mail gauntlet, pal.' She patted my arm as she passed, laughing affectionately. 'Long may it last.'

THE END

Printed in Great Britain
by Amazon

57791024R00162